THE LIGHTHOUSE

The LIGHTHOUSE

Christopher Parker

BEACON PRESS

Cover design by James T. Egan (bookfly.com)
Book design by Anna B. Knighton (annaknighton.com)
Map illustration by Karl Whiteley (who587.com)

ISBN 978-0-9951495-0-2 (paperback)
ISBN 978-0-9951495-1-9 (ebook)
ISBN 978-0-9951495-2-6 (hardcover)
ISBN 978-0-9951495-3-3 (audiobook)

Beacon Press Limited

christopherparker.com

3014 Dauphine Street
New Orleans, LA
70117

For Lucy

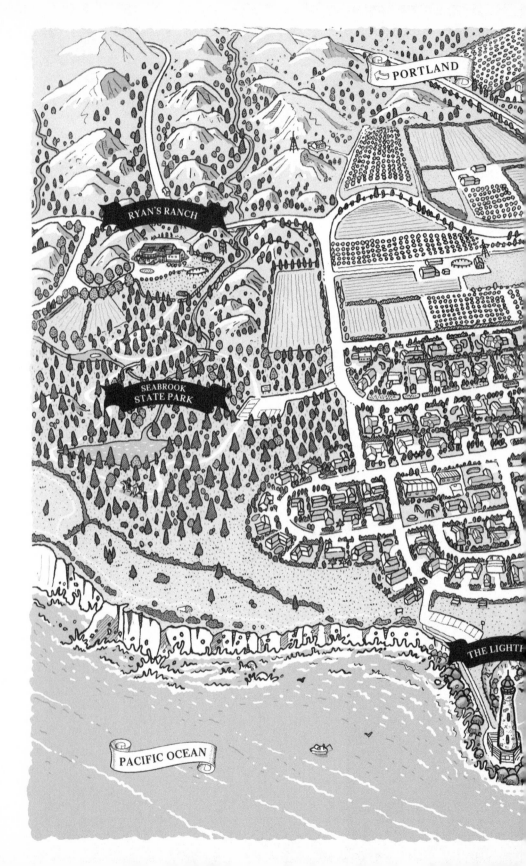

THE LIGHTHOUSE

IN THE TOWN OF SEABROOK, there stands a lighthouse.

Perched on an outcrop of jagged rocks, the derelict tower was condemned over half a century ago and has been bruised and battered by the wind and sea ever since.

Some say she's a relic of a bygone era, an eyesore that should be torn down. Others believe she's a symbol of the town's heritage, a pillar of the past that should be protected and saved. And there are those who think she should be left to the mercy of Mother Nature.

Crumbling brick by brick, the building is too dangerous to enter, and longstanding rumors of a ghost lurking within have meant that it's been years since anyone has stepped inside.

Few even remember the last time she shone.

But the horizon has yet to see the last of her light, and just as she once helped sailors navigate the treacherous waters off the bay, Seabrook's famous lighthouse will soon be called upon one more time, to help those in need find their way home.

PART
ONE

1

"A MY, WHERE ON EARTH have you been?"

Amy didn't know what had given her away—the security light, the creak of the gate, or the sound of her footsteps as she'd snuck along the pebbled path. The truth was that she hadn't meant to come home so late. She had been visiting her mother and simply lost track of time, a mistake she instantly regretted when she discovered her father anxiously waiting for her on their front porch.

"Well?" he growled. "Speak up."

Amy stuck her head down and tried to squeeze through the narrow gap between him and the door. "I'm sorry," was all she could say.

"You're sorry? That's it?"

"I'm tired, Dad. I just want to go to bed."

Amy pushed her way inside and made straight for her room, desperately hoping that he would save his interrogation for morning. But considering her father's line of work—he was a detective in the

Criminal Investigations Division of the Oregon State Police—that seemed highly unlikely.

"I asked you a question. Where were you?"

"Can we do this tomorrow? Please?"

"No, we can't." He chased Amy down the hall and into her bedroom, his tone growing more tempestuous. "Do you have any idea how worried I've been?"

Amy drew her curtains shut, plugged in her phone, switched on her lamp—whatever she could do to avoid eye contact.

"Amy, are you hearing me?"

"Yes," she snapped. "I hear you."

"Well? Will you tell me where you disappeared to?"

"I didn't disappear. I was visiting Mom."

"You can't be serious. You mean to tell me you've been at the *cemetery* this whole time?"

She turned to face him. "Is there something wrong with that?"

"Aside from the fact that you should have called to let me know? Why haven't you been picking up your phone?"

"The battery died. I didn't realize it was so late. I didn't know you'd be so worried. I'm *sorry*, all right?"

"Sorry isn't good enough, Amy. You're eighteen years old. I know you miss your mother, but it's completely irresponsible for you to be wandering around the cemetery by yourself at this ridiculous hour."

And there it was again, thought Amy, the beginning of yet another lecture. He'd been like this since the day of the funeral: critical of almost everything she did. If he wasn't micromanaging how much she was eating, or fussing over how much sleep she was getting, then he'd be second-guessing her every decision, just as he was doing tonight, or like yesterday when he'd urged her to "take some more time" and not to "jump the gun" after she'd announced her plans to withdraw from college. They'd sparred over it for the better part of the day, and Amy wasn't even sure why. The decision wasn't permanent; it was, as the university soberly called it, a "special dispensation for a life-changing event," which meant she could return to her studies whenever she wanted, and yet the most her father could offer in response was a resigned, "All right, Amy, whatever you think is best."

On the one hand she shouldn't have been surprised. The two of them weren't close, hadn't been for a long time. Still, she'd never thought they'd end up like this, that they would become so . . . distant. It was as though the death of her mother had left a crater so wide and pushed them so far apart that neither one of them knew who the other was anymore.

"Do you know what I was about to do?" Her father's rising voice urged Amy back to the present. "I damn near called this in. I was *this* close to sending out a patrol to look for you."

She shot him a stunned glare. "You've got to be kidding me."

"What did you expect? I couldn't reach you."

"I expect you to trust me, not order a citywide police hunt whenever I leave the house!"

"This isn't about trust, Amy—it's about me having some clue about where you are." He paused to take a breath. "Look, I'm not pretending any of this is easy. I'm still trying to come to terms with the loss of your mother, just like you are. And, yes, I realize I'm doing a damn poor job of it. But despite everything that's happened, I am *still* your father, and I don't appreciate being treated as though I don't exist."

Amy resisted the urge to fight back and instead marched across the room and swung open her door. "Would you mind just leaving me alone? *Please?*"

"Why won't you talk to me?" he said, making no effort to move. "All I want to do is help."

"What's the point, Dad? It's not as if you can fix what's happened."

"I can't fix anything if you won't let me try."

Amy rattled the door hard and pointed to the hall, a stampede of tears building behind her eyes. "I said you *can't*, okay? This isn't another case for you to solve. You *can't* help, you *can't* fix this—and

I'm pretty sure you can't bring Mom back—so will you *please* just leave me alone?"

"All right, Amy, fine—if that's what you want."

With his arms raised in surrender, her father turned and trudged out of the room.

And as soon as he was gone, Amy slammed the door.

2

THAT NIGHT, Kevin Tucker didn't sleep a wink. His daughter's
words had set off a fire of disquiet in the pit of his stomach that three
shots of bourbon and a handful of sleeping pills wouldn't extinguish.
Not even the arrival of morning could lessen the sting of what Amy
had said.

In desperate need of a distraction, he phoned his older brother,
Jack, and asked to meet for a drink. The venue was one of their regular haunts, a cozy whiskey bar in downtown Portland. Jack, also a
detective in the same division of the state police, came charging in
thirty minutes late, fell into his seat, and brought Kevin up to speed
on what had been happening at work, beginning with a rant about
one of his junior detective's recent slipups. Kevin raised his hand
for the bartender to bring over two glasses while he waited for his
brother to get everything off his chest.

"I tell ya, Kevin," Jack said, slurping his drink between breaths,
"damn Rodney screwed up the wording of the warrant so bad that

Judge Norton tore it up and threw it straight back in his face—
literally ripped it in two—and the task force that was all geared to
rock 'n' roll at dawn had to park up for another twenty-four hours.
Cap was spitting tacks like you wouldn't believe, and the feds were
too. I'd have written the warrant myself, except it's not the only thing
I've got going on, you know?"

To underscore his point, Jack then summarized everything else
he had on his plate: a double homicide in East Burnside, an ongoing
drug ring investigation, and, finally, a missing person case he'd been
overseeing down the coast.

"Anyway," he said, straightening his back, "you don't need me bleat-
ing on about work. Tomorrow you'll be back with me at the grind, so
how about we save the unpleasantries till then."

Kevin stared ahead, throwing back the last dribble of his drink. He
had completely forgotten that it was a mere twenty-four hours before
he was due back at CID. The thought landed in his gut like a heavy
rock. He'd been trying to reassure himself that work would help distract from the grief of losing his wife, but the truth was that he felt
apprehensive about returning to the bleak realities of his job. With
Helen gone and the way things were with his daughter, he wasn't
sure he was ready, wasn't sure how he was going to cope.

He raised the empty glass in the air, signaling the bartender for
another.

Jack folded his arms and rested them squarely on the table, as
though to communicate disapproval at the vigor with which Kevin
was putting away his liquor. "How are you doing, buddy? Are you
okay?"

Kevin winked and raised a thumb. "Superb," he drawled.

"I'm serious. I'm asking as your brother, not as a cop. How are you
holding up . . . in general, I mean?"

"In general? What exactly do you want to hear?"

"How about the truth? How are things at home?"

The question made Kevin retreat into the pit of his seat and start picking at the edges of his soggy coaster.

"Not good, huh?" Jack said.

"Let's put it this way—after what happened last night, I'm not sure things can get much worse."

"Want to tell me about it?"

Kevin shook his head, his expression grim as the bartender arrived and poured a fresh glass.

"Damn, Kev, I'm sorry."

"Not your fault. Besides, I shouldn't be surprised. Amy and Helen were very close, and now all she's got left is me, and, well, let's face it, we both know I'm not exactly father of the year." He tipped his head back and took another generous gulp.

"It won't last forever, Kev. Amy is dealing with some heavy stuff right now. You both are."

"To tell you the truth, I'm actually getting really worried about her. She's becoming more and more withdrawn. She spends all her time either locked inside her room or down at the cemetery."

"Tried talking to her?"

"Of course, but whenever I do, we just end up arguing. I only want to help her, you know? I'm her father. I want to be there for her. The problem is I haven't the slightest clue what to say to an eighteen-year-old girl who's just lost her mother."

"Hey, if it's any consolation—and I know it's not—I've got a forty-five-year-old brother who's just lost his wife, and I haven't got a clue what to say to him either."

Kevin managed a small smile. "Well, Jack, you're doing a damn sight better than me."

Jack reached across the table and put his hand on his brother's arm. "Doubt that very much. But do you know what? I think I've just had an idea, something that might help."

"Oh?"

"It's a bit out of left field, but will you hear me out?"

"Right now, I'd consider anything."

Jack gave a tense smile and reached for his keys. "Stay put. I'll be right back."

Two minutes later, Jack returned from his car clutching a manila folder. He dropped it in front of Kevin and sat back down.

Kevin studied the front cover. It was a case file—the emblem of the Oregon State Police was emblazoned at the top, and there was a file number scribbled in red at the bottom. Kevin didn't recognize the number, but he did recognize the handwriting—it was Jack's.

"Say hello to your new assignment," Jack said.

Kevin's eyebrows ticked up. "My new assignment?"

"Before you say anything more, just take a look."

Confused, Kevin flipped the cover and started reading. It was the missing person case Jack had mentioned a moment ago. The file was two months old and wafer thin, containing only a half-dozen pages that for the most part consisted of interview transcripts and county search reports. From what Kevin could gather, the investigation had been coordinated from Portland, despite the fact that the disappearance had taken place in a small town a couple of hundred miles to the south. Straightforward enough, but it begged the obvious question: What did any of this have to do with him and Amy?

"I'm lost, Jack. Why are you trying to pawn off one of your cases?"

Jack shifted his drink to one side. "I won't bore you with all the details, but this one's a dead end. The consensus among the team is that the kid has skipped town. I was supposed to be driving down there tonight to formally notify the family that state police are shutting up shop, but . . ." Jack paused and cleared his throat. "I think you should be the one to go instead."

"Me?" Kevin looked down at the file again and reread the notes, just to make sure he wasn't missing something. "Jack, this is a copyboy errand. You actually want me to get in the car and drive three hours to a town in the middle of nowhere, just to pass that message on in person?"

"Yes, I do."

"May I ask why?"

"Because I think it might be a good idea if you got out of the city."

Kevin leaned back in his chair and gave his brother a long, dubious glare. "You must be kidding. What is sending me away going to achieve? I can't leave Amy on her own, not now."

"Of course not. I'm not suggesting you do."

"Then what *are* you suggesting?"

"That you take her with you."

Kevin would have laughed had his brother not sounded so serious. "You're not kidding, are you?"

"No, I'm not. And I think you should take your time too. Take a couple of days."

Kevin flipped the folder shut and slid it back across the table. "Sorry, I know you mean well, but the last thing Amy will want to do is pack a bag and go on a holiday."

"It's not a holiday. It's work." Jack slid the folder right back. "Tell her you've got to go away to close down an investigation—which is the truth—and tell her that you want her to go with you."

"And this is somehow going to bring us closer together? That's your great plan?"

"I never said it was great, but it's the best I can come up with."

"Jack, I'm not sure."

"Come on, think about it. Some time away from the house and a bit of ocean air might be just what you both need."

Kevin rested his elbow on the table and sat quietly for a moment, mulling the idea over. He did have to admit, begrudgingly, that his brother might have a point. Perhaps a change of scenery would do him and his daughter a world of good. After all, what did he have to lose? Persuading Amy wasn't going to be easy, though, and there was a high chance it could all backfire the moment they stepped out the door, but Jack was right—it could be worth a shot.

"All right, Jack. But if this whole thing goes south, I'm blaming you."

Jack winked as he threw back the rest of his drink. "Happy to take responsibility."

Kevin opened the folder and glanced over the case notes one last time, just to remind himself where he and Amy were headed. Then, to acquaint himself with the shortest possible route, as well as to defer the task of heading home and convincing his daughter of their impromptu road trip, he pulled up the map function on his phone and typed in the name of the town.

Point of destination: *Seabrook*.

3

IT HAD BEEN THREE WEEKS since the accident, and not a moment went by when Amy didn't feel like bursting into tears. All she could think about was her mother—about how much she loved her and missed her, and how much it hurt that they never got a chance to say goodbye.

The funeral hadn't helped, not that Amy thought it would. No amount of flowers, kind speeches, or sympathetic hugs could possibly bring her any comfort, or change the fact that her mother would still be here if she hadn't gotten in the car that morning, or if she'd left just one minute earlier, or one minute later, or if the driver of the other vehicle had bothered to look up from their phone and see that the light was red. If any one of those things had happened then her body wouldn't be buried in the ground, and Amy wouldn't be forced to endure this nightmare, forced to confront a future that now seemed so unbearably bleak.

Sometimes she wondered if the pain would ever go away. It was constant, like being stuck on a treadmill, a vicious cycle of anger and sorrow with no finish line in sight and no way of getting off. And what made it worse was that everyone seemed to want to help. Her father was on her case all the time, incessantly trying to get her to start "living normally" again, as though doing so might fast-track her through her grief, and her best friend had made a point of turning up every day to check in on her, a routine that seemed to imply Amy was fragile and delicate and in constant need of being watched. Amy appreciated that people were worried, and she was sure they meant well, but their persistent efforts to try to steer her through this emotional minefield only made the road ahead seem even more daunting and hopeless.

Like clockwork, though, while Amy was locked away in her room, staring at her laptop and perusing yet another website dedicated to "overcoming loss," the familiar rattle of Sam's car could be heard pulling up outside. Amy considered crawling under her sheets and pretending she wasn't there, but Sam was nothing if not persistent. And it seemed today would be no exception.

"I know you're in there, Ames, and I know you probably want to be left alone," Sam called out, knocking firmly on Amy's bedroom door. "But you should know that I'm not leaving without seeing my best friend, and she can't hide either—trust me, I still remember what she looks like. Let's see, she's about five foot four, with mousy brown hair, and green eyes, and she's also got this flawless skin that has always kinda bugged me because I know she loves french fries just as much as I do. But I'm taller. So I guess that balances it out. Except . . . being taller doesn't really balance things out, does it? It just makes me taller. And I think I'd much rather have perfect skin. But anyway . . ." Sam took a breath. "I'm worried, and even though she's the most amazingly brave person I know, I really want to see her, just to make sure she's okay." Sam paused again, waiting for a response. "Amy?"

Resigned to the fact that her friend wouldn't take no for an answer, Amy reluctantly closed the lid to her computer and went to let her in.

"There you are!" Sam cried out, falling into the room like a tower of stacked boxes and wrapping her arms around the back of Amy's neck. "How are you? Are you doing okay?"

"I'm okay," Amy replied, resting her chin on Sam's shoulder. "I'm okay."

As Amy propped a pair of pillows against the wall and climbed back into bed, Sam rolled a chair out from beneath Amy's desk and wheeled herself into the center of the room. On her lap was a paper bag from which she promptly removed a white carton, a napkin, and a plastic fork.

"I wasn't sure whether to keep turning up like this," Sam said breathlessly. She offered the carton and fork to Amy, then spent the next few minutes espousing how much self-control it had taken for her not to flood Amy's phone with messages and call every hour of the day. "I don't want you to think I'm checking up on you, but I think it's important you see someone regularly. And I figured you could do with something yummy to eat, too. Wasn't sure what you felt like, so I got something simple."

Though she wasn't hungry in the slightest, Amy indulged Sam's whim and peeled back the folds of the lid.

"It's just a noodle salad. But if you feel like something else, I can head back out. I can go to Bec Sucré and get some of those pain aux raisins that you like? Or maybe some sushi? You name it."

Amy sat in silence, twisting the soggy noodles into clumps around her fork while at the same time trying not to wince at the overpowering scent of soy and garlic wafting up from the box. She plucked out a solitary cube of celery and placed it in her mouth.

"No, this is good," she said, crunching slowly and getting the distinct impression that her every move was being closely evaluated.

"Are you sure?"

"Yeah. Haven't got much of an appetite, that's all." Amy stuck the fork in the food and closed the carton.

"I can see that," Sam said as she began inspecting Amy from head to toe. "There's hardly anything left of you."

"Don't you start too. You sound just like my dad."

"Speaking of him, where is he? Didn't see his car out front."

"Dunno."

"Is he back at work already?"

"Probably."

"Things still not great between you two?"

Amy shook her head, in no mood to recount the details of their most recent argument.

"Right. And are you still finding it hard to sleep?"

Amy nodded.

Sam took a sweeping gaze around the room and cleared her throat. "And I guess you still haven't been getting out of the house all that much either?"

"No," Amy answered softly. "I haven't."

"Ames, what would it take for you to come out with me? It doesn't have to be anything major. We could do whatever you want. We could go for a walk in the park. Maybe catch a movie? Or, hey, here's an idea . . ." Sam leaned forward, her eyes flickering with enthusiasm. "Why don't I get your gear together and we go for a drive out to Cannon Beach for a swim? Might feel good to get some fresh air, get your body moving. What do you say?"

"I don't think so, Sam. I'm sorry."

Sam got up and sat beside Amy, putting an arm around her friend. "I can't imagine what any of this must be like. I really can't."

"I'm scared, Sam . . . I just miss Mom so much. I'm scared it's always gonna hurt this bad. I'm scared I'm gonna feel this way forever."

"Oh, Ames."

Amy laid her head down on Sam's shoulder, unable to stop herself from crying. She was so upset that she didn't hear her dad's car pull into the driveway. She didn't even hear the front door open. It was only when she heard her name being called from downstairs that Amy blinked away her tears, slid off her bed, and poked her head into the hall.

"What is it?" she called out.

"Pack a bag," he answered. "We're going on a small trip."

4

TIME WAS RUNNING OUT for Ryan Porter. The storm that had struck Seabrook was only getting worse and his missing horse, Little Dipper, was nowhere to be found. She had bolted from their ranch and led Ryan on a frantic chase—but three hours had passed since he'd last caught sight of her and he didn't have a clue where to search next.

"Come on, Lil' Dip, you've got to be out here somewhere . . ."

Ryan tugged the reins of his own horse and took cover by a nearby tree, one of the few that hadn't been pulverized by the wind. Sheltering beneath a mangled mess of half-naked branches, he cupped his hands around his mouth and screamed as loud as he could over the roar of the rain.

"*Please*, Little Dipper!" he cried out. "Tell me where you are!"

The sky answered with an almighty growl, a sound so fierce it snatched the air from Ryan's throat. His steed, Bella, cowered against the trunk of the tree and thrashed her head, equally frightened.

"Easy, girl," he whispered, stroking her neck. "It's only thunder . . . just a little bit of thunder."

It must have been close to midnight, but Ryan couldn't be certain. He didn't have a phone on him. He had no way of calling for help, no way of knowing where they were. All he had was a flashlight, but its batteries were drained and the beam was pitifully faint, nowhere near strong enough to punch through the gloom. The situation seemed hopeless. There was no chance of picking up on a trail, if Little Dipper had even left one, or any way of knowing which areas they had already searched. Visibility was so poor, Ryan couldn't even be sure which way was home. But what frightened him the most was the fact that he had no clue how far they were from the edge of the cliff. Somewhere in the darkness loomed an unnerving drop, a two-hundred-foot plunge straight down to the ocean.

"Come on, Bella, we have to keep moving. If we stay here, we'll never find her." But Bella must also have sensed the danger they were in because she wasn't budging. "I know you're scared. I am too. But we can't give up. Lil' Dip needs us!"

But then, a miracle! Just as Ryan was smacking the flashlight against the palm of his hand, willing it to turn on, he glimpsed something in the distance: a shadow shifting in the rain. He lunged forward and fixed his gaze on the dark shape, certain his eyes were deceiving him, but then the shadow moved again, this time more erratically, and it was all Ryan could do not to leap out of his saddle.

I can't believe it! We found her!

Without taking his eyes off the moving shadow, Ryan fumbled for the rope hanging off his waist, hurriedly tied together a lasso, then pulled on Bella's reins to quickly maneuver her into position.

"Easy does it, girl. Easy does it . . ."

Edging closer, his hands shaking from adrenaline, Ryan sat up straighter and began swinging the rope in a wide clockwise motion high above his head. He knew he wouldn't get too many shots at this. Just finding her wasn't enough—if he messed this up, if he couldn't land his throw, Little Dipper could bolt and he might never see her again. Every move was critical.

"We can do this," he whispered to Bella. "Please, whatever you do, just stay very, very still."

Once in striking distance, Ryan readied himself and took a deep breath.

The first two attempts failed miserably. One throw fell woefully short, the other got caught by a blustery gust of wind and flew straight into the side of Little Dipper's stomach. The third, however, much to Ryan's relief, sailed through the air with perfect aim and fell cleanly around her head.

Before Little Dipper had a chance to react, Ryan jerked on the rope, snagging the neck of the noose tight, then coiled his end of the rope around his forearm and looped it up and over his wrist, tethering him to his frightened horse. Little Dipper spun around at once, nostrils flared, eyes white with panic.

"Whoa, easy girl. Relax. It's okay, it's me . . ." Ryan raised one hand in the air, desperately trying to calm her, while his other hand kept a deathlike grip on the rope. "I'm here to help, Lil' Dip. I'm here to get you home."

How Ryan managed to do that, though, he honestly couldn't say. Riding one horse while wrangling another was difficult enough, but add a storm, the dark of night, and three miles of impossibly dense forest—it was a miracle they made it back at all.

When the ranch finally appeared through a clearing in the trees, Ryan let out an exhausted sigh of relief. He dismounted, led the two horses into the barn, showed them to their stalls, set them up with some food and water, then dashed straight to the house, where he knew his father would be nervously waiting and no doubt wondering where he had been.

All the lights were off except in the kitchen, which was where Ryan found him, sitting in a chair with the telephone gripped in his hands.

"Son! Thank God, you're okay!"

"Everything's all right, Dad." Ryan rushed over and gave him a hug. "Sorry I'm so late."

"What happened?"

"You wouldn't believe it . . ."

Ryan made a pot of tea, pulled out two mugs, then sat down and told his father an elaborate story—not about rescuing Little Dipper, but instead a complete fiction about his truck breaking down.

"Out of nowhere the engine seized, right by milepost thirteen," Ryan explained, making up the details as he went along without so much as a blink or a sideways glance. "Had to hitch a ride back into town. Thankfully, the garage hadn't closed yet. One of the mechanics offered to drive out and give me a tow. They brought her back and diagnosed the problem—carburetor, I think they said it was? Anyhow, they stayed open and kindly replaced it for me. All fixed now."

His father listened intently throughout, saying nothing except at the end when he pointed to the phone and confessed he was only moments away from dialing 911. "You were gone so long. What with this weather we're having, I was beginning to fear the worst."

"Sorry, I should've called. Anyway, come on, I'll help you to bed. It's late, and you know what the doctors say about you not getting enough sleep."

"The doctors say lots of things," his father grumbled as Ryan stood behind him and helped him to his feet.

"Yes, for good reason."

"I suppose so."

"You know so, Dad. Don't you ever forget how far you've come. Now, come on, do as you're told."

Ryan slipped his arm around the crook of his father's elbow and escorted him to his room, gently easing him down onto the bed.

"Don't worry about me, Son. You need your rest too. I can manage."

"I know you can, but how about you let me help you tonight?"

After removing his father's slippers and lifting his legs up, Ryan pulled up the sheets, double-checked that the medical alarm cord was hanging within reach, then went to fetch a glass of water. When he returned, his father had rolled over to his side and was staring out the window. The view was pitch black but for a silver curtain of rain, visible whenever a crack of lightning lit up the night sky.

"Don't you think it's time?" his father whispered as Ryan drew the curtains shut, sealing the room off from the storm raging outside.

"Time for what, Dad?"

"Time to start thinking about what you're doing with your life."

Ryan turned and tossed him a curious glance. "I don't understand."

"You've got it all ahead of you. You should be out there chasing your dreams and kissing girls, all the things a young man should be doing." His father paused and looked away, his head sinking low. "Sometimes I feel like this place is holding you back. Like *I'm* holding you back."

"Dad, don't be ridiculous—"

"I mean it. I don't want you staying in Seabrook for the rest of your life, looking after me, working all the time, running yourself ragged. You do too much. This isn't the life I wanted for you."

Ryan stood in the doorway, surprised. His father had never spoken like that before, and the words gave him pause. Despite the guilt, he indulged the thought for a moment, wondering what he'd do if he really could choose differently. Where would he even begin?

He'd be lying if he said he'd never asked the question before, but the answer was never simple. Any path he chose invariably meant cutting ties to home, which was something he knew he could never do. He could never abandon the ranch, or say goodbye to Seabrook, or leave his father to fend for himself, and yet the idea that his father thought he could left Ryan speechless, even a little hurt. Maybe it was the meds talking, or maybe his father was just having one of his off days; whatever the reason, Ryan did his best to shrug it off.

"Don't talk nonsense," Ryan said. He flicked off the lights and moved into the hall, but not before popping his head into the room one last time.

"I'm your son. My place is here with you."

5

*L*AST NIGHT'S RESCUE had certainly left Ryan feeling worse for wear. Aching muscles and blistered hands were just some of the ailments greeting him when he woke the next morning, never mind his bruised and numb backside. Little Dipper was safe, though, and that's all that mattered—even if his body had paid a hefty price.

Stifling a groan, Ryan sat up and rubbed his eyes, then turned to check his bedside clock. The sun was already up, but the digits on the clock's display—which appeared to be unstable and flickering— were stuck on the wrong time. He wondered if a storm-related power surge had caused a fuse to blow, perhaps fried the clock's circuitry. Curious, he leaned over and gave it a shake, even tried hitting the reset button a few times, but each time the display returned the same digits: 10:57.

Great, just what I need, he thought with a sigh. *Something else around here that needs fixing.*

After leaning over to switch the clock off, Ryan dragged himself out of bed, threw on some pants and a shirt, and headed downstairs.

"Morning, Dad."

His father was seated at the dining table working on a crossword with a cup of tea cradled in his hand. Wispy threads of steam wafted out of a ceramic teapot, lending the room a sweet, fruity smell.

"Good morning, Son."

Ryan took a mug out of the cupboard and poured himself a cup too. "Sleep well?" he asked, pulling out a chair.

His father nodded, his eyebrows knitted together while he pondered one of the clues. Crosswords had been recommended by the doctors as an important recovery exercise—useful for re-familiarizing with words and helping to rewire the brain when recovering from a major stroke, they'd said. In those difficult early days of rehabilitation, Ryan had needed to sit beside him, work out the answers, and write them down. But now, four years on from that catastrophic event, his father was completing the puzzles all by himself. Well, almost by himself.

"Six letters," his father said, chewing the nib of his pen. "*Remain,* ending with *r.*"

Ryan scratched his jaw. "Hmm. Linger?"

"Ah! That's it."

Ryan blew the steam off his tea and glanced out the window. All was calm in the valley; the slopes of the hills were bathed in the sunlight, the sky cloudless and icy blue.

"Looks like the storm has cleared off. That sure was a nasty one, wasn't it?"

"Haven't seen one like it for a while," his father agreed as he scribbled letters into the empty boxes. "The trails won't be in good shape. Might even be a few trees down."

"Good point. I'll go take a look after I turn the horses out."

"Many bookings for today?"

"I'm not sure. Haven't had a chance to check."

"Been awfully quiet of late."

"Has it?"

"You haven't noticed?"

"It comes and goes . . . you know how it is." Ryan took his unfinished mug to the sink and abruptly changed the subject. "Hey, it's Friday, remember," he said, turning on the tap. "Don't forget you've got the physio coming this afternoon."

"Haven't forgotten."

"And you need to make sure you head outside for a walk today, okay? At least fifteen minutes."

His father responded with a mock salute. "Yes, sir."

"Good for you, Dad." Ryan dried his hands on a kitchen towel and made for the door, but not before his father reached out and grabbed his arm.

"Ryan, what I said last night, about how I thought you should leave the ranch . . . that wasn't what I meant to say. It came out all wrong."

"Don't worry about it."

"No, please, let me finish. All I meant was that you don't have to be trapped in this town forever, not if you don't want to be. I want you to know that you're free to make anything of your life, anything at all."

"And that's exactly what I'm doing," Ryan replied, giving his father a kiss on the forehead. "Seabrook is where I belong. There's nowhere else I would rather be than here at home, on this ranch, with you."

———⟨⟩———

Short work was made of the morning chores; Ryan filled the troughs, restocked the feeders, and mucked out the stalls in less than an hour. After setting the horses loose in the field, he then grabbed his hat and journal from the tack room, dragged his chair into the sun, and sat down to check the day's bookings. But when he flipped to inspect the entries, he discovered that both the morning and afternoon columns were empty. No groups were due to come through. Not one single rider.

Ryan slammed the journal shut and sank low into his chair, frustrated, but not entirely surprised. This was how the ranch made its money—scenic treks across the valley and trail rides around the neighboring state park forest—but visitor numbers had been dropping for a while and blank pages like these were becoming increasingly common. In fact, business had been so quiet that days on end could go by without a soul coming through the gate.

When this first started happening, Ryan had shrugged it off, trying to convince himself that it was nothing more than a seasonal blip, but it was getting harder to stay positive when each month the business seemed to plunge to new lows. The reason for the downtrend? He honestly couldn't say. Perhaps they needed to advertise more. But how? The ranch probably needed a page on the Internet to promote itself, but Ryan didn't have the first clue about setting up something like that. Computers were like voodoo to him. Their business had always survived on word of mouth and a stack of flyers inside the town hotel. In the past, that had been enough. Not anymore, it seemed.

But that wasn't the worst of it—what Ryan found most difficult was hiding all this from his father. When it came to anything to do with money, Ryan had made it a rule to always keep him in the dark. The doctors had said that avoiding stress and high blood pressure was critical to his long-term recovery. Fifty percent of people who had a stroke went on to have another, and they warned that it would be unlikely his father could survive a second one. Worrying over finances was the last thing he needed. But keeping up this charade was becoming more and more difficult, particularly on days like today when the ranch sat conspicuously empty.

"It's just a quiet patch," Ryan would often say. "Plenty of bookings coming up."

Lies.

All of them.

And the slump in business wasn't the only problem. The horses were aging and experiencing a growing number of health issues, which meant the expenses associated with their care were forever mounting. Month on month the bills were piling higher and higher, and Ryan's strategy of pretending "the check was in the mail" while pleading with the bank to borrow more money was no longer working. He was now over ninety days late on every single account, all the credit cards were maxed out, and he had borrowed against everything they owned, from the property itself to the ranch machinery, even down to the twenty-six-year-old skid steer rusting behind the shed. There was literally nothing left to draw against. And to make matters worse, just last month the bank had started sending letters, formal notices issued in stark white envelopes, bearing red stamps marked *Urgent*. He couldn't even bring himself to open those. Then, just the other day, someone had phoned the ranch and left a solicitous message on their machine, a problem that had required Ryan to dig deeper into his vault of cunning.

"A fellow from the bank got in touch," his father had said. "He wanted you to call him back."

"Oh?"

"Why would the bank be phoning?"

"You know what they're like, Dad—they'll be trying to sell us something, some newfangled insurance product probably. Waste of time if you ask me."

Desperate to stave off disaster, Ryan had even landed a part-time job at Rosie's, the diner in town. Joe and Linda weren't hiring, but they were willing to give him whatever work they could spare, running tables, working the till. During the last few weeks, he'd even become a half-decent fry cook. But it wasn't enough, not even close.

The dollars he scrimped and saved may as well have been pennies for all the difference they made. Short of looking to the sky and hoping for a miracle, he didn't know what to do. The ranch was in dire trouble, he was the only one who knew anything about it, and he feared it was only a matter of time before someone came knocking on their door.

In a futile attempt to distract himself, Ryan spent the rest of that day tending to odd jobs around the ranch. He replaced two rotting fence posts, repaired the broken hinge in stall seven, tore out some weeds, and washed down the horses. He even dragged himself into town to pick up a shift at the diner—but no amount of flipping burgers or making milkshakes seemed to do him any good. Ryan agonized over his predicament so much that by the time he had finished his shift, his overcooked brain must've resembled any one of the hundred patties he'd spent all afternoon turning on the grill. How much longer could this go on? Did he *really* think he could keep the bank at bay forever? Had he done the right thing by not telling his father the truth? He'd realized a long time ago that there were no easy answers.

A little after six, exhausted from all the worrying, Ryan hung up his apron and said farewell to Joe and Linda, thanking them for the shift. They gave him his usual wage and said there was more work tomorrow if he needed it.

"Whatever you can spare," he told them.

Before heading home, he crossed the town square and called in on the general store, where once a week he collected the mail. He received the usual across the counter—another wad of bills, some glossy brochures, the latest edition of the local newspaper, the *Seabrook Beacon*—but today there was something else: an unsealed white envelope.

Dropping the brochures in the bin and shoving the bills and the *Beacon* into his back pocket, Ryan stepped out onto the sidewalk and flipped over the envelope. No stamp, no postmark, but there was a worryingly familiar logo printed in the left corner.

Oh no.

His heart beating fast, he removed the contents of the envelope and found a note handwritten by Tom Tippenworth, branch manager of Pacific First & Mutual, Seabrook's one and only bank.

It read: *Ryan Porter, come and see me . . .*

Hands shaking, Ryan swallowed hard and tried to breathe, but his chest, already agonizingly tight, felt like it was about to cave in.

. . . to discuss a matter of utmost importance.

6

"WHAT DO YOU FEEL LIKE listening to, Amy?"

Kevin's finger rested on the radio dial; the Portland station had just fizzled into static and he was searching for something else to fill the air.

Amy curled up her legs, twisted her body toward the door, and said nothing. They had been driving for over an hour. Long since free of the interstate, they were now speeding through open country on a narrow two-lane road. She had no idea where they were headed, and she wasn't sure why she had agreed to come. Her dad had made the announcement with an air of finality, saying the excursion was "police business" and "only for the night," but that it would also be a chance for them to "spend some time together." How that would be possible if he planned to be working a case at the same time, Amy didn't know, but the last thing she wanted to do was put up a fight, so she had offered no objection and instead resolved to make it through the weekend with no arguing and as little drama as possible.

"Amy?"

He was still flicking through the stations, waiting for an answer.

Amy folded her arms in such a way that she could rest her head on the flat of her hand and muttered, "Anything, I don't mind," then spent the rest of the drive staring out the window.

—◈—

The journey neared its end some 120 miles later, when the road Amy and Kevin were on brought them to the outskirts of a small coastal town.

Noticing the car decelerate, Amy sat up straighter and saw that the view, previously a rotating scene of trees and rolling hills, now offered a glimpse of the Pacific Ocean. A large sign loomed ahead—a bright circular motif featuring the image of a blue-domed lighthouse, with a golden sun, squiggly blue ribbons of water, and a message arched above the lighthouse: *Welcome to Seabrook*.

They continued for another few miles, passing a church and a school, then navigating a series of tree-lined streets with porch-fronted cottages and farmhouse-style homes, before arriving in the center of town. The town square was quaint and equally picturesque; a generously proportioned redbrick town hall loomed over a large grassy plaza, surrounded on the fringes by a pastiche of wooden buildings. One of those, according to the robotic voice on her dad's phone, was their destination.

"There, that's it," he said, lifting one finger off the wheel and pointing toward a grand, four-level hotel with a black awning out front, marked in gold lettering with the words *The Lookout*.

They parked, grabbed their bags from the trunk, and headed inside.

The lobby was a wide-open space with a low vaulted ceiling and halls leading off to the left and right. One hall led to a corridor of guest rooms, the other toward the bar. There was an unmanned concierge desk over by the stairs, on top of which was a small rack of brochures, a banker's lamp, and a notice that read *Hotel Customers—See Bar* with an arrow pointing to the left. Kevin and Amy duly followed.

The bar was nautically themed, a kind of cross between a saloon and a beach hut. Drooping sheets of drift net covered the ceiling, surfboards and canoes adorned the walls, and two giant ships' wheels, upcycled into chandeliers, hung from above. In one corner was a small stage with a lone microphone stand, but tonight music was coming from a retro jukebox sitting pride of place beneath a framed photograph of a man holding an impressively large fish. The place was busy too, every stool and chair occupied.

Setting the bags at his feet, Amy's dad leaned across the bar countertop and made eye contact with a burly lady pouring a pint.

"Evenin'," she said in a deep Southern accent as she sidled toward them, locks of wavy hair billowing behind her. "What'll it be?"

"We're checking in. We have a room booked."

"Right you are." The bartender squatted and pulled out a hefty tome from somewhere down below. She cleared her throat, licked her thumb, and flipped through the pages. "Last name?"

"Tucker."

Her roving finger found the booking with minimal effort. "There, got ya." She grabbed a pen from her pocket and scribbled something down. "Now I just need to take a peep at your credit card and identification, if you don't mind."

"Yes, of course."

While Amy's dad reached for his wallet, the bartender tossed a glance at Amy and cheerfully asked if it was their first time in Seabrook. Amy forced a smile and nodded.

"Wow, you folks sure have picked a fine time to visit! Tomorrow we've got a big festival that'll be running all day long, right outside in the square, so you needn't go far if you're short of something to do. And if that's not in your wheelhouse then make sure you check out the brochure rack by the stairs, right where you came in. There's plenty"—she paused to take Kevin's credit card, which she inserted into a machine—"to do," she continued, punching in a series of numbers into a keypad. "Fishing charters, guided walks, great trails up in the woods, easy hikes, if that's your sort of thing. Otherwise, closer to town, we've got the beach just a hop, skip, and a jump down the street."

"We'll be sure to keep that in mind," Kevin said.

"There, you're all done," she said, sliding back the credit card. "Your room is on the second floor, end of the hall: 212. Breakfast is from six until nine. We run a light dinner service here in the hotel, but there's also a grocer two doors down, and Rosie's Diner is over yonder. If you mention you're staying at The Lookout, you'll get ten percent off your check." She placed a pair of silver keys on the counter while at the same time affording Amy a quick smile and a wink. "If you need anything, anything at all, just come and talk to me—the name's Peggy."

"Thank you," Kevin said.

Amy followed her dad out of the bar, back through the lobby, and up the stairs. The age of the hotel quickly became apparent; floorboards creaked and groaned, and the balustrades wobbled the higher they went. Their room was at the end of a dimly lit corridor, its walls covered in equal parts warped wainscoting and maize-colored wallpaper. When they reached their door, Amy's dad did his best to put on a brave face.

"Okay, so it's obviously not the Ritz," he remarked as he twisted the key and proceeded to give the bottom of the door a persuasive kick. "But it's only for one night."

In contrast to the rest of the hotel, however, their room was distinctly contemporary and pleasant. Polished floorboards and modern furniture indicated that it had recently been refurbished. On one side was a generously sized cream-colored sofa, and on the other a writing desk that doubled as a stand for a newish-looking television and lamp. There was a glass table positioned near the window, through which Amy caught a glimpse of the ocean and the lighthouse. While her dad poked his head outside and admired the view, she wandered into the adjoining room, where she found a modest bed, two bed-side tables, and a tall freestanding wardrobe. A vase of dried flowers provided color, as did three framed prints hanging on the walls that portrayed differing versions of the same blue-domed lighthouse.

Her dad set their bags down in the room and told Amy she could have the bed, and that he was happy sleeping on the couch. "It's coming up seven," he added. "I don't suppose you're hungry?"

Amy shook her head and looked out the window. After a long afternoon stuck in the car, all she wanted was fresh air and time alone.

"I might go for a walk," she said.

"Are you sure?"

"Yeah," she replied, staring at the beach. "Need to stretch my legs."

He stepped to one side as she retrieved her jacket from her bag and made for the door. She had expected to hear an objection, a question, or at the very least a disapproving comment, but none were forthcoming. To her surprise, he just reached into his pocket and handed over one of the keys.

"Take this with you in case I decide to head downstairs for a drink. And please don't go far, okay?"

Amy put the key in her pocket. "I won't."

The walk to the beach took only a few minutes, but it was surprisingly busy, full of couples strolling hand in hand, people playing fetch with their dogs, children splashing about in the shallows. Hoping for some solitude, Amy's attention was drawn to the northern end of the bay, where she spotted a rocky outcrop protruding into the ocean, at the very end of which stood the town's lighthouse. Seeing as the tower appeared to be deserted, Amy buttoned up her jacket and set off straight for it.

The lighthouse was farther from shore than it initially seemed, and up close it bore little resemblance to the pristine tower depicted in her room. Its circular wall was pockmarked with cracks and holes, giving the impression that a single tap from a hammer would be enough to bring the whole building crashing down. The domed roof had faded to pale gray, and the lantern room, teeming with gulls that had made it their home, appeared as though it had taken artillery fire, such was the damage to its glass surrounds. Guarding the base was a tall fence that wrapped all the way around, and through diamond-shaped holes in the wire mesh, fixed with permanence to the building's boarded-up door, Amy could see a sign that read:

NO PUBLIC ACCESS

DANGER——UNSTABLE STRUCTURE

BY ORDER OF SEABROOK COUNTY,
ENTRY INTO THE LIGHTHOUSE
IS STRICTLY PROHIBITED.

Heeding the warning, Amy traversed a path around the fence, climbed down some jagged rocks, and found a quiet place to sit. The sun had already set behind a wall of clouds and there was hardly any wind, leaving the ocean looking cold, flat, and ominously gray.

Staring at the distant horizon, it wasn't long before Amy's thoughts turned to her mother. Amy missed her like always, but sitting here, far from home on the edge of this small, remote town, the ache seemed almost unbearable. Not since the day she lost her could Amy remember feeling so low. Even her pendant, which she had so often turned to for comfort, brought little respite. The beloved jewel, given to Amy by her mother, had been hanging around her neck since she was a little girl. Small, silver, and intricately detailed, it depicted a mermaid perched on a rock, her long hair frozen in the wind and her tail curled into a perfect circle around a luminous blue moonstone. It had always been a symbol of her mother's love, a precious object connecting them both—but its power and magic were gone. Now, touching her pendant felt like falling through a trapdoor, instantly transporting Amy to a place filled with nothing but pain and heartbreak. What had once been a source of comfort had become nothing more than a cruel reminder of everything she had lost, a souvenir of the hole in her life that could never again be filled.

7

*O*BEYING TOM'S NOTE was the last thing Ryan felt like doing. The situation was grim enough; meeting face-to-face and getting a lecture from the bank manager was hardly going to make it any better. So, to avoid the unpleasantness, Ryan threw the note in a garbage can and double-timed it back to the lot behind the town's hotel, where he had parked his truck. *Better to drive home*, he thought— he would find a way to deal with this problem in the morning.

But that wasn't going to be possible, because it just so happened that Tom was working late that night, and from inside the glass-walled office of the bank he had spotted Ryan making a hurried dash across the town square.

"Well, look at that . . . if it isn't Ryan Porter."

Ryan's stomach lurched as he turned around and locked eyes with the bank manager. "Oh, good evening, Mr. Tippenworth," he replied, doing his best to feign surprise. "Fancy seeing you, sir."

Tom, who wasn't the least bit swayed by Ryan's attempt to cloak himself in geniality, stared at him grievously, saying nothing, waiting to see if Ryan had any excuse for why he'd been ignoring him for so long. But Ryan didn't, and the silence that prevailed in those interminably long few seconds was deafening.

"You're alive and well, I see."

Ryan met the comment with an awkward laugh. "I am."

"We really do need to talk."

"Oh, sorry, Mr. Tippenworth, but I don't think I can right now. You see, I've got to get—"

"Would you prefer I came to the ranch?" Tom interrupted sternly. "Perhaps we can discuss the matter there instead?"

The threat made Ryan freeze.

"Didn't think so." Tom stepped closer and folded his arms. "As I'm certain you're aware, I've been"—he stopped to correct himself— "the *bank* has been trying to reach you for some time now."

"Yes, and I'm very sorry—I know what this is all about."

"You do?"

"I'm behind on payments, I realize that, but it won't be long now, business will pick up and we're gonna get back on track." Even Ryan had to admit the conviction in his plea was sorely lacking. It sounded rehearsed and robotic and he wasn't fooling anyone.

"Behind on payments? Ryan, do you know how long it's been?"

"We're going through a slow patch, that's all," Ryan said, courageously rebuffing Tom with the same lies he'd told his father.

"I'm sorry to be the one to tell you this, but I'm afraid it's worse than that. Am I to take it that you haven't even been opening the mail?"

Ryan shook his head.

"So, you're not aware. Well then, this is going to come as quite the shock."

Something of a gulp sounded from inside Ryan's throat.

"As you rightly know, you were already dangerously overextended, long before this 'slow patch' of yours, but the lack of cash flow isn't the only issue the bank is concerned about. The other part of the problem is that your drawings have continued to increase, which has been compounded by the fact that your interest rates went up when we resettled the loan last year." Tom drawled on for another minute, drifting into technical territory and citing terms like "loss mitigation" and "negative equity" and "margin of risk," none of which Ryan understood.

"Just be straight with me," Ryan blurted out. "In English, please."

Tom bowed his head and took a step closer. "It's bad."

"What do you mean it's bad? How bad?"

"Bad . . . as in, I'm afraid the bank must now take action."

"Action? What kind of *action*?"

"The ranch has reached the point where it now owes more than it's worth. It's no longer viable for the bank to provide you the loan. Do you understand what that means?"

Ryan swallowed and mumbled something inarticulate.

"It means that, in three days, a foreclosure notice will be served on your property. The bank intends to put the ranch to auction and sell before the month is out."

"No, no, there must be some mistake." It took Ryan a considerable length of time to work his way through the shock. His heart was up somewhere near his throat.

"I'm afraid not."

"But three days? That's far too soon."

"Ryan, this has all been explained to you," Tom said, his tone beginning to harden. "If you'd only opened the letters, you would have had more time."

Ryan shook his head violently. Shock gave way to panic when he began thinking of his father. "Please, Mr. Tippenworth, you can't do this to us. There must be something I can do. *Anything*." His voice began to break.

Tom placed his hand on Ryan's shoulder. "The wheels are already in motion. Barring a miracle, your ranch *will* be sold. My advice is that you get your affairs in order. Come clean with your father—and do it soon."

Ryan's spirits were so crushed that he couldn't stay steady on his feet. The asphalt suddenly felt like it was shifting and sinking beneath him.

Come clean with your father.

Tom delivered those words so freely, yet he had no idea what they meant, what grave ramifications could likely result.

"I beg of you. You don't understand what this will do to him."

But Tom was resolute and stood there shaking his head, unwilling to hear any more of Ryan's pleas.

"What exactly did you think was going to happen?" Tom countered. "How did you imagine this would all end? I understand your reasons for needing the money, and I understand why you couldn't tell your father, but why on earth have you kept it hidden from him for this long? Didn't you ever worry about what would happen if one day he decided to check the account?"

"I . . . I don't know. I have to have more time—anything you can spare!"

"Three days, Mr. Porter, that's all there is left. I'm sorry. I truly am. If you need to speak with me, you know where I am."

And with that, Tom turned and walked away.

Ryan grabbed the side mirror of his truck and leaned on it for balance, fearing he was about to faint. It was like a bomb had just gone off, obliterating everything but for the small plot of gravel on which he stood.

Foreclosure. In three days.

The shocking news left his head throbbing with pain. He couldn't think straight. He rubbed at his temple, imploring the ache to subside, when suddenly he looked up and saw a neon sign fixed to the façade of the hotel: *BAR OPEN*.

Though he rarely felt the draw of alcohol, Ryan gravitated toward those bright letters like a moth to a flame, in desperate need of something—*anything*—to numb the shock.

8

*A*MY FLED THE LIGHTHOUSE in a cloud of sorrow, desperate to get back to the hotel. A shortcut across the dunes took her down a quiet, windswept street, which snaked its way behind the beach and led her back to the town square. Keeping her head down so that nobody could see that she was crying, she crossed the lobby, hurried up the stairs, then rushed down the hall and disappeared inside her room. Thankfully, her dad wasn't there; it seemed he had gone downstairs for a drink, just as he had suggested he might.

Unable to hold in the emotions any longer, Amy collapsed onto the bed and burst into tears. She was so upset that she ripped the chain from around her neck and clenched her mother's pendant in her fist, squeezing so tightly that its jagged points dug deep into her flesh. She just couldn't bear it, couldn't bear the agony of missing her mother a moment longer. The grief was unrelenting. All she wanted was an escape, a chance to shut off her mind, to close her eyes and get just the tiniest bit of sleep, anything that would let her go one damn minute without having to be constantly reminded of her loss.

Then, amid her despair, Amy realized that her dad had something that could help.

Sniffing back the tears, she leapt off the bed and ran into the other room, straight for his duffel. She unzipped it and pulled out his toiletry bag, inside of which she found a small container full of white tablets: his sleeping pills. He had been taking these for as long as she could remember. They went with him everywhere.

Acutely aware that he could return to the room at any moment, and preferring that he not know she was pilfering his medication, Amy rushed to unscrew the cap, then went to the bathroom to pour a glass of water. She didn't bother searching the label's tiny text for directions, didn't bother counting the pills; instead, she tapped out a small handful, chucked them into her mouth, took a gulp of water, then swallowed. She returned to the room, lay down on the bed, and closed her eyes.

But nothing seemed to happen.

Half an hour passed.

Still nothing.

How long was this supposed to take?

Despite taking them on an empty stomach, Amy didn't feel the slightest bit drowsy, couldn't even muster a single yawn. Taking an extra dose crossed her mind, but she decided to wait. To pass the time, she would run a bath, maybe try to eat something, and then if she still wasn't feeling tired, she'd swallow a couple more.

She stumbled out of bed and headed back into the bathroom. The tile floor was like ice against her bare feet. Against the wall sat an old claw-foot tub. She leaned over and secured the plug, twisted the faucets, then sat on a stool and waited. But just like the pills, the bath filled excruciatingly slowly. When it was barely a third full, Amy undressed and hopped in, laying her body flat with her head arched against the rim. As the water rose against the flesh of her skin, she became restful, and her thoughts began to drift and wander.

Soon her eyes began to feel weak and heavy. Amy dragged her gaze around the room, which had become cloaked in a strange haze. It seemed the walls were shifting in and out of focus, the ceiling arching and bowing, the room bending out of shape. Her mind soon followed, shrouded in the same thick fog.

Where am I?

Amy tried to search her memory, but her concentration was slipping. She couldn't grab hold of a thought. She had no recollection of where she was, how she'd come to be there, nor could she recall the tablets she had digested a short time ago, which were now invading her bloodstream. She drew a long breath, watched her chest rise and fall through drowsy eyes, but the movement seemed to last forever. Everything became distorted. Her stomach was starting to hurt.

A small fragment of awareness told Amy that she needed to get out of the tub, but the water rising around her body felt thick and gelatinous, almost like glue encasing her limbs. She was drained of energy and couldn't move. Her heartrate was so slow she could mark entire breaths between the beats. Soon she couldn't even remember her own name. In a fog of complete delirium, only one discernible thought remained:

Please . . . I just want to go to sleep.

9

RYAN GAWKED at the dazzling array of bottles on the wall, dumbfounded. Alcohol wasn't his thing. His only goal was to ingest something so potent that it might dim the sound of Tom Tippenworth's voice, if such a feat was even possible.

Three days.

The words were reverberating in his head, the grim news still sinking in. The sentence had been handed down. In three days, his father would learn the truth, every shameful last detail.

That it was going to happen was a certainty; Ryan had accepted that. The only question left was which revelation would devastate his father more: learning that the ranch that had been in the family for generations—the ranch he thought would one day be passed down to his son—was about to be seized by the bank and sold, or finding out that it was Ryan who bore the responsibility. That he had borrowed the money and put the property into debt and then spent the next four years trying to cover it all up. What would his father say? How would he react? How would a man so fragile and vulnerable, a man whose body had already conspired against him in the past by way of inflicting a catastrophic stroke, bear the weight of such news?

Just imagining the possible repercussions made Ryan feel so sick to his stomach that he didn't notice when Peggy, the hotel proprietor, whom he had spoken with on occasion whenever he stopped by to restock flyers for the ranch, greeted him from the other side of the bar.

"Why, hello there, young Ryan."

"Peggy—um, hi."

"I must say, this is a surprise." She slid a giant clamshell filled with an assortment of salty nuts in his direction.

"Oh?" he said distantly, still trying to wrangle back his thoughts. "Why's that?"

"Only because I don't think I've ever seen you come into our fine establishment this late in the evenin', and certainly never without a stack of flyers in your hands." She grabbed a wet tumbler from a rack and started twisting a rag inside it while fixing him with a stare. "You know, math was never my thing, but even I can put two and two together and see you've got the look of a man with something on his mind."

"It's just been one of those days," Ryan lied, manufacturing a smile, one that he hoped would mask any evidence of the turmoil going on inside his head.

"We all have 'em," Peggy said as she reached for a nearby bottle. She twisted the cap and poured a glass of amber liquid. "Here, see if this'll make you feel better."

It didn't. Seconds after taking a sip, Ryan experienced what he could only describe as a caustic trail of fire blazing down the back of his throat, followed by a spirited bout of coughing.

"Whoa there, cowboy! You okay?"

Ryan pushed the glass aside. He felt ridiculous, even a little embarrassed. What exactly was he trying to accomplish? Here he was trying to distract himself from his problems at home, when all this was doing was making him miss the ranch and his father more. He coughed again more forcefully before sliding off the stool.

Peggy looked at him. "Everythin' all right?"

"Everything's fine. I just need to be getting home."

The pain in his head worsened when his feet hit the floor. Squinting from the discomfort, he slid a ten-dollar bill across the counter and asked after the restroom.

Peggy emptied the glass into a sink. "You'll need to go that way," she said, pointing out toward the lobby. "Use the one on the second floor—the one down here is on the fritz."

"All right, thanks."

"You take it easy now, ya hear?"

Ryan made his way upstairs and found the bathroom down the far end of the hall. He hunched over the sink, cupped his hands beneath the faucet, and spent a minute freshening up before making a slow stride back toward the door. He tugged a paper towel from a dispenser, dried off his face and hands, then stepped back into the hall.

"What the—"

His eyes darted to the floor. Water was gathering around his shoes. The puddle, which was growing quickly, appeared to be seeping out under the door of a nearby room. Had someone left a tap on? Was there a leak coming from somewhere? Prompted to investigate, Ryan approached the door and knocked.

"Hello?" he called out.

No answer.

"Hello?" he yelled, a little louder. "Is anyone inside?"

Again, no answer. Ryan glanced up and down the deserted corridor, unsure what to do. Meanwhile the deluge continued unabated, water spreading farther out into the hall. He banged on the door with the side of his fist, much more firmly.

"Is everything all right in there? Hello?"

Still nothing.

He reached for the handle, expecting it to be locked, but instead it turned freely.

As the door swung open, an empty room was revealed before him, spotless but for a duffel lying in the middle of the floor. Ryan stepped inside, his eyes immediately traveling along the ground, following the trail of water that led to another closed door to his left. White tiles were visible beneath the threshold. The bathroom. He called out once more, but there was still no answer, just the same unsettling sound of running water, now noticeably amplified.

Ryan pushed down on the handle. This door wasn't locked either. Peering through an inch-wide gap, he glimpsed a bathtub. It was of the vintage sort, with ornate faucets and a thick roll around the edge. Two taps were running full bore, a curtain of water spilling over the rim. He nudged the door open a little more, holding his breath.

Oh no.

There was a girl lying in the bathtub. Her whole body was submerged except for her head, which was arched back over the rim. The water had risen to her chin. Her eyes were closed. She was very still. *Too* still. Was she . . . asleep? Ryan's thoughts spun out in a hundred different directions. He couldn't make any sense of this. How could she be oblivious to the running water? How could she have not woken up?

"Hello?"

His voice was barely a whisper and failed to elicit a response, so he tried again, this time a fraction louder.

"Excuse me. Hello?"

The girl remained motionless. He took a step closer. He could see that her skin was pale and her lips tinged purple. The tension inside his chest ratcheted up even higher. Fearing the worst, he spoke much louder, projecting his voice high above the roar of the taps.

"Are you all right? Wake up. *Please*, wake up!"

10

AMY HAD ONLY a vague awareness of the emptiness surrounding her. Nothing made any sense. Thoughts were indistinguishable. They flew in and out of her head without leaving the slightest trace of meaning behind. There was nothing she could latch on to. Nothing seemed real, nothing except for a faint, distant sound, shapeless and obscure . . . a voice.

She didn't know where it was coming from or to whom it belonged, but through the darkness, with words that weaved in and out of her ears like ghostly ribbons, Amy was sure the voice was calling to her.

"Hello," the voice said. "Are you all right?

Scraps of thought began falling like confetti, fleeting images, fragments of memories. Amy could see her pendant, could remember ripping it off her neck, and she could also see a lighthouse: a dark tower with a golden beam that was slowly glowing brighter and brighter against an inky black sky. Then, suddenly, as though she was stumbling out of a cave, the darkness began to recede.

———

Ryan was about to flee the room to call for help when he spotted the girl's eyelids twitch. He inched closer and saw her lips begin to move, saw her cheeks begin to redden and fill with color.

Oh, thank God.

Not wanting to do anything that might startle her, he tiptoed back to the doorway, unsure whether to make a discreet exit or stay to make sure she was okay. But before he could decide what to do, the girl was opening her eyes. A second later she was gripping the rim of the tub and trying to pull herself up. Had she looked to the right, she would have seen Ryan standing by the door, but she was too pre-occupied with the sight of the overflowing tub and running faucets.

Ryan had no choice but to announce himself. He leaned forward slightly, hoping to alert her to his presence in the gentlest way possible.

"Hello?" he softly called out. "Are you all right?"

———

Amy twisted her head and locked eyes with a figure standing by her door. She had no idea who he was. Had no idea where he'd come from. How did he get in their room? And why was he just standing there in her bathroom . . . *watching her*!

"What the hell . . ."

"Hey, my name is——"

"I don't care what your name is! What are you doing in my bath-room?"

"No, wait, this isn't what you think . . ."

Amy lunged to snatch a towel from the railing and covered herself as she jumped to her feet. She then let out an ear-popping scream, one that rang like a siren inside the small room.

"No, please don't do that . . ." The intruder showed her his open palms and staggered backward, colliding with the doorframe and tumbling to the floor. "I was only—"

Amy thrust a finger in the air while simultaneously trying to keep the towel in place around her middle. "*Get out!*"

"Please—"

"*I said, get out!*"

"But you've got it all wrong!"

"*Now!*"

The intruder continued rambling through some incoherent explanation, but Amy wasn't the least bit interested and let loose another scream, followed by a string of colorful expletives.

"If you could just let me explain!"

"I don't care! *Just go!*"

The intruder hobbled to his feet, his face flushed red with embarrassment. "Honestly, I meant you no harm! I'm so sorry!" he yelled, and he stumbled out of the room and took off, his apology continuing even as he was halfway out the door.

Amy turned off the taps and jumped out of the bath. She twisted the knot in her towel tighter, which only made her heartbeat even faster. It took her a good minute to catch her breath. She didn't know whether to call for help, give chase, or jump straight on the phone and dial 911. How did that creep get in? How long had he been standing there? Had she really forgotten to lock the door? And where on earth was her dad?

After hurriedly toweling off, Amy slipped on some clothes and left the bathroom in search of her phone. She found it fast and was about to dial, but then she saw the extent of the flood she had unwittingly created. Not only had water spread out into the main room, but it was also seeping beneath the door and traveling out into the hall. She hesitated before dialing, considering the possibility that the intruder's motives mightn't have been so sinister after all. Maybe this was why he had come into her room? To help?

But whether that was the case or not, it didn't matter; the priority right now was getting this mess cleaned up before her dad came back. Amy could only imagine the questions she'd face if he saw this, never mind how worried he'd be if he spotted his half-empty pill container and found out she had fallen asleep in the bath. Knowing him, he'd undoubtedly jump to the worst possible conclusion.

Amy moved fast and grabbed as many towels as she could find, first by exhausting the supply in the room, then raiding the hotel's laundry cupboard down the hall. She got down on her hands and knees and soaked up the water as best she could. Thankfully, it lifted from the tiles and hardwood floors with relative ease, leaving behind only a mild dampness that she hoped would dry by morning.

When she was done, Amy stowed her dad's pill container back in his duffel, closed the door, switched off the lights, and climbed back into bed. Still drowsy from the drugs, she yawned deeply and fell asleep with no trouble at all, not stirring even once. She was so tired that she completely forgot about the intruder, nor did she think to question the whereabouts of her dad, who still hadn't returned. And she certainly didn't notice the light emanating from outside, a golden beam that cut through the night sky and was pointed at the first floor of the hotel . . . straight at her bedroom window.

11

*K*EVIN'S MIND was stuck on Amy. He had just seen her return to the hotel and rush up the stairs, but from the way she had kept her arms folded and head down, it seemed that she might have been upset, and that left him feeling unsure about what he should do next.

His instinct was to give chase, but there was a voice in his head telling him to refrain. After all, the last thing Amy would want was him knocking on the door checking if she was all right, smothering her with questions. And the last thing *he* wanted was for yet another one of their conversations to end in an argument. This trip was supposed to give them a change of scenery, a chance to reconnect, and while he'd been skeptical of Jack's idea at first, they were here now and he was determined to give it his best shot. If that meant staying put and giving Amy some space, then that's what he would try to do. He only wished it wasn't so damn hard.

Hoping to take his mind off things, Kevin pulled out his phone and once again reached out to his brother.

"Hey buddy," Jack answered. "How's everything going down there?"

"Hard to say right now. Amy was quiet on the drive down. I'm trying to let her be, which seems counterintuitive to this great plan of yours."

"Keep your chin up. You two are going to be fine."

"Yeah, we'll see. Ask me again in twenty-four hours."

"Still, must feel better to be getting out of that house for a bit, don't you think?"

"What's that supposed to mean?"

"Nothing. Just that there are probably lots of reminders of Helen."

"And?"

"And that some breathing room might do you some good, that's all. Hence the whole point of the trip, you know?"

"I thought the point of this trip was for me to run one of your errands."

"You know what I mean, Kev."

Kevin sighed into the phone. He couldn't argue Jack's point. It was true, reminders of his wife were everywhere back home, made even worse by the fact that the house had remained largely undisturbed since her death. Upstairs on her bedside table, the book she had been reading was still sitting underneath the lamp, marked at a page somewhere near halfway. Her wardrobe was exactly as she'd left it, shoes and clothes ordered neatly, and in the bathroom, her toothbrush remained perched next to his. The smell of her soap and shampoo still lingered, her fragrance trapped in pockets of the house, thick in the air. Even the oversized day planner on the refrigerator had yet to be wiped clean, and its schedule, which Helen had studiously kept up to date, eerily taunted the days ahead. There was no escaping it—you couldn't turn a corner without coming across something.

"You're right, Jack. I'm sorry."

"Don't apologize."

"No, it was a good idea for us to get away from it all. I shouldn't be biting your head off."

"Forget about it. Tell me about the place you're staying? What's it like?"

Kevin leaned back in his chair and glanced around the large, crowded room. "It's pretty old but has its charms. Kind of reminds of me that old Victorian Helen and I had in Buckman. Do you remember?"

"Sure. That was after you joined the department, that little fixer-upper."

"That's right," Kevin mused, his head now swimming with memories. "Helen was so excited when we bought that place. It wasn't much to look at. The gutter was hanging by a thread and the roof probably had half a dozen holes in it. There was a big storm one night and I remember the two of us running around at two in the morning, trying to catch all the leaks. In the end we just gave up, collapsed on the ground, and started laughing. Maybe it's because we were young and didn't know any better, but we felt invincible, like there was nothing that could hurt us. As long as we had each other, we would be all right. I guess that all sounds a bit silly now, doesn't it?"

"No, it doesn't. Sounds like two young people who were in love."

"We really were." Kevin lowered his head and dwelled on the memory for a moment longer, and as he did his gaze drifted to his wedding ring. "The day we got engaged, I knew I was going to love that woman forever."

"You mean the day that Helen proposed to *you*," Jack said jokingly.

"That's right," Kevin admitted, his throat tightening at the memory. "And to think we'd only been together a year when she popped the question."

"It happened on her parents' farm, right?"

"Yeah. We'd been staying there for the week. It was my first time meeting her folks—never been more nervous in my life. It was the very last day of our trip when she woke me up early, stuck a spade in my hand, and told me she had a surprise waiting outside."

"Classic Helen."

"I know. She marched me out to this tree—a huge cottonwood on the edge of their property—then pointed to the ground and said, 'Start digging.' Didn't take me long to find the box with the letter inside."

"How long had it been buried again?"

"Nine years."

"Wow. And you still carry it around with you, right?"

Kevin reached into his pocket, pulled out his wallet, and saw the letter peeking out from the main compartment like a small sail, a sliver of yellowish paper with the ghostly strokes of Helen's handwriting faintly shining through.

"Of course," he said. "It's never left my side."

"I know I've told you this before, but my wife always thought your engagement was the most romantic story she'd ever heard. You two were lucky to have found each other."

Kevin folded the letter and tucked it safely back inside his wallet.

"We were," he said, bravely trying to mask the scratchy pain in his throat. "Until everything changed. Until *I* changed."

"We all change, Kev, sooner or later."

"No, not all of us. Helen never did. She never lost sight of what was important. She always knew what she wanted, so much so that she wrote a letter to someone she hadn't even met yet, buried it in the ground, and vowed only to dig it up once she knew she'd found the person she wanted to spend the rest of her life with. That's the kind of woman she was. She was always so strong, so incredibly sure of herself. Me on the other hand, sometimes I look in the mirror and don't even know who I am anymore. Sometimes I feel so far away from where I started, so far from the man I always thought I'd turn out to be.

When I agreed to marry Helen, I promised her the world. I promised I would make her proud. But all I ever really did was let her down. And now I'm letting Amy down too."

"Kev, that's not true."

"It sure feels like it. My little girl is all grown up. I was never there when it counted. Now it feels like our relationship is broken beyond repair."

"Amy loves you. She's just hurting right now, and she's gonna need some time to process the loss. You both do."

"I wish that were true, Jack, but Helen was the glue that held our family together. I'm lost without her."

There was silence for a moment as Kevin's thoughts were derailed by the jovial chatter filling the bar. He moved the phone away and quietly sniffed back a tear before wiping his nose on the cuff of his shirt.

"Can I ask you something, Jack?"

"Anything."

"Do you ever stop and think about it?"

"About what?"

"About this job we do, and why we do it."

Jack went silent for a moment, needing a moment to process the sudden swerve in the conversation. "You know why we do this," he finally said.

"To protect the ones we love, right?"

Jack hesitated again. "Don't go there, Kev. There's no use in beating yourself up over what happened. Helen's death was a tragedy, a terrible car accident. She was in the wrong place at the wrong time, that's all. There's nothing you could've done."

"I know, but that's not what I mean. I want to know if you've thought about what this job does to you. The sacrifices we've had to make, the time away from our families, the awful side of humanity we've had to bear witness to."

"It's not an easy life, I won't deny that."

"But do you ever wonder if it's all been worth it?"

"Kev, where exactly are you going with this?"

Before Kevin could answer, he was interrupted by the bartender, the same overzealous woman who had checked him and Amy in earlier.

"Something wrong with the pour, mister?"

Kevin stared at her for a moment. "Jack, we'll have to pick this up later." He ended the call and put his phone down. "I'm sorry?"

The bartender gave a not-so-subtle nod at Kevin's whiskey, which had been sitting untouched for so long that the ice had melted and the liquid inside had turned a pallid shade of yellow.

"Your drink," she said. "Something wrong with it?"

"Oh, not thirsty, I guess."

"Would ya like another? On the house?"

"Thanks, but no."

"You're a cop, aren't you?"

"Pardon me?"

"Saw your badge when you checked in, right there in your wallet."

"Just here to enjoy a quiet drink," Kevin said, mustering a smile that was obviously fake.

"Except you're not. You haven't touched it." She kneeled next to his table, her voice dropping to a whisper. "I'm not one to pry, but you wouldn't be down here in some official capacity now, would ya? Perhaps investigating that big case?"

"Really, ma'am, if you don't mind."

The bartender straightened and threw a rag over her shoulder.

"Suit yourself," she said, and walked off.

PART
TWO

12

MANY HOURS LATER, Amy was stirred awake by an unusual hum of activity coming from outside. There was laughter, chatter, and, if she wasn't mistaken, the rumble and beeping of trucks. Still half asleep, she rolled onto her side and rubbed her eyes, uncertain as to where she was. The lumpy mattress and spongy pillow told her she wasn't at home, but it wasn't until she blinked away the last remnants of sleep that she remembered she was in a hotel, in a town far from Portland.

Must be morning, she thought as she glimpsed a wedge of blue sky from behind the curtains.

Amy sat up at once and scrutinized the clock beside her bed, which seemed to confirm that it was in fact morning. But if that were true, if it really was morning, then that could mean only one thing—she had finally managed to get a full night's sleep!

Admittedly she may have needed some pills to do it, but that didn't matter because the results felt spectacular. Every part of her had been rejuvenated. Her head felt clearer, her heartrate seemed steady and calm, and even her stomach, which had been nigh on dormant for nearly a month, was growling with an urgent craving for food. Even the desperate pain she had felt for her mother the night before seemed oddly diminished. As ridiculous as it sounded, it was as though a miraculous and profound sense of renewal had taken place. Had she known to expect *this* sort of outcome, she would have raided her dad's pills a great deal sooner!

Come to think of it—where was he?

Amy got out of bed and headed into the adjoining room, which she found strangely empty. His bag lay on the floor, untouched, as was the arrangement of the cushions on the couch, where he had said he was going to sleep. Puzzled by his absence, Amy reached for her phone and sent two text messages to him, five minutes apart, but both went unanswered. She tried placing a call but could only reach his voicemail. *You've reached the phone of Kevin Tucker. Please leave your name and—*

Amy terminated the call and glared at the screen, thinking it a little odd that he would disappear without letting her know where he was going, or when he would be back. She supposed she should be concerned, but then she reminded herself that he had come down here on police business. He hadn't mentioned what the job was— all he'd said was that Uncle Jack had wanted him to "take care of something"—but Amy had been on the periphery of his work long enough to know this could mean anything. Growing up, she had gotten used to him slaving away on whatever his latest case was, sometimes vanishing for days on end, so even if this excursion was supposedly meant for them to spend some time together, it wouldn't surprise her if it turned out that work had once again stolen his attention.

Rather than sit and wait for him to make contact, Amy decided to focus on her growing hunger pains instead, so she freshened up, slipped on some clothes, and vacated the hotel in search of something to eat.

—◦◦◦—

The lively atmosphere outside was in stark contrast to when they had arrived the night before. The town was bustling with activity, every sidewalk a busy thoroughfare humming with people jovially anticipating the sunny day ahead.

Preparations for the 64th Annual Lighthouse Festival, as confirmed by the sign hanging between the pillars of the town hall, were underway in the square. An army of volunteers in high-visibility vests was completing a variety of tasks: stringing up banners between the streetlights, threading fairy lights and lanterns through the trees, and unpacking colorful rides—a Ferris wheel, a carousel, flying scooters, and a miniature pirate ship—from a flotilla of flatbed trucks. They were inflating bouncy castles, rolling food caravans into position, and laying a series of cables between a portable generator and the copper-domed bandstand where a group of musicians was plugging in instruments and beginning a sound check.

Escaping the throngs of people, Amy headed for the first store she could find, a charming bakery with cabinets full of delicious-looking breads and pastries. There was so much on display that she couldn't decide, so she took the recommendation of the portly man behind the counter—whom she presumed to be the baker himself, based on the dusting of flour coating the tips of his chevron moustache—and went for a strawberry-and-cream-cheese muffin.

She left the store, paper bag in hand, and found a park bench on the edge of the square, beneath the shade of a tree. As she tore chunks off her muffin and watched the last-minute preparations taking place for the festival, Amy couldn't help but eavesdrop on conversations of townsfolk passing by, all of whom, despite their varied ages and genders, seemed fascinated by one common but mysterious topic.

"It's been over a quarter of a century," mused a middle-aged couple with two young children in tow who were each slurping through coiled straws from giant milkshakes. "Why now? Who's behind it? Think of the effort involved. Who would dare?"

And a moment later, from the other direction, Amy saw a girl younger than her tugging on a boy's hand as she passed by. "Be brave, let's go down and take a look," the girl was saying as she urged him in the direction of the beach.

"No way," he protested. "There's no way you're getting me near that thing."

Then, a more serious assessment, that of an old man as he grumbled to his wife: "If this is someone's idea of a joke, then I don't find it the least bit amusing. Really, have people no respect for . . ."

The more Amy listened, the more intrigued she became. Whatever phenomenon had swept through the town, it sure had everyone talking. *Must be pretty major*, she thought. She wondered what on earth it could be.

Finishing the last of her muffin, she turned her attention back to finding her dad. She brushed the crumbs off her hands and pulled out her phone, but there were still no calls or messages. She tried his number a second time, but it was still going to voicemail.

This was starting to feel a little strange. Amy threw her rubbish in a nearby garbage can and made her way back to the hotel, hoping she might find some answers there. In the lobby, she spotted the familiar face of the bartender, the one who had checked them in last night.

"Excuse me . . ." The woman, whose name Amy couldn't remember, was moving so briskly across the lobby that Amy had to lightly grab her by the arm just to snatch her attention. "I'm sorry to bother you, but can I ask you a question?"

Carrying a large pile of freshly folded towels, the bartender came to a sudden halt and focused on Amy through a pair of distant eyes.

"Yes?" she answered as beads of sweat trickled down her temples.

"This might sound strange, but I haven't seen my dad since last night, and I was wondering—"

"Your dad?"

"I just wanted to know if you'd seen him at all?"

The bartender's face blanked over in confusion. "Forgive me, but my memory ain't what it should be at the best of times, and as you can plainly see it's utter bedlam around here—you'll have to help me out some. You are . . . ?"

Amy volunteered her name and reminded the bartender that both she and her father were staying in the hotel. "You checked us in. Don't you remember?"

This did nothing to diminish the woman's vacant expression. "Really? I did?"

"Um, yes? We're in room 212."

After a moment's hesitation, her eyes sprung open. "Oh now, hang on just a moment . . ." She set the towels down on a nearby table. "Room 212, you say?"

"Yes."

"Then I have something for you. It's a message for the 'girl from 212,' so that must be you. It's from young Ryan. I almost clear forgot. Now, just give me a moment and I'm sure I'll remember what it was."

Amy hesitated. A message? For her? She didn't know anyone in this town, and she definitely didn't know anyone by the name of Ryan. Why would some random guy named Ryan be leaving her—

Oh.

Suddenly the events of last night came rushing back, and it dawned on Amy, rather obviously, that Ryan must have been the guy who was in her bathroom. She was shocked that she had forgotten about it. How that was possible, she had no idea, for it wasn't the sort of thing one could easily forget—but somehow she had.

"Ahh, that's it, yes, yes." The bartender lifted her head and looked at Amy. "Somethin' must have happened between the two of you last night because he rushed down to speak with me and then flew outta here at a rate of knots. I swear, I've never seen that boy move so fast. Anyhow, I haven't the foggiest idea what he was talkin' about—he was beside himself, truly he was—but he wanted me to tell you this . . ." She took Amy's arm and guided her to the corner of the room, away from the swaths of people making their way through the lobby. "Ryan is very sorry. He knows he gave you a scare, but he only meant to help, nothing more. He hopes you can understand why he did what he did. He said if he were you, he would have reacted in the exact same way. Does that make any sense at all?"

"Um, yeah, it does."

"Really? Because it's all a mystery to me."

"No, it's clear. We had a misunderstanding."

Upon hearing this, Amy admitted to feeling somewhat relieved. The whole thing was innocent after all. Ryan wasn't an intruder. He must have seen the water in the hall and come inside to check if everything was all right, just as she had suspected. Of course, she now felt a little bit embarrassed for reacting the way she had, hurling obscenities at him when it was obvious he was only trying to help. Still, what else was she supposed to have done? She'd awoken to find some strange guy standing in her bathroom! It sounded like he understood where she was coming from, though, and she had to admit she was pleased he hadn't gone into any specifics with the bartender. The last thing Amy wanted to do was contrive an explanation for how she had flooded the room, let alone be unmasked as the guest responsible for cleaning out the entire upstairs laundry cupboard.

"He meant it all, he really did," the bartender continued. "He made me promise to pass it on. Thank goodness I remembered. Oh, wait, there was one more thing."

"Yes?"

"He wanted me to say that he hopes you're okay."

"That's kind of him," Amy said, a faint smile beginning to show on her face.

"If you want to reach him," the bartender said, picking up on Amy's favorable expression, "I can tell you how."

"What? Oh, no, that's okay."

"You sure about that?"

"Next time you see him, tell him no harm done. All's forgiven."

Grinning to herself, the bartender leaned over the concierge desk and grabbed a flyer from the brochure stand. She thrust it into Amy's hands, cleared her throat, and pointed to a photo of a young man standing outside a barn. "That's how you can find him, just so you know."

Amy couldn't resist taking a quick look at the flyer. In the photo, Ryan was standing beside a horse, one hand holding the reins, the other shoved in his pocket. Broad shouldered and tall, he was wearing a blue-and-white plaid shirt, jeans, and an old-fashioned cowboy hat, the brim of which cast shade over his eyes, though not enough to hide his smile. As Amy studied the picture, she reflected on how different he looked from last night; she wasn't sure she would have known it was him had the bartender not pointed him out. Below the image, in yellow writing over a blue background, was a message that said *Horseback Riding*, followed by a description of services and activities, then an address and phone number. Amy smiled and tried to hand the flyer back.

"Thanks, but I don't need this. Like I said, it was just a misunderstanding."

"Sounds to me like a little more than that."

"It wasn't, really," Amy insisted.

"All the same, you hang on to it just in case you go changin' your mind," she said, and she picked the fresh towels off the table and scooted away before hearing any further objection.

Amy shrugged off the bartender's not-so-subtle insinuations and returned upstairs, realizing halfway down the hall that their conversation had resulted in no progress whatsoever concerning the whereabouts of her dad. She slid the key into the lock and stepped inside their room.

"Dad? Are you here?"

He wasn't.

She rang his number again, this time from the hotel phone, but the result was the same. Though she was beginning to worry, she reminded herself that he had come down here for work. While the circumstances were admittedly unusual, there would be a perfectly good reason for him disappearing and not answering his phone. He'd turn up soon and explain everything, she was sure of it.

Casting the mystery aside, Amy lay down on the couch and searched for a distraction. She began by clicking through the limited range of channels on the television, but the only options were info-mercials and football. She then flicked through the scant selection of tabloid magazines left on the coffee table, though it soon became apparent that none of the latest trendy diets, self-help quizzes, or gossip over which Hollywood starlet had checked themselves into rehab was going to hold much interest either. Bored and restless, Amy threw the magazines to one side, closed her eyes, and sighed in contemplation of the long day ahead, when an image of Ryan unex-pectedly popped into her mind. She sat up and reached for the flyer. Studying his photo again, it seemed crazy to think this was the same person she had been screaming at twelve hours earlier. He appeared perfectly normal—approachable, even—certainly nothing like some late-night prowler.

Oh, the poor guy. He probably wished he'd never tried to help.

As Amy replayed the encounter in her head, she wondered if her response might have been an overreaction. Yes, the sight of him standing there had scared her witless, but maybe she should have taken a moment and listened to what he had to say rather than send him barreling out of the room. Had she given him a chance to speak, or had she seen the extent of the flooding, she would have realized that his intentions were noble and that he was only trying to do the right thing. But instead, what did he get for his troubles? He got screamed at, shouted at, and Amy was pretty sure he got called some rather unpleasant names.

Ugh, now I really do feel terrible.

Dragging her gaze to the bottom of the flyer, to the address below

Ryan's photo, Amy realized what she needed to do. Turning up on his doorstep to clear the air might well be awkward, but it would surely be better than sitting around the hotel feeling guilty all afternoon— so she grabbed her wallet, phone, and room key; swept her hair back into a ponytail; swapped her flats for boots; and made for the door.

13

RYAN HAD BARELY had any sleep. Since the crack of dawn, he had been lying on the grass in one of the fields near his house, lamenting the mess he now found himself in. And it wasn't just the threat of foreclosure stressing him out—he was still dwelling on last night's run-in at the hotel. He'd been keeping a nervous eye on the driveway all morning, convinced that the local sheriff was going to show up and arrest him for trespassing, or invasion of privacy, or harassment, or whatever the appropriate charge was for entering someone's bathroom. His only hope was that the poor girl wasn't staying in Seabrook long. With any luck she was already on her way home. He couldn't remember ever feeling so embarrassed, and he was sure she felt the same way. If they never saw each other again, it would be far too soon.

But his primary concern wasn't her—it was Tom Tippenworth.

With a deadline now hanging over Ryan's head, there appeared to be only two viable options: either man up and confess everything to his father, or cower in silence and wait for an eviction sticker to be slapped on their front door. Suffice to say neither scenario appealed. He briefly considered finding a lawyer—perhaps there was a legal way to halt the foreclosure process?—but who was he kidding? He had no money for that. Could he plead hardship with the bank? Not likely. Given Tom's demeanor last night, the time for clemency had come and gone. It seemed this was really it: the end of the road.

Ryan stuck his hat over his face, closed his eyes, and let out a frustrated sigh. The day he had feared for so long was finally coming to pass. Unless a miracle presented itself, and soon, his world would turn to ruin. If only he'd told his father the truth. If only he'd been honest about the choices he'd taken, the mistakes he'd made, then he wouldn't be stuck in this—

"Wake up, mister!"

Ryan got such a fright that his hat bounced clear off his face. He bolted upright and searched for the source of the voice, which seemed to be a little girl presently skipping in circles around him.

"Hi Ryan!"

"What in the blazes . . . Who are you?"

It was only after Ryan stood and scooped his hat off the ground that she paused long enough to introduce herself.

"I'm Chloe," she announced exuberantly, oblivious to the fact that she had frightened him half to death with her theatrical entrance.

Ryan hesitantly shook her tiny hand.

"I think you're supposed to say, 'Hi, I'm Ryan, nice to meet you.'"

"I'm sorry?"

"You do know your own name, don't you?"

"Of course, I do, but—"

"Could've fooled me!" She continued skipping with gleeful abandon, her plaited blonde pigtails flying up and down as she went. Wearing a blue-and-yellow polka-dot dress, she couldn't have been more than seven or eight years old, much too young to be at the ranch by herself.

"Um, little girl, where are your parents?"

The girl stopped in her tracks and rolled her eyes. "I'm eight and three-quarters, mister," she said, correcting him. "And my name isn't 'little girl'—it's *Chloe*."

"Chloe, sorry, right."

The smile returned to her face and she continued skipping, feasting her eyes on Ryan as though he were a present she might open at Christmas.

"It's just like the book," she added, humming a tune.

Ryan spun on the heel of his boots, trying to keep up with her as she whirled around. "Come again?"

Chloe paused to give him a weighty glare, then burst into laughter, hopping from foot to foot and swinging her arms as if she were wielding a giant sword. "The book, silly! About the girl who steps through the mirror and becomes a princess who can ride dragons!" She moved to slice his arms off with her imaginary sword, then sheathed her weapon, stood directly in front of Ryan, hands on hips, and said, "You must remember it?"

"Um, no, I'm not sure I know that one. Listen, how did you get here?"

Chloe laughed. "Mom brought me."

"Your mom?" Ryan cast a confused look around the ranch. "And where might I find her?"

"You can't, sorry."

"Why not?"

"Because she's not here right now. But she'll be back later to pick me up."

"I see." Ryan scratched his chin. "And you're here—because?"

She rolled her eyes again. "Because you're going to teach me to ride horses."

"Me?"

"You *are* Ryan, aren't you?"

"Yes, but listen, we don't do lessons. I mean, we used to, a long time ago, but not anymore."

"Well, I'm definitely here for a lesson. Do I get to choose my own?"

"Choose your own what?"

"Horse," she said merrily, spinning her gaze around the field.

"Whoa, can we slow down a moment? No one is picking any horses. I think there's been a misunderstanding. We do treks and trail rides here, that's all. Now, I'm not quite sure exactly how you got here or why you—"

"I'm not here for any of that. I'm here to learn to ride, you know, properly. It's all been arranged."

Ryan raised his eyebrows. "It has?"

She nodded.

"Are you sure?"

"You don't believe me?"

"It's not that . . ."

"What is it?"

"Well," he started to say, speaking with an air of importance, "if you'd made a booking, I'd know about it, and I definitely don't recall there being one for you."

"Well," she said, parroting him, "maybe you should take another look?"

After a lighthearted standoff, Ryan cleared his throat with an incredulous "ahem" and led his precocious visitor over to the barn. While she went up and down the stalls saying hi to all the horses, he disappeared inside the tack room and flipped back through his journal. He stopped at today's page, drew his eyes across the booking column, checked the entries, then froze. *Impossible*, he thought. Right there in front of him, in blue ink, and in his own handwriting no less, was the young girl's name booked for a riding lesson at 11:00 a.m. It was an entry he had absolutely no recollection of making.

"Told you!" Chloe yelled, apparently supremely confident in what he would find. "Guess this means you have to teach me, right?"

Ryan tucked the journal under his arm and stared at her somewhat dumbfoundedly. "Chloe, when was this booking made?"

"You'd have to ask Mom."

"Did she phone it in? Maybe she spoke to my father. Do you remember?"

Chloe thought about that for a while, even though she projected a look suggesting she wasn't really thinking about it at all.

"I'm not sure," she finally said. "But that doesn't matter because my name is in your little book, so that means you can teach me, right?"

"Not so fast. I really do need to talk to her first."

"About what?"

"Well, for one, why she left you here on your own. And another, aren't you a little early?"

"Am I?"

"Yes, you are," Ryan said, except when he looked down to check the time, he realized his watch was broken. But that wasn't the strangest part—the strangest part was that his watch had seemed to have stopped ticking at the same time as the clock in his attic. What a crazy coincidence, he thought, that both his wristwatch and bedside clock should fail within hours of each other, and both precisely at the exact same time: 10:57.

"Come on, let's start," Chloe said. "I want to choose my horse."

Ryan found it hard not to get swept up in her enthusiasm, despite the fact that he was still trying to make sense of this bizarre sequence of events.

"All right, Chloe, listen, because you're here, and because you somehow seem to have a booking, I'll take you through a lesson. But when we're done, I'd really like to speak with your mother and get all of this straightened out, okay?"

That answer elicited a squeal of delight. "Yep! Sure thing. Okay, so which one will be my horse?"

"Hold on. Have you ever ridden before?"

She shook her head.

"Best to pair you with a horse that's suitable, then." Ryan showed Chloe down to stall three, where Bo, his twenty-one-year-old Appaloosa, was milling quietly and chewing on his breakfast. "There, how about him?"

Chloe climbed to the top of the stall gate and watched Bo lazily munch on hay. "He looks really old."

"Bo's a good horse," Ryan said. "He's friendly and kind and likes to take things slow."

"You mean like an old person?"

He grinned. "Yeah, I guess so."

After patiently listening to Ryan's safety briefing, Chloe was brimming with excitement when it finally came time to start riding. The first few minutes in the saddle were a little overwhelming, but she soon got comfortable and settled into Bo's rhythm. In fact, by the time Ryan had brought Bo to a gentle trot, she was already rising and falling to the beat of his gait as though she'd done it a hundred times before. She was a natural, exuding such confidence that it wasn't long before she could balance on three gaits and had the basics of horsemanship well in hand. It seemed the girl had riding in her blood. He was impressed.

Later, after they had de-tacked and were escorting Bo back into his stall, Ryan heard an engine idling down by the ranch gate. Two toots of its horn rang out across the valley. Chloe handed Ryan Bo's reins.

"I have to go," she said.

"Wait, what about your mother? I wanted to speak with her."

"Maybe next time." She wrapped her arms around his waist and gave him a hug. "We're kind of in a hurry. Sorry!"

And before he could say another word, she had spun and run off.

Ryan's father came out of the house just moments after Chloe disappeared. A car door opened and closed, then an engine could be heard trailing off into the distance.

"Who was that?" his father called out as he limped slowly across the porch.

As Ryan walked up the steps, it occurred to him that while he had spent most of the morning with Chloe, the only thing he really knew was her name.

"Honestly, Dad, I have no idea."

14

ITH NO CAR at her disposal and the flyer stating that Ryan's ranch was "only five miles from town," Amy opted for a cab. She considered calling for one but decided to chance her luck on catching one from the sidewalk instead.

Over in the square, the Lighthouse Festival was officially being opened on the steps of the town hall with the cutting of an enormous ribbon. Fanfare erupted as the rides, which had been dormant earlier, grunted into life. The rainbow-colored carriages of the Ferris wheel began carrying pairs of dangling legs into the sky, while over by the fountain the old-fashioned carousel chimed circus-style music as it began the first of many revolutions for the day. Children swelled into the midway, hurling hoops at bowling pins and shoving Ping-Pong balls into the mouths of clowns, and the food caravans were slowly being inundated with crowds of people drawn toward the sweet, sugary smells wafting across the square.

The town's entire population seemed to be in attendance, leaving the roads notably empty. Amy doubted a cab would be driving by anytime soon. But while she was waiting by the side of the curb, Amy caught the eye of a young girl watching her from the opposite side of the street. For some reason the girl had turned her back on the festivities and appeared to be fixated on Amy. What Amy had done to earn the girl's inquisitive stare, she didn't know, but nevertheless she responded with a smile and a polite wave.

"You're lost!" the girl called out.

"Excuse me?" Amy answered.

The girl looked both ways before skipping across the street, a candy apple clutched in her hand. She took a bite as she approached. "You're not from around here, are you?" she mumbled, her small jaw working overtime to chew up the toffee.

"What makes you say that?"

"It's kinda obvious."

Amy's eyebrows ticked up. "It is?"

The girl smiled mischievously before twisting a finger inside her mouth, trying to loosen chunks of toffee lodged between her teeth. "Yep."

"You're pretty clever, then."

She shrugged her shoulders. "Where are you from?"

"Portland."

"When did you get here?"

"I arrived last night."

"How did you get here?"

"We drove, why?"

Laughter tumbled out of the girl's mouth.

"What's funny about that?" Amy asked.

"Nothing," the little girl replied, unable to stifle her own giggling.

Amy laughed as well. "Okay, what about you?"

"Me?"

"Yes, where are *you* from?"

"I'm not from around here either."

"You're not?"

Her blonde pigtails flew in the air as her head whipped from side to side. "Nuh-uh." A coy look swept across her face. "Kinda like you." She twisted the stick of the candy apple in her hands, searching for a prime section of toffee to sink her teeth into. "If you're not lost, what are you doing just standing here looking up and down the street?"

Amy told the girl that she was waiting to catch a cab, and in that very moment, as though it had materialized at her very command, an old Chevrolet, with smatterings of rust over the roof and a faded logo on the passenger-side door that had the words *Seabrook Taxis* wrapped around the now-familiar lighthouse motif, rattled to a stop beside the curb. Its driver—an older man with a long face, sallow skin, and gin blossoms on his nose—emerged from the car and limped his way to the sidewalk. He greeted Amy with a pleasant smile.

"You headin' someplace, miss?" he asked, his voice warm and gravelly with the rasp of an ex-smoker.

"Um, yes, I am." She pulled out the flyer and drew the driver's attention to the address at the bottom. "Could you take me here please?"

"Let me see . . ."

Amy was so surprised by the fortuitous timing that she failed to notice that her new friend was no longer by her side. When she looked around, Amy saw the little girl had returned to the square and was happily playing by the fountain. Amy looked back at the driver, who was now holding open the passenger door.

"I know it well. It's not far," he said. "Hop in. I'll have you there in under fifteen minutes."

"Thank you."

The car was hot and stuffy. Amy buckled up while the driver clumsily poked his finger at the buttons on the meter before stretching out his arm in lieu of raising the turn signal and slowly pulling away. They left the bustling town square behind and were soon on the outskirts of town, traveling at a leisurely pace through a sun-filled valley on a road bordered by tree-covered hills.

"Beautiful day for doin' some horse riding, ain't it, miss?"

Amy smiled, but didn't bother to correct him. "You've come this way before, I take it?"

"To the Porter Ranch? Yes, miss, I've taken a few in my time, though, come to think of it, you're the first in quite a while." He went silent, then mused, "Beautiful country up there."

Amy looked around the car, which she guessed he had owned for a long time. Two dream catchers hung from the rearview mirror, family photos adorned the vinyl dash, and a large pickle jar, full of coins and curled-up dollar bills, sat snug in a drink holder.

"You sound like you know them?" she asked, picking up on the informality with which he'd referred to the family.

"Me? Not really. Just part of livin' in a small town, you see. We all know each other to some degree."

"Right, of course."

"Especially the Porters," he added. "Almost all of Seabrook knows about the Porters."

"They do?"

"Oh, most definitely."

Though the unprompted comment left Amy a little intrigued, she thought it best not to pry.

The journey continued in silence, the road straight and uneventful until they took a left turn and headed deeper into the valley. Lofty trees cast slanting shade on the road, the surface of which had become soft, crumbly gravel. Amy sensed they were close.

"How long you visitin' us for, miss?"

"Just the one night."

"Where's home?"

"Portland."

"Ahh, City of Roses. Well, you chose the right time to visit. Our town put on quite the show last night, wouldn't you say?"

"What do you mean?"

"You didn't see it?"

Amy met the driver's eyes in the mirror. "See what?" She wondered if what he was referring to could be connected to the townsfolk and their feverish discussion. "I overheard some people talking, but I wasn't sure what had happened."

"The lighthouse, miss. Late last night it started shining." His grip on the wheel tightened as the road narrowed and turned from gravel into dirt. The coins in the jar started to rattle. "Lit up the sky like a torch from heaven. Damn bright. Kept me up half the night, the cursed thing. First time in almost thirty-five years too. *Thirty-five years*. Can you believe that? Whole town is talkin' 'bout it."

"The lighthouse? Are you sure?"

"I know what I saw," the driver insisted.

Amy was confused. She'd seen the building up close and clearly remembered its crumbling walls, wire fence, and smashed-up lantern room, not to mention the sign on its boarded-up door warning people to keep out.

"But how would that be possible?" she asked.

"Someone with far too much time on their hands would be my guess," he grumbled. "Some little scoundrels, no doubt."

"You mean someone did it as a hoax?"

"You bet your last nickel. But you be careful who you talk to. You're bound to get some interesting points of view, depending on who you ask—ghosts and spirits and hogwash like that. Don't believe a word of it. Oh, look, here we are."

The driver pulled off the road and brought the car to a stop, nudging its nose into an opening between two sentry-like trees. Amy leaned forward and saw a rusted gate guarding a long, dusty driveway. To the left, creeping out from a dense thicket of bushes, was a paint-chipped letterbox with the words *Porter Ranch* stenciled in white, and to the right was a sign fixed to the trunk of a tree and held in place by two threads of wire. That, too, was hand painted and plainly said *Horseback Riding*.

"This is the place," the driver confirmed.

"Would you mind keeping the meter running?" Amy asked, unbuckling her belt. "I won't be long."

"Sure, no problem. I'll be waitin' right here for you."

The entrance to the ranch resembled a lime-and-emerald tunnel, an effect created by the arching canopies of the trees that flanked the driveway. Amy followed the shaded path on foot, passing by fenced-off fields until she came to a small bend that rose over a small ridge. As she came down the other side, the tree cover disappeared and she was presented with a striking view, a scene resembling something out of a storybook.

The ranch, tucked away between majestic hills, was exquisitely beautiful. In front of Amy was a circular forecourt, headed by a pristine Colonial-style farmhouse. Single level, with a steeply pitched roof, the house had a white coat of paint, creamy-blue windows, and a generously proportioned wraparound porch, the banisters of which were being strangled by the twisting branches of a nearby creeping tree. To the right, set farther back from the forecourt perimeter, were two sheds, a round pen, a greenhouse, a dusty arena, and a large red barn, all connected in a sea of grass and flowers and woven together by pea-gravel paths. Green pastures completed the view, fields the color of shamrock, leading off to a towering wall of trees beyond which lay a world of dense woodland.

But it was the barn where Amy headed first, for she had heard the enticing neighs and whinnies of horses coming from inside and couldn't resist taking a peek. She strolled over and was about to stick her head in when she heard the smack of a screen door. She stopped and looked back at the house.

It was Ryan.

She recognized him at once. Like in the photo, he was wearing a wide-brimmed hat, the same stone-washed denim jeans, and a nearly identical plaid shirt; even the sleeves were rolled up in the exact same way, just past his elbows. He did, however, look taller than she remembered, probably owing to the fact that he was standing up on the porch, a position from which he had not yet budged. She gave a small wave, took a deep breath, and began walking in his direction.

Ryan stood flat-footed, unable to believe his eyes. *It's her*, he thought with a quiver, *the girl from the hotel!* His mind instantly curdled with visions of last night. Surely after all the distress and embarrassment he had caused, wouldn't he be the last person she'd want to see? Unless she had come to scream at him some more? Or worse, maybe she'd come to perform some kind of citizen's arrest! Why else would she come all this way to find him?

"Ryan?"

Ryan felt his throat constrict as she approached. He made his way down the steps, swallowing uneasily.

"It's me," she added. "My name's Amy. From last night?"

When the ice finally melted from around his vocal cords, he managed to mutter, "Yes, I remember."

"Have you got a moment to talk?"

"You want to . . . talk?"

"If that's all right?"

"Uh, I guess."

Amy unfolded her arms and reached out her hand, briefly touching his arm. "It's okay, you can relax. I haven't come here to accuse you of anything or to bite your head off. I came because I got your message."

"You spoke with Peggy?"

"This morning, yes. She passed along everything you asked her to say, and I wanted to let you know that I'm not mad. I get it. I understand what you were doing in my room."

The knots in Ryan's stomach finally began to unwind as he exhaled a big sigh of relief.

"Are you okay?" she asked.

"Yeah, I am." He wiped his brow. "For a second there I wondered if you might still be upset, which would be completely understandable, you know, if you *were* still upset."

Amy stepped closer. "Completely the opposite, believe me. I'm grateful for what you did."

"Well, thanks, but I only did what anyone else would have done."

"Don't be so sure. If you hadn't woken me, who knows what might've happened. The situation could've been worse. Like, a *lot* worse."

Ryan fidgeted with the brim of his hat; for a moment, he didn't know what to say. "It's my pleasure. But really, you didn't need to come all this way just to tell me that."

"Yeah, I did, especially with how I reacted. You were only trying to help, and instead you got me screaming my head off, which, can I just add, I feel really bad about. *Really* bad."

"Honestly, it's okay. You had every right."

"Doesn't change the fact that I feel terrible about it."

"Trust me, you needn't."

"Even still, for the record, can I just say that I'm sorry?"

"It's really not necessary. Truly." Ryan wholeheartedly meant that; her assertion that he was due some kind of apology was patently ridiculous. "I'm just pleased you're okay."

"Thanks. I am."

After shuffling his feet through an awkward silence, Ryan gathered up the nerve to ask her if she'd like to come inside for a drink. After coming all this way, he figured it was the least he could do. "I don't have much to offer, but I've got lemonade? It's fresh."

Amy tilted her head to one side. A lock of hair fell across her face. "That's kind of you, but I should really get going."

"Are you sure? So soon?"

"Yeah, my ride is waiting, and I don't want to take up any more of your time. That's all I came to say." She shoved her hands in her pockets, rocked back on the heels of her boots, then flashed him a smile that made his throat go dry. "So, no hard feelings?"

"Course not."

"And next time you're about to save the day, you won't go stopping on my account, okay?"

"I won't."

"Great. I feel much better now."

He laughed. "Likewise."

They exchanged one last smile and shook hands.

"Nice to meet you, Ryan. Take care."

"You too, Amy."

15

AMY MADE HER WAY down the driveway with a smile on her face. Coming to the ranch had been the right thing to do. She could tell that the poor guy had been nervous and no doubt regretful over what had happened, so she was pleased to have set the record straight. The visit had been short, but at least she could head back to town with a clear conscience, knowing she had put her mind—and his—at ease.

But it seemed returning to Seabrook mightn't be so simple, because when Amy reached the ranch gate, she discovered that her cab had disappeared.

Huh, that's strange.

Figuring the driver must have repositioned and parked someplace else, Amy exited through the gate and crossed to the middle of the road. She stood and peered in either direction, expecting she would spot him, but the road was quiet and deserted—no sign of a cab, no trace of a nearby idling engine, nothing.

You've got to be kidding. Didn't I tell him to stay and keep the meter running? I'm sure I did.

Complicating matters further was the fact that there was a *No Service* message flashing on Amy's phone, meaning she couldn't get a call through to the cab company. Not even the tried-and-true method of waving her phone in the air worked. She persisted for a few minutes longer, walking up and down the street, pointing her phone this way and that, hoping to catch a measly bar, but she had no luck. It seemed Amy had no choice but to turn around and seek help back at the ranch.

Ryan was in the barn tending to the horses when he heard the footsteps. He walked outside, surprised to see Amy back so soon.

"Hey! Did you leave something behind?"

"No," she grumbled, "but my cab driver did—*me.*"

"Seriously?"

"He's taken off. Didn't even wait for his fare."

"You're joking."

"Nope." She fumbled for her phone and held it in the air. "And I can't get any service."

"I'm afraid those toys don't work so well out here in the valley, but you can go old school, if you like—we've got a phone inside the house."

"You don't mind?"

"Of course not."

Ryan led Amy inside and showed her to the phone, which was sitting on top of a sideboard cluttered with empty vases and framed photos. He pulled out a phone book from the drawer below, a publication no thicker than a magazine, and left Amy to search for the listing for Seabrook Taxis. She located and dialed the number.

"Thank you," she mouthed silently to Ryan, who smiled and indicated he was returning outside.

While the phone rang, Amy heard a noise from another room. Through a gap in a door she glimpsed a man seated at a table in the kitchen. Wearing corduroy pants, an oversized polo shirt, and a misshapen baseball cap, the man staggered to his feet, gripped a cane, and hobbled out of sight. She assumed he was Ryan's father, though by the way he was moving he seemed a little too old and frail.

"Thank you for calling Seabrook Taxis," a rehearsed voice said. "Please leave your name and number, and we'll return your call as soon as we can."

Amy relayed her name and circumstances into the machine and said she would start walking back in the direction of town. "If you could have the driver return along the same road he brought me in on, that would be appreciated, thanks."

After hanging up, Amy returned outside and found Ryan escorting a horse toward the field. The exquisite animal, striking with its mocha-colored coat and inky-black mane, warmed her spirits and instantly made her forget about her drama with the disappearing taxi.

"She's gorgeous!" Amy called out.

"Don't say that too loud, might inflate her ego."

She laughed. "May I?"

"Sure. Go right ahead."

Amy stepped up to the horse and ran her hand down the animal's silky neck. "She looks young?"

"Just gone three, which for her breed is pretty much a baby."

"What's her name?"

"Bella. There's more in the barn. You're more than welcome to take a look?"

Amy nodded enthusiastically.

"Come on, then, follow me."

The shade of the barn was a pleasant respite from the midday sun. Freshly cut hay made the air inside smell lush and sweet, and the sounds of the horses, who were composing their own brand of music with their steel shoes and playful whinnies, created an ambience that made Amy's heart sing.

She listened with interest as Ryan took her on a tour of the stalls. There were eight in total, four on either side of a wide central alley, with horses inside all but two. Ryan reeled off each of their names, ages, breeds, some other statistics, and even shared a few anecdotes. He did, however, face a stiff challenge when it came time to introduce the horse in stall number seven—the stubborn animal was ensconced in the corner and in no mood to come forward.

"Is she feeling okay?" Amy asked.

"Oh yeah, she's fine. Just not what you'd call a people horse." Ryan started making clicking noises with his mouth, trying to coax the horse out. "Come here, Lil' Dip, come say hi to our new friend," he said, but the horse wasn't budging.

"Maybe she doesn't like me."

Ryan shook his head. "The opposite. The fact she hasn't charged at the door or kicked up her legs means she likes you quite a bit."

When Amy had toured the rest of the barn, having asked a flurry of questions concerning the horses' diet, grooming, and exercise routines, and after finding out why all the horseshoes on the wall were hanging the wrong side up (which Ryan explained was to catch all the good luck), they finally returned outside. Amy had enjoyed herself so much that she could have stayed the entire afternoon, but the taxi would probably be along soon, and she didn't want to overstay her welcome.

"Thanks. That was so much fun."

Ryan lifted his hat. "My pleasure."

They strolled back across the forecourt.

"And thanks again for letting me use your phone."

"Did you have any luck?"

"No one answered, but I left a message. Hopefully someone will be along soon."

"You're welcome to wait up here."

Amy smiled. "That's kind of you, but I really should let you get back to your day."

"What'll you do, though? Wait down by the gate?"

"No, I'll start walking."

"You can't do that."

"Why not?"

"Because you're a long way from town. What if they haven't picked up your message yet? Actually, what will happen if no one collects it till morning?" Ryan nodded ominously toward the hills. "It's over five miles to Seabrook—if no one comes, you might end up walking the whole way back, and with the way the roads are out here that could be pretty dangerous." He came to a stop and turned to face her. "Of course, you could stay here, and if you want you could come out riding with me instead?"

Amy, who suddenly had visions of being stranded on the edge of a deserted dirt road, thumb out, hitching for a ride, hadn't registered a word of what Ryan had just said.

"Sorry, what was that?" she asked.

Ryan cleared his throat. "I said that you should stay and come out for a ride. I was heading out on the trails, so how about I saddle up another horse and you come along too? I can give you the guided tour, show you around the place, and as soon as we're done, I'll drive you back into town myself. How does that sound?"

"You're serious?"

"Of course."

"But you can't."

"Why not?"

"You hardly know me for a start, never mind that it sounds like a pretty big imposition on your time."

"It's not, and besides, you'd actually be doing me a favor."

"How so?"

"If you came along then that would mean another horse could get some exercise too."

"But what about the part where you have to drive me back to town?"

"It's really no trouble, no trouble at all." He tilted his head, gesturing back toward the barn. "Come on, what do you say?"

Amy didn't need to deliberate for long. "All right, you've twisted my arm. I'll come. As long as you're sure you don't mind?"

"Positive. I'd be glad for the company. Now, let's choose you a horse."

Amy returned with him to the barn, perused the stalls, and selected Snowflake, a fourteen-year-old gelding with a white coat, friendly eyes, and a relaxed disposition. Ryan tacked him up, and in no time at all they were ready to ride.

"Step forward," he said.

Nervous but excited, Amy took Ryan's hand, slid her left boot into the stirrup, and launched herself into the saddle.

"You should know it's been a long time since I last rode a horse," she said with a dash of uncertainty as she took a moment to acclimatize to the height. "I'm not sure I remember what to do."

Ryan smiled as he bent down to inspect the length of the stirrups.

"We're not going for a gallop," he said, "just a slow walk along the trails. I'll show you some basic tips once we're underway: stop, go, left, right. But for the most part, Snowflake'll be following my lead, so all you need to do is keep a loose hand on the reins, relax, and enjoy yourself."

After checking both sides and shortening the leathers of the stirrups, Ryan slid the heel of Amy's boots in a little farther so that the ball of her foot was comfortably resting on the iron. "How does that feel?"

"Good," she said, wriggling around. "I think."

"Ready to go?"

She laughed. "You tell me."

Ryan put a finger to his chin. "Actually, wait, there's one more thing."

He disappeared into the tack room and returned a moment later with a hat, one of his favorites: diamond style, ruddy brown with a pinched front, the kind John Wayne liked to wear. He offered it to Amy. With a bashful smile she slid her hair tie out from her ponytail, shook out her hair, then fit the hat snugly over her head, adjusting the brim while at the same time invoking her best cowgirl impression.

"How do I look?" she asked, unable to contain her grin.

Coolly and casually, Ryan gave her a thumbs-up and told her that she looked good, which was a lie.

She looked better than good.

She looked *perfect*.

16

$\mathscr{S}$EABROOK STATE PARK, as Ryan informed Amy during his rolling commentary, was a three-thousand-acre forest dominated by Douglas firs, cedars, and red alders. There were nine creeks and tributaries, thirteen sub-varieties of trees, and numerous types of wildflowers carpeting the forest floor. Although deforestation and two major fires had decimated much of the area during the 1920s and '30s, the resulting replanting efforts allowed for the inclusion of a network of trails, forty-seven miles in total length, one of which they were traversing right now.

Only a short distance into the ride, Amy could already tell that Ryan was a most accomplished guide. His breezy narration, which she suspected had been delivered countless times before, illuminated points of interest along the way, as well as facts about the area's history. He was showing himself to be thoughtful and kind too, pausing on more than one occasion to ask whether she was comfortable, if the saddle was in need of adjustment, whether she needed to take a break, and if she had any questions.

Amy found herself both charmed and intrigued. Was he this attentive with everyone he rode with, she wondered, or was it because he still harbored some lingering awkwardness over last night? Maybe this was his way of defusing any perceived tension? But there existed another possibility: that this was just the type of person he was, old-fashioned and polite. Compared to the guys she knew back in the city, the ones obsessed with football and fraternity life, Ryan might have come from a whole different world.

Amy mused on these thoughts as she cast her gaze into the forest, and as Ryan continued with his commentary, describing with enthusiasm paradoxical to the topic (some 1935 agreement between the state and the county that had resulted in the area being declared a protected woodland park), she realized that she was having a good time, that she was remarkably at ease in her guide's company, and that she held not the slightest hint of regret about agreeing to come along.

Meanwhile, Ryan, who was riding next to her, no more than three feet away, was becoming increasingly conscious of the tiring effect his narration might be having on his guest. He had started reciting from his script only as a means to spark conversation, expecting they would soon branch off into more interesting topics, but what he hadn't counted on was Amy's conspicuous silence. They were over a mile into the trail and he was still rambling on about the not-so-scintillating subject of parkland politics.

"I'm boring you half to death, aren't I?"

"What?" She turned and looked straight at him, lifting her chin, her green eyes lighting up from beneath the brim of her hat. "No," she hastened to add, but with what sounded to him like mock sincerity. "Of course you're not."

"I'm sorry, I really don't mean to. It's my job, you see. Whenever I'm out on the trail, I tend to turn into a robot and start jabbering away. Half the time, I don't even know I'm doing it."

"You're not boring me, I promise."

"You've been very quiet, though."

"Only because I'm trying to take it all in," she said, sealing her answer with a courteous smile. "And I'm trying to get used to the idea that this is all basically your own backyard. Where I'm from, that's kinda crazy."

"A little different from what you're used to, huh?"

"You could say that. About the closest thing we've got to something like this would be Forest Park, but it's not the same if you have to get in a car and drive there, is it?"

"I guess it's not." Ryan found himself watching her for a moment as she stared out into the woods. He wasn't blind. He could see how pretty she was, something he had failed to register last night when her face had been contorted in fear.

"Forest Park, that's up in Portland, right?"

"Yep."

"So that's home?"

She nodded.

They approached a narrow hairpin in the trail; Ryan drew on the reins and eased Bella off to let Amy maneuver her horse through the turn first, which she did confidently. As the trail widened again, he came back up alongside, remarking to himself, not for the first time, how comfortable she seemed in the saddle.

"What keeps you busy up in the big city? Are you in college?"

"Freshman year," she said, before reminding herself that she had put a temporary hold on her studies. "At least I was," she added a moment later. "Kind of taking a small break right now."

"What were you studying?"

"Liberal arts, which in my case really means a little bit of everything." She needed to pause to search through her memory for the complete list. "My subjects last semester were twentieth-century literature, art history, life science, and environmental studies."

"And what's your major?"

"Haven't chosen one yet. If I'm being honest, I still don't know what I want to do. Figured I'd take my time, try a few different things, see if anything sticks."

"Makes sense. There's no point rushing anything, is there?"

She smiled. "My thoughts exactly. And what about you?" she asked, moving the focus away from her. "Done the whole college thing?"

He shook his head. "Hasn't ever crossed my mind, to be honest. The ranch, the horses, they've always kept me plenty busy."

Amy freed one hand from the reins and stroked the back of Snowflake's head, from his crest down to his withers. "How long have you lived here?"

"Seabrook's been my home forever. Our ranch has been in the family for four generations."

"Wow, that's amazing."

"Eighty-three years," he added, his face flickering with pride. "My great-grandfather was the one who purchased the land and built the original house. It operated as a farm for thirty years, beef cattle mostly, then my grandfather inherited it and set up the riding arena and converted the barn to stables, and then it was passed down to my father. The rest is history, as they say."

"And these trail rides are what you do? They're your full-time job?"

"That, and anything else that needs doing around the place."

"I think I read in your flyer that you also do riding lessons?"

"Used to, a long time ago. Really should get those flyers updated. These days I try to keep the focus on getting people out on the trails."

"How come?"

"Just the economics of it. Don't get me wrong, though, I enjoy the lessons. Had a young girl come by this morning, and her enthusiasm reminded me of how rewarding it can be. But the math doesn't add up—there's little sense in me spending an hour with someone one-on-one, not when I can take a whole group out and charge five times the price."

"I guess that makes me pretty bad for business then, huh?"

"How so?"

"Well, here I am, monopolizing your afternoon, and I haven't paid a dime."

Ryan twisted in the saddle and glimpsed Amy's shrewd grin. "It's not quite like that," he said, smiling back. "There's always exceptions to the rule. Besides, don't forget, you're doing me a favor."

"Oh yeah," she said with a wink. "A favor, that's right, I forgot."

—⁓—

The scenery was ever changing; one minute they were riding through dense forest, traversing narrow trails choked over by rhododendrons, and the next they were crossing sunlit glades. At the bank of a stream, they diverged from the trail and started heading west, a direction that took them into a disorientating maze of red alders. As Amy surveyed the myriad columns of stilt-like trunks surrounding them in every direction, she wondered if Ryan actually knew where they were.

"You do know where you're going, right?"

"Good point. Didn't we just come through here?"

She laughed. "Honestly, even if we were going in circles, I don't think I would know."

He laughed as well. "You can relax. We're nearly there."

"We're heading back already?" Amy shot back a startled look, surprised by how much disappointment this news stirred up. She wasn't ready for the ride to end, not so soon.

"Not quite," he said. "I've taken us on a small detour. Hope you don't mind. There's something I want to show you. It'll be worth it, I promise."

He was notably coy on detail, but Amy needed little persuading. "You're the guide," she said happily. "You lead, I'll follow."

The trees thinned and before long they found themselves at the forest's edge, confronted with a series of sloping, grassy hills, bare but for a speckling of shrubs and some scrawny, windblown trees. In the distance, their destination was revealed: an expanse of water shimmering in the sunlight, stretching from one side of the horizon to the other: the Pacific Ocean.

They rode until they could go no farther, coming to a stop ten yards from the precipice of a cliff. The view was spectacular. Amy could see for miles up and down the rugged coast and far out across the windswept sea.

"You were right," she said, staring in wonder at the ocean, its surface frothing with a million whitecaps. "This was worth it."

"It gets better," Ryan said, jumping out of his saddle. "Come with me, let's go in for a closer look."

Amy took her time to dismount safely—the grass was wildly overgrown and she made sure her foot found solid ground before releasing the other from its stirrup. Ryan tied both horses to a nearby tree before taking confident strides toward the cliff edge. Amy however lingered a few steps behind. She contemplated the steep terrain and decided she could see just as well from where she stood.

He turned around. "You all right?"

"Yep."

"Scared of heights?"

"No, just scared of falling."

He grinned. "Come on, it's safe."

Amy took Ryan's hand and joined him at the edge, but the stomach-churning sight of the plunging cliff face had her quickly reaching for his arm instead. A stiff breeze swirled around them, conspiring to knock them off their feet.

Ryan stood steadfast and strong, though her touch had his stomach stirring with a flutter of nerves.

"How far down is that?" she asked.

"Two hundred feet, or thereabouts."

"Whoa."

Amy craned her neck and tipped her body farther over the edge. Her grip on Ryan's arm turned clawlike at the sight of the ocean slamming against the rocks below.

"If you think that's scary, you should've seen this place a few nights back when that big storm blew through. Pitch black, howling wind and rain—couldn't see a thing."

"What on earth were you doing out here in all that?" Satisfied at having proven her mettle, Amy let go of Ryan's arm and retreated a few steps back.

"Remember back at the barn, the horse that wouldn't say hi? Little Dipper?"

Amy nodded, still giddy from the view.

"Poor girl escaped the ranch. She spooked at a clap of thunder and that was it—she was gone. She bolted all the way out to this very spot. Took me hours to track her down. It was only through sheer dumb luck she hadn't already wandered off the edge."

"Thank God you found her."

"You're telling me. Anyway"—Ryan shook off the memories and pointed south, far into the distance—"look down there, tell me if you can spot it."

Amy squinted, searching the coast. Her eyes landed upon a thin sliver of beach and beside it a tiny settlement that was barely discernible in the seaside mist.

"I think so. Wait, that's not—"

"That's Seabrook."

"Are you serious?" From this vantage point the town looked comically small, a child's play set almost—the buildings could have been Lego blocks and the lighthouse a stick of chalk.

"Crazy how tiny it looks."

"You know something," he said, staring at the town, "I just realized I don't even know why you're here in Seabrook. Are you in town on holiday or something?"

She shook her head. "I'm here with my dad. He had to come down for work. I'm just tagging along."

"What does he do?"

As Amy mulled over her answer, a strong gust of wind came barreling through, nearly lifting the hat clear off her head.

"He's a detective with the state police," she said.

Ryan fell silent.

A detective.

To him, the word almost sounded exotic and conjured up images from movies and comic books, shadowy figures in trench coats and fedoras. *But what would a big city detective be doing all the way down here in Seabrook?* he wondered. And why hadn't he heard anything about it? Surely, in a small town where everyone knew each other's business, where every disturbance, no matter how indiscriminately small, was trotted out in the local paper for all to see, wouldn't the visit have set a few tongues wagging?

"Obviously I need to start reading the *Beacon* a little more closely."

"Huh?"

"Our paper. You know, to get a clue as to why your dad might be here."

"Oh right."

"I don't suppose you know anything, do you?"

"No, sorry, I don't."

"Hope it's nothing serious."

"Your guess would be as good as mine." Amy looked again upon the distant town, then grinned. "Hey, maybe it's got something to do with that lighthouse of yours."

"Come again?"

"Just kidding."

"No, tell me, what do you mean?"

"I'm only making a joke, you know, with what happened there last night and all."

"I'm not following."

"Oh, sorry, you haven't heard. Everyone in town was talking about it, and I just assumed you would have known. Probably not, though, if you live all the way out here, huh?"

"Known what, exactly?"

"That it turned on last night."

"Say that again?"

Amy described everything she had heard from those in town, as well as from her cab driver.

One of Ryan's eyebrows instantly arched up. "Forgive me, but that's a little hard to believe."

"Hey, I'm only the messenger."

"That's really what people were saying happened?"

"That's what I heard."

"They've all lost their minds, then. There's no way the lighthouse could have done that—no way, no how."

"Yeah, I went on a walk and saw it for myself. It's pretty beat up."

"That's only the half of it. The place is a complete ruin. There's a wire fence around the building, no staircase on the inside, and even if someone found a way to get into the lantern room, there's no lamp."

"There isn't?"

"Nope. The lamp was dismantled and removed after the building was condemned back in the late 1970s."

Amy stared at the horizon, thoroughly confused. If the lighthouse wasn't capable of producing a beam, then what was it that everyone thought they had seen? Even her cab driver's explanation, which had sounded somewhat plausible at the time, no longer made any sense: How could the town have been fooled by some hoax if the apparatus no longer existed with which to achieve it?

"I must be missing something, then," she said.

"There'll be a perfectly reasonable explanation."

"But all the people I overheard seemed so convinced. Some of them even sounded genuinely frightened."

"Rational thought flies out the window when it comes to the folks in this town and that lighthouse. Put it this way, I'm not surprised to hear that's the conclusion everyone's jumped to."

"Okay, I'll bite. What's behind the fascination? I've only been in Seabrook one night, and yet I don't think I've gone five minutes without seeing a picture of the lighthouse or hearing a reference to it. Is it just me or is the town a little obsessed?"

Ryan took off his hat and nodded to the ground. "If you want to hear the story, then we'd better sit."

17

So, it all begins with a lighthouse keeper," Ryan began, "a man by the name of Theodore Booth. Theodore had been manning the Seabrook lighthouse for over forty years, but during the last year of his watch, in 1907, right in the middle of a big winter storm, his lamp failed. No one knows exactly why, but at the time people suspected he'd lost the flame by trimming the wick too closely, and because of his mistake, a passing vessel—a fishing boat named the *Lady Madeline*—smashed into the rocks and sank. Eight people died. It took two weeks for all the bodies to wash ashore."

"Oh no," Amy whispered. "That's terrible."

"Awful, I know." Ryan wedged his hat between his knees to stop it from blowing away. "Anyhow, the tragedy took a toll on Theodore. He blamed himself, and over the following weeks and months his mental state deteriorated. He spent all his time inside the lighthouse, refusing to come out. The guilt drove him mad. He became so detached from reality that he was convinced the spirits of the dead crewmen were visiting him, haunting his lighthouse as punishment. 'It's them,' he scratched into the walls of the tower, the 'ghosts of the *Madeline*,' 'they're here again.' He quite literally lost his mind. It got so bad that his wife, who was probably worried sick, broke down the door so she could reach him. She went up those lighthouse stairs to confront her husband, but unfortunately that's the last anyone ever saw of her alive."

"Why? What happened?"

"Her body was found on the rocks not far from the wall of the lighthouse, with injuries consistent with someone who had suffered a fall."

Amy gasped. "What! You can't seriously mean that Theodore was responsible?"

"No one knows exactly what happened, but there's one common theory."

"And that is?"

"'That Theodore snapped, that when his wife appeared before him in the lamp room, he was probably in the middle of a psychotic break. People think he might've mistaken his wife for a ghost, believed her to be an evil apparition, and in his desperation to rid himself of his demons, he threw her from the top of the lighthouse. It's all specula-tion, of course, but Theodore made one final etching into the wall: 'My God, forgive me,' and his body was found washed up on the beach two days later, with many convinced that this was proof that he had thrown himself into the water and drowned once he realized the grave mistake he'd made." Ryan paused and registered the look of horror sweeping across Amy's face. "Not the most pleasant story."

"That's the most tragic thing I think I've ever heard!"

"I know, right? Anyway, the whole affair was so sad that nobody in Seabrook could bring themselves to talk about it. The very men-tion of Theodore's name became taboo, and the town tried to move on. Decades went by, memories faded, and by the time the light-house was decommissioned in 1956, the story of Theodore was all but forgotten. Then, fifteen years later, a group of boys came up with a plan to fool the town. On the anniversary of Theodore's death, under the cover of night, they broke into the lighthouse with a bucket of kerosene and a fresh wick and managed to fire up the lamp. It blazed all night long and rumors quickly circulated, all of them started by the boys, of course—whispers of a ghost and the forgotten story of a mad lighthouse keeper. Come morning, Theodore was the talk of the town, and it wasn't long before everyone in Seabrook was discussing the possibility that his spirit still lurked inside the lighthouse, that he had returned to resume his watch."

"That actually gives me shivers! Pretty imaginative on the boys' part, I have to say."

"It was, but they didn't stop there. They were so keen to keep the charade alive that they repeated the hoax the next year on the very same day, and as you can imagine, this really set the cat among the pigeons. News spread and soon people were traveling from far and wide to witness the phenomenon. As a result of all the attention, the symbol of the lighthouse became synonymous with the town's identity. Its image was used to promote Seabrook, an annual festival was established in its honor, and as for those boys, well, this growing obsession only spurred them further and they continued their deception for years to come."

"How were they never caught?"

"People became so afraid of the building that the boys were able to use the town's fear to their advantage. They later bragged about how easy it all was."

"What finally made them stop?"

Ryan took a dramatic pause. "The lighthouse itself."

Amy's eyes grew wider. "Come again?"

"On the seventh year, as the boys were making their way up to the lantern room, the staircase broke away from the wall and collapsed to the ground."

"Were they all right?"

"Aside from some broken bones and one hell of a fright, yeah, they were okay—but that put a definite end to all their fun."

"And what was the reaction from the town? Was everyone furious once they found out the whole thing had been a sham?"

"The opposite, actually—attention on the lighthouse only intensified. People could not be dissuaded—they saw what happened to those boys as a clear sign that the building was haunted, or at the very least that a curse had been placed upon it. No one dared to go near it after that, not even those who might have doubted all the stories before. The incredulous few who rolled their eyes at talk of ghosts and dead spirits—even they became avid believers."

"And then what? What happened next?"

Ryan shrugged. "Nothing," he said. "That's pretty much it. As a result of the incident, the town erected a fence around the building, boarded up its doors, and left it to slowly decay. Decades have passed, not a soul has been inside since."

"No one?"

"No one."

Amy put her arms out and leaned back, meditating on what she'd just been told. A flock of gulls swooped overhead and disappeared below the precipice of the cliff, their squawking still audible. As she gazed out at the ocean, she thought back to what she'd overheard in town and understood at once why the beam of light had caused such a fervent stir.

"Quite the story, huh," Ryan said.

She nodded. "Kinda makes a lot of sense."

"You mean about what happened last night?"

"Yes. Now I really wish I'd seen it for myself."

Ryan coughed loudly, not bothering to conceal his skepticism. "Yeah, so do I," he quipped.

"How can you be so sure it didn't light up?"

"I'm not saying it didn't."

"Oh, so you *do* think it's possible?"

"The jury is out, let's put it that way."

"Interesting," Amy said with a smile. "That's different to what you said before."

He stared back at her. "What did I say before?"

"I believe the phrase you used was 'No way, no how'—wasn't it?" She leaned in a little closer, playfully nudging him in the ribs. "Has someone changed their tune?"

"If I may——" he started to say, eager to rush to his own defense but caught off-balance by the mischievous glint radiating from her eyes. "When I used those words——"

"Hmm?"

"——it was merely to dismiss any suggestion that a ghost would have been involved, which I'm sure is the prevailing consensus going around town."

"And how can you be sure it wasn't? You don't believe in ghosts?"

"I'm quite sure the tower is haunted—heck, you wouldn't ever catch me going inside—but the suggestion that a ghost can fire up a lamp that isn't even there sounds a little bit too kooky to me."

Amy agreed, but that didn't preclude the possibility of another scenario, the one first suggested by her cab driver.

"All right," she said, "ghosts aside, what do you think about this being a case of history repeating itself?"

"Someone trying to fool the town again?"

"Why not? There's probably a lot of people out there who would want to re-create the excitement of what those boys did. It sure has got everyone talking, hasn't it? And with that big festival going on in town, it seems like perfect timing. Perhaps even the mayor is involved. I smell a conspiracy."

Ryan drew back his head, confused. "Wait, the Lighthouse Festival? Has that come around already? I was sure that wasn't for another couple of months."

Amy laughed. "Well, either they decided to put it on early or you probably should update your calendars."

He laughed along with her. "Wow, time really does fly."

He fell silent and tossed her theory around in his head for a moment; if the festival really was on today, it would indeed provide a captive audience for any would-be tricksters.

"Anything's possible," he conceded, "but if it were true, and that's a *big* if, you're forgetting something—no lamp."

"Right, I forgot." Amy sat up and crossed her legs. "What if they improvised? I'm thinking aloud here, but couldn't someone just rig up a spotlight? Wouldn't that have the same effect as a beam from a lamp?"

"I suppose. But without a staircase, how would they get something like that all the way to the top? Sounds like an awful lot of effort to me."

"Oops—no staircase. Forgot about that."

Ryan plucked a blade of grass. "You know, we could always get your dad on the case. I'm sure he could solve it for us."

She laughed. "Good thinking, I'll get him on it."

The conversation lulled into a comfortable silence. As Ryan glanced up at the sky, it occurred to him that they should be saddling up and heading back; the sun was making a quick descent toward the horizon and there was still an hour of riding ahead. That time had slipped by so quickly was a testament to how much he was enjoying himself, as well as the fact that he hadn't spared one single thought to the problems waiting for him back home. And little did he realize that Amy felt the same; that she had managed to go an entire afternoon without the loss of her mother constantly clouding her thoughts made her feel incredibly grateful, more grateful than Ryan could possibly know.

"We ought to get moving," he said, putting his hat on. "If we stay out any longer, it'll be near dark by the time we get you back."

Amy checked her phone, noting how rapidly the hours had advanced, but also noting the continued absence of any attempts at communication from her dad. Probably not surprising given the poor reception, though. In any case, if her dad *was* trying to make contact, best the excursion came to an end and she got back into cellphone coverage before he contemplated sounding any alarms.

"Yeah," she said, "you're probably right."

They stood up and walked the short distance over to the horses, across grass now striped in long shadows. Ryan untied the horses, coiled up the rope, stowed it in his satchel, then gave Amy a boost into her saddle. As she took the reins and wriggled to get comfortable, she directed her attention one last time to the distant lighthouse.

Ryan climbed into his saddle and drew up alongside, picking up on her distracted gaze. "Don't like a mystery you can't solve, huh?"

She blinked and let her eyes wander back toward his. "There's still time. Who knows, maybe I'll get lucky. Maybe it'll light up again before I leave."

"Twice in two days," he said, his lips curling into a smirk. "Now wouldn't *that* be something."

18

AMY AND RYAN ENJOYED a pleasant, meandering ride back
through the forest. Conversation flowed freely between them, and
while the topic continued to center on the mystery of the lighthouse,
all manner of things spooky were soon being discussed, from their
favorite ghost stories when they were growing up, right down to their
biggest pet peeves in horror films.

"Do you know what really bothers me?" Amy said. "When the
family chooses to stay in a house that is clearly haunted. I don't know
about you, but if I saw a face in the window, or found some creepy
doll watching me while I slept, I'd be out of there in a flash."

Ryan laughed. "I know, right? Or why does someone always have
to go down into the basement? You know there's nothing good down
there, so why do it?"

"And of course the lights never work."

"And if there's a flashlight, it's always just about to run out of
batteries."

Amy laughed along as she bobbed up and down in her saddle. "I swear, I wouldn't stay in the house at all. Wouldn't even be hanging around town. I'd be straight to the airport and on a plane and getting as far away as possible.

Ryan nodded in agreement. "The idea of flying has always terrified me, but in that situation, I'd be right there with you."

Amy gave him a surprised look. "Wait, you've never been on a plane?"

"Never had the chance, plus the thought of speeding through the sky in a metal tube has never sat too well with me."

"Well, when you put it like that!"

"Sorry, didn't mean to put you off."

"Nah, you haven't. I'd love to see the world one day, so I plan on doing plenty of flying."

Ryan steered his horse and led them both onto the last length of trail. In just a few minutes they would be emerging from the forest and arriving back at the ranch.

"Anywhere in particular you want to go?" he asked.

"Oh, somewhere in Europe. Anywhere in Europe, really. I'd love to see all the museums, art galleries, churches and castles that are thousands of years old, be surrounded by all that history. Wouldn't that be amazing?"

As someone who hadn't even been out of the state, Ryan couldn't begin to comprehend the idea of traveling to such faraway places.

"Sure would," he said.

For the next few minutes, he rode in silence and listened to her talk about towns and places he'd never heard of, exotic parts of the world he'd never imagined he would get to see. He had known this girl for only a short amount of time, but it was amazing how relaxed he felt around her. They chatted as though they were long lost friends. Ryan had never experienced such an instant connection with anyone like this before.

His good mood, however, was short-lived. When they reached the outermost field of the ranch, he heard a clamorous sound coming from inside the barn. Amy could hear it too, a chorus of impatient nickering and neighing.

"Oh no," he said.

Amy looked across at him. "What's wrong?"

"Me being forgetful is what's wrong. I didn't think we'd be gone so long."

It was all Ryan's fault. He had been so distracted with Amy that he had forgotten about his other horses—horses who had just spent the entire afternoon confined to their stalls, bored, hot, and no doubt very hungry.

"Would you mind waiting a few minutes before I drove you back?"

"No problem. Is everything okay?"

"I need to let the horses out into the field, give them a chance to stretch their legs." With dusk settling over the valley, Ryan figured there might only be thirty minutes of light left—just enough time for a short wander and graze. It wasn't much, but it was better than nothing.

"Of course," Amy said. "Do what you need to do."

Turning the horses out didn't take long. After the last one entered the field, Ryan swung the gate shut and pointed Amy toward his truck, which was housed in a rickety carport beside one of the sheds.

"It's unlocked," he said. "Hop in and I'll grab my keys."

"Sure."

As Amy headed over, she couldn't help but notice that the truck's best days were behind it. Its mudguards were caked in dirt, chassis pockmarked with dents, and the paintwork had faded to the point that it was impossible to be sure of its original color. Once seated inside, however, she found the interior surprisingly comfortable. She settled into the cozy vinyl seat, which was peeling along the edges, then rolled down the window and waited for Ryan's return.

"Dad?" Ryan had found his father in the living room, slumped in his favorite chair, eyes closed, with his favorite show playing on the television and a book splayed across his chest.

His father gave a start.

"Sorry, I didn't mean to wake you." Ryan crouched beside the chair, switched off the television, and placed a hand on his father's arm. "How are you feeling?"

He propped himself upright using his good arm and cast a sluggish gaze around the room. "What time is it?"

"It's nearly six."

"Have you"—he took off his glasses and rubbed his eyes, looking confused—"been out? Have you been in town?"

"No, Dad, I've been out on the trails. We had a booking today."

"Oh. How many?"

"Just one—a girl. She's visiting from Portland."

"Right. Good." His eyes were heavy.

"Have you eaten? Have you had anything since lunch?"

The question went unanswered. Whether his father was slipping back to sleep or taking an inordinately long time to question his own stomach, Ryan couldn't be sure.

"Why don't you go and lie down? I'm going to drive our visitor back to town. I won't be long. Have a snooze, and then when I get back I'll fix us something for dinner. I'll fry a steak, boil up some potatoes—how does that sound?" The suggestion was greeted with a lazy nod of the head. "All right, let's get you into bed."

Ryan helped his father to his feet and walked him to his room. Conscious not to keep Amy waiting, he hurried through the rest of the goodbye, kissing his father on the forehead and drawing the curtains shut.

Amy's face brightened at his return.

"Everything okay?" she asked.

"Just fine," he answered, climbing inside the truck. "Thanks for waiting."

"No problem. It's you I should be thanking for driving me back."

"More than happy to."

He shut his door and slipped the key into the ignition, but his attempt to turn on the engine was greeted with a whiny revving sound followed by a mechanical splutter and cough.

Amy threw him a worried look. "Out of gas or something?"

"No, nothing like that," he said as he gave the dash a pat. "She'll start. Sometimes she just needs a little encouragement." He looked over and pointed to Amy's open window. "Some friendly advice, though—best you wind that up."

After a few more attempts, Ryan was finally able to coax the engine to life. "Ah, there we go." He pumped the gas pedal harder, which brought forth a heavy rumbling from beneath Amy's feet. There was an almighty grunt, the truck's chassis momentarily shook, and then a plume of brown smoke erupted out of the exhaust. Even with the windows up, the acrid stench managed to seep its way inside. Amy put her hand to her mouth and coughed as Ryan wrenched the gear-stick into reverse and rolled the truck out of the carport.

"Sorry about the smell," he said.

Amy rolled down her window in a desperate attempt to cleanse the air of fumes. "Hey, if it gets you from A to B, then that's all that matters, right?"

His mouth dropped open. "She can do a great deal more than just get from A to B! Don't be fooled by her looks now, this truck has got all the same fancy extras of those flashy ones you get up there in that big city of yours."

She grinned as she contemplated the cab's sparse, utilitarian interior, which seemed void of anything built during her lifetime. "Uh-huh."

"It does!"

"I believe you."

Ryan brought the truck to a stop outside the main gate. With the engine idling anemically, he leaned over and popped open the glove box. "Look there," he said wittingly, "it's got full navigation."

Amy pulled out an oversized, crumpled map of Oregon. "Very funny."

"A little cumbersome and unwieldy, sure, but it works." With a self-satisfied grin, Ryan stepped on the gas and headed off down the road. "And that's not all," he said as he rolled down his window and stuck his hand outside. "There's air-conditioning too. And none of that recirculated air, only the good stuff."

"Thought of everything, haven't you?"

"No, wait, there's one more thing." He tapped the central console of his dash, drawing her attention to the radio. "See? There's even music as well. All the modern comforts."

Amy leaned forward to inspect closer. "Is that—"

"—a tape deck?" he said, taking his eyes off the road for a moment. "Yes, it is."

"As in . . . cassette tapes?"

"You say that like it's a bad thing."

"I didn't know they *were* still a thing!"

Ryan let out an audible gasp. "This might be hard to believe, but there was a time when that there would have been a luxury addition to any vehicle. That's how people used to listen to music before everyone started carrying those fancy toys around."

"Phones, you mean?"

He laughed. "Yeah, those."

"All right, let's hear it, then. Play me something. Where are all your tapes?" But no sooner had she started searching than she noticed his expression turn bashful. "Ah, you don't have any, do you?"

"I do, actually."

"Come on, put one on then."

The cab suddenly fell silent as Ryan began fidgeting with the dial. "How about we listen to the radio instead?"

"The tapes, Ryan—come clean—where are you hiding them?"

Again, he went suspiciously quiet.

"You're not embarrassed, are you? Is it all country music or something?"

He looked at her innocently. "Why would I be embarrassed about that?"

Amy suppressed her urge to giggle and mustered up a straight face. "Fess up, then! Where are they?"

"Well, if I'm being honest, there might be a small problem."

"And that would be?"

He exchanged an exceptionally dark look with the tape deck before admitting, meekly, that the machine "might've chewed them up."

Amy looked away at once, clamping her hand across her mouth.

"It's okay. You can laugh."

"No, I shouldn't."

"I know you want to."

"No, really—" But Amy was unable to hold it in, and she doubled over in her seat, snickering uncontrollably. Her convulsive giggling was so distracting that it drew Ryan's gaze away from the road. His grip on the wheel slackened, and he started laughing as well.

"It's great you find it so amusing!"

"I am so, so sorry." Her eyes filled with tears. "I don't mean to find it funny. Not at all. I feel terrible!" Her hand flew across her mouth as she tried taking a few short breaths, a desperate attempt to regain some composure. But when she rubbed her eyes and looked to the road, her laughter ended abruptly—they were straying from the road and heading straight for the grassy embankment!

"*Ryan!*" Her spine stiffened like a rod and she slapped both hands on the dash. "*Turn!*"

Ryan swung his head.

"Whoa! *Hold on!*"

He gripped the wheel and pulled hard, but the gravel was loose and the tires wouldn't stick. They both drew back panicked gasps as the heavy truck skidded toward the wall of dirt. With no time to brake, Ryan's only option was to lay his foot heavy on the gas and hope like hell the burst of acceleration would help them draw traction. Thankfully, it did—the tires connected with the gravel at the last second and the truck made a violent swerve back onto the road.

Ryan shrunk in his seat, his expression sheepish as he tried to regain his composure and center the truck back in its lane.

"Are you all right?" he asked.

Amy unglued her hands from the dash and placed them flat across her chest. "I'm okay."

"Are you sure?"

"Yes," she said, breathing heavily.

"I'm so, *so* sorry." He adjusted his grip on the wheel and sat up straighter. "Thank goodness you looked up when you did. Now really isn't the best time for me to go crashing my father's truck!"

She gave an awkward laugh. "It's okay. Just make sure to give me warning next time you plan on going off-road." When he glanced in her direction, Amy planted her finger on his cheek and nudged his head back the other way. "And you might want to keep those eyes straight ahead, cowboy."

He laughed too, not realizing that his cheeks had just turned rosy.

19

FOR THE NEXT MILE or so, neither of them said a word. Amy
focused on the view out her window, giving a chance for the adrenaline to settle. It wasn't long before her thoughts began to wander.
Traveling back down this road made her think of the journey she'd
taken to get here, which in turn reminded her of the cab and its
driver, who had rudely taken off. What an unwelcome surprise that
had been, abandoned at the ranch gate, and probably for no other
reason than a more lucrative fare!

Still somewhat miffed, she gave a passing thought to the message
she'd left and contemplated what, if anything, had come of it. Had
anyone actually listened to it yet? Had another cab even been sent
out? Somehow, she doubted it.

She then found herself thinking about that person she had seen
while on the phone, the man in the kitchen. His physical condition
was what had stuck in her head the most—the difficulty he'd had
standing, how poorly he'd seemed, his labored movements, the cane

he'd leaned on when he'd walked. Who was he? Could he have been Ryan's dad? She remembered discarding that possibility at the time, but twice Ryan had brought up his father in conversation: first in the forest, now again in the truck. Maybe Amy had been wrong? Perhaps the man was younger than she had initially thought.

Naturally, she then thought of her own father and was abruptly reminded of the fact that her phone *still* hadn't buzzed, which seemed even more peculiar considering she now had reception again. This meant one of two things: either he was still off working on his mysterious assignment, or he had returned and was waiting for her in their room, silently stewing with annoyance that she had gone and done the same thing—disappeared without letting him know. Either way, she would find out once she got back to the hotel. Shifting her mind elsewhere, she turned in her seat to face Ryan.

"Can I ask you a question?"

Ryan, now driving with hypervigilance because of their near-miss, flicked Amy a quick glance before returning his eyes back to the road. "Sure, anything."

"There was a man back at the ranch, a man with a cane?"

"My father?" He looked sideways at her, frowning. "You saw him? When?"

"Earlier," she said, "when I was inside using the phone."

"Ah, okay."

"It was only a quick glimpse, and I don't think he even knew I was there. He was in the kitchen. I saw him stand and walk, and I couldn't help notice . . ."

"That there might be something wrong?"

"Tell me if it's none of my business. I don't want to pry."

"It's okay, I don't mind."

"Are you sure?"

"Yes, I'm sure."

"So, is he all right? Was he in some kind of accident?"

Ryan brought the truck to a stop at a quiet T-junction, leaving the engine to idle. The indicator ticked back and forth, hypnotizing him for a moment. "You're close. An accident was how it was first described to me by the doctors—a 'cerebrovascular accident' were the exact words, as I recall—which is really just a fancy way of saying he had a stroke."

She looked at him with astonishment. "When was this?"

"Four years ago. He was forty-seven."

"I'm sorry—that's terrible."

He nodded, still staring ahead. "Scariest thing I've ever seen in my life."

"You were there when it happened?"

"I was." As Ryan recalled the moment, his grip on the wheel tightened and his knuckles turned bone white. "We were out on the trails at the time, near where we were today. We hadn't been riding long when all of a sudden he just tipped sideways out of his saddle and fell to the ground. No warning, nothing. A helicopter had to come and airlift him to the nearest hospital. I'll never forget what that felt like, that hollow sensation in the pit of my gut as I watched him fly away."

"You couldn't go with him?"

He shook his head, sensing Amy's gaze heavy on him. "There wasn't any room. I had to make my own way there. It was awful. I had no idea what condition he'd be in, or if he was even still alive. For all I knew, he was already in a body bag. I swear, I don't think I've ever been so frightened."

Unbidden, the emotion of Amy's own experience came rushing back to her, the moment her dad told her about the death of her mother. Sharing the weight of his sadness, she reached across and put her hand on the side of Ryan's arm; without explaining why, she wanted to let him know that she knew *precisely* how he felt.

"What happened when you got to the hospital? Were you able to see him straight away?"

"No, he was in surgery . . ." The words were sticking in his throat.

"I didn't see him for a few hours. And before I could, the doctor had to prepare me."

"Prepare you?"

"For what I'd find." Ryan looked over at her, his expression grim. "I hardly recognized him at first—there were tubes coming out of his head, wires all over his chest. But the worst part was the damage the stroke had inflicted on his brain. His speech was slurred, a problem the doctor called 'aphasia.' Communicating with him was very difficult. He was disorientated, confused—just bringing a single word to his lips seemed to take a herculean effort. And then there was a raft of physical issues, problems with his mobility, coordination, balance, muscle movement—all brought about by severe hemiparesis."

"Hemi-what?"

"Partial paralysis down one side of the body," Ryan clarified, giving her an apologetic smile. "Sorry, I don't mean to rehash all the medical terms, but it's like being dropped into another world when something like that happens—you suddenly learn a whole bunch of words you never even knew existed."

"I can imagine." Amy fell silent as she watched a big rig trundle down the main road, roaring past like a freight train, four bright headlights cutting through the darkening air.

"After that came rehabilitation, and lots of it." Ryan's head sank a little lower, dragged down by the memories. "It wasn't an easy time," he said, his voice nearly breaking. "He really struggled."

"Must have been hard for you too, watching him go through all that."

Ryan shrugged his shoulders. Through a tightened throat he told her it was mostly just a blur, but that was a lie. The truth was that he remembered nearly everything from inside that hospital, some of it in granular detail—from the shade of beige on the corridor walls, to the stench of disinfectant, right down to the taste of the stale crackers from the vending machine and the bitterness of the burnt coffee. He remembered the view out the window of the small, pebbled, walled-in courtyard. He remembered the army of therapists. He remembered wheeling his father back and forth between them all, from one long, draining session to the next, the exercises, the repetition, the feeling that they weren't getting anywhere. He remembered the despondency in his father's eyes, the look of a man broken, defeated. But most of all, Ryan remembered what happened six weeks into rehabilitation when he received a visit from a man in a suit, a man who delivered news that no son would ever want to hear.

"Anyway." Ryan snapped himself out of it and tried to force the memories from his head, even though the expression on his face telegraphed the fact that there was a great deal more being left unsaid. "He pulled through, and that's all that matters."

Amy let a moment of silence pass. "So, you've had help through all of this? I mean, it's not just you and your dad, is it?"

"No, it's only us."

"No other family nearby?"

"Closest relation I have is an uncle in Montana. He owns a farm up there, a place called Darby, I think. But I've never met him. He and my father haven't spoken in twenty years. A falling-out over something or other, I'm really not sure. I don't think they remember anymore either. There isn't anyone else. It's just us."

"But what about the ranch?"

He looked at her tentatively. "The ranch?"

"Yeah."

"What about it?"

"It can't just be you running that place? Not all by yourself?"

"It's a lot of work, sure, but not more than one person can handle."

"But wouldn't it be easier with some help? Why don't you have anyone working for you?"

"We did for a while, but business has been kind of quiet lately— not much spare cash lying around—so for the most part it's just been me."

Another car pulled up behind with its headlights shining. The driver waited all of two seconds before leaning on the horn. Ryan waved an apology, hit the pedal, and drove forward.

"Okay, let me get this straight," Amy said as they pulled onto the main road, the truck rumbling up to full speed. "You care for your father, you look after all the horses"—she was counting these off on her fingers—"and you're responsible for running the ranch."

"Yes."

"*And* you do all of this on your own?"

"Yes."

"With *no one else* around to help?"

"It sounds like a lot when you say it like that, but yes, I guess I do."

Amy was so impressed that she felt a sudden compulsion to prod her finger into the side of Ryan's arm, just to check if he was actually real.

"That's pretty remarkable."

"Is it? Not really."

"Are you kidding? Doing that much all by yourself?" She could barely keep the astonishment from showing on her face. "It's kind of incredible, actually."

Ryan could only politely smile and squirm in his seat. "Remarkable" and "incredible" were hardly words he'd choose to describe his efforts, particularly since the net result was that they were being thrown out of the ranch in three days—no, strike that, *two days*.

"Okay, enough about me, and enough about my father. Let's talk about something else. Your father—tell me more about him."

Her head whipped around. "*My* father?"

"Yes!"

"But, why?"

"There must be some crazy stories? With his job and all, I figure there's gotta be one or two, right?"

"Not really."

"There's nothing?"

"What were you hoping to hear? It's not as if I ride shotgun helping him solve cases, you know."

He laughed. "Yeah, I know, but it must've been kinda exciting growing up, having a detective for a dad."

"Hardly. He was never around. Still never is around. It's the kind of work that doesn't leave much room for anything else."

"Sounds like you resent him a little for it."

Amy shook her head with indifference and turned her gaze to the road. At that moment, the truck passed by the *Welcome to Seabrook* sign. Night was falling fast; darkness had slid across the sky, and through the grimy windshield she could see a galaxy of stars waking from their daytime slumber.

"I don't resent him. This might sound a little cold, but when it comes to Dad, I've just learned to manage my expectations. His work matters. People rely on him. It always seemed a little selfish of me to resent him when him not being with us meant he was out there helping people and making the world a safer place."

"Still, he's your dad—doesn't mean you're not allowed to feel let down."

Amy shrugged her shoulders. "It is what it is. But, hey, if you really are desperate for a story, turns out I might have one for you."

Ryan leaned forward in his seat. "You do?"

"It's not much of a story, nor is it particularly 'crazy' or 'exciting'— but it *is* a little odd. And it's probably gonna turn out to be nothing at all . . ."

"Go on, I'm listening."

She cleared her throat. "I'm not sure how best to say it, but I think, *maybe*, that Dad might be up to something."

"Up to something? Like what?"

"You know how I said he was down here for work?"

He nodded.

"Well . . . ugh, now I feel silly even talking about it."

"It's okay," Ryan said, growing more intrigued. "What's happened?"

Amy shared the details of her dad's disappearance, beginning with the previous night—the moment she saw him last. "We'd just checked in to our room. I said I was going for a walk along the beach, and he said he was heading downstairs for a drink. But when I got back, he was nowhere to be found."

"Gone? Just like that?"

She nodded. "I thought nothing of it at the time. I assumed he was down at the bar. But what's strange is when I asked the bartender about it, she couldn't remember him at all." Amy then explained about her numerous failed attempts to reach him by phone.

Ryan looked across at her. "Okay, that's a little weird."

"I know, right?"

Ryan tapped the wheel with both thumbs, his imagination running riot as he prognosticated over the likely scenarios. "Hey, what if something's happened and he's had to go undercover?"

Amy would have laughed had she not already considered the very same thing. "I thought so too, but if he were here for something *that* serious, then why bring me along?"

"True. Especially if he planned to disappear the moment you arrived." He scratched his chin. "You're right. Definitely a little odd."

"Yeah, you're telling me."

Speaking of the hotel, there it was dead ahead.

Ryan broke from his theorizing to scan for a place to park. He found a spot just shy of the entrance. With a heave of the parking brake, he turned the key and switched off the engine.

"There we go. Door to door, almost."

She turned and smiled but quickly found herself distracted by the commotion in the town square. The festival she had seen getting underway this morning was still going strong, the crowd even bigger than before.

"That's some party your town is throwing," she said, gazing up at the Ferris wheel. The ride looked even more impressive at night, like a giant neon parlor machine with its brightly lit steel arms swinging carriages high into the sky.

"Hey, you should know by now that if it's got anything to do with that lighthouse, Seabrook takes it *very* seriously."

Amy smiled. "Yeah, I'm starting to get the idea. Anyway, I should go. If Dad's back, which he probably is, then he'll definitely be wondering where I am."

"Of course."

She slipped off her seat belt and turned to face him. "I guess this is goodbye."

He nodded slowly. "I guess it is."

"Once again, thank you—for everything—for inviting me out riding, for driving me back, and, of course, for what you did last night. You were a lifesaver."

He waved a hand through the air. "Think nothing of it."

"I'm being serious. Today's been fun, lots of fun. I can't begin to explain to you how much I needed this, how much I needed . . . a distraction." She looked straight at him, one hand on the door handle. "Truly, I mean it. Thank you."

"It's been my pleasure," he said. "And believe me, I know what it's like to need a distraction. If you ever need another one, then you know exactly where to find me. You're welcome back to the ranch anytime you like."

Amy stepped out onto the sidewalk, her dark hair dancing around her shoulders, caught by a swirling breeze.

"Hypothetically," she started to say, holding the door open, "let's say that I do. Let's say I show up one day—does that mean you'll take me riding again?"

A smile spread wide across Ryan's face. "Of course."

"Good, because I think I'm beginning to miss those trails already!"

"Hey, who knows, we might even find some new ones for you to explore. There are plenty of them."

"Forty-seven miles, right?"

"You remembered."

"I heard every word." Smiling back at him, Amy closed the door and stepped forward, resting her arms on the frame. "Ryan, listen . . ." She leaned in so she didn't have to shout over the noise of the festival. "I have no idea how often you make it up to Portland, or if you ever do, because I know how much you've got on your plate, but next time you come—*if* you ever come—why don't you give me a call? Let me take a turn showing *you* around. I admit, it won't compete with where you've taken me today, but at least I can repay the favor."

Ryan's response was swift, the answer leaping straight from his lips. "Yes, okay," he blurted out. "I mean, *yes*, absolutely. I'd like that. Very much."

She opened the door and climbed back inside. "Do you have a pen?"

"Huh?"

Her eyes zipped about the cab.

"You know, something you write with."

"A pen. Right, yes." Ryan collected himself and popped open the glove box. He reached for a ballpoint and handed it over to Amy, who proceeded to take his arm in her hand and scribble down her details, signing off with an *A* and a smiley face.

"There you go. That's how you can reach me."

Ryan stared at the series of numbers on his skin, making a mental note to transfer them to paper at his earliest opportunity. Amy, meanwhile, had already stowed the pen back in the glove box and was exiting the truck. By the time he looked up, she was standing on the sidewalk, her hand raised in farewell.

"Till next time, then," she said.

"Till then."

She stepped back and slid her hands into her pockets.

They shared one more smile, said a final goodbye, and then, from behind the wheel of his truck, his heart thumping heavy and fast, Ryan watched as she turned and walked away.

20

$\mathcal{A}$MY WASTED NO TIME returning to her room. As fond as her thoughts were of Ryan and the afternoon they had shared, the focus now was finding out where her dad had been. Discussing the situation with Ryan had only heightened her curiosity. If she was being honest, she was beginning to wonder if what her dad had said was true—had he really come down here to work on some case? Or was there something more mysterious at play, something he hadn't told her about their spontaneous trip to Seabrook? The circumstances surrounding his disappearance led her to believe that all was not as it seemed. Determined to get some answers, she unlocked the door to their room and stepped inside.

For Ryan, saying goodbye to Amy was already feeling bittersweet. They had parted ways with a promise they might see each other again, and while the prospect of a future meeting had momentarily catapulted him into a stratosphere of joy, reality was quickly bringing him back down to earth. He wasn't a fool. He knew it would be a long time before Amy found herself back in Seabrook again, if she ever did. And as for him visiting Portland? Not likely. With everything going on at home, the city might as well be on another continent. Besides, he could count on one hand the number of times he'd been there. Two trips were related to his father—one to purchase some second-hand therapy equipment, the other a visit with a stroke specialist—and the third was even longer ago, when he was eight and his mother had taken him to visit the planetarium after a book given as a birthday present had sparked a childhood obsession with the stars. Although that memory was one of the strongest he had of his mother, what Ryan remembered most from that trip was how much he had wanted to come home. The city was too intimidating— the rows upon rows of imposing buildings, the people, the clogged freeways, the incessant noise. Even now, he could remember how much he had looked forward to getting back to Seabrook, back to the sanctity of the ranch.

The ranch.

Ryan's heart sank when he thought of home. What was he doing? Had he lost all common sense? Here he was, thinking about a girl he'd only just met when a far greater problem was looming: *imminent foreclosure*. A feeling of dread churned inside his chest, the same as when Tom Tippenworth had first delivered the news. How much longer was he going to pretend this wasn't happening? No one was going to wave a magic wand and make his problems go away. There were only two days left. The clock was ticking. He had gone past the point of no return, and if he didn't do what had to be done, if he didn't confess the truth to his father once and for all, then he risked him finding out from someone else, and that was a thought far too horrifying to contemplate.

Ryan shoved his key into the ignition, willing himself to switch on the engine. Deep down he knew what he needed to do—he needed to forget about Amy and head home.

Except he couldn't.

It was as if he'd been put under a spell. Not even the prospect of losing the ranch could make him stop thinking about her.

As his fingers slipped off the keys, Ryan glanced up at the hotel and wondered what Amy was doing right now, whether she might also be thinking about him. He also wondered if she had gotten some answers as to the whereabouts of her father. Ryan had to admit, even he was curious about what was going on. But then another thought occurred to him—*what if her father still wasn't back?* What if she had stumbled into an empty room? What if he was still AWOL? Might that not mean her plans would have changed? Could that mean she would need to stay in Seabrook for one more night?

Ryan sat up straight and took a deep breath. He decided that he wasn't going home. Not yet.

———

Amy closed the door behind her and ran her fingers along the wall of the dark room, feeling for the lights.

"Hello? Dad? Are you here?"

With a flick of the switch, she saw the room was empty. Everything was the same as when she had left: magazines scattered on the couch, his duffel lying on the floor.

Amy walked across the room and set her keys down before heading into the bedroom. The window was ajar, a cool breeze rustling the curtains. She put her hands on her hips and stared at the ocean, feeling more confused than ever. She couldn't shrug it off anymore; her dad's behavior wasn't just a little strange—it was downright odd. It didn't make any sense. If he had wanted the two of them to spend some time together—which she assumed was the reason for this trip in the first place—why disappear the moment they arrived? What possible reason could he have for leaving her behind in a strange town with no warning, no explanation, and no means of communicating with him?

Wait a minute.

Hadn't they come down to Seabrook for only one night? They were supposed to be on their way home by now, so why wasn't anyone knocking on the door to bundle them out of the room? Amy grabbed her key and marched back downstairs.

"Peggy, isn't it? We spoke earlier?"

The bartender was midpour of four large jugs of beer when Amy presented herself at the counter of the bar.

"Of course, you're from room 212, right? Can you give me a moment?" She finished serving her customer, closed the till, then shuffled sideways toward Amy, wiping the countertop with a rag as she spoke. "What can I do for ya? Is everything all right with your room?"

"Everything's fine. My room's fine."

"Would you like a drink? You look too young for the strong stuff, but would ya like a soda?"

"No, no soda. Thanks. I just want to ask you something . . . it's about my dad."

"Your dad? Weren't you asking about him this morning?"

"Yes."

"And he still hasn't shown up?"

"No, he hasn't. You haven't seen him come through, have you?" Amy pulled out her phone and swiped through her photos, searching for a recent picture. "There, that's him."

Peggy didn't seem interested in looking at the screen. "This place has been like a way station all day long, what with the festival and all, so even if I passed right by him there's every chance I wasn't paying the least bit of attention."

"I know, but if you don't mind, could you take a look?" Amy forced the phone closer. "Please?"

"All right then, let's see if we can't jog this ol' memory of mine." Peggy slung the rag over her shoulder and took the phone from Amy's hands. Her eyes narrowed and she fell silent. For a moment, Amy thought the image might have triggered a memory, but . . . "Sorry, wish I could tell ya otherwise, but his face ain't ringin' no bells."

"Not even from last night? Don't you remember checking us in? I was with him. *You spoke to him.*"

"I did? Really?"

"Yes, he was standing right here."

Her eyes traveled around the room. "Sorry, mind's gone a complete blank."

"What about our booking?"

"Mmm?"

"Our booking. Could you check it for me? Could you tell me what it says?"

Peggy disappeared below the counter and produced the hefty tome. "Room 212," she said after opening the book and running her finger across the page. "Tucker, Kevin. That your dad?"

"Yes."

"Says here we have you checking out in the morning."

"What?" Amy spun the journal 180 degrees. "That can't be."

Peggy slapped her finger down. "Two nights—says it right there." She gave Amy a moment to verify the details before closing and returning the book to the shelf underneath. "Don't be takin' this the wrong way, but are you quite sure everything is all right?"

Amy muttered "uh-huh" and stumbled two steps back from the bar.

"Are you sure you're okay?"

"I'm fine. I'm sorry for wasting your time."

Peggy waved her rag. "It's no bother. And now I know what your dad looks like, don't I? If I catch a glimpse, I'll be sure to let him know you've been looking for him."

Amy slid her phone into her pocket, smiled, thanked Peggy for her help, and turned to leave. But as she turned to face the crowded bar, a room full of patrons mixing and mingling and sipping on drinks, she spotted something odd. There was a man looking in her direction. Looking *directly* at her. He was middle-aged, with a long, thin face and a tuft of receding brown hair. He was staring at her from one of the small tables along the window. There was someone else with him—a woman—but he didn't seem to be paying her the slightest bit of attention. His gaze was locked on Amy. Despite the commotion and activity inside the bar, his eyes never shifted, never wavered. A chill raced up Amy's spine. She wondered if she knew him from somewhere, but nothing about his face sparked any recognition. She had half a mind to walk over and ask what his problem was, but the truth was that there was something off about him, something that made the hairs on the back of her neck stand up.

"Amy, over here!"

Someone was calling her name.

"Amy!"

There it was again.

Rising above the din of the bar, the voice sounded bright and young, and even a little familiar. Amy broke off her stare with the man and looked around the room. Over by the door to the lobby, she saw a young girl—the same one she had spoken to this morning while waiting for her taxi. The one who had spouted all those strange questions.

The girl skipped over, zigzagging a path through all the tables and chairs. She drew up right in front of Amy, smiling gleefully.

"Hi! It's me!"

"Um, hi?"

"Amy? It *is* Amy, right?"

"That's right."

"Do you remember me?"

"Yes, I do. But wait, how do you know my name?"

"You told me, silly!"

"I did?"

Amy wasn't sure if that was true. She couldn't remember. The truth was that she couldn't concentrate on anything but that strange man. She glanced back at him to see if he was still watching her, but to her surprise he was smiling and chatting happily to the woman at his table, acting as though nothing had happened. Still suspicious, Amy watched him a moment longer, waiting for his beady eyes to swing back in her direction, but they never did.

"Hey, I really need to talk to you."

Amy blinked and turned her attention back to the girl. "Me?"

"Yes, you!"

"Why?"

"I can't say—not in here."

Before Amy could gather her thoughts, the girl grabbed her by the hand and started dragging her through the crowd. Amy tried to shake her loose, but her grip was surprisingly strong.

"Whoa, what are you doing?"

"This way."

"Wait! Can you stop, please?"

"Can't, need to talk to you." The girl's head was down; she was on a warpath for the exit.

"What's this all about?"

"It's important."

"But what's it got to do with *me?*"

"You'll see."

As soon as they reached the lobby, Amy wrestled her hand loose and folded her arms, refusing to take another step. "Will you just tell me what's going on?"

The girl's sprightly expression faded; she suddenly looked nervous, skittish, her small blue eyes darting left and right and all around. When Amy asked if she was lost or needed help, the girl became agitated.

"No, I'm not lost. But you need to come with me."

"If you're not lost, then who are you with? Where are your parents?"

"Never mind that. There's no time." She tried to take Amy's hand.

"I'm not going anywhere until you tell me exactly what you want."

The girl spun her head and glanced at the hotel entrance. "Okay, but not here. Can we go upstairs?"

"Why upstairs? What's up there?"

"Your room."

"Are you kidding? No. We definitely cannot go up to my room. Are you in some kind of trouble?"

"No, silly, nothing like that. There's just something I really need to tell you."

"Go on, then." Amy dropped her head and leaned in closer. "Whatever it is, you can tell me. Just say it."

The girl stood on tiptoes, cupped her small hands around Amy's ear, and, in a hushed voice, whispered: "It's about the lighthouse."

Ryan tilted his head, straightened his collar, ran his fingers through his hair, checked his teeth, did everything he could to make himself as presentable as possible—not an easy task when the only tool available was the rearview mirror in his truck.

He turned his attention back to the hotel, sizing it up as though it were some kind of fortified stronghold. What was he going to say to Amy? And what if her dad was back—what then? And why was he this nervous?

After gathering his composure, Ryan haphazardly tucked in his shirt and decamped from his truck. He crossed the sidewalk and reached the canopied entrance of the hotel in just a dozen steps. He approached the door, gripped the handle. From his vantage point he could see through the glass and straight into the lobby. The room was busy with visitors and guests crisscrossing from one side to the other and moving up and down the stairs. And among the hustle and bustle, he spotted Amy. Except she wasn't alone. Her head was bent down, and she appeared to be engaged in conversation with a young child. Ryan couldn't see the child's face, but he didn't need to—he recognized those blonde pigtails from earlier that same day.

21

BEFORE AMY HAD A CHANCE to get anything further out of Chloe, she felt a tap on her shoulder. She held her breath and spun around, nervous it might be the strange man, but she was greeted with a familiar face instead.

"Ryan!" she said, happily surprised. "Wait, you're still here?"

"I am," he answered, smiling back.

"How come? Is everything okay?"

Ryan hesitated for a moment, trying to come up with an excuse. "It's my truck," he said at last. "Cursed thing won't start again."

"Oh no . . ."

"She'll be fine. Probably just needs a moment to cool down." He gave a casual shrug of the shoulders before shifting his attention to Chloe. "Hello, you."

"Um, hi," Chloe replied.

"This is quite the surprise."

"What is?"

"Seeing you in here."

"It is?"

"Yes."

"Wait a second," Amy said as she waved her finger back and forth between them. "You two know each other?"

"We certainly do." Ryan ruffled Chloe's hair affectionately. "This one was with me at the ranch this morning. She's the girl I was telling you about earlier—my student—and a great one at that. Isn't that right, Chloe?"

Chloe nodded while averting her eyes, appearing to be a little rattled by this turn of events.

"That's odd," Amy remarked. "We ran into each other this morning too, just as I was on my way up to see you."

"Oh?" An uncertain silence followed. Ryan looked at them both. "You two know each other as well?"

"I wouldn't say we know each other, but what's weird is that just now she came rushing in to find me, saying there was something she had to tell me."

"Really?" His frown sharpened. "And? . . . What was it?"

"Beats me. You'll have to ask her. I have yet to find out myself. But she did say it had something to do with the lighthouse."

Chloe looked down at her shoes and began twirling one of the loose buckle strands of her dress around her fingers. Ryan could see she looked uncomfortable. He hadn't a clue what it was, but it was obvious she was hiding something.

"Is something going on, Chloe?"

"Nothing's going on."

"Nothing?"

"Nuh-uh."

"Are you sure? Because you look a little nervous."

"I'm sure."

Ryan fixed her with a stare. "The lighthouse, huh? This wouldn't have something to do with what happened last night, would it?"

"I don't know what you mean," she said in an innocent-sounding voice.

"I'm sure you've heard."

"Heard what?"

"Apparently, the lighthouse switched on. Some people think they saw a beam. Can you believe that?"

Chloe's eyes began skipping about the room.

"Sounds to me like you're playing games with the out-of-towners," Ryan said, "perhaps spreading rumors and trying to scare the visitors. Because what better place to do that than here in the hotel, right?" He gave her a knowing smile, but she shook her head.

"I wouldn't do that," she said.

"Then what's the big secret? What did you want to talk to Amy about?"

"I thought she ought to know something, that's all."

"And that would be?"

"It's just this thing that I heard."

"Okay, and what did you hear?"

Another long silence followed. Chloe snuck a glance outside and postured for a few seconds as though she were trying to come up with something to say. Finally, after sneaking a few looks around the lobby, she leaned in and started whispering.

"All right, this is what I know. Later tonight, when the festival is finished, there's a group of people who are gonna go down to the lighthouse." And then, even more quietly, she added: "They're on some kind of mission."

Despite himself, Ryan started whispering too. "A mission? To do what?"

"What do you think, silly? They want to find out how it turned on! Everyone wants to know what happened."

Amy shuffled closer too, her own interest piqued.

"And how exactly are they going to do that?" Ryan asked.

"Dunno. Someone mentioned they were gonna climb the fence and break in."

"You're kidding."

"Nope."

"Who have you heard talking about this?"

"Lots of people."

Ryan rolled his eyes. "I suppose that's hardly surprising in this town," he said. "But why are you in here? And why are you involving Amy? What's she got to do with this?"

"Umm." Chloe looked skyward, a poor attempt to bide some more time.

"Come out with it, Chloe."

"I just thought she ought to know, that's all."

"But why?"

"Because I thought she might be interested."

"Interested in *what*, exactly? I hardly think Amy wants to get involved in the nefarious activities of some spooked townsfolk." Realizing that he was sounding a lot like a disapproving parent, Ryan paused for a moment and took a breath. "Look, while I'm sure you mean well, and while I'm sure Amy appreciates the gesture, I really don't think—"

"You know what? I don't think it sounds all that bad," Amy interjected. "Actually, if you're asking me, it sounds like a bit of good-natured fun. And after what happened last night, who could really blame everyone for wanting to get to the bottom of it?"

This contribution won a conspiratorial smile from Chloe but a wide-eyed glance from Ryan.

"Not helping!" he said.

Amy threw back an innocent smirk. "What can I say? I'm intrigued!"

"You just want to know if your theory is right and see if someone's rigged a spotlight up top."

"Like you said, I'm a sucker for a mystery."

"Hey, speaking of mysteries, have you been upstairs yet? Was your dad there?"

Amy shook her head and went on to explain about the empty room upstairs and the change to their booking.

Ryan kept a steady face, doing his best not to smile too broadly when he realized what this news meant: that Amy would indeed be staying one more night.

"Question, please." Chloe's small face was scrunched in confusion. "What does 'nefarious' mean?"

"It means something bad—*illegal,* even—which is why you shouldn't be getting yourself involved in this kind of thing."

"Would we say it's *that* bad?" Amy teased.

Ryan gave her another long, grinning look. "All right, maybe I'm overreacting. But, Chloe, you really shouldn't be running about town trying to recruit people. Where are your parents?"

"Over in the square. Mom thinks I'm riding the teacups."

"Probably best you get back, don't you think?"

"Good idea. I will." She sprang forward and wrapped her arms around Ryan's middle, hugging him goodbye the same way she had that morning. "See you soon."

"All right, take care." He hugged her back and nodded to the door. "Now, go find your mother before she starts to worry. And say hi to her from me, okay?"

"Okay."

She gave a smile and a wave to Amy, then spun on her shoes and skipped away.

"She's fond of you," Amy remarked as they watched her leave the lobby.

Ryan smiled. He waited to watch Chloe make safe passage across the street before turning his attention back to Amy. "So, it seems our town's lucky enough to have you one more night?"

"Seems that way."

"I take it you'd rather be heading home?" he asked, registering the flatness in her voice.

"No, it's not that. It's just confusing, this whole situation with my dad. He's a workaholic for sure, but this isn't like him. I haven't got a clue what's going on."

Ryan looked around. "This might sound silly, but is it worth asking someone? Who knows, maybe someone saw him, or spoke to him? Anything that might shed a clue?"

"Tried that."

"Didn't get you anywhere?"

"No, all it did was raise more questions. To tell you the truth, I'm actually starting to feel a bit like Alice—every answer I get sends me deeper down the rabbit hole."

"What are you going to do?"

"Nothing. I can only assume this has got something to do with work, but until he decides to show up or call me and actually tell me what's going on, there's not a lot I can do."

Ryan turned to the door, where the lights of the festival could be seen shining through the glass. "Sounds to me like you need a distraction."

"Is that so?" Her eyes lifted. "Sounds to me like you've already got something in mind."

"I think I do. But it depends."

"On what?"

He grinned. "Whether or not you like to fish."

22

"Very clever," Amy said.

Ryan paid the operator of a carnival game a five-dollar bill and in exchange received two flimsy plastic rods, one of which he stuck in Amy's hand.

"You didn't really think I was going to take you to the beach and cast a line out into the ocean, did you?"

"I didn't know what to think!" she replied, thinking that she didn't expect to find herself standing in front of an inflatable pool, comically labeled *The Lucky Lagoon*, either.

"This is even better. At least here you know you're gonna catch something." He alerted her to the prize shelves, headed by a sign that said *Guaranteed to Win!* "Blue ducks win the top, green the middle, yellow the bottom."

Amy had always prided herself on her competitive streak and quickly warmed to the challenge. Tempering the excitement, how-ever, was the dearth of prizes on display. It was a rather sad-looking collection, with the winning shelf offering a choice between a plastic ukulele, a bag of marbles, or a cheap-looking teddy bear. Before she cast her line, she leaned over and suggested to Ryan that they up the ante.

"All right," he said, "what do you have in mind?"

"Hmm, let's see, how about the loser has to buy us something to eat?"

"Sounds like a win-win to me. I'll take that bet."

In no time at all, Amy was sporting a victorious grin. She had managed to reel in the proverbial big one, the sought-after blue duck, while Ryan's efforts had earned him only a yellow one, securing him second place and the indignity of having to choose between a miniature water pistol and a pair of fluffy dice.

"Don't suppose there's any hope of redemption?" he asked as they handed their rods back.

"You bet there is."

They crisscrossed the midway, visiting every game they could find. Keeping record of who was winning their wager was difficult, though, as the spoils were going back and forth. While Ryan proved adept at popping balloons with darts and throwing rings (which he joked must be residual skill from many hours of horseshoe throwing), Amy surprised even herself by her precision with the toy gun and rubber bullets in Tin Can Alley. There was plenty of friendly pushing and shoving in the Whack-a-Mole; Ryan prevailed easily there on account of his longer reach—but Amy pegged him back in Skee-Ball, making a succession of pinpoint rolls. After a number of prizes had been accumulated and donated to passing kids, they paused to tally up the scores. They were locked at four wins apiece. A tiebreaker was needed, and Amy found the perfect game: the Laughing Clowns.

"What's this one all about?" Ryan asked.

"You've never played? It's easy. You stick the ball in the clown's mouth and it falls out there." She pointed down to the numbered columns. "Add them up at the end, highest total wins."

"That's it?"

"That's it."

Ryan gathered up a handful of Ping-Pong balls and began studying the clown's head as it swiveled back and forth. "Sounds a little rudimentary, but all right."

"By all means, show me how it's done."

Ryan got off to a good start, with his first attempt landing in the highest-numbered column. Believing he'd already mastered the game, he then timed his next roll and waited for the clown's head to turn back into the same position, except this produced a completely different result—the ball rolled into the *1* column. He gave Amy a sideways look.

"This game is rigged."

Amy, meanwhile, was employing a different strategy and shoving balls into the clown's mouth as fast as she could. "You're overthinking it."

"No, I'm putting it in at the exact same spot." He tried again, and again, and again, but each time the ball tumbled out into a completely different row.

"Not kidding, there's been some serious tampering going on here." He held up one of the balls to the light. "Are you sure they don't put weights in these things or something?"

Amy made a noise, which was intended to sound like a laugh but instead came out more like a snort. "I'm not sure what the right etiquette is, but don't you normally wait until *after* the game is finished before you start making excuses?"

"True," he said, smirking as he lined up his last two balls. "Not another word, then."

It was Amy's scattergun approach that sealed her victory. There was a witty suggestion from Ryan that they go best of three, but she wasn't interested. Besides, all this excitement was making her hungry.

"Dream on, cowboy. If I remember the terms of our deal, you're the one who's buying!"

"And it was a well-earned victory too. You're a formidable oppo-nent. Come on, follow me."

Ordering food meant lining up at one of the caravans parked along the fringe of the square. The lines were long and they must have been waiting for fifteen minutes before progressing far enough to get a glimpse of the garishly bright menu board. Choices were limited to the usual festival fare: burgers, curly fries, corn dogs, funnel cakes, and cotton candy.

"Do you know what you're getting?" she asked.

"Yes, I do." He pointed straight to a giant yellow star that, in red lettering, screamed the words SEABROOK'S FAMOUS DEEP-FRIED SURPRISE. "I think you should try one."

"What's in it?"

"That's the surprise."

"But it's deep-fried, so it'll be chicken or fish or something, right?"

"Not quite."

"What, then?"

"All I'll say is that it's a local delicacy, and as a visitor to the town, it's only right that you experience it."

Amy's eyes narrowed. "What *exactly* is the surprise, Ryan?"

"It could be anything. They take a mystery ingredient and fry it in batter. You don't find out what it is until you bite into it."

"Are you for real?"

His lips curled into a smile. "Yep."

"And that's what you're having?"

"That's what *we're* having."

"Ugh, um . . . I'm not sure."

"Trust me, you'll enjoy it."

She felt her stomach turn. "Can I have a clue at least? What kind of things could they use? You know, hypothetically?"

"I'm not sure you understand the meaning of the word *surprise!*" The line shifted; they were only a few feet from the counter. "Now, before I order, I do need to ask you a couple of questions. Are you allergic to anything?"

"No."

"And on a scale of one to ten, how adventurous would you say you are with food?"

"Is negative one hundred a valid answer?"

"It's not."

"Oh God." Amy craned her neck and tried to catch a whiff or a glimpse or anything, but the frying station was guarded behind a plastic wall. All she could hear was the sizzle of hot oil. "Is it too late to go back on our deal and buy myself a corn dog instead?"

"Of course, if that's what you really want, but then I'd ask you to think of what would happen next—the regret you would have, the questions, the lifetime of endless wondering, all because of that one day in Seabrook when you didn't trust me enough to buy you that Deep-Fried Surprise."

She rolled her eyes. "All right, *okay*, order it. But if it's something gross—like, really gross—well, I can't promise what will happen."

After placing their order, they joined a semicircle waiting around a small window. Amy watched with jealousy as others went to the counter when their numbers were called and walked away with deliciously plain-looking fare. When their turn came, they were presented with a fistful of napkins and two hockey-puck-sized creations coated in layers of glistening golden batter so dense that you'd need to have X-ray vision to see what might be lurking inside.

"Come on," Ryan said, "let's find somewhere to sit."

That, however, was easier said than done—every park bench was occupied, as were all the spots along the edge of the fountain. Ryan glanced at the Ferris wheel and spotted empty carriages. A minute later they were seated and buckled in.

"You're okay with this?" he asked as a steel bar lowered over their laps. The giant wheel began to turn, lifting their carriage toward the sky.

"Why wouldn't I be?"

"Last time we were up high, you looked a little green."

He was of course referring to their excursion by the cliff, specifically when she had leaned over the edge to take in the view of the ocean swirling two hundred feet below. To Amy's surprise, though, the danger of that plunging drop was not what she remembered most. Instead, it was clinging to Ryan's arm, the comfort of knowing he was there, knowing she would be okay. She trusted him. More than that, she felt *safe*—a sensation she hadn't experienced since the day she'd lost her mom.

But how far did that trust extend? Enough to put this grotesque combination of batter and *God knows what* into her mouth? That was another question entirely.

"All right, now you gotta commit," Ryan said. "No nibbling and then trying to peek. One big bite. Straight in."

Their carriage began to swing back and forth as the Ferris wheel hit its stride.

"Believe me, I don't intend to drag this out any longer than necessary!"

"Here we go then, three . . . two . . . one . . ."

With one hand underneath the napkin, soggy from the grease already seeping through, Amy closed her eyes and sank her teeth into the batter. Her senses were on high alert as she scrutinized what she had just started to chew. It tasted familiar. Soft, kind of crumbly, even a little sweet. She chewed a few seconds more before daring to look, and when she did she saw a small stack of Oreos caked inside the batter.

Ryan leaned over. "What did you get?"

She showed him. He nodded with delight and then revealed his— a deep-fried peanut-butter sandwich.

"Not as bad as you first thought, am I right?"

She took a second bite and mumbled, "I'm reserving judgment for now."

"Ha! I knew it."

For a while they ate in a comfortable silence, enjoying the rotating view. The Ferris wheel was by far the largest Amy had ever ridden. Buildings fell away like magic whenever their carriage sailed across the top, revealing a picturesque parade of trees, sloping roofs, and lit streetlamps. They could see the entire town, from the hills to the east and back across to the ocean.

"So, what's the verdict?" Ryan asked. "Aside from the exotic food on offer, how are you enjoying our little festival?"

"I like it, it's cute." She finished another mouthful, the sickly sweet taste of chocolate and cream and soft batter sliding down her throat. "And if I'm being honest, the food's not half bad."

Ryan's eyes widened, his expression triumphant. "What did I tell you? They're good, huh? It's a combination you think just can't work, and yet somehow it does."

"Don't get too ahead of yourself. Remember, you haven't been right the entire night. Do the words 'sabotage' and 'laughing clowns' ring any bells?"

Ryan jokingly hung his head in shame. He wasted no time conceding defeat on that one, admitting that he was wrong, maybe even "reaching a little" with his conspiracy theories.

"A little?"

"All right, a lot."

"Okay, so we're clear, then—the clowns are innocent?"

"Whoa, innocent? We're talking about clowns here."

"Fair point."

As they laughed, there was movement on the ground. Two young boys had approached to board the Ferris wheel. Ryan didn't recognize them, but their father, who was standing on the ground with his back turned, struck him as being oddly familiar.

"Do you know those boys?" Amy asked.

Ryan dragged his eyes back to her. "Not them—thought I recognized someone else."

"Must happen all the time," she said as the wheel started turning again.

"What does?"

"Coming across people you know. Isn't that how it goes in small towns? Everyone knows everyone?"

Ryan smiled. "I suppose we do. I guess that sounds scary to someone who comes from the city?"

"Not at all," she said. "The opposite. It actually sounds kinda comforting. Portland's great, but sometimes it can feel a little impersonal. There must be hundreds of people living on our street back home, and yet none of us know each other. We don't even know each other's names. To me, that seems kinda sad."

"It's certainly different down here. We don't have many neighbors in the valley, but if you take all the stores in this town square, for instance, I could probably tell you not only the names of the people who run them but a whole lot of other useless information as well."

"Oh yeah, like what?"

"Point to one, I'll show you."

"All right." The first store Amy laid her eyes on also happened to be where she had bought the muffin. "There, that one."

"Easy, that's the bakery. It's owned and run by Oscar Pipps, famous for his mustache and his key-lime pound cake. On his days off he likes to take his boat out and go fishing. Once caught a thirty-pound steelhead right out in the bay. There's a photo of it inside the hotel."

"Wow, and do you know his star sign too?"

He laughed and waved his hand. "Try another."

Amy pointed to the adjacent block next, singling out a narrow store with a busy window display and a frilly peach-colored canopy.

"Haberdashery. Mrs. Mallory is the proprietor, but because of her other pursuits—co-editing the *Beacon* and curating the local community theater group—the store is left to her daughter, Leslie, to run."

Amy drew her head back, impressed. She wouldn't know the first thing about the people who owned and ran her own local shops, never mind what hobbies they kept.

"Shall I keep going?" he asked.

"Sure, who's next door?"

Ryan scanned the block and told her it was Handsome Frank's Hardware.

"Wait, let me guess . . . run by Frank?"

"Correct, but don't forget the *Handsome*!"

"Is there a reason for that? Or is Frank just not the modest type?"

"Little bit of both. Frank came third place in a competition way back in the late eighties—Most Eligible Bachelor in the Pacific Northwest—and from that day on, he's been known around town simply as Handsome Frank. He's even got his winning photo on the door of his shop—denim blazer, mullet, the works—it's great, you should see it."

Amy smiled. "And what about that one?"

"Ah, that one I know particularly well. That's Rosie's, our diner— Seabrook's *only* diner—owned and run by Joe and Linda Petersen. It's named after Joe's grandmother, who first opened the doors back in—" Ryan's voice suddenly died in his throat, not because he couldn't remember the year but because he'd just realized who that man on the ground was.

"Ryan? Are you okay?"

With a sinking stomach, he peered over the railing of their carriage, and there, standing thirty feet below, waving and pointing a camera, was the father of the two boys who had just boarded a carriage: Tom Tippenworth.

"What's wrong, Ryan? You look like you've seen a ghost."

If only, he thought.

If only.

23

*R*YAN TWISTED NINETY DEGREES, nodded to Amy's side of the carriage, and politely requested to swap sides.

"Do you mind?" he asked, "and quick, before we reach the ground."

"Why?" she asked, tempted to lean across him so she could see for herself. "What's down there? What did you see?"

"I just really would like to sit there."

"But how?" Amy asked, who thought the idea of switching seats to be entirely impractical. They were squeezed together in a tiny carriage with a steel bar across their laps, swinging some fifty feet up in the air. This didn't seem to bother Ryan, though, not judging by what he did next. Without any warning, he reached out, grabbed hold of the lap bar, gave it a shake, and wrestled it free from its locked position.

"Hey! Are you sure you should be doing that?"

To Amy's astonishment he then swung the bar over their head and perched himself on the open edge of the carriage, motioning for her to slide over. The brazen act hadn't gone unnoticed. By dislodging the bar, he'd set off a chain reaction: red lights were blinking, a siren was wailing, and the ride was beginning to slow.

"Okay," she said, looking around, embarrassed, "you *definitely* weren't allowed to do that."

The occupants of the other carriages all turned their heads as the giant wheel ground to a halt.

"Hey! What's going on up there!"

Awkwardly, the two of them quickly switched places and pulled the lap bar back down, though this now left Amy in the unenviable position of having to deal with the wrath of the ride operator, who was squawking at them from down below.

"You two! You two up there!" a high-pitched voice shrieked. "Yes, I can see you!"

"Oh no," Ryan whispered, now cowering in his seat. "Please don't let him kick us off."

"The guy and girl in carriage number seven, the green carriage! Don't think I don't know it was you!"

Gritting her teeth, Amy turned and poked her head over the side and made eye contact with a pimply faced teenager, who was scowling at her.

"I am *so* sorry," she called out. "We didn't—"

"You can't do that!"

"It was an accident—"

"Those bars have to stay down whenever the ride is in motion!"

"Yes, I know. It was my bad. It won't happen again. I promise." She flashed her friendliest smile.

"Yeah, well . . . all right. But stay in your seats or else you'll have to come off. I'm not kidding."

She gave him a salute. "Got it. You have my word."

He punched a button on his console and buried his head in a comic book. As soon as the Ferris wheel started turning again, Amy heard Ryan let out a relieved sigh.

"Thank you," he said.

"You're welcome, but what was all that about? Who are you hiding from?" Amy put her head back over the side and searched the ground; there was only one other person standing near the ride: a nondescript middle-aged man in a brown sweater. His most distinguishing feature was the old-fashioned camera draped around his neck. "Is it that guy down there?"

"Did he see me?" Ryan whispered.

Amy snuck a glance over her shoulder. "No. I don't think so. Why, who is he?"

"His . . . his name's Tom."

"Okay, and who is Tom, exactly?"

"Tom . . . is the bank manager."

"You're telling me that all that was to avoid being seen by your bank manager?"

"Aren't most people afraid of their bank managers?"

"Sure, but by the way you reacted, anyone would think you'd gone and robbed the place. Why are you so desperate to avoid him?" When he didn't answer, Amy took a guess. "Do you owe them money? Are you behind on a credit card or something?"

Ryan went ominously quiet.

Amy was inclined to leave the matter there, and normally that was what she would've done—after all, a person's financial affairs were their own business—but there was something about Ryan's demeanor that made her want to delve deeper.

"Tell me to butt out if you want, but I get the sense this is something serious."

Ryan gave her a look, a kind of half smile, half grimace, then turned away and drew in a deep breath, which seemed to stick awkwardly as it traveled down his throat. "I can't talk about it," he said, his head stooping lower. "I shouldn't."

"Why not?"

"Because this isn't something you want to hear."

"Maybe it is."

"Trust me, it's not."

She waited for him to lift his chin and look at her. "Because?"

"Because we've only just met. And because the last thing you want is to sit here and listen to a stranger prattling on about his problems, especially when they're about something as tedious as money."

"Firstly, you're not a stranger, not anymore, and secondly, in case it slipped your mind, I just watched you break this Ferris wheel in order to hide from your bank manager, so it seems pretty clear that this is a problem in desperate need of some solving."

"And believe me, if talking could solve it then I'd tell you everything right now, really, I would, but the problem I'm facing is serious—it's *foreclosure*—so unless you're actually a law student or someone with knowledge of a loophole that might help me get out of this mess, then honestly there's not much point."

Amy's eyes sprang open. "Wait, did you just say foreclosure?"

Ryan dropped his gaze and tried to look away.

"*Foreclosure?*"

"Please, forget it."

"But that's . . . that's when you lose your home. That's when the bank comes in and takes everything. Isn't it?" She fixed him with a look and turned her body as far as the carriage would allow—any farther and her feet would be crossing over his. "Ryan, that's not about to happen to your ranch, is it . . . ?"

Ryan's silence was answer enough.

"But you grew up there, Ryan. Your ranch has been in your family for generations. Isn't that what you told me? How can something like this be happening?"

"Because they're the bank. They can do whatever they want."

"And that's it? There isn't anything you can do to stop it?"

"I wish there was."

"There must be *something*."

He shook his head. The defeat in his eyes was plainly evident.

"But that's not fair," Amy exclaimed. "Ask them to give you some more time. If they knew everything, if they knew how long the ranch has been in your family, surely, they would—"

"Believe me, I've tried, but it's just no use. They know all that. They've already given us time, and the time they've given us has all but run out."

"What? When's this supposed to happen?"

"Soon."

"*How soon?*"

He clasped his hands together. "The day after next."

Amy recoiled in shock, too stunned to speak.

"What are you going to do?" she finally asked. "And what's going to happen to your business?"

"I—I don't know—"

"What?"

"I said, I don't know."

She made a face. "You can't say that, Ryan."

"But it's the truth. There aren't any easy answers."

"I get that, but you still must have *some* idea about what you're going to do. What does your father say about this? The two of you must have talked about it at the very least."

"No, we haven't . . . um . . ." A quiver broke in his voice, and the words came out all shaky. "We haven't talked about it."

Amy leaned forward so fast that the carriage lurched and creaked on its hinges. "You're *kidding?*" She could hear the exasperation in her own voice. "You're both about to get kicked out of your home."

"I know."

"And you'll have nowhere to go."

"Amy, I know."

"So how can you not be talking about this?"

"Because . . ." Ryan closed his eyes and swallowed hard, the uncomfortable kind, the kind that catches the tongue. "Because he doesn't even know, okay? Because I haven't discussed this with him. Any of it . . . not *ever.*"

There was an abrupt silence.

The words had escaped Ryan's lips in a breathless blur, and the moment he realized what he was saying, that he was admitting aloud his most personal and private secret, he felt his heart leap halfway up his throat. He wanted to take it back, but it was too late.

Next to him, sitting in silence, Amy was perched forward, her jaw dropped and her eyes radiating shock and dismay. Ryan couldn't blame her for looking as surprised as she did. No doubt she'd be asking herself how anyone could end up in such a mess, but she must also be questioning *why* it was only him who knew anything about it and *why on earth* he would be keeping it to himself. And what was he supposed to say? Changing the subject wasn't going to work. There was no brushing this revelation aside. Which really only left him with one choice: tell Amy the truth. Tell her everything. *All of it.* The idea of confiding in her made him nervous, but what choice did he have? After four years of living with this secret, he couldn't keep it buried a moment longer.

"Amy, there's a reason my father and I don't talk about this . . ." Ryan turned to face her and took a deep breath. "There's a reason he doesn't know."

Amy studied him, her expression steady, her eyes resting gently on his. He looked vulnerable, and she noticed his hands were shaking, which told her that whatever he was about to say was probably something big, something very important.

"Okay . . ."

"I need to tell you something. It's about something I've done.

Something I've never spoken about before. Not with anyone, not ever."

Even though their carriage was tiny and the gap between them was only a few inches, Amy acted on impulse and wriggled closer, laying her hand on his knee.

"Go on," she said. "Whatever it is, you can tell me."

24

$\mathcal{O}$N THE WAY HERE," Ryan started, "back in the truck, when we were talking about my father's stroke, do you remember when I spoke about his stay in the hospital? His rehabilitation?"

"Yes," Amy said, "but you didn't say much. All I remember you saying was that it was mostly a blur but that he managed to pull through?"

"That's right. That's what I said. That's what I always say whenever someone asks me about it, because until now I've never been able to say what really happened."

Amy held his gaze. "Okay, what did really happen?"

Ryan blinked hard and ran both hands down the length of his face. Exhaling heavily into his palms, he closed his eyes, gathered his thoughts, and began.

"After the stroke, my father was in a bad way. The damage to his brain left him needing around-the-clock medical care. Rehabilitation was his only chance at a future, but the six weeks he spent in that hospital were a complete disaster. He didn't respond to any of the treatments. He had the best physical therapists, the best equipment, yet by the end of the program he was no better than he was when he started. The toll of the experience left him severely depressed."

As he spoke, Ryan's eyes drifted west across the dark horizon. "On the inside, mentally, I knew what agony he must have been in. Here was a physical man who had loved the outdoors and spent every day riding horses—and now he was suddenly confined to a hospital, stuck in a small room, incapable of standing up by himself or even tying his own shoelaces or reciting the alphabet. His whole world had been turned upside down."

"That must have been awful, having to watch him go through that."

"It was, and there wasn't much I could do to help. I did what I could. I got him out of the hospital as often as possible, wheeled him around the park, fed him his lunch, read him the news. Sometimes we'd just listen to the birds and watch clouds roll across the sky. I talked about the ranch, about Seabrook, filled him in on how the horses were doing, and talking about home never failed to lift my father's mood. It was the only time I ever saw him relax. His eyes would brighten, and for a few minutes he seemed to forget about everything that was going on. For a fleeting moment, I caught a glimpse of the man I knew from before, the man who used to be— who *was*—my dad."

The emotion of that memory stung deep and interrupted Ryan's train of thought. Putting all of this into words was much harder than he'd expected, and the rigid seats of the Ferris wheel and the noise of the festival weren't making his job any easier.

Amy might have been reading his mind. She broke the silence and suggested they hop off and go someplace else, somewhere a little quieter. "If you're happy to walk and talk, why don't we go down to the beach?"

"Perfect," he said.

After exiting their carriage and stepping off the gangway, they fled the festival and headed in the direction of a narrow, sand-blown road that connected the town square to the beach. When they reached the end, they climbed over the dunes and began walking up the beach, the soles of their shoes sinking into the soft sand. They headed toward the outcrop at the northern tip, where the lighthouse stood. Neither one of them was paying any attention to the weather, or bothering to notice that the sky, clear and starlit since nightfall, had suddenly clouded over and gone black.

Amid the sound of crashing waves, with his hands stuffed in his pockets, Ryan resumed his story.

"Anyhow, Wednesday morning, week six of therapy, that's when the bombshell dropped."

"What happened?" Amy asked as she stepped closer to him to avoid the advancing water.

"This man in a suit came to see me. He was from the insurance company. His name escapes me now, probably because I've blanked it out, but he came to the hospital and was there to inform me that, in line with the conditions of our policy, coverage for my father's treatment had been canceled. They were pulling the plug on his care. We had seventy-two hours, and then we needed to be gone."

"Seriously? Throwing you out, just like that?"

"According to them, it was in my father's best interests that his therapy be discontinued and that the focus of his care be shifted toward managing his quality of life."

"What did that mean?"

"They wanted to put him in a nursing home."

"They could do that?"

"Standard practice, apparently. The insurance people talk to the doctors, and if it's clear the patient isn't improving and has reached a plateau in their recovery, then they have the right to trigger that clause in the policy. It's all in the fine print. The man in the suit flipped open his briefcase and flashed the paperwork in my face, but by that point I was too distressed to take any of it in."

"What a nightmare. What did you do?"

"I lost it, had a meltdown right there in the hall. I pleaded, I begged, tried to tell him he was making a huge mistake, but he wasn't going to change his mind."

"And what happened when you told your father? How did he react?"

Ryan thrust his hands deeper into his pockets and dropped his head, admitting with a shameful sigh that his father never found out. "I mean, I did try to tell him. I started by saying there were about to be some changes, changes that meant he'd be saying good-bye to the hospital . . . but before I had a chance to finish, he reached out for my hand and asked me if this meant he was going home. I should have corrected him, but I froze. It was the first time I'd seen his face light up in weeks, and even though I should've told him the truth right there and then, I just couldn't bring myself to do it. He really believed he was going back to the ranch. So, I lied. I said I didn't know. I made up something along the lines of 'they're still working out the details.' Then I kissed him goodbye and I left. Got in my truck. Drove straight home." Ryan shook his head, chastising himself. "I was a complete coward."

They were approaching the end of the beach, the last sliver of walkable sand. They could barely see a thing. The tide was encroaching and rocks were getting in the way of their feet, jagged, porous heads rising out of the ground like tiny black icebergs. Rather than continue on this path, which would have taken them toward the outcrop, they turned and searched for a place they could sit. They headed up the beach to the dunes, where the sand was soft and full of buried shells. The breeze was getting stronger and colder, and brought with it the smell of the ocean's tide and the sound of a faraway amplified guitar.

"After you," Ryan said, nodding to the slope.

Amy sat and tucked in her legs, noticing for the first time the chill in the air but too absorbed in the story to care. She was still puzzled;

the connection to the foreclosure had yet to be made clear, but she sensed she was about to find out how the pieces fit together.

"All right," she said, "what happened next?"

"Well, as you might expect, I was up that entire night. The hospital had given me brochures for every nursing home within a hundred miles, and my job was to find one where my father would fit in best. But instead, all I could think about were the what ifs. *What if* this was a big mistake? *What if* the doctors were wrong? *What if* they were acting too quickly, giving up too soon? Yes, they knew the science, they knew the odds, but I knew my father, and what if all he needed was another chance at treatment, not in the hospital but somewhere different . . . somewhere he could feel safe, somewhere quiet. A place where he could look out the window and see fields and trees and not a walled-in courtyard. A place where he could go outside and listen to the birds, watch the horses play, see the sun setting behind the hills. A place where, instead of air freshener and disinfectant, he could smell the sweetness of hay curing in the mow, or the soil after a spring rain. What if *that* was what my father needed for the rehabilitation to work? And that was when I had my epiphany—that was when I knew what had to be done. Despite the risks and despite the costs, I knew that somehow I had to get my father back to the ranch and give him a second chance at therapy."

"But your insurance? They had already canceled on you."

"Yes, it meant I needed to go private."

"Pay for it yourself?"

"That's right. So, the next thing I know, I'm on the phone— I'm calling up the hospital, treatment centers, speaking with doctors, nurses, therapists, care providers—anyone who could help me organize what I needed. And none of it was cheap. Just two months of treatment was going to empty our savings account, and that was without factoring in the extra expenses like equipment and supplies, nor did it include the nursing care he'd need or the travel costs of bringing these people to Seabrook."

"How could you afford all that?"

"We couldn't. I needed a loan. And the only way to get one big enough was to borrow against the ranch."

"Oh, I see . . ."

"I put my head down, made a plan, and soon had it all figured out. According to my calculations, if we trimmed our costs, lived frugally, and if I was able to keep the business running, then I could borrow what we needed and have the entire amount repaid in under five years. My father would never need to find out. So off I went, armed with my budget, straight to the bank. Everything was put into motion, and the next day I was approved for the loan. I had the cash. I was ready to bring my father home."

"Wait a second. You went by yourself and the bank said yes, just like that? They let you sign off on something like that on your own?"

"They had to because of the stroke. Being his son, his next of kin, I had automatic power of attorney over my father's affairs."

"You didn't need his permission?"

Ryan shook his head. "Not even his signature. That's how I've been able to keep it a secret. As far as he's concerned, we've never borrowed a cent. He's been under the impression that all his rehabilitation has been covered by insurance. Because that's the lie I told him. And I know that sounds terrible, and I know that it makes me sound like this horrible human being, but—"

"No, it doesn't," she said, cutting in. "You did what you had to do. I get it. I understand."

"You do?"

"You were trying to help him, trying to protect him."

"Yes, yes, that's . . . that's exactly what I was trying to do. All I ever wanted was for him to get better, to have my father back."

"And that's what happened? The plan worked, didn't it? You got him back?"

Ryan permitted himself a small smile. "Yeah, I did. He's obviously not the same as he was before the stroke, but the results have been amazing. He can stand and move around on his own without any need for a wheelchair, and where words used to get stuck in his throat, whole sentences now roll off the tongue. Don't get me wrong, he still struggles—his memory is patchy, and he gets extremely tired, needs about fourteen hours of sleep a day, and every now and then he'll slur a word or lose hold of a thought, but as time goes by, even that's becoming more and more rare. Our neurologist says he's one of the most remarkable recovery stories he's ever seen. To get from where he was to where he is now, no one can quite believe it."

"Then why did you say you feel like a horrible human being? Look at what's happened. Your father got better because of you. The only reason he isn't stuck in a nursing home somewhere is because of *you*."

Ryan's smile faded. "But I lied, Amy."

"Only because you felt there was no other way."

"Because I wanted him to concentrate on his recovery and not be thinking about me and the ranch and this stupid thing I'd gone and done."

"How can you call it stupid when you were the one who made all the difference? You knew what your father needed, and you went with your gut. If anything, I call that brave, Ryan, not stupid."

"At what cost, though? We might lose the ranch because of me."

"Except it *isn't* because of you."

"Yes, it is. It's me who's been lying about this, keeping it a secret for years, doing everything in my power to keep my father from our accounts, from opening the mail, from anything that might circle back to the truth. That's all my doing. How can anyone call that brave when my lies have led us to the brink of foreclosure?"

"Okay, can you explain that to me, because there's something I still don't get. Wasn't the plan to get the loan repaid?"

"Yes, that *was* the plan," Ryan said, before giving Amy the abridged version of how, due to the slowdown in business and the increased expenses, his once-modest loan had grown to be so stupendous in size. "It got away from me. Week after week, month after month, year after year, it just got worse and worse. Soon I was borrowing just so that we could live."

"And the whole time, while all this was going on, you never once came close to telling your father?"

He shook his head.

"Not even later, when he started getting better?"

"I was just too scared."

"But it's not like you meant for any of this to happen. You did what you did because you love him. Anyone can see that."

He dropped his head. "I'm not sure any of that matters anymore."

"It matters. Of course it matters. It's everything."

"Remember, we're not talking about some innocent little lie. We're talking about losing the ranch. And if he hears about what I've done, if he reacts the way I think he's going to react, then I don't think I could live with myself."

"You think he'd never forgive you?"

"Not that. Worse."

"Worse, how?"

"Worse as in I'm scared he'll have another stroke. I'm scared that when he finds out the truth, he won't be able to handle it. I'm scared the shock is gonna be too much and his brain will seize up and explode."

Ryan wrapped a blade of grass around his finger. He looped it around as many times as possible, as tightly as he could, until the tip of his finger burned a dark scarlet red. "You probably think that's irrational."

"Not at all," she said. "But I do think you're afraid, and because of that, you're imagining the worst-case scenario, which isn't likely to happen."

There was a grim look in his eyes. "Don't be so sure. Nearly half of stroke victims have a second one within five years. Did you know that? And the vast majority of them don't survive. And I'm pretty sure none of them had to confront news like this. If you put it all together, what other conclusion is there to reach? My father is strong—he's the strongest man I know—I just don't know if he's strong enough to get through *this*."

Amy tilted her head toward him as waves crashed along the beach. She smiled supportively but said nothing. She figured it was better to commiserate in silence than to keep on talking and pretending she had any answers. Because she didn't. The truth was that she didn't have the slightest clue what Ryan should do. She understood the dilemma and felt sympathy for him. She understood why he had borrowed the money, and she couldn't blame him for wanting to keep it a secret. But had he really needed to leave it so long? By waiting until the last minute, until the bank was literally breathing down his neck, had he not made the problem exponentially worse?

She reached down and pulled a shell out of the dune, and as she emptied out the sand and turned it over in her hands, her thoughts turned to the weather and how cold it was getting. The wind was blowing harder and no longer carried any trace of music. Had the festival come to an end? Was it that late already? She then wondered, rather despondently, whether that meant the evening would soon be coming to an end too. She also wondered about her dad. Her phone still hadn't made a sound. No messages, no missed calls. Despite reminding herself again and again that there must be a reasonable explanation for this continued radio silence, the unsettling feeling in her stomach surrounding his disappearance was only getting worse.

Then, from out of nowhere, she heard something—voices—the sound of an approaching crowd. Amy looked down the beach and spotted a large contingent of people emerging from out of the darkness.

"Oh wow," Ryan said. He had just seen and heard them too. "I don't believe it."

"You know who they are?"

"Of course. You don't?"

"Should I?" She frowned as she gave the moving mass of shadows a closer look. There must have been hundreds marching up the beach, raucous and fizzing with excitement, wielding flashlights with great enthusiasm.

"Look where they're headed," Ryan said as he pointed to the lighthouse.

"Oh of course." Amy was instantly reminded of their conversation with Chloe, those whisperings of that "nefarious" late-night plot. "Wow, they're like an actual mob."

"I know, right? All they're missing are some placards and pitchforks."

Amy smiled, though deep down she couldn't help but feel ambivalent about the crowd's arrival. The mystery they had come to uncover seemed like a distant concern when compared to the problems Ryan faced.

"What happens now, then?" she asked, nudging the conversation back to him. "Tomorrow, what will you do?"

"Talk to my father, I suppose, though I'm open to other ideas if you've got any."

"You know that you *have* to talk to him, don't you?"

It took a moment for him to answer. "Yeah, I do."

"And you know you can't leave it any longer, right?"

"I know. Shouldn't have let it drag out this long."

The wind roared a little louder, whipping up the sand and slamming waves against the shore. In the distance, the crowd had just arrived at the lighthouse, surrounding the building like a swarm of insects, flashlights buzzing like fireflies around its dark walls.

"You know, being in this mess makes me think about my mother," Ryan said wistfully. "She's been gone for a long time—died when I was young—but I can't help but wonder what advice she would give me if she were here." His gaze was drawn to the lighthouse and the activity unfolding there, which meant he hadn't noticed the sudden change in Amy's expression, how a wave of sadness had just swept across her face.

"She was always the wise one," he continued, "the kind of person who never saw problems, only solutions. You could be having the worst day ever, and she'd find a way to make everything seem okay. What I wouldn't give to have her here right now, to have her tell me exactly what I need to do."

Amy looked away at once as a tear escaped down her cheek.

Ryan turned back at her. "Amy? Hey, what's wrong?"

"Nothing."

He looked at her more closely. "Something's upset you."

"I'm okay," she said, even though her eyes were red and watery and she had an awful pain in her chest. His story about his mother had come from nowhere and she hadn't been the least bit prepared.

"Is it something I said?"

"No," she lied.

"It seems like it."

Amy shook her head, sniffing as she wiped her eyes with the sleeve of her top. To distract herself, she tried to reach for her mother's pendant, but got a fright when she discovered that it wasn't hanging around her neck. There was a moment of panic before she remembered why she wasn't wearing it—she had torn the chain from her neck the night before after she had been at the lighthouse. It must still be back in her hotel room.

"This is all my fault," Ryan groaned. "I knew I shouldn't have dumped all this on you. This has ruined the whole night, hasn't it?"

"Don't say that."

"You didn't need to hear all my problems."

"I'm pleased you told me. I wanted you to. And I basically made you, remember?"

"Yeah, but I invited you out promising that we'd have some fun, not make you cry." And then, without any warning, he leapt straight to his feet, dusted the sand off his jeans, and offered her his hand. "Come on, up you get. You're coming with me."

"Where are we going?"

He turned and gestured straight at the lighthouse.

"You can't be serious," Amy said. "You actually want to go out there?"

"You bet I do. Let's go see what all the fuss is about."

"I don't know. It feels strange. It doesn't seem right."

"You were curious a few hours ago."

"Before our big chat, sure. But the mood's changed, you know?"

"And that's *exactly* why we should, if for no other reason than to try to lighten up the evening." Ryan gave his hand a shake, urging her to take it. Amy couldn't help wonder if this was a diversionary tactic so he could avoid dealing with the bigger issues waiting for him back at home.

"Come on. How about it?"

"But what about everything you said to Chloe—that it's wrong, that you don't think they're going to find anything, that you think they're all wasting their time?"

"And I still do, but that doesn't mean it'll be any less fun to go and watch, right?"

He folded his hand around hers, and Amy felt his strength as he pulled her to her feet. Standing inches apart, she looked straight at him and saw that his eyes were glowing, bright and blue and full of adventure.

"You're sure about this?"

He had a look on his face that was starting to feel familiar, a smile that felt oddly comforting.

"Absolutely," he said.

They set off at once down the dune and across the beach, negotiating a path through the rocks. And as they climbed their way to the top of the outcrop and headed for the tower, Amy noticed that Ryan had made no effort to let go of her hand, that his fingers were now entwined with hers.

And she didn't mind at all. Not one bit.

25

THE MOOD at the lighthouse was quieter than Amy and Ryan had expected. The crowd, which had been full of bravado a few minutes ago, now seemed uncharacteristically subdued, as though it was only just dawning on them what they were there to do. They had organized themselves into a semicircle behind the ringed wire fence and were barely making a sound. The only murmur of conversation came from a few near the front, too far away for Amy and Ryan to make out. Amy stood on her tiptoes and craned her neck, but they were stranded at the back and couldn't see a thing—just a sea of heads, hundreds of them.

"What's going on?" she whispered into Ryan's ear. "Why's everyone so quiet?"

"I'm not sure. Maybe they've got cold feet?" Despite his height advantage, Ryan couldn't see much either. "Come with me," he said, tightening his grip on her hand. "Let's get closer."

With Amy following in his slipstream, Ryan squeezed and bumped through the mass of bodies and staked out a spot right up against the fence, a perfect place from which to see everything going on. Ryan took a moment and looked around. A quick glance at the crowd confirmed to him what he already suspected: these were all locals. He recognized every single face, including one of particular interest: Handsome Frank. Seeing Frank wasn't any great surprise—he was a stalwart of the town and a long-time believer in the spooky folklore of the lighthouse. But what interested Ryan was *where* Frank happened to be standing (front and center) and *what* he'd brought with him (a considerably large toolbox).

"Ah, there's the culprit," Ryan said.

Amy turned around. "Who?"

"Frank from the hardware store. Guarantee you he's the one who has spearheaded this."

"You mean Frank, as in Handsome Frank?"

"That's him."

Frank was tall, standing well over six feet, with a perfectly manicured pencil mustache and a head of slick brown hair that was evenly swept back. Next to him, standing just as tall with a baseball cap spun backward, was someone younger and strikingly similar, far too similar not to be related.

"I'm guessing that's his son beside him?"

"Yep, Frank Junior."

"Of course."

The two Franks and a few others appeared to be engaged in a serious discussion. The focus of the deliberations, which were taking a very long time, seemed to concern the issue of who was going to break in.

"Are they actually going to do anything?" Amy remarked. "Or are they are going to spend the night talking about it?"

Ryan nodded in agreement. "Don't be surprised if they chicken out. Remember, most people here believe the ghost of Theodore is rattling around inside, which is why no one wants to be the first to go in. And, not to state the obvious, but the tower isn't the easiest place to get into. She's buttoned up pretty good."

Amy pressed her face against the mesh of the fence. Indeed, the building looked as impenetrable as it had last night. The door to the lighthouse was the only way in and completely hidden, boarded over with thick planks of timber, and the fence around the perimeter was bolted into the rock, at least ten feet tall, and crowned with a nasty clump of razor wire, negating the possibility of anyone climbing over the top.

"Lord almighty," a voice heckled from the back. "Is there a reason why this is taking so long?"

There was a murmur of agreement.

"Yeah!" another voice cried. "What are we waiting for? We'll all turn into ghosts ourselves by the time someone finally goes inside!"

As the complaints grew louder and more impatient, Amy whispered into Ryan's ear and suggested he be the one to volunteer.

"Me?" His expression turned cold. "Why *me*?"

"What's the matter?" she teased. "You're not scared, are you? You didn't think there was anything going on, right? Weren't you the one who thought everyone was just seeing things?"

"Was that me? Look, I'm happy just standing here with you. Happy to watch."

"Is that so? Hmm, if I didn't know any better, I'd say someone's a bit scared of a little ol' ghost."

"Not all ghosts," Ryan quipped. "Just the psychopathic lighthouse-keeper variety of ghost—for them I make an exception."

As Amy laughed, the announcement finally came, the one everyone had been waiting for:

"I'll do it! I'll go inside!"

A cheer erupted through the crowd. Amy and Ryan looked around. The boyish shriek had come from Frank Junior.

"That's my boy! My son will do it!" Beaming with pride, Handsome Frank clapped his son on the back and fished out a pair of wire cutters from the toolbox. "Go get 'em, Son!"

There was a rumble of enthusiasm from the crowd as Frank Junior stepped forward. He began at the bottom of the fence and started snipping his way through the wire. Once he'd cut a hole big enough, he stepped through to the other side and was showered with rapturous applause. He heaved his chest and raised his hands triumphantly in the air, and the roar grew even louder. Anyone would have thought he had just stepped foot on the moon.

Emboldened by the cheers, he exchanged the cutters for a hammer and turned his attention to the next challenge: the boarded-up door. But this didn't go as smoothly. He stuck the claw of the hammer underneath one of the planks and pulled as hard as he could, but the plank was fixed to the wall with large nails and refused to budge. He persisted for a while longer, but it was clear he was going to need some help.

"Wait there, Son! I'm coming!"

Handsome Frank rummaged in his toolbox. He pulled out a crowbar and clambered through the hole to join his son. Coordinating their efforts, they wedged their tools behind the timber and, with brute strength and clenched faces, managed to rip the plank clear from the wall. A small glimpse of the lighthouse door was revealed.

The Franks stepped back to admire their handiwork. However, it soon became obvious to everyone watching that something wasn't right. A section of the door was peeking out, a sliver of blood-red wood, but unlike the rest of the building, which was in a crumbling, decrepit state, this particular piece looked immaculate. The wood was unblemished, the paintwork almost glistening.

Frank Junior stepped closer and ran his fingers across the lustrous surface. "It smells fresh!" he shouted. "Like it's just had a brand-new coat!"

His father did the same. "Good Lord, you're right."

"How's that possible, Dad? How?"

Handsome Frank was shaking his head. "I don't know, Son. But let's keep going."

Amy didn't know what to make of it, and as she looked around at the crowd, she realized they didn't either. Hundreds of awestruck faces surrounded her, countless pairs of eyes, puzzled and perplexed, every one of them glued to the lighthouse in anticipation of what was going to happen next. All except for one pair of eyes—a pair fixed on *her* instead.

Through the sea of bodies and shadowy faces, she spotted him: that same man she'd seen earlier at the bar. A plunging sensation took hold in her stomach. There was that same ice in his gaze, cold and empty, just like before.

"Ryan, who is that?"

But Ryan couldn't hear her over all the noise. The two Franks had just pried away a second plank, and the crowd was once again finding its voice, erupting into a cheer so loud that it completely drowned her out.

"*Ryan,*" she said louder, squeezing his hand tighter.

He turned at once. "What's wrong? Are you okay?"

Amy pointed her finger straight into the crowd, to where the man had been standing. But it was too late—he had already disappeared.

"I don't believe it."

"Huh?"

"He's gone . . ."

"What?"

"The man I saw. Where did he go?"

"Amy, I can't hear you."

The Franks were working double time—another plank had just come off and the applause was growing louder.

Amy shook her head. It was pointless trying to talk with the commotion unfolding around them. She mouthed the words "It's okay," then returned her attention to the lighthouse. She tried telling herself that this was all in her head, that it was just her imagination running wild, but she had enough sense to know what was real and what wasn't, and that man, with his dark and sinister stare, was most certainly *real*. She resolved to tell Ryan as soon as she could.

When the job was done, when the last planks had been torn from the wall and the crimson door was fully exposed, the two Franks gave each other an enthusiastic high five.

The door was almost twice the size of an ordinary one, with an arch at the top and an iron latch for a handle. Upon giving it a twist and seeing that it was locked, Handsome Frank made for his tools and returned with a sledgehammer.

"Step back now, Son."

Frank Junior did as he was told.

Wielding it like a baseball bat, determination etched into his face, Frank lined up the head of his hammer with the iron lock and took a few mock swings, then steadied his feet for the real thing.

One swing was all it took. The brute force of his strike blasted the door open.

Everyone fell silent. For the first time in decades, the townsfolk of Seabrook were getting a look inside—and what they saw drew a unified gasp. The interior was spotless! What should have been a room of dust and rubble appeared to have been perfectly preserved. The walls shone brilliant white, the checkered floor sparkled with polish, and even the staircase, which was said to have collapsed over thirty years earlier, was completely intact. Everyone was dumbfounded. It was silent enough to hear a pin drop. Even Ryan, who counted himself one of the biggest skeptics of all, was lost for words. Handsome Frank stepped toward the threshold, put one hand on the wall, and tentatively leaned in.

The sight of someone about to enter the lighthouse had transfixed the crowd so fully that hardly anyone noticed the first drops of rain. Amy felt one land on her head then another splatter on her shoulder. Then, without warning, the sky bellowed with thunder and the heavens spilled open. No one had a chance to catch their breath. Rain started pouring down so thick and fast it was as if a dam had burst in the sky.

Amy buried her face into Ryan's chest. Those around her began pushing and shoving, trying to escape and make for the shore. But there wasn't room for everyone, not all at once. An impatient bunch climbed down and clambered over rocks; others were so desperate for shelter they were trying to get inside the lighthouse, tangling themselves as they pushed through the fence. Then, as the rain came down even harder, and as lightning cracked all around, someone let out a wailing, high-pitched scream.

"Look up! Look up!" came the terrified cries.

Everyone shuddered to a halt and glanced skyward.

A column of light was blazing across the sky—a bright, powerful beam emanating from the top of the lighthouse.

The sight unleashed utter panic. Even Handsome Frank, who had been so intent on getting inside, abandoned his efforts and scampered away from the building. There were screams and shouts and shrieks of horror as the scene quickly devolved into chaos. People couldn't get off the outcrop quickly enough. They slipped over rocks, stumbled, fell, and trampled over each other, desperate to get away.

"Hang on!" Ryan yelled as he wrapped his arm around Amy and drew her in close, as they too were swept up in the stampede.

Once they had escaped the outcrop and were clear of the crowd, they headed down the beach, straight for the nearest lifeguard tower. The base of the tower was only a few feet high off the sand, but it provided the perfect place to take refuge from the rain and all the hysteria. They crawled underneath and huddled next to each other, both needing a few minutes before they were able to catch their breaths.

"Excuse me for cussin'," Ryan said with a splutter, planting his hands on his knees, "but *Jesus Christ*, what just happened?"

Amy wiped the rain from her face. Her heart was racing, her spine still tingling from everything that had just happened. "I . . . have . . .

no idea," she answered, gasping for air. "But there's no question—there's something *seriously* wrong with that lighthouse!"

Ryan stared out at the eerie sight of the lighthouse all lit up, its beam of light slicing through the stormy sky like a giant amber sword. "You know what? I think so too."

"And what's with this weather?"

"I know, right?"

"I've never seen a storm hit so fast! It's like it just came out of nowhere."

Ryan was about to agree with Amy when he realized that he *had* seen a storm like this. Only two nights ago, in fact, the one that had caused Little Dipper to bolt from the ranch. Come to think of it, this one felt eerily similar. The rain was intensifying by the minute and the wind gusts were so fierce that Ryan could feel the lifeguard tower creaking and buckling under the pressure. He only hoped his horses back home were calm and that the barn was holding up okay. But then Ryan cast his mind back a few hours to when they had left the ranch, and suddenly he remembered that the horses weren't in the barn at all. They were outside. *Still in the field.*

"Oh no . . ."

Amy looked at him. "What's wrong?"

He slapped a hand over his mouth. "I can't have. . . . How could I . . ."

"What is it?"

"It's the horses. I've forgotten about the horses!"

"What's wrong with them? What's happened?"

"I let them out for a graze, remember? But I was supposed to bring them in. When I got back from bringing you into town, I was going to bring them in!" Ryan couldn't believe he'd been so forgetful and careless. It made him feel sick. To think he had repeated his mistake and left Little Dipper stuck outside *again*, in *this*!

"I have to leave," he said. "Right now."

"Of course. They'll be okay, though, won't they? They're safe, right?"

"No. Not Little Dipper. Not her. She can't be outside in this weather. She could spook and run off again, just like she did before. I have to get back to the ranch."

Amy didn't think twice. She grabbed him by the hand and squeezed tight.

"Then I'm coming with you."

26

$\mathscr{T}$HE TOWN SQUARE was deserted. Ryan's truck was still parked outside the hotel, its windshield plastered with food wrappers, fluorescent streamers, and other soggy remnants of a festival hastily abandoned. They cleared away the debris, jumped inside, then took to the road.

Conditions were treacherous, visibility next to nothing. Even Amy, who wasn't behind the wheel, kept her eyes fixed ahead to help Ryan steer through the maze of potholes, fallen trees, and other obstacles littering the road. Once back at the ranch, Ryan brought the truck to a skidding stop outside the field gate and turned his headlights to full.

Horses!

He could see them huddled by the gate, but by his count there were only six.

"Little Dipper's not there. She's gone!" He turned off the engine and grabbed a flashlight from the glove box. "Wait here for me."

"Where are you going?"

"To the field! I have to find her."

"I'll come too."

"No, it's not safe. She'll be frightened and unpredictable. It's too dangerous."

"But there must be something I can do—anything—I want to help."

"Actually, yes—the other horses." Ryan twisted around and checked that the barn was open. "Could you get them inside?"

"Okay, I can do that. But how?"

"There's a strap beneath their chins. Hold it tight and lead them over one at a time and put them in a stall, any stall, doesn't matter which."

"All right, no problem. Go, Ryan, go find her."

"Thank you, Amy. Back soon."

They jumped out of the truck and went their separate ways. Amy went for the horses while Ryan ran for the field, the beam of his flashlight getting swiftly swallowed up by the darkness.

Amy had no problems getting the horses to safety. They obeyed her commands and were so keen to find shelter that she had trouble keeping up. Once they were all locked away in their stalls, she returned to the entrance of the barn, where she stood guard and waited. The storm was relentless. The rain was falling in sheets and the wind, now even fiercer than before, was bulldozing through the valley, sending haybales cartwheeling across the grass and making light work of anything that wasn't tied down. It took everything Amy had just to stay upright. Her clothes were sodden and she was shivering with cold, but she didn't care—all she could think about was that poor horse and how frightened she must be. She only hoped that luck was on Ryan's side, that he would return soon with good news.

Thankfully, after a brief but nervous wait, Ryan emerged from the darkness with Little Dipper thrashing next to him. She appeared to be highly agitated and in no mood to cooperate.

"Can you believe it!" Ryan called out as he jostled and wrestled the frightened animal through the gate and across the forecourt.

"Where was she?"

"Way, way back! Right by the fence line. It's amazing she hadn't gone any farther. But keep your distance. She's still really freaked out."

Amy stood back, marveling at Ryan's ability to hold on and keep the powerful animal under his control. The horse was kicking her legs and swinging her head; how he was able to coax her into the stall, she had no idea.

"I need to stay with her a moment," he said as he locked himself inside the stall and began stroking Little Dipper's neck. "Just till she's calm."

"Of course."

By the time the horse was settled, Amy was so cold and wet that she wondered if she might be on the cusp of hypothermia. She had goose bumps over her arms and her teeth were chattering between her pale blue lips.

"Look at you, you're freezing."

She smiled and pointed out that so was he.

"You need to get warm. Come on, I have dry clothes in the house."

Ryan locked the barn and hand in hand they made another dash through the rain.

The lights were off inside the house, curtains still open. Ryan figured his father was probably still where he'd left him, in his room, asleep. They tiptoed their way to a dark hall at the back of the house. Ryan reached up and grabbed a rope that was dangling from the ceiling; he gave it a pull and a ladder unfolded.

"After you," he said.

Amy got a surprise when she climbed to the top. The space, which spanned the entire breadth of the roof, felt less like an attic and more like a self-contained home. Strings of lights hung from the rafters and enormous rugs covered the floor. There was a bed wedged into a corner, a couch and table in another, and various pieces of mismatched furniture—a cupboard, a chest of drawers, and two bookcases—stacked against the sloping walls.

Ryan went to the drawers and pulled out some clothes: a blue checked shirt; a pair of gray pants, which he admitted were going to be far too big; some wool socks; and a towel.

"It's the best I can do, I'm afraid," he said. "Get changed into these and I'll be back in five minutes. I've got to go check on my father."

Amy thanked him with a smile. After he climbed back down the ladder, she kicked off her shoes and stripped off her wet clothes, wriggling out of her jeans and pulling her top over her shoulders. She toweled off and threw on his spare clothes, grinning at how stupendously big they were, then moseyed around the room while dabbing her wet hair with the towel, waiting for him to return. Her curiosity led her over to a small writer's desk, which was covered in a mountainous mess of paper. Crumpled envelopes, stacks of overdue bills, letters, notices of demand—many bearing the logo of the bank, Pacific First & Mutual—spread to every corner of the desk. Amy's heart sank at the sight of it all. Seeing firsthand the trouble he was in made her feel sad. She wished there was something she could do. She really did feel sorry for him. It wasn't fair what was happening, that he should be punished like this. He was only in this situation because of his love for his father. He only ever wanted to see him get better. He'd been brave and bold and he'd acted with his heart, and for that he was about to be thrown out of his home. The world, she decided, really was a cruel and unfair place.

"Are you decent?" Ryan called out.

Amy stepped away from the desk and pretended to be looking out the window. "I am."

Ryan walked over carrying a pair of mugs. "I wasn't sure if you liked tea or coffee best," he said apologetically, slipping one of the mugs into her hands, "so I made you a hot chocolate."

Amy brought the mug to her lips, blew off the steam, and took a long, heavenly sip.

"That's sweet," she said.

"What, too much sugar?"

"No, I mean, sweet of you to think of me, and sweet of you to lend me these clothes." As Amy said this, she had to reach down and hike up the pants, which were nearly falling off her hips.

"Wow, they're even bigger on you than I thought."

She laughed. "They're a little generous in the waist, but they're dry, so thank you." She wrapped her hands around the mug and made a glancing nod to the window. "Little Dipper is gonna be okay?"

"She'll be fine. Don't worry."

"The storm won't be scaring her?"

"Not anymore. Now that she's inside and locked up with the rest of the herd, her anxiety will be under control."

"What happened to her?" Amy asked, taking a second sip. "What caused her to become this way?"

Ryan set his mug down on the desk. "She's had a rough past. Not cared for properly, badly mistreated."

"She was born someplace else?"

"Yes, I rescued her from a farm, next county over. I was driving past and nearly put the truck in a ditch when I first saw her, I was that horrified." He stepped closer to the window, his somber expression reflected in the glass. "She was wilting by the side of a fence, ribs showing through her stomach, with barely enough energy to shake off the flies buzzing around her ears. Her hooves were so overgrown that she could hardly walk, and she had deep harness sores running along her shoulders, probably a result of being overworked. The grass in her field had been grazed down to the nubbins. Hadn't eaten in days, would be my guess. As soon as I saw that poor animal, my heart bled."

"That's awful. Where was her owner?"

"Up in the house. I went to see him, and boy was he a nasty piece of work. He flashed me this greedy, yellow-stained grin and told me to mind my own business and get off his property and never come back."

"What! Did you report him?"

"And risk him getting off with a warning? Not a chance. That horse's life was at stake. She needed help right away. I told the man I'd buy her off him, told him he could name his price. I did what I had to do to get Little Dipper out of there. Didn't think twice. Money was already tight by that point, but I didn't care. I paid him what he wanted."

That came as no surprise to Amy, not anymore, not after hearing about Ryan's other selfless acts. He was that rare breed of person: the kind who put everyone else ahead of himself, the kind of person who wore his humanity like a second skin and couldn't shed it if he tried.

He continued. "Anyway, getting her out of there turned out to be the easy part. Getting her to trust another human being again? Not so much. Her sense of self-preservation was almost that of a wild horse's. She hated being touched, hated the round pen—she double-barreled me to the ground the first time I tried to get her in there. I broke three ribs, and you can *still* see the spot where the bruise was!"

"Ouch! Can I look?"

Ryan lifted his shirt up high and pointed to where the hooves had struck, a discolored patch an inch or so down from his chest. Amy looked a little closer. His skin was tanned and he was strong and muscular, probably a natural result of being outside and working with horses.

"Looks sore," she said, dragging her gaze back up to meet his.

"Tell me about it."

"How did you get through to her?"

He dropped his shirt. "By keeping my distance. I didn't force it. All I did was keep her fed and warm and let her get used to me being around. I made sure she saw me each and every day, made sure she knew that I was one of the good guys."

"And that worked?"

"That and a lot of patience. Unfortunately, though, her scars run deep. I'm still the only one she'll trust. She won't let anyone else near."

Amy smiled as she took another sip. "And the name?"

"Little Dipper?"

"Yeah, where did that come from?"

"Oh, that came easy. She's named after the constellation. How well do you know your stars?"

"Not very."

"But you know the Little Dipper?"

"No."

"But you've heard of it?"

"Yes, but I couldn't point it out."

"Come, I'll show you."

He took her by the hand and led her to the couch, then shuffled off to a corner of the attic where he pulled out a cardboard box. He carried it back across the room and opened it up. Peering inside, Amy saw its contents were random—record albums, books, framed photos, a diary, some handwritten notes, and one object that looked out of place: a sheet of X-ray film tucked at the back. The box appeared to be a collection of keepsakes, belonging to or in memory of someone.

"There it is." Ryan reached in and pulled out one of the books, titled *The Shapes in our Stars*. "My mother gave this to me when I was eight," he said as he flipped through the pages. "Had me totally obsessed for a while. Even had a telescope, which I pointed out through that very window." He soon found the page he was looking for. He placed the book in Amy's lap and opened to a page headed *Ursa Minor (The Little Dipper)*.

"On Little Dipper's forehead," he said, "right above her blaze, she's got a cluster of white spots that closely matches the shape of that constellation. The resemblance is uncanny; it's almost identical."

Amy studied the picture, an image of the night sky. In it, a trail of stars shaped into a long-handled ladle had been highlighted in yellow.

"Wow, that's neat," she said.

"I know, right? When it came time to think up a name, what could have been better?"

"Nothing," she agreed. "The name is perfect."

Ryan thumbed through the pages and gave Amy a crash course in some other constellations, focusing particularly on the brighter ones she might have a chance of spotting in the light-polluted skies above the city. Amy was listening closely and trying to take it all in—really, she was—but no amount of smiling and nodding could disguise the fact that her eyes kept sliding off the page and drifting to the inside of that box. After a while, her curiosity got the best of her and she interrupted him, just as he was talking about Sagittarius and a story about a man who had the body of a horse.

"Everything in there—it belonged to your mother?"

Ryan stopped midsentence. He looked down. "Most of it, yeah, or it's stuff that reminds me of her."

Amy spied a photo. "Is that her?"

"Yes."

"May I see?"

"Sure." He set the book aside and retrieved the framed photo. The shot was of him when he was very young, perhaps only five or six years old. He was sitting on a fence with his father and mother on either side. Horses were milling about in the background. Tall and dark-haired, his mother had one hand on her hip and the other around Ryan's shoulders.

"She's pretty. You've got her eyes."

"Do you think so?"

"Definitely. Do you have any others?"

"Lots."

Ryan reached for another photograph. As he handed it to Amy, he remarked that this was the last photo he had of her, that it had been taken shortly before she died. Amy held the frame with care. In this photo Ryan was sitting on the back of a horse with a rider's cap on his head and reins in his hands. He looked much older in this one, though probably not quite a teenager. His mother was standing next to him, strands of dark hair blowing across her face.

"Wait." Amy peered closer. She could see that one of his mother's hands was placed on Ryan's knee, but the other was resting on her very pronounced stomach. "Your mother was pregnant?"

Ryan reached back into the box and pulled out the X-ray film, which, seen properly and in the light, clearly wasn't an X-ray film at all—it was a sonogram. He showed it to Amy. "Yes, she was pregnant with a baby girl. She was five months along."

Amy stared at the sonogram then back up at him, confused. "I didn't realize that. I . . . didn't know you had a sister."

"I don't. I mean, in a way, yes, I did, but I never got to meet her. Never got the chance."

"Oh no. She lost the baby?"

"There were complications," he said, his voice broken and scratchy. He tried to clear his throat. "Six weeks after that photo was taken, Mom went into labor. But the delivery was very premature and there were serious problems. I can't remember the exact name for it, but it had something to do with the fluid for the baby ending up in my mother's bloodstream. It's one of those things that's very rare. There was nothing anyone could do."

Amy covered her mouth. "Ryan, are you saying that's how your mom . . ." She couldn't bring herself to finish the sentence.

"We lost them both," he said, and he closed his eyes.

"Oh my God."

He fidgeted with his hands. There was a long silence.

She reached over, touched his arm. "I am so sorry."

Ryan rubbed his face and set the sonogram to one side. "It was a long time ago now."

"Yes, but still, that's awful. How old were you again?"

"Thirteen."

"And you were able to make it through? How did you come out the other side of something like that?"

"I'm not sure I know."

Amy looked him deep in the eyes. She didn't think it could be possible, but she felt even deeper levels of admiration for him.

"How much about her do you remember?" she asked.

"Lots."

"You think about her often?"

"All the time. Every day. I've never stopped thinking about her. Never stopped missing her."

"And that doesn't make you sad?" Amy knew she might start crying soon if they stayed on this topic for too long, but she didn't care. These were things she really wanted to know—things she *had* to know.

Ryan stared at the photo again. "Not so much anymore. There's a bit of sadness, sure, but the hurt doesn't sting like it once did. Clichéd as it sounds, I guess time has helped to heal the wounds." He glanced back up, held her gaze, but this time, he saw something different in Amy's eyes—an undercurrent of sorrow. Her eyes still glowed, were still magnetic, but there was something there that he hadn't noticed before, a buried sadness.

"Amy, are you all right?"

She shook her head.

"What is it?"

She could feel the pinch in her throat, tears welling in her eyes. Despite herself, her defenses were beginning to break.

"It's my mom," she whispered. "I—I lost her too."

"What?"

"It happened a month ago."

"Seriously? Why didn't you—"

"It was a car accident," Amy said, swallowing hard, doing her utmost to keep a level voice. "Wasn't even her fault. If she'd left work just a minute later, she'd still be alive. She'd still be with us. But she didn't. And now she's gone."

"Amy, I'm so, so sorry." Ryan moved closer, put his arm around her, and they were silent for a moment while Amy wept. "I don't know what to say. Here's me going on about my father and my mother and here's you dealing with this."

"It's awful, Ryan. I'm trying to be brave, trying to be strong, but I just miss her so much." Again, she went to reach for her pendant but burst into tears when she remembered that it wasn't there.

"Hey, what's wrong?"

"It's nothing," she cried, burrowing in closer to him.

"Please, tell me."

"It's my mom's pendant. I just really wish I had it with me right now. She gave it to me when I was a little girl, and last night I was so upset that I tore it off my neck and left it back at the hotel."

Ryan brought her in even closer, leaning her head into his chest. "Why don't you tell me about this pendant of yours, tell me what makes it so special."

"It'll sound childish."

"Don't be silly. Tell me."

Amy took a deep breath, dabbing her eyes with the cuff of her borrowed shirt. "I was seven at the time. It was just before Christmas. We were on holiday, in a village near Mount Hood, and the day before we headed home Mom took me to a Christmas market. I remember it so clearly: the smell of apple and cinnamon, the snow falling, everyone singing carols. There were lots of stalls too, lots of people selling little trinkets, and just as we were about to leave Mom spotted this pendant—a mermaid sitting on a rock with her tail wrapped around a moonstone—a beautiful blue moonstone. I had this terrible fear of the water when I was young, so Mom bought the pendant and then sat me down and told me a story. She told me that this mermaid had also been afraid of the water, just like me, and that she'd never had the courage to dive into the ocean to find her way home. The mermaid had cried and cried, night after night, until one day she decided she wasn't going to be afraid anymore, so she closed her eyes and made a wish, and the next morning, when she woke up, all her tears had dried up. But they weren't gone—they had been collected to make her moonstone, which then became a reminder of how special and brave she was, and from that day on the mermaid was never scared of the water again. Mom then told me whoever wore the pendant would also have the mermaid's powers . . . not to be afraid." Amy sat up and tried to compose herself, even though her voice was still choked up with tears. "It might sound ridiculous, but to a seven-year-old girl, that story changed my life. It was magic."

"And I bet you were never scared of the water again."

"Nope, never."

At that moment, it seemed Ryan's eyes were glistening with tears too.

"She sounds like a wonderful person, Amy, and a wonderful mother."

Amy collapsed back onto his chest.

"It hurts, Ryan. Whenever I think about her, it just hurts so much."

"And it's probably going to hurt for a while longer yet, but trust me, it will get better. Right now, everything is raw, but this pain you're feeling *will* soften. I promise."

"But what if it doesn't?"

"It will."

"I . . . I wish I could believe that. I want to, but—"

Ryan lifted her head and told her to wait right there.

"Where are you going?" she asked.

"Sit tight, I want to show you something."

Ryan got up from the couch to retrieve two mysterious objects sitting on a far windowsill. When he returned, Amy could see they were two small rocks—one black, volcanic, covered in divots and holes and jagged edges, and the other gray and sleek and perfectly rounded, the kind you could skip across a lake.

"My father showed me this not long after my mom died," he said. "He probably doesn't even know that I kept these. It's a little corny in an obvious kind of way, but it made all the difference in the world."

"I don't understand."

"Just go along with me, okay?"

Amy nodded.

"What I need you to do is think of that memory of your mom, the day she gave you that pendant."

"All right."

"Now, hold out your hand and close your eyes."

Amy did as he asked. He took her hand and gave her one of the rocks. Without peeking, she knew it was the volcanic one; she could feel its rough, scarred exterior against the palm of her skin. Next, he folded his hand around hers, encasing the rock.

"Try to ignore what I'm doing. For this to work, all you need to do is concentrate on your mom. Don't think about anything else. Just focus on the memory as hard as you can."

Amy nodded. She closed her eyes, already lost in her thoughts. But while she replayed that memory in her head, imagining the sights and sounds of that day and listening to her mom's voice in her ears, Ryan was slowly squeezing her hand, quietly applying pressure, tighter and tighter. He'd been doing it gradually, deftly, without her even noticing. But now he was squeezing so tight that the rock's angular edges and sharp points were pressing deep into her flesh. And now it was *really* starting to hurt.

"Ouch! All right, that's enough." When Amy opened her eyes and looked at her hands, she saw her skin was covered with countless dimples and tiny indentations. "Um, what was the point of that?"

He apologized, then took the rock from Amy's pockmarked hand and swapped it for the other, urging her to close her eyes again. "This next part won't hurt."

She gave him a cautionary glare.

"It won't, I promise. Now, exactly like before, Amy—same memory."

Again, she did as she was asked, closing her eyes and conjuring the memory again, and again, like before, she felt Ryan's hands fold around hers, felt the pressure of him squeezing tight. Only this time the sensation was different. This time there wasn't any pain. This time the rock fitted snugly into her hand, its sleek, polished surface pressing comfortably into her skin.

"There," he said, still holding her hands tight. "Think about what's changed. Nothing's really changed. The memory is still the same memory, except time has now smoothed over its edges. Now it doesn't sting so much. Now you're free to remember. Now you can think about your mom as much as you want." He eased the pressure and left his hands resting gently on top of hers. "Does it make sense now? Do you see?"

Amy slowly opened her eyes. There were thoughts in her head, things she wanted to say. She wanted to tell him that she got it, that it all made perfect sense, that she understood him, that for the first time since her mother died, she had finally caught a glimpse of a future that didn't feel so overwhelmingly bleak. But Amy couldn't muster a single word because all she wanted to do was kiss him.

And it seemed he wanted to kiss her too.

His warm blue eyes were circling her face, drifting low, down to her mouth. Amy leaned in. The rock fell from her hand and hit the floor with a thud. Neither of them noticed or even blinked. She put her hand around the back of his head and pulled him in closer, so close that only a whisper of a breath separated their lips. Her inhibitions melted away. Surrendering to the moment, she closed her eyes and she did it, she kissed him, and for the next few seconds thought of nothing else but the heady sensation of her lips pressed against his.

With the same longing and desire, Ryan kissed her back. He pulled her toward him, drawing her body against his. She let him. She folded her leg over his and let his fingers brush her face, let them trace the contours of her cheek, her jaw, down her neck, lower. She opened her mouth wider. As she ran her fingers through his wet hair and down the back of his neck, she began kissing him harder and hungrier. Her craving was so deep that she didn't stop—she *couldn't* stop, not until there was a roar of thunder outside, loud enough to split their lips apart.

Amy sat up in a hurry. "This is a mistake," she said as she disentangled her legs from around his. "We shouldn't be doing this."

Ryan let the question settle in the air for a moment. His expression was soft, his eyes quiet and still. "Why shouldn't we?"

"Because we only just met. Doesn't this feel a bit crazy to you?"

"Not particularly."

Amy watched his mouth as he spoke, only an inch away from hers. She felt like she could still taste him, could feel his warm breath mixing with her own. "It's not that I don't want to . . ."

"I don't not want to either," he replied, his lips curling into a smile as he kissed her again, tenderly, softly.

"But it's not that simple, Ryan . . ." Her words came out in broken whispers, straight from her lips to his, straight into his mouth. "Think about the bigger picture, think about the ranch. The next few days are important for you, too important for you to be thinking about anything else. I'm not sure a distraction is what you need right now."

Ryan shook his head, smiled, then tucked a strand of Amy's damp hair behind her ears and planted his lips on hers once more. "It's *exactly* what I need."

After losing themselves for a few minutes longer, they fell sideways, lower into the couch. Amy tucked her head into the nook of Ryan's neck, and he slid his hand over hers, threading their fingers together as they lay and watched the rain lash at the windows, listened to thunder rippling through the clouds.

"What are you thinking about?" she asked after a long, comfortable silence.

"That you'll be gone in the morning," he answered with a sigh. "That this time tomorrow you'll be hundreds of miles away."

"This isn't the last you'll see of me," she said, propping her head up and looking him in the eyes. "You know that, right?"

"How can you be sure?"

"Because it's not as if we're on opposite sides of the world. You've got my number. I want you to call me tomorrow. And the day after that. I want to know you're all right. I want to know what's happening here with you and your father. And my invitation still stands— I want you to come see me in Portland as soon as you can."

"And if I can't?"

"Then I'll find a way to come back and visit you."

"Do you mean that?"

"Of course."

"Do you promise?"

Amy squeezed his hand tighter. "I promise."

They sat quietly for a moment, hands threaded together, watching the storm continue to rage outside, when another jolt of thunder shook the attic and knocked down one of Ryan's mother's photos. The frame fell from the couch and hit the wooden floor hard, cracking the glass.

"Ugh, damn—" Ryan reached for the fallen picture, wincing when he saw the damage. "I should really get all this packed up."

"Here, let me help."

Amy dragged the box closer and helped him gather up the photos and stow away the sonogram and the astronomy book. Ryan was just about to close the lid to the box when something inside caught his eye.

"Hey, wait a minute," he said as he perched forward on the edge of the couch.

"What is it?"

"This book . . ." His voice trailed off as he reached in to grab it.

"What about it?"

"I'm not sure."

Amy leaned over and saw that Ryan had retrieved a children's book. Titled *Chloe & the Magic Mirror*, the illustration on the front was of a young girl riding on the back of a dragon. The two of them were flying high above a land of lakes and castles and snowy mountains, the girl waving a sword, the creature breathing fire. It looked like a typical fairy-tale scene, a perfectly normal picture book. Except what really stood out was the depiction of the book's heroine.

"Hey, that's weird," Amy said. "That girl looks just like the girl from the hotel . . . Chloe."

"You noticed that too, huh?"

Amy nodded. And it wasn't just referring to the fact that they shared the same name. Physically they bore a striking resemblance to each other. Not only did they appear to be of a similar age and height, but Ryan's young student had also been wearing the same polka-dot dress, the same pig-tailed blonde hair, and, if Amy remembered correctly, the same sparkly shoes. Amy knew that kids dressed up as their favorite fictional characters all the time, but this was impressive on a whole other level—the girl could have literally stepped right off the page.

"Well, I guess we know who her hero is. Whose book is this? Did it belong to your mother?"

"No, it belonged to me," Ryan said quietly. "I bought it while Mom was pregnant, soon after I found out she was having a girl. I wanted to get something for when she was older, a gift from her big brother, so my father took me to the bookstore, and I chose this. I remember liking this picture. I'd forgotten all about it. It's been so long since I've seen it. Years."

Amy put her arm around him and rubbed his back. "I'm sorry you never got the chance to give it to her."

Ryan shook his head. "No, you don't understand. There's something very strange going on. Something's not right."

"What do you mean?"

"It's Chloe. It's something she said." His eyes were glued to the cover, his gaze sinking deeper into the picture. "When she first introduced herself this morning, she told me she was named after the girl in this book. But then—and here's the weird part—she acted like I should have known, like it was the most obvious thing in the world. Her exact words to me were, 'You must remember it?'" He looked at Amy. "It was as though she knew."

"Knew what?"

"That I had this book."

"A book you bought nine years ago?"

"Yes."

"But how could she know something like that?"

He shrugged. "Don't know. But somehow she knew."

"And the two of you had never met before today?"

"No."

"You're sure?"

"Positive. I'd remember."

Amy stared back at him. "Then what you're saying doesn't make any sense. Maybe you misheard."

"I didn't. That's what she said, I'm sure of it. It had sounded so strange at the time, which is why I remember it so well. I'm not making this up."

"Okay, then what happened?"

"Nothing. I told her I didn't remember, and she laughed at me like it was the funniest thing she'd ever heard, then we got on with the lesson." Ryan buried his eyes back into the book, staring as though the answer might somehow be lurking inside. "Something's going on with her, Amy. I don't know what it is, but there's something."

Not knowing what else to say, Amy looked down at the book too, and as she studied the cover once more, she noticed something unusual.

"Hey, what's that?" she asked, pointing at a small bulge near the spine. "There's something stuck inside the book."

"Yeah, you're right." Holding the book in the air, Ryan opened the covers and gave it a good shake. Something small and silvery dropped to the floor.

Amy bent down and searched the ground beside Ryan's feet. When she saw what it was, her heart nearly stopped. It was a pendant— a mermaid perched on a rock, her tail wrapped around a moonstone. At first Amy thought it was just a bizarre coincidence, but when she picked up the pendant and examined it more closely, she quickly realized that every mark, every scratch, every tiny imperfection— from the scuff marks on the tail, right down to the discolored specks on the moonstone—were identical to hers. Even the chain was the same. *Everything* was the same.

No, thought Amy, *it can't be possible.*

She turned to face him.

"Why do you have this?"

"Why do I have what?" Ryan reached out his hand. "Can I see it?"

Amy gave the pendant to him and watched him closely, following his expression as he turned it over in his hands.

"I have no idea where this came from."

Amy snatched it back, securing it tightly inside her fist. "You're not playing games with me, are you?"

"Games? What?"

"Don't tease me. Is this some kind of joke?"

"A joke? Amy, what are you talking about?" Ryan tried to reach out and touch her leg, but she shifted away. "Whoa, what's going on?"

"You tell me."

"What?"

"Tell me the truth, Ryan."

"The truth about *what*?"

"About why you have this pendant. This is the pendant my mom gave me."

He frowned hard. "But how can that be?" Again, he tried to move closer, but Amy continued her slide down the couch. "Amy, listen to me, you're not making any sense."

"You're seriously telling me that you don't know how you got this?"

"Yes, that's what I'm telling you."

"You don't know how something of mine ended up here in *your* attic?"

"No, Amy, I don't. That's the honest truth."

"Wait, did you take this from my room?"

"What?"

"You were at the hotel," Amy muttered as a chill raced across her skin. "Exactly how long were you in my room before you woke me up? Is that when you took it?" She faced Ryan front on, squaring her shoulders, her heart thumping harder. "It's a simple question."

"I don't understand why you're asking me this."

"Then why aren't you answering me? What were you even doing at the hotel?"

"This is crazy."

She studied him for a long moment, her eyes locked on his in a cold and distrustful glare. "You *live* in Seabrook. Why did you need to be there? Were you stalking me? Did you see me out by the light-house and follow me back?"

Ryan didn't even pause to consider the question. His lips started moving fast. "*What?* No, Amy, I was not *stalking* you. I was at the hotel because I needed a drink. I went in there because I had just seen Tom, because he had just told me about the foreclosure, and because I needed a moment to myself before—"

"But you *weren't* in the bar. You were upstairs."

"Yes, I know, I *was* in the bar, but then—"

"And then . . . and then you were in my room."

"Because water was coming out into the hall, for Pete's sake! You left the bathtub running! You flooded the room! Don't you remember? Amy, where is this all coming from? Why are you acting like this?"

Amy launched herself to her feet. "How else should I be acting? You have my pendant, Ryan. Mom gave me this pendant. It's my most precious thing in the world. And now I find it up here, up in *your* attic!"

"I *promise* that I had nothing to do with it." He jumped to his feet too, pitching his hands together as he spoke, begging her to listen. "Amy, please, hand on heart, this hasn't got anything to do with me!"

Amy could feel her legs beginning to shake. Her breathing was getting shallow, her doubt growing deeper by the minute. Despite Ryan's impassioned denials and protests of innocence, she couldn't bring herself to believe him. She couldn't put her finger on it, couldn't rationalize it in her head, but deep in her gut she knew there was something wrong, knew there was *something* he wasn't telling her. She suddenly felt very alone and uncomfortable—even a little afraid.

"I want to go, Ryan. I need to go." She grabbed her phone and clothes.

"Hold up, stop for a second, okay? There's no need for you to go anywhere. Just stay calm."

"I *am* calm, and I want to go."

"But where?" He waved his hands at the window. "Look, it's pouring out!"

"Back to town," she declared, and she started for the staircase.

Ryan followed her across the room, pursuing her as she climbed down. "Don't leave like this, Amy. Let me try to figure this out." He kept pleading as she stormed down the hallway and out the front door.

"At least get in my truck, at least let me drive you back," he cried out as they crossed the front porch and stepped into the blustery rain. "We can talk. We can get this mess all straightened out."

"No, no, Ryan, I can't." Rain was pelting her skin, wind whipping up her hair. Her legs were moving faster, nearly a run now as she fled down the driveway.

Ryan wasn't giving up and ran beside her, protesting the entire way. "Amy, what exactly do you plan on doing? Are you going to walk all the way back? Stop, will you, *please?* This is ridiculous. It's crazy. It's the middle of the night!"

Admittedly Amy hadn't thought that far ahead, hadn't thought much of anything beyond her immediate need to get down from that attic and out of the house, which was why her heart swelled with relief when she spotted a pair of headlights by the ranch gate. There was a vehicle parked there, its engine idling. Amy ran straight for it.

"Careful, Amy! We don't know who that is!"

But Amy believed she did, because as she drew closer to the mysterious vehicle, she recognized the logo on the door: *Seabrook Taxis.* The same driver who had driven her to the ranch was seated behind the wheel, greeting her with a raised hand. Amy made for the rear of the car, opened the passenger door, and climbed in.

"Amy, please don't leave," Ryan cried out. "We can talk about this, we can fix—"

Amy slammed the door before he could finish. She locked it and glanced to the mirror, exchanging a look with the driver. He smiled and spoke with the same gravelly voice. "Hello, miss. Good to see you again. Everything all right?"

"Hi, yes, hello," she blurted out. "You came back. Thank God you came back."

His eyebrows pinched together. "Been here the whole time."

"What?"

"Meter's been running too. You sure did take your sweet time."

Amy didn't look at the meter. She didn't stop to think about why the cab was now here when it hadn't been here before, and she didn't look at Ryan, who was hovering right outside the window, his voice muffled but still cutting through the rain and the glass.

"Amy! Please, will you get out of the cab! I don't know what's going on! I swear to you, on the life of my father, I don't know what I've done!"

Amy couldn't take it a second longer. She was so confused and upset she was about to cry. She turned her face to the rain-striped glass and gave Ryan one last look, her voice breaking as she gave the cabbie her order.

"Can we go? Now, please."

"But is everything all right, miss? He sure does seem upset about something?"

"*Please. Just drive.*"

27

*A*MY COULD THINK of nothing else as the cab wound its way back down the narrow country roads. All she wanted to know was *why*? Why did Ryan take her pendant from her room? Why hide it from her? Why play dumb and pretend he'd never seen it before? Was that really the sort of person he was? Just some opportunistic petty thief? Granted, they hadn't known each other long, but the last thing she would have pegged him for would be a liar and a crook. It didn't make any sense. None whatsoever. Much like everything else going on in this damn town.

"Miss, you sure you're okay?"

Amy didn't answer. She turned inward to the door, away from the driver, and pulled out her phone. She needed to speak to her dad. She needed to make sure he was back from wherever he'd been. She desperately needed to hear a voice she could trust.

The moment the car emerged from the valley and joined the main road, Amy hit the green button and held the phone to her ear. She caught the driver's eyes lingering on her in the rearview mirror as she waited impatiently for the call to connect.

"Come on," she muttered under her breath, "please go through, please go through."

The number you have dialed is not in service. Please check the number and try again. The number you have dialed is not in service. Please—

Amy ripped the phone from her ear and glared at the screen. She assumed she had messed something up, but the signal bars were at full strength and the number she had called was most definitely her dad's. She hit the call button and tried again, but again she was thwarted by the same robotic voice crackling in her ears.

The number you have dialed is not in service. Please—

Amy terminated the call and swiped through her contacts, hurriedly searching for her uncle's number. He was the reason they were here. He was the one who had sent her dad down to Seabrook. If anyone knew what was going on, it would be Uncle Jack. But her attempts to reach him were met with the same response.

The number you have dialed is not in service.

"What the hell . . ."

With her heart beginning to beat unnervingly fast, Amy tried phoning a bunch of her contacts at random, including her best friend, but nothing was getting through. Text messages weren't sending either. Contact with the outside world had seemingly been cut off. Ordinarily she would have assumed it was some fault in the network, but there was too much weird stuff going on for this to be a coincidence. She was so disturbed by it all that she considered calling the police, even pulled up the keypad and entered 911, but before she had a chance to hit dial, the cab came to a stop.

"We're here," the driver said.

Amy had been so lost in her head that she hadn't realized they had already made it back to Seabrook. She glanced out her window, her eyes widening at the sight of the hotel's brightly lit lobby. She unclicked her seat belt and tried to exit the cab, but the driver hit a button and locked the doors. She met his eyes in the mirror and furiously shook the handle, pleading with him to let her out.

"Aren't you forgetting something?" he said, rubbing his fingers together, signaling that he'd yet to be paid.

"Right, sorry." Amy pulled out her wallet and asked how much she owed.

"Well, like I was sayin', miss, you ran her up pretty high." He grumbled as he tapped the meter with his finger. "Three hundred and twenty-two dollars."

"*What?*" Amy slid to the middle seat and lunged forward to inspect the meter herself. "Are you kidding me?"

"I beg your pardon?"

"I don't have that much."

"That's the fare."

"That's ridiculous."

"That's what happens when you hire a cab for half the day."

"But you *disappeared* on me!"

The cabbie shook his head. "I went nowhere, miss."

Amy glared at him. "Is this some kind of joke? Three hundred dollars? How am I even supposed to pay that?"

"Not my concern—you just better come up with something."

"Then let me out so that I can go up to my room. I'll try to find a credit card or something."

"Don't you think I haven't seen that one before? As soon as I do that, you'll make a run for it. You asked me to wait for you, and I did, so you'll pay up or else I'll have to put in a call to the sheriff."

"Look for yourself!" Amy shouted impatiently. "I have nothing. I have twenty dollars. Call the sheriff. Call him if you want. Please do, actually, because I'd like to talk to him myself." She slumped back into her seat and folded her arms.

"As you wish." But just as the driver was fiddling with an old flip phone, a figure appeared outside the driver's side window. There was a tap on the glass. Amy leaned forward to see who it was.

Chloe.

She was standing in the pouring rain, absolutely soaked, pointing at the driver to wind down the window. The driver huffed under his breath and waved his hand to shoo her away, but Chloe only rapped on the glass harder.

"Yes, yes, all right!" the driver barked. He rolled the window down a few inches, and as he did wind and rain swirled into the car. "What is it, girl? What do you want?"

Chloe slipped her hand through the gap and dropped a stack of hundred-dollar bills into the driver's lap. "Here, take it," she said.

"What is all this?"

"It's for the fare, and you can keep the change." The driver stared down at all the money, speechless. As he began counting, Chloe reached in and pushed the button that unlocked Amy's door.

"Psst, get out," she said. "*Now.*"

Amy didn't hesitate. She nodded and flung open the door.

"You need to come with me," Chloe ordered, grabbing Amy firmly by the hand. "You're leaving soon and there isn't much time."

"Time? Time for *what*?"

"Time for you to help! He needs you, Amy." Chloe dragged Amy toward the hotel entrance. "If you don't help him soon, it's gonna be too late." She stormed inside and cut a path through the lobby.

"What does *that* mean? Someone's in trouble? Who—who's in trouble? My dad?"

"No, not him."

Amy hastened after Chloe as she charged up the stairs, leaping two at a time just to keep up, firing questions as they sped down the hall. "Talk to me, Chloe! Who needs help? *Who?*"

Chloe stuck her finger on her lips. "Shhh! Not here. Wait till we're in your room."

They snuck inside and shut the door. The room was empty. The curtains were billowing in the wind, their shadows playing on the walls. Amy switched on the lights and looked around. It took just a fraction of a second to see that something wasn't right.

"Hey, wait. My dad's bag, his stuff . . ."

"What about it?"

"It's not here. It's gone!"

Chloe froze on the spot while Amy made a frantic search around the room.

"Are you sure, Amy? Are you absolutely sure?"

"Yes!" Amy peered into the bathroom, checked the spare room, checked the cupboard, even checked under the bed, but there was nothing of his anywhere. "I don't believe this. He's really gone. He's left me in this town. He's just left me here."

Chloe went quiet for a second. "Okay, I think this is bad." She stared at the floor, eyes busy, blinking fast. "Yes, this is definitely very bad."

"What are you talking about! What does *that* mean?"

"It means we don't have as much time as I thought." Chloe rushed over to Amy. "Your phone, do you have it on you?"

Amy fumbled in her pockets. "Yes?"

"Check the time, check it now."

Amy's hands were shaking. She pressed a button to light up the screen. Four digits shone back at her: 10:57.

Chloe saw them. "Yep, I was right. We have to leave. Now."

Amy felt a shiver come over her. She couldn't take much more of this. Her patience had run out and her sanity, or what was left of it, was wearing very, very thin.

"Forget it. I'm not going anywhere."

"But you have to, Amy. If you don't, you won't be able to—"

"No, I'm not moving. Not until I find out what the hell is going on."

"I promise you will, soon, but first I need to get you out of this hotel. It's not safe for you to stay here."

"It's not safe? *It's not safe?* What's happening in this damn town?

First my dad disappears, then there's some creepy man staring at me, and then my pendant shows up, and now *this*." She buried her head in her hands and let out a muffled groan. "I know what's happening. I'm losing it . . . I'm going crazy. I'm actually losing my mind."

"Someone's been watching you?" Chloe leaned in closer. "Someone's been watching you . . . *already*?"

Amy's heart was thumping hard. "Yes! What does he *want*?"

Before Chloe could answer, there was a loud noise, one single heavy knock on the door.

Someone wanted to come in.

Amy jumped and ran over. "Oh, please, *please* let that be my dad!"

"No, Amy, stop!" Chloe leapt in the way, wedging her body between Amy and the door. "Let me check who it is first." She turned around, opened the door a sliver of a crack, and peeked out into the hall. Her face paled as she slammed it shut.

"Chloe, who is it? Who's out there?"

Chloe shook her head. "Doesn't matter. We can't go that way anymore. We need a new plan."

Amy stared at the door, inching closer. "Chloe, tell me who's out there."

There was another knock.

"Don't look, Amy. I mean it."

"Why not?"

"Because they'll only frighten you."

"*They*?"

Then another knock.

Amy put her eye to the peephole. What she saw nearly made her scream. On the other side of the wall was a crowd of people, though they really didn't look like people at all—more like a horde of barren statues. There were so many of them. They filled the hall and were all facing the door, motionless, staring with that same cold glaze in their eyes as the man from the bar, that same lifeless expression.

Amy leapt backward, nearly tripping over her own feet as she stumbled away. She wanted to throw up or run or scream, but she was too scared to do any of those things, too scared to make a sound.

"Amy, don't freak out."

Another knock.

"It's *really* important you stay calm."

Another.

Amy fled across the room, going as far back as she could go. Her legs buckled as she hit the wall. She fell to the floor.

Another.

Her heart was thumping so hard she thought it was about to explode out of her chest. Chloe, in the meantime, was busy racing around the room, shifting furniture and stacking it against the wall. Displaying unnatural levels of strength, she made light work of the couch, the chairs, the dining table, the small fridge, even the portable safe—anything that could be moved, she used to fortify the door.

"There, that's the best I can do, but it's not going to hold them for long." She ran back across the room and clapped her hands at Amy, who was still cowering in the corner. "Stand up. We have to leave. We can go out the window. There's a fire escape. We can climb down that."

Amy was almost hyperventilating. "Chloe, I beg you—please, will you just tell me what's happening? You know something. Can you *please* tell me what's going on?"

"There's no time. They're already on to you. They know you don't belong here. This is only making it worse." The next knock was so strong that the stacked furniture rattled and shook and nearly tipped over. Chloe grabbed Amy by the arms, lifted her to her feet, and dragged her to the window. "Come on, you go first. I'll follow."

Steeling her nerves as best as she could, Amy climbed out the window and put all her weight on the narrow gangway, which was caked in rust and wobbling in the strong wind. She gripped the railing with both hands. She was only one floor up, but the street looked a long way down. The storm had cut the power to the streetlights. She could barely see a thing. Chloe stepped out behind her. Suddenly there was a crash from inside the room. One of the chairs had fallen to the floor. The knocking was getting worse.

"Go, Amy! Hurry!"

Amy hustled along the gangway and down the plunging steps as fast as her shaking limbs would allow. There was a gap between the staircase and the sidewalk. She held her breath and jumped. Chloe did the same and didn't waste another second before grabbing Amy's hand.

"Come on!" she yelled. "This way!"

They fled the hotel and made a breathless dash down a dead-end street, away from the town square, straight for the beach. Amy couldn't breathe for all the wind and sand blowing in the air. She couldn't understand why they were going this way. There was nothing down here, nothing but the ocean. Soon there would be nowhere left for them to run.

"This is it," Chloe said, coming to a sudden standstill. "This is as far as I can go. The rest you have to do alone."

"What am I supposed to do now, Chloe? *Where* am I supposed to go!"

Chloe pointed her finger and cried out, "That way!"

Amy wiped her eyes, which were filled with tears and rain and confusion. She turned her face to the wind. All she could see were sand dunes. "The *beach?* But *why?*"

"No, not the beach—the *lighthouse!*" Chloe took hold of Amy's hands. "You have to listen to me, listen very carefully—there's someone waiting for you inside the lighthouse, someone you can trust. They're going to help you, okay? All of this is going to make sense very soon, I promise—but you have to go now. You have to run, and you have to run fast, and no matter what, whatever you do, *don't look back.*"

28

AFTER SPRINTING the length of the beach and climbing over the outcrop's slippery rocks, Amy was once again face-to-face with the lighthouse. She looked around, just to make sure she was alone, then pressed her face against the wire mesh fence and stared at the tower's giant door. Who was waiting inside that building? Who could Chloe possibly have meant when she said, *someone you can trust?* Amy was all alone. With her dad now gone, vanished without a trace, there wasn't a soul in this town she dared trust.

Her heart beating impossibly fast, she glanced skyward to the top of the lighthouse. Its lamp room was still aglow. The same column of light that had caused everyone to flee in terror was still blazing across the sky. Common sense told her that she shouldn't be there, and yet at the same time, for some strange, unknowable reason, this powerful beam seemed to be calling to her, beckoning her to come inside.

Come on, she told herself. *You can do this.*

Amy stumbled along the fence line and found the spot where

Frank Junior had cut through the wire. She stepped through to the other side and cautiously approached the door. With a small push, she nudged it open.

The first thing she noticed was a flickering light coming from an old-fashioned lantern, sitting on the lowest step of the staircase. She bent down to pick up the lantern, but the moment she had it in her hands a monstrous gust of wind blew through and slammed the door shut. She spun around and lunged at the door, but it was too late—the lock, which had been obliterated by the nub of Frank's sledge-hammer, had somehow materialized back into place. She twisted the latch and tried to jimmy it open, but it was no use—it wouldn't budge. She had been sealed inside the building.

Amy nervously turned around and tried not to panic. The room was much darker now. She couldn't hear a whisper of what was going on outside. For all she knew the storm might have stopped, it was that quiet.

Clutching the lantern in her clammy hands, which were shaking along with every other part of her body, Amy glanced at the staircase, the last place left for her to go. She put her foot on the first step and slowly began the ascent. Less than a minute later, she found herself standing in the tower's glass-walled lamp room. In the middle of the room was a giant lens. It was a few feet wide, at least six feet tall, and was covered in arc-like patterns of glass radiating out from its center. Inside the lens was a powerful lamp, pulsing brightly and rotating with a mechanical purr. Amy stepped to the right and tried to peek around the lens. She sensed she wasn't alone. There was someone else up there with her. She could feel it . . . another presence.

"Hello," Amy called out, her voice trembling. "Is someone here?" She took another small step, then another, and then she saw someone standing on the opposite side of the room. A heavy lump solidified in her throat. She couldn't make out who it was; the figure, looming on the other side of the lens, was obscured by all the reflected light and luminescent glass.

"Please," Amy whispered, "tell me who you are."

And then, from out of the silence, a voice answered, a voice from beyond the grave, a voice that couldn't possibly be real . . .

"Amy, it's me."

Amy froze.

No, it's not possible . . .

A woman moved from behind the lens and stepped into view, a woman with sandy-blonde hair and dark-green eyes. Dressed in a dark gown that seemed to shimmer with translucency when it moved, the woman whispered to Amy as she reached out her hand, her voice soft, surreal, and familiar.

Amy couldn't breathe. Her throat shriveled up. She stepped backward and stumbled and hit the wall, mumbling "no" over and over and over, louder and louder, as an avalanche of fear and shock and confusion crashed inside her head.

"Don't be frightened, sweetheart."

"Stay back!" Amy fled along the wall, waving her hand in the air as the woman—the ghost, apparition, whatever she was—tried to follow. None of this was real. None of this could *possibly* be real. "Whoever you are, stay back!"

"It's me, Amy."

"*No!* Don't come any closer! You're not *her*! You're not my *mother*!"

"Yes, I am."

"My mother was in a car accident! We buried her! I was at her funeral! You *died*!"

Amy's heart was pounding fast, every beat a chest-rattling tremor. She fell to the ground and began sobbing uncontrollably, the raw emotions spilling out.

"That's right. I did. But see, I'm here now, I'm here with you." The woman knelt down, hand outstretched. "Breathe, Amy. Just breathe." She placed her hand on Amy's cheek, ran her finger down Amy's nose. "Feel my touch, see? I promise, it's me. I'm here."

Amy stared into the woman's eyes, her *mom's* eyes, while spluttering through tears, which were coming faster than she could sniff them back. "It can't be you. It's not possible."

"It *is* possible," she answered, "and in a moment, I'll tell you how—but right now, I need to hug you, and hold you. Sweetheart, come here."

"M-M-Mom . . . is it you? Is it really you?"

"It's me, it's really me."

Amy couldn't endure it any longer. The torment was too much. Her resolve crumbled away, and in a bluster of tears she collapsed into her mother's arms. The room fell silent as they embraced. Amy was so bewildered and overwhelmed that she couldn't stop crying.

"Oh, Mom . . . I've missed you. I've missed you so much."

"And I've missed you too, my precious girl. More than you can know."

"This can't be real. It can't be happening." Amy buried her face deeper into her mother's chest, muffled sobs ringing out around the room.

"It's real, I promise."

"But how? How is this possible? How can you be here?"

"Shh, don't think, don't talk, don't worry about any of that just now." She drew Amy in closer. "Let me just hold you for a moment. Let me hold my baby girl."

29

Since watching Amy's cab speed off, Ryan hadn't moved. He was still standing by the gate, oblivious to everything going on around him—to the darkness, the storm, the wind, the rain, even the puddles rising around his feet.

He couldn't comprehend what had happened. One minute they were locked in each other's embrace, the next Amy couldn't get away quickly enough.

And all because of a *pendant*.

If Ryan had known how that pendant had gotten inside his mother's old box, he would have said so, but the truth was that he didn't have a clue. He'd never seen it before. And he certainly hadn't taken it from Amy's hotel room! Did she honestly believe he was capable of that? He'd poured his heart out to her. He'd told her secrets he'd never uttered to anyone. Heck, they had just kissed! And yet despite all that, Amy had felt her only choice was to get away from him as fast as she possibly could, without hearing him out, without even saying goodbye. Ryan felt like his heart had been ripped out of his chest. Their perfect day had been destroyed in the blink of an eye, and all he wanted to know was *why*.

Desperate not to let the evening end in disaster, Ryan left the road and rushed back to the house. He made straight for the phone. The rain had washed Amy's number from his arm, but maybe she had already arrived at the hotel? Maybe he could reach her there? He grabbed the phone book, found the number, then picked up the receiver and dialed the hotel. But when he got patched through to her room, no one answered. She should have been back by now. Unless she was purposely not picking up. He phoned three more times. Still no answer.

Could it be that she'd finally found her dad? Maybe they were already in the car and on their way back to Portland. This was a troubling thought as it had just dawned on him that he didn't even know Amy's last name. If she were to leave then he'd have no hope of tracking her down. He needed to act. He needed to do *something*.

Ryan slammed the phone down and fetched his keys, then raced outside to his truck, which was still parked by the field gate. Plan A was to drive straight to the hotel—if Amy wasn't there then plan B was to try to find them on the road. There wouldn't be many vehicles about, not in this weather. Maybe he could get lucky and catch up with them before they hit the highway.

Ryan twisted the key, revved the engine, spun the wheel, and punched the gearstick into first, ready to pull away. But as he was about to drive off, he saw that his father's bedroom light was on. *That's odd.* It wasn't normal for his father to be awake at this hour. Had the storm woken him? Perhaps the sound of the truck? Whatever prompted it, Ryan had a strange feeling that he needed to go check.

Pulling the parking brake, he ran back inside the house and made straight for his father's room. It was empty. The curtains were drawn, sheets neatly tucked into the mattress. Ryan checked elsewhere—the bathroom, then the living room—but found nothing.

"Dad?" he called out, beginning to worry. "Where are you? . . . Are you all right?"

Ryan passed through the living room and made his way into the kitchen. The room was dark, but he could make out a shadow sitting in a chair.

"Hey . . . Dad? What are you doing?"

There was no answer.

A sick feeling took hold in Ryan's stomach. He reached for the wall and switched on the lights.

"What the hell . . ."

The room was a mess. Documents were strewn across the floor. Everywhere Ryan looked, every letter from the bank, every overdue bill, every red-stamped notice of demand—they were all out in the open, all in plain sight. And sitting in the middle of the room, adrift in the white sea of paper, was his father. His head was bent low with tears running down his cheeks, and in his trembling hands he held one of the letters. Even from across the room, Ryan could make out the scrawl of Tom Tippenworth's signature and that dreaded word emblazoned across the top of the page: *FORECLOSURE.*

30

*H*UDDLED TOGETHER on the lantern room's cold concrete floor, neither Amy nor her mother spoke, not for a long time. The outside world seemed to fade away. Time itself ceased to feel real. Only the rotation of the lamp gave any clue to the seconds passing by. Each time the beam swung over their heads, Amy sank deeper and deeper into her mother's arms, praying in her heart that this reunion wasn't a dream, wishing she could bottle this moment and make it last forever.

"Is this real, Mom? Are you actually here?"

"I'm here, Amy."

"I'm not losing my mind?"

"No," her mother said, smiling. "You're not."

"Are you . . . a *ghost?*"

"No, I'm not a ghost. I'm really here, sweetheart, here with you now."

Amy didn't want to open her eyes in case doing so might bring an end to this beautiful, impossible dream. She had so much she wanted to say, so many questions, but the sensation of being held in her mother's arms made it impossible for her to speak. Tears kept coming thick and fast. It took a long time before she dared to believe any of this was actually happening.

"Mom, can you explain what's going on? Have you come back . . . *for good?*"

"I wish that were so, Amy. Since I left you, I've felt your pain. I know how much you've been hurting. But I won't lie to you—I'm not back for good, and I can't stay with you for very long either. I can't hide up here forever."

"Hide? What do you mean, *hide?*"

"I need you to listen carefully because there's something important I need to tell you."

Amy felt a lump catch in her throat. "What is it?"

Her mother tucked back a strand of Amy's hair and gently kissed her on the forehead. "What I'm about to say isn't going to make a lot of sense, but I want you to know that I love you very much, and that we're going to find a way through this, okay?"

Amy took a deep breath, a gulp of air that seemed to fly through her chest and land heavy in her stomach. "You're scaring me, Mom. Please tell me what's going on."

"Last night, shortly after you arrived in Seabrook, you crossed paths with a young man."

"Why are you asking—"

"Isn't that right?" her mother asserted. "When you were at the hotel, someone came into your room?"

"Yes, that's right. That was Ryan. But I don't understand—how do you know about Ryan? And what's he got to do with this?"

Her mother drew a breath through pursed lips, trepidation brewing in her eyes. "There's no other way for me to say this, so I'm just going to come out with it."

"Say what? . . . Mom?"

"That young man, Ryan . . . he's hiding a secret."

"I know all about his secret. He told me about the ranch, and his father. He told me everything."

"I'm not talking about *that* secret."

There was a crash of thunder; it rumbled across the sky, reverberating violently inside the glass-walled room. The hairs on Amy's neck stood up.

"Mom, I don't understand what you mean. I don't get what Ryan has to do with any of this. What's he got to do with you being here?"

Her mother hesitated again, her gaze drifting toward town before returning to Amy. "Two months ago, while Ryan was out riding his horse, he suffered a terrible accident."

"Okay . . ."

"It happened late at night, during a big storm, just like this one. He was out riding by the cliffs, trying to find a horse that had escaped from his ranch."

"Are you talking about when he rescued Little Dipper?"

"Yes."

"But that wasn't two months ago—that was just the other night."

"Let me finish. When he found his spooked horse, Ryan tried to get a rope on her so that he could pull her in, but in the process he was pulled off his own horse and dragged over the edge of the cliff. He fell into the ocean . . . and he drowned."

"He . . . what?"

"He drowned."

Amy's head jerked back. She had to let the nonsense of that statement settle for a moment before she could respond. "No, that's not right. Ryan told me all about that night. He even took me to those same cliffs. He said he found the horse; he saved her and brought her home. They both made it home. That's what he told me."

"And when he told you that, he would have believed what he was saying was true because that's how *he* remembers it, but that's not what actually happened."

"Mom, you're not listening to me. I've been with Ryan all day. He took me out riding, and we went to the festival and spent the whole day together. You've got this all wrong. He made it home that night. He didn't *drown*." The words were so ridiculous, Amy could hardly get them out.

"I know this is confusing."

"Confusing? Why would any of this be confusing? I'm sitting in a haunted lighthouse talking to my mother, who I thought I'd never see or speak to again, and she's trying to tell me that the guy I met today actually died two months ago, which seems a bit strange seeing as I'm the one who just spent the day with him, and he looked pretty alive to me. And I'm pretty sure he thinks he's alive too."

"I'm sure he does, but that's because he's fooled himself into remembering a different version of events. Ryan died on that night, Amy—I'm afraid he just doesn't realize it."

Amy threw her arms up in the air in frustration. "This is *crazy*. Will you *please* just explain what's going on? Why have you come back? How can I be talking to you right now? And why are you trying to tell me that Ryan is dead even though he's walking around town and living his life as though everything is normal?"

"Well, that's the thing—everything's not normal, is it? Nothing about this town is normal."

"Mom, I've just escaped a hotel full of creepy people who were trying to bust down my door, and now I'm sitting here talking to *you*. I'm fully aware none of this is normal. But what's that got to do with Ryan? Or you? What's any of this got to do with *anything*?"

"Stand up, sweetheart—let me show you something."

Amy stood and followed her mother to the other side of the room, where they stopped by the window and glanced back down the beach.

"Look closely," her mother said, "tell me what you see."

Amy ran her eyes along the coastline. Through the wind and rain, she spotted the faint glow of streetlights, the distant outline of buildings as they became briefly illuminated by the beam of the lighthouse.

"I see Seabrook."

"It may look like Seabrook, but the truth—and this is going to sound a little strange—is that it's not the *real* Seabrook."

"Say that again?"

"The town you're staring at is a fake. Everything you see out there, from the buildings, to the ocean, to the sky, right down to every single grain of sand on that beach—not one bit of it is real."

Amy turned away from the view and raised her eyebrows at her mother. "You can't really be serious."

"I'm afraid so."

"But if it's not real . . . then what is it?"

"An elaborate illusion, designed to look and feel just like the real thing."

"An *illusion?* Mom, this isn't making any sense."

Her mother gave a tentative smile and invited Amy to sit back down. "All of this was created by Ryan," she said. "On the night he died, at the very moment of his passing, his spirit made a choice not to cross over."

"Why?"

"Because his spirit refused to accept what had happened. It rejected the idea that Ryan's time on earth had come to an end, and so this fantasy was created instead. Ryan's been trapped here since the night he drowned, imprisoned inside this false existence, tricked into thinking that life has carried on."

Amy gave herself a moment to fully digest the absurdity of that statement. She'd never heard anything so bizarre. It set off so many questions, she didn't even know where to begin.

"I don't understand how something like this is even possible."

"The human spirit is capable of some incredible things."

"What, like being able to create entirely fake towns?"

"We create elaborate dreams when we're asleep—this is simply another level beyond that."

"Okay, but . . . *still* . . . isn't this a little extreme? Even if what you're saying is true, why would Ryan go to such lengths just to fool himself?"

"Well, in Ryan's case there were factors that prevented him from being able to move on, reasons why his spirit felt it needed to take these drastic measures."

"Like *what*?"

"Like his deep love for his father, his devotion to him, his need to protect him from the problems facing the ranch, problems for which he blamed himself. This is what interfered with his transition."

"You're saying he ended up in here as punishment just because he loved his father too much?"

"It's more than that, Amy. You saw it for yourself—Ryan's world was centered around his father. His singular purpose in life was to care for him, to make sure he got better. His father was everything to Ryan, and so the notion that he couldn't protect him anymore, particularly from the catastrophe about to descend upon the ranch, wasn't just incomprehensible—it was, quite literally, a fate worse than death. And that's why, when death *did* come, Ryan's spirit did what it had to do—it built this place to save him from having to confront the truth. Don't think of it as punishment. Think of it as an act of self-preservation."

Lost for words, Amy fired a stunned glance back toward the shore, past the beach and the dunes, to the dark cluster of Seabrook's shadowy buildings.

"I can't believe this," she mumbled. "If what you're saying is true, then what about all the people that are in here? I've seen them. I've *spoken* with them. Who are *they*?"

"They're part of the illusion too. They're just projections of Ryan's memory—echoes of people he knew or met at some point in the past. Try to think of this place as a giant snow globe made up of all the people Ryan knew, an exact version of his world as it was at the time of his death."

Amy fell silent again, deep in her own thoughts. She didn't know what to say. If what her mother said was true, what did that mean for *her*? Why was *she* here? More to the point, *how* did she end up in here? Had something happened on the drive in? Had her dad taken a wrong turn? Had they gone through some portal? Was there some flash from the sky that struck their car and magically transported them into this other dimension? Normally such thoughts would sound ridiculous, but considering she had just found her dead mother hiding at the top of an abandoned lighthouse, Amy didn't know what to think anymore. Nothing was beyond the realm of possibility.

"You're going to have to explain this all again," Amy said, "and I mean from the beginning, from when Dad and I first arrived. How did *we* get mixed up in all this? I need to know *exactly* how we got here."

"There's no *we*," her mother said softly. "Only you made the journey to this place—just you." There was a wary look in her eyes, as though she had known this question was coming. "Sweetheart, how much do you remember about last night?"

Amy's throat tightened. "Uh, everything . . . I think."

"Tell me, then. Tell me what you remember."

"We drove here, checked in to the hotel . . ."

"And then?"

"And then I went for a walk along the beach. I came here, to the lighthouse . . . and then I went back to the hotel."

"Keep going. Tell me exactly what happened next."

"I got to my room and ran a bath, but I must have dozed off because I spilled water everywhere, and that's how I first met Ryan, because he saw the mess and knocked on my door."

"But there's something else, isn't there? Before you got into the bath, you went searching for something in your father's bag, didn't you? You found his pills."

Amy's heart skipped a beat. She opened her mouth to speak, then hesitated for a moment. "The . . . sleeping pills?"

"Yes—and you took some."

"I did . . ."

"Do you remember how many you took?"

"No . . . I don't. A few, I guess. A handful? I don't know." Amy blinked rapidly. Her chest was feeling sore, her stomach suddenly full of knots. "Mom, what's happening? Why are you talking about those pills?"

"Because you swallowed too many of them. Those pills you took didn't send you off to sleep—they knocked you unconscious. You slipped under the water, you didn't wake up, and that's when your spirit made its way here. Your body is still in that bathtub, sweetheart. Right now, as we speak, that's where you are. You're back at the hotel, still lying in the water."

31

*R*YAN COULDN'T believe his eyes. All his private paperwork—months' worth of bank statements and letters and overdue bills—dumped across the kitchen floor. And there was his father, sitting in a chair right smack in the middle of it. Ryan had known this moment would come, had dreaded it for four years, but this was the absolute worst of worst-case scenarios. Never had he imagined confronting such a situation; in all his days and nights of lost sleep, never had he pictured his father finding out the truth like *this*.

"Dad?"

Ryan entered the kitchen, traipsing lightly across the sheets of paper. His father wasn't answering him. His gaze was locked on the letter in his hands. Ryan resisted the urge to deconstruct the scene and start asking questions. Exactly how this had all happened was irrelevant. His father's world was in the process of being turned upside down and the only thing that mattered now was minimizing the damage.

"Dad, it's me. Are you okay?" Ryan knelt beside the chair and examined his father's face for clues, for traces of anger, sadness, confusion, any sign at all that would let him know what was going on inside his head. "Can you hear me, Dad?"

But his father, who hadn't acknowledged Ryan's presence, remained deathly silent for a few seconds longer, until he finally said quietly, "What's the meaning of all this, Son?"

Ryan put a hand on his father's back. "Dad, listen, there's something I need—"

"This letter here says we have to vacate the property, they say we have to l-leave . . . The bank, they want to th-throw us out."

Ryan could hear the cracks in his father's voice, the fracturing in his words, his faintly slurred speech. Swallowing hard, he nervously put his other hand on his father's arm and tried to extricate him from the chair. "How about we get up, huh? Let's go someplace else, okay?"

His father didn't budge. "This can't be right," he protested. His lips were quivering, and his eyes were making frenetic dashes back and forth across the page. "There must be . . . a m-mistake . . . a t-t-terrible mistake. Right, Son?"

Ryan hadn't a clue what to say or do; all he knew was that he couldn't stand to watch his father struggle like this. He squeezed his arm. "Please, Dad. Put that letter down. Come with me. I'll try to explain what's going on."

"No, Son, we need to f-fix this . . . need to fix this now."

"We can't, Dad."

"But we have to. We must."

"There's nothing we can do right now. There's nothing we can fix."

His father looked down at the letter, then back up at Ryan; confusion was etched into every line and wrinkle on his face. "But, Son, this is our home."

"I know."

"Then have you read this?"

"I know what it says."

"They can't come and take our home, Ryan."

"Listen, Dad . . ."

"They can't s-send . . . a letter like this . . ."

"Dad, please . . ."

"This place belongs to us, Son . . . to *us* . . ."

"Dad, stop! The ranch doesn't belong to us, not anymore."

"What?"

"That letter's real. The ranch . . . it's gone."

"How c-can it be gone?"

"Because it is, okay? Because of *me*."

His father fell silent. Even his hand stopped shaking for a moment. "S-S-Son . . . wh-what do you mean?"

"I've ruined everything, Dad. The bank's evicting us and it's all my fault. I've been lying to you, lying about what happened after your stroke, about the business, about everything."

Ryan held his father's gaze for a moment, his voice dissolving into a whimper. "There was never any insurance. When you left the hospital, you were supposed to be placed into a nursing home, but I borrowed the money so that I could bring you back to the ranch, because I knew this was where you needed to be. I took out a loan against our home and paid for your therapy, paid for all of it. I never told you because I didn't want you to worry, because all I wanted you to do was concentrate on getting better. I love you—you're all I've got. I let you think the insurance had taken care of everything because I thought I could pay it all back. I thought you would never need to know. Except I couldn't pay it back, and now we're about to lose everything. This is all my fault, Dad. All me. I'm sorry. I'm so, so sorry."

His father sat motionless, numb from the shock.

"Please realize that I never meant for this to happen. I never meant for you to find out this way. You have to know that I've been trying to get us out of this mess. For years, I've been trying, Dad, every single day. But business has been drying up, and I've kept needing to borrow more and—"

"St-st-stop . . . t-talking . . ."

"I took a part-time job at the diner. I've been doing everything I possibly can to—"

"I said stop." His father dropped the letter and put his hand across his forehead, covering his eyes. "I n-n-need . . . I . . . need . . . a m-m-moment . . ."

There was a crippling pain inside Ryan's chest, a pain beyond words. His guilt had never hurt this much; the shame of what he'd done had never cut so deep. If he didn't know any better, he'd think his heart was being torn in two. He couldn't bear this, couldn't bear to imagine what havoc this news must be wreaking inside his father's frail mind.

"Talk to me, Dad. Please. Say something."

But his father didn't say anything, not a word. He remained silent for an agonizingly long time. Then, suddenly, his arm dropped lifelessly by his side.

"Dad, hey . . . are you okay?" Ryan leaned in and grabbed his father's chin, turned his head, and saw trouble right away—the distant gaze in his eyes, the frozen, constricted pupils. He felt a surge of panic. "What's happening, Dad? What's going on?"

In one sudden movement, his father thrust out his hand and grabbed hold of Ryan.

"S-S-on . . . I don't . . . f-feel . . . right . . ."

"Dad? *Dad? What's wrong?*"

His grip on Ryan's arm tightened and became viselike. He was trying to talk but seemed unable to move his lips. "I . . . I can't . . . I can't s-see."

"*You can't see?* What do you mean? *Dad?*"

Without warning, his father's weight shifted and he tipped out of his chair. Ryan threw his own weight behind his father, wrapping both arms around his torso and breaking the momentum of his fall. Laying him on his back, Ryan slapped his father's cheek and gave him a shake, frantically trying to draw a response, but his eyes were closed and his body had gone limp. His chest was flat. No pulse. It was all Ryan could do not to scream and go into an all-out panic.

"You're gonna be okay. Listen to my voice. You're gonna be fine. I'm calling for help. Dad, I'm getting you help. Stay with me, Dad. Stay with me!"

Ryan rushed to the other side of the room, nearly falling over as he tore across the sea of paper. He yanked the telephone off the wall and punched three numbers into the handset. He waited. A moment later, the phone began to ring.

"911, what's your emergency?"

"Please! We need help!" Ryan screamed. "Someone has to come quick! Now!"

"Tell me what's happened, sir?"

"It's my father. He's in trouble. Please, someone needs to get here fast."

"Sir, I need you to slow down. Take a breath and tell me what's happened. Is your father in need of medical attention?"

"Yes!"

"Is he breathing? Can you tell me if he's conscious?"

"No, no, he's not. He's not all right." Ryan began to simultaneously cry and hyperventilate into the receiver as he looked at his father lying on their kitchen floor, his body in a crumpled heap. "My father is having a stroke," he cried in agony. "Please, *please*, someone help us!"

32

AMY CLAPPED HER HANDS over her mouth and drew a shuddering breath through the cracks in her fingers. The revelation that she was still lying in the bathtub had raised a frightening thought, one that shook her to her core, one too terrifying to even say aloud.

"M-Mom . . ."

Her mother placed her hand on Amy's cheek, caught a tear with her thumb. "It's okay. Stay calm."

"But is that why I'm here? Because I overdosed on Dad's pills? Am I here because . . . I died?" Just saying those words made Amy's body go numb; she had to grab on to her mother for fear she was about to faint.

"No, no—not that, not at all, listen to me—"

"But if I'm talking to you, then—"

"You're talking to me because your spirit was momentarily set free, *not* because you died."

"But if I'm still lying in the water, and if it's already been a whole day, then that means nobody has found me, which means I *can't* be alive . . . it just isn't possible."

"No one's found you yet because time is at a standstill. While you've been stuck in here, the world you left behind has been frozen at the precise moment you blacked out."

"Wait . . ." Amy tried to calm herself, tried to focus on what her mother was saying. "Let me get this straight. . . . My body's in the bathtub . . ."

"That's right."

"But you're telling me that I'm still alive?"

"Most definitely."

"Even though my spirit has been set free, or whatever it was you just said . . . I'm not dead?"

"Unequivocally, one hundred percent *not dead.*"

"But if I'm stuck in here and my body's back there, what's going to happen to me? How am I supposed to leave wherever this is and get back?"

"Don't worry about that right now. When this is all over, I'm going to make sure you find your way home. The important thing is that you're here with me, and that you're safe."

"You promise?"

"I promise."

Amy turned away from her mother and faced the window. Shock, confusion, relief—she was experiencing a collision of conflicting emotions. She didn't know what to say or how to react. All she could do was stare at her reflection, breathe, exhale, and watch the mist fog and fade across the glass.

"This must all be very confusing," her mother said. "Anything you want to know, please, ask."

"I need a moment, Mom."

"Of course."

Amy had questions. Lots of questions. But what she struggled with the most wasn't that she was talking to her dead mother, or that she had overdosed on some pills—it was the revelation about Ryan. To think that the guy she had spent all day with, the guy she had just kissed, had not only *died* but had also spent the last two months living out some deluded fantasy in a town that wasn't even real—she just couldn't believe it. Could he really have been stuck here for that long without realizing something wasn't right? But as Amy looked around the room, even she had to admit she couldn't spot anything that looked odd or out of place. From the chill in the air to the uneven streaks of paint on the ceiling, even the smell of kerosene burning beneath the lamp, everything about this illusion seemed utterly real. Even the most minuscule details, like the trails of rain running across the windows, or the way the lighthouse beam shone through them and created flecks of prismatic light in the glass, were astoundingly intricate. It was no wonder Ryan had been fooled.

But what was Amy's part in all this? She took some pills and blacked out, she got that, but if this illusion was created to deceive Ryan, then what was *she* doing in here? How exactly did she end up sharing his snow globe with him? That question was put straight to her mother.

"Well, it certainly wasn't by accident," she answered. "The truth is that your spirits latched on to each other in a very strong way, and this connection between you is how Ryan was able to draw you in."

"Wait, are you saying *he* did this? He brought me in here on purpose?"

"No, at least not on a conscious level. Remember, to him, you were just a girl he found in a bathtub. He hasn't got a clue where you're really from."

Amy replayed that moment in her head when she saw Ryan standing at the doorway . . . the moment she had left the real world behind.

"But we're complete strangers," Amy said. "How could there be such a strong connection between us if we hadn't even met yet, when he didn't even know who I was?"

"Let's back up and talk about the reason you came down to Seabrook in the first place."

Amy raised her eyebrows. "It was for Dad's work, wasn't it?"

"Yes, but it was actually because of your uncle."

"Uncle Jack? What's he got to do with any of this?"

"Quite a lot," her mother said. "Jack was the one first assigned to Ryan's case. Ryan's body was never found, which made him a missing person, but because the local county lacks the resources for that sort of thing, the case fell to the state police to investigate."

"Wait, Ryan's body still hasn't been found? Even after all this time?"

"I'm afraid not."

"Then what does everyone think happened to him?"

"No one's sure. When the investigation first began, there was suspicion of foul play."

"Why?"

"Because *two* horses were found wandering in the forest the morning after he died—the one Ryan was riding, and the one he saved—which led some to believe a second person might have been involved. But with no other leads or evidence, the investigation quickly dried up. Your uncle was about to close the file. The last thing left to do was to formally notify Ryan's father and advise him that the investigation was being shut down. This was a task he had originally planned to do himself, but at the last minute he decided to give this job to your father, and, well, here you are."

Amy ran her hands down her face, her head spinning. "So that's why Ryan's spirit latched on to mine?" she muttered. "That's how I ended up in here? Just because Dad is connected to his case?"

"It's part of it, yes, but remember—you were drawn to *each other*. You latched on to Ryan, just as much as he latched on to you."

"I did? But why?"

"Because trauma has a way of marking us—that history of loss you share is something that connects both of you on the deepest of levels. That, together with your father's involvement in his case, and the fact that you were here in Seabrook, physically present in Ryan's hometown, is what made it possible for you two to find each other. A natural tether formed between your spirits, Amy, and that's why, the moment yours had a chance to wander, it went straight to his."

Amy's eyes, red and sore, welled up once more when she stopped to think of Ryan and everything he'd been through. She had been too distracted by this reunion with her mother to fully process what had happened to him. Until this moment, she had not confronted the painful truth that his life had come to an end, that it wouldn't be possible to go to see him once she got back home. Who knew if she would ever get to see or speak with him again? Given that she had known him for less than a day, the sadness of that realization hit her unexpectedly hard.

"Are you okay?" her mother asked.

Amy nodded, sniffing back tears. "Ryan and I had become really close, that's all, and to think that no one knows what happened to him, to think his body is just lying somewhere and no one knows where . . . it's really heartbreaking." She fell back into her mother's arms, deep into the comfort and warmth of her embrace. "Oh, Mom. I still can't believe that you're really here, that any of this is actually happening."

"Neither can I, sweetheart. To see you, to be holding you again— this isn't something I thought would happen for a very long time."

"But why wait so long? Why didn't you try to reach out to me as soon as I got stuck in here?" Amy's voice was almost lost behind the sound of rain and thunder; the storm, never-ending in its fury, continued to rage outside.

"I did try. The moment you arrived, I found my way inside this lighthouse, switched on the lamp, and I pointed the beam at the hotel. My hope was that you might see it."

"Why couldn't you just come to my room and knock on my door?"

"Because this lighthouse is the only place I'm allowed to be. I can't go outside. Come, I'll show you." She led Amy to the other side of the room, to a door providing access to the circular platform. She opened the door and tried to stick her arm outside, but doing this caused her arm to completely disappear. It happened right before Amy's very eyes. It was as though her mother was pushing her hand through a wall of nothingness—first her skin turned translucent, then one half of her limb, from her fingertips to her elbow, evaporated into thin air. A plume of twinkling dust was all that remained.

"*Mom!*"

"It's okay, Amy. It doesn't hurt."

"*But, Mom! Your arm!*" Amy grabbed her mother and pulled her back. As she did so, the dust flickered, became bright and ember-like, then sparkled and magically coalesced back into flesh. Inch by inch, her mother's arm rematerialized.

"What the hell?" Amy screamed. "*Are you okay?*"

"I'm fine."

"But your arm! It vanished! I saw it!"

"What you saw is exactly what happens when an outsider— someone unknown to Ryan, someone he's never met before—tries to infiltrate the town. I wasn't brought in here like you were, and because I occupy no place in Ryan's memory, his spirit isn't able to recognize my presence."

"But that doesn't make sense because you *are here*," Amy said as she continued to inspect her mother's arm, pushing and prodding the skin. "You're here with me right now."

"Here in this lighthouse, yes, but this place is different from any-where else in Seabrook. The town has a fear of this building, a fear that stretches back many years."

"I know. Ryan told me all about what happened with the light-house keeper and how everyone thought the tower might be haunted, but what's that got to do with you?"

"It's how I was able to sneak in. That fear the town has—the fear that made the lighthouse off-limits for Ryan and for everyone else—

created a blind spot, a sort of hidden back door into this snow globe. Ryan's fear of what might be lurking behind these walls makes it the one place his spirit can't see into, the one place where his defenses are weak."

"You're invisible in here, is what you're saying?"

"From the gaze of Ryan's spirit—yes."

Amy took a long look around the lantern room, shaking her head, somewhat shocked that she was actually comprehending any of this.

"But it didn't make it any easier to reach out and make contact," her mother continued. "Even though I found a way to slip in here unnoticed, I'm powerless to help. Switching on the lamp and pointing it at your hotel was the most I could do, but then half the town saw what I'd done, and it kicked off an enormous fuss. And then this morning you went to see Ryan, and the two of you struck up a bond, and that only destabilized things even further. From the way the people behave and interact, all those strange looks you've been getting, even down to the flow of time itself—your presence here has seriously disrupted everything."

"The flow of time?" Amy shot back a confused look. "What does *that* mean?"

Given the explanation that was to follow, Amy soon wished she hadn't asked. As it turned out, this place had been confining Ryan by repeating the same twenty-four hours over and over, trapping him inside a cruel loop. The loop began at the point when he arrived back at the ranch after rescuing his horse, and then restarted the next day at three minutes to eleven, the exact time he had perished. But when Amy showed up, it became impossible for this cycle to continue. Because she had come from a point two months in the future, time inside Ryan's world was forced to start marching forward. The day she and Ryan had spent together, the festival—these things were never meant to happen.

"Can't you see, Amy? Your arrival put a big crack in his snow globe, and it's only getting bigger."

Amy glanced up at the sky, at the black ceiling of thunder and rain covering the town. "And if it breaks? What then?"

"Think not *if*, but *when*," her mother said through gritted teeth. "The cracks are spreading; the damage is accelerating. It won't be long now before this illusion completely breaks down, and when that happens Ryan will be forced to confront what really happened to him that night out by the cliffs."

"But isn't that for the best? Isn't it better that he learns the truth than go on like he is now, pretending that nothing happened?"

"Absolutely, but the question is whether he can accept that truth and leave this place behind, or if his spirit will kick us out and double down on this illusion, reforging the town, but this time with stronger walls, which would make it almost impossible for Ryan to ever get out, or anyone else to get in."

Amy gave a little shudder. "That could really happen? He could actually end up trapped in here forever?"

Her mother nodded and gave a slight grimace. "Remember, his spirit believes it *is* helping by keeping him stuck in this fantasy. That's why he's been stuck in here for two months already, and that's why—if he isn't able to find a way to make peace with his fate—he could be stuck in here a lot longer—possibly an eternity."

Amy dropped her head, her stomach plunging at the thought of Ryan being stuck in here . . . alone . . . reliving the same twenty-four hours . . . never being able to escape.

"Then why isn't *someone* doing something to help him?" she asked. "Where's *his* mother? Why isn't she helping him the same way that you're helping me?"

"She's been trying, sweetheart, but for her it's even harder—she can't even get inside the lighthouse, never mind the town. Chloe, her daughter, was able to use her unique connection to Ryan to infiltrate the snow globe, but it's not as if she can reveal who she is and tell her brother what's going on."

"Hang on—did you just say *Chloe*? The same Chloe, as in . . ."

"As in the young girl you met this morning, the one who helped you get out of the hotel."

"You mean Chloe is actually Ryan's *sister*?" Amy blurted out. "His *unborn* sister?"

"This is a lot to take in, I know."

Another understatement, she thought.

Amy glanced out the window and stared into empty space, in desperate need of a break. She felt utterly dazed, almost as though her head was about to burst. She didn't know what was more alarming: the nature of the information being heaped upon her, or the fact that she was actually taking it in. Some of it, she had to admit, was even starting to make sense. She understood why Ryan had found himself in this predicament. She had seen for herself the depth of love he had for his father, the sacrifices he had made to protect him from the mess they were in. That Ryan had unwittingly created this charade didn't surprise her in the slightest. Even in death, he had done what he needed to do to stay with his father—if only just to pretend he could still keep him safe.

But that still didn't make any of this right. No matter how heartfelt the reasons might be, confronting the truth was more important than living this lie. Ryan *deserved* to know the truth. He deserved to be with his mother and his sister, deserved to be able to move on in peace, not be condemned to eternity inside a prison that wasn't even real. But how could he break free? It was obvious he needed help, but could Amy and her mother do anything? Could they make any difference at all? Amy wasn't sure, but she knew that Ryan deserved nothing less than her best effort to try. This entire town, this fantasy, though borne out of Ryan's best intentions, borne out of the love that he held for his father, *needed* to come to an end.

"All right, Mom, I have no idea how any of this works, but Ryan means a lot to me and I can't just stand by and leave him to suffer like this." Amy stood a little taller, lifted her a chin a little higher. "Is there anything we can do?"

"There is, but we don't have much time."

"Then tell me what it is. I want to do whatever I can."

Her selfless words drew a smile of pride from her mother. "First, you must get yourself to the ranch. The most important thing is that you find Ryan, and quickly. He's going to need you, Amy. He's going to need you by his side."

Amy felt her heartrate quicken. "All right, and when I get there, what then? What exactly am I supposed to say? 'Hi, Ryan, sorry I ran out on you before. Oh, by the way, you died, and you've been living in wonderland for the past two months, and the little girl you met this morning is actually your unborn sister?'" Just saying those words aloud had Amy helplessly shaking her head. "He's going to think I'm crazy, Mom. I mean, listen to how that sounds."

Before she got an answer, a commotion rocked the sky: more thunder, more lightning, this time centered to the north. Her mother's face dimmed with worry.

"At this rate, you won't need to tell him anything," she said. "This storm is exactly the same as the one the night Ryan died, and it's only getting worse. This world is unraveling fast. Ryan's on the verge of discovering everything out for himself. Any moment now, the truth is about to be revealed. What you need to do is make sure you're there with him when it happens."

"That's it?" Amy asked, surprised by the simplicity of the plan. "How long do we have?"

"Not long, but you must listen carefully—" Her mother stooped her head and lowered her voice. "From here on out, you need to be extra vigilant—no talking to anyone. I'll do what I can to help from here, but there's little chance of you standing up to the scrutiny of someone's gaze, not with the information you now know, so it's very important you try not to let anyone see you outside this lighthouse."

"But the ranch is miles away. How am I supposed to get there?"

"Take your father's car. You'll find it waiting for you on the same street, parked near the hotel."

"It's still here?"

"Yes."

"But keys . . . I need keys."

"They're in your room."

"No, all Dad's stuff is gone."

"You'll find the keys if you look for them. Trust me."

"They're just going to magically appear?"

"Remember, none of this is real. It may be Ryan's illusion, but you're a part of it too, and you have more control in here than you think." She stood and helped Amy up. "Now, come on, you need to start moving."

Amy swallowed and stared at the ground. She wanted to stay and find out exactly what her mother meant, but it was clear from the urgency in her voice that they couldn't linger in the lighthouse any longer. She followed her mother's gaze and glanced at the stairwell, trying to rally her thoughts.

"I'm worried, Mom. What if I mess this up? What if I somehow make everything worse?"

"Amy, what you don't realize is that you're the reason he has this chance in the first place. The connection forged between the two of you changed everything. You've awoken his heart. You helped him open up about his father and free him from the guilt he's been carrying all these years. You've given him a glimpse of the world beyond Seabrook, a glimpse of a future that he didn't even know existed. Because of you, he's been empowered to fight, and now all you need to do is be by his side and help him take that very last step. Go to him, Amy. Go help him shatter this snow globe into a thousand pieces."

Amy nodded and took a deep breath. She turned her attention to what lay ahead, to the prospect of venturing outside and making her way back to the ranch. She was visualizing the two previous journeys, reminding herself of where she needed to go, the roads she needed to take, when a new problem presented itself: Wasn't helping Ryan break free going to create a dilemma for her and her mother?

Without this town and the protection of its lighthouse, where were the two of them supposed to go?

"Mom, wait—once I've seen Ryan, how will I be able to find you?"

"Sweetheart, you won't."

Amy froze. "What?"

"I'm afraid this is where we must say our goodbyes."

"No, Mom. *No.* You can't be serious."

"I'm sorry, Amy. I wish we had longer."

"But this isn't fair! This can't be it! *This* is all I get to see of you?"

"It's how it has to be. Once this is over, we need to go our separate ways. It won't be possible for us to see each other again."

"No . . ." Amy shook her head, the weight of this news too heavy for her heart. She collapsed to the ground, every part of her aching. "I can't do that. I don't want to say goodbye, not yet. You only just got here. There's still so much I want to say."

"Amy, please . . ." Her mother knelt down and brushed Amy's hair back, put her hands on her cheeks, though this did nothing to distract from the knifelike agony burning inside Amy's chest. "It's not goodbye forever, it's only goodbye for now."

"No, I don't want to leave you like this. I don't want to go home."

"Don't say that, sweetheart."

"I mean it. I don't want you to leave me again," she cried, choking on the words, her throat swollen in despair. "I can't do this again."

"You've been so brave through all of this, Amy. I couldn't be more proud of you."

"Stop it. Stop talking like that. There has to be something else I can do to stay with you."

"No, Amy, don't—"

"But this is *my* choice, isn't it? Why can't I just decide to stay with you just a little bit longer?"

"Please, it doesn't work like that."

"I don't care how it works! I have to see you one more time before I go. I *have* to!"

"You don't know what you're asking. You don't know what that means. It's not safe for you to say things like that, it's not safe for you to linger."

"I don't care what it means! I've already lost you once without saying goodbye properly, and I'm not doing it again! I'm not!"

"Amy . . ."

"*Please, Mom!*"

Amy's plea echoed loudly throughout the tiny room. They stood in silence, staring at each other, the beam of the lighthouse sweeping across them, illuminating the desperation on Amy's face, and the heartache on her mother's.

"All right," her mother whispered. "After you've been with Ryan, I'll find a way to see you."

"You will? You really mean it?"

She bowed her head and closed her eyes. "I will."

Amy lunged forward and threw her arms around her. "You have to promise. Please. You have to promise me you'll be there."

"I promise. You have my word. Come now, it's time for you to leave. Before it's too late." She grabbed Amy's hand and led her around the lamp. They paused by the uppermost step of the staircase, both pondering the passage down.

"Time is running out. Ryan really needs you. His mother, his sister, they need you too. Go to him, Amy. Go as fast as you can."

Amy took her pendant from her pocket and tied it around her neck. Taking a deep breath, she hugged her mother one last time, drawing from her whatever strength she could, then cast her teary eyes down the plunging stairwell, her thoughts shifting from her mom to the world waiting outside, to the town of Seabrook, to the ranch, to the boy she now desperately needed to see.

33

*A*MY HAD BEEN outside for only a few minutes, but already her mind was playing tricks. The disembodied notion of being in two places at once was really messing with her head, as was the fact that she no longer had the protection of the lighthouse, which left her feeling as though a giant spotlight had been thrust upon her, as though a thousand eyes were now watching her every step.

She sensed it as she ran back down the beach, the weight of this strange world pressing down upon her, its suspicion penetrating the air. It was as though every gust of wind was on the verge of swallowing her whole.

One step at a time, she told herself. *Just take one step at a time. First find the car keys, then worry about what happens next.*

Running as fast as she could against the barreling wind, Amy made it back down the beach, over the dunes, and into the street that led to the town square. The hotel loomed ahead on her left, the fountain and the grassy plaza—still a windswept mess of rubbish from the festival—just beyond. Thankfully, the sidewalks were all empty and the square looked deserted. *So far, so good.*

Staying hidden in shadow, she approached the hotel and crept along the wall, then snuck up the fire escape and climbed back into her room. Making as little noise as possible, Amy checked her bag, opened all the drawers, peered beneath the bed and the couch, looked everywhere she could think to look. She then spied the magazines on the coffee table, the ones she had been flicking through earlier, and to her relief she found the keys hiding at the bottom of the pile. They made a heavenly jingle as she scooped them into her hands. But when Amy turned to the window, preparing to make a swift exit, the room suddenly fell silent.

Amy didn't need to turn around to know she wasn't alone. A group of people had somehow infiltrated the room. She could see them in the reflection of the glass. They were standing by the door. Half a dozen of them, each focused on her with that same empty, ominous glare.

"Leave . . ." one of them said.

Another pointed a finger.

"Leave . . ."

They began moving in her direction. It took every ounce of control Amy had not to scream. She made a desperate lunge for the window, grabbed the handle, and pulled hard on it, but the lock had jammed and wouldn't budge. In a panic, she even tried smashing the pane with her elbow, but the glass wouldn't break. As the intruders were approaching, as Amy watched them in the reflection, converging on her, only a few feet away, the beam from the lighthouse swung in her direction and flooded the room with light. The intruders stumbled backward, shielding their eyes. Then Amy heard the window slide back open, and she felt a small hand tug on her arm.

"Saving your butt three times in one night. You owe me!"

"Oh my God, Chloe. *Get me out of here!*"

"Come on, let's go!"

Amy climbed out the window and followed Chloe along the fire escape. They leapt down the stairs several steps at a time. When they reached the sidewalk, Chloe yanked Amy's arm and pulled her into the middle of the street. Rain swirled around them, the wind roaring in their ears.

"Where's the car?" Chloe yelled.

Amy fumbled for the keys and pressed down; from out of the darkness, a hundred yards away, a pair of orange lights blinked back at them.

"There it is! Come with me, Chloe!"

"No, I can't. It's up to you now."

"Come, please!" Amy tugged on Chloe's arm, but Chloe stepped away and shook her head.

"I can't, Amy! This place is falling apart. I need to find somewhere to hide. You're the only one who can help my brother!"

Behind them, the crowd began spilling out of the hotel. They had spotted Chloe and Amy and were charging toward them, blocking the path to the car. Chloe gave Amy a hard shove.

"You're on your own, Amy!" she cried out. "Go find him! You can do it! I believe in you!" Without any warning, Chloe threw her hands in the air, hollered at the crowd, then began running in the opposite direction. "Just get in the car and start driving!" she yelled, her voice fading into the distance. "Go!"

The crowd swerved and followed Chloe down the street and out of the town square, gifting Amy a few precious seconds, which she was determined not to waste. She sprinted to her dad's car and jumped straight in. She shoved the keys into the ignition and switched on the engine, but she was so desperate to get away that she planted her foot too hard and lost control. The car roared forward, veered to the right, then mounted the curb and plowed straight into the town square's grassy plaza. Amy shrieked as she yanked the wheel this way and that while the car skidded across the lawn and crashed through abandoned food stands and arcade stalls. Once she had made it to the other side of the square and regained control, she slammed her foot down on the accelerator and sped out of town. She wasn't stopping for anything.

—◦◦◦—

The roads leading to the ranch were in even worse condition than before. Hunched over the wheel, Amy drove as fast as she could without sending the car into a ditch or crashing into one of the many fallen trees. Finally, she rounded the last bend and saw the entrance to Ryan's ranch.

Okay, here goes nothing . . .

Amy steered the car through the gap, zoomed straight up the driveway, made a turn right over a small crest, then made a second turn and caught her first glimpse of the house: a sliver of its roof. But then she saw something she wasn't expecting: flashing lights. She slammed on the brakes and lunged forward. An ambulance was parked directly in front of the house, its rear doors wide open, rooftop lights silently spinning.

What the hell. What's happened? Was someone hurt . . . ?

There was no way of knowing without getting closer to the house, but how was she going to do that when there were people inside? They might have already heard her coming up the driveway.

This was a problem.

A big problem.

Slipping off her seat belt, Amy swung open her door and leapt from the car. She jumped the fence and ran into the field, taking cover behind a low ridge, then popped her head up and peeked at the house. The lights were on and the front door was open, but there was no sign of movement. She was still too far away. With the wind and rain lashing her face, it was impossible to see anything. She needed to get closer.

Rising to her feet but still staying low, Amy made her way to the edge of the forecourt and hid behind a tree. She lay flat on the grass and wiggled around the trunk, closer to the fence, squinting through a narrow gap between two slats of wood. She still couldn't spot any activity. She contemplated scaling the fence and sneaking a look through a window when suddenly a figure stepped out onto the porch—a tall man wearing a cap and dark-blue uniform with badges on his sleeves—a paramedic. He was walking backward holding the end of a stretcher while another man, identically dressed, held the other end. There was a fluorescent-yellow body bag resting on the stretcher. Amy stared in horror. *Who was sealed inside the bag? Ryan? His father?* Her mother had given no warning that something like this might happen. Did this signal the end? Had Amy failed before even making contact with Ryan? Had she not made it to him quick enough?

Sadness and panic tugged inside her chest as she watched the paramedics descend from the porch and load the stretcher into the ambulance. While one paramedic went to the driver's side door, the other returned to the house, and that's when Amy saw Ryan.

He emerged from the house and stumbled down the steps, visibly distraught. Collapsing to the ground with his arms around his stomach, he rocked back and forth as though his whole body were writhing with pain. His cries pierced the air. Amy was desperate to rush to his aid, but it was impossible with the paramedics still on the property. She couldn't risk being seen, couldn't risk giving herself away.

But then, without warning, just as one of the paramedics was walking over to console him, Ryan jumped to his feet and sprinted to the barn. He disappeared inside. Amy lay frozen on the grass, her heart in her throat, each second passing by unbearably slowly as she waited for him to reappear. But when he did, the situation only got worse—he was on the back of a horse. He came charging out at breakneck speed, so fast that it was only a matter of seconds before he had jumped the fence, galloped across the field, and vanished into the night.

Amy acted without thinking. She jumped up and screamed, "No! Ryan! Come back!" But it was too late. Ryan was gone. And all her outburst had done was alert the paramedics to her presence.

Amy nervously turned toward them, and they turned to face her. After a long stare, they climbed the fence and began marching into the field. Amy felt a strange sensation take hold in her body: an emptiness spreading through her limbs. She looked down at her hands and saw tiny specks of light glowing on her palm, little dots flickering, just like her mother's arm before it had disappeared. Was this it? Was this how it happened? Was she already being pulled away from Ryan's world?

No, please . . . not yet . . .

She frantically evaluated her options, which seemed to be dwindling fast. Her only option was to get to Ryan, but there was no hope of catching him now, not anymore, not unless she too could somehow get on a horse . . .

Amy looked toward the barn. Stealing her one last chance, she broke to the right and made a daring dash across the field, cutting in front of the stony-faced paramedics, who promptly spun around and took up pursuit. She flung herself over the fence and ran across the forecourt, straight for the barn. She darted inside. Among the rows of stalls, one horse stood out: Little Dipper. The horse's eyes were large and alert, and her head was craned over the edge of her door, seemingly eager to attract Amy's attention.

Amy remembered what she'd been told, that this horse trusted no one, to be wary and keep her distance, but there was something about the intensity of Little Dipper's gaze that made Amy believe she was the horse for the job.

"You know where he's gone, don't you?" Amy said, rushing up to her. "Will you take me to him?" Little Dipper's ears pricked forward. She blinked her brown eyes and pawed at the ground, swishing her tail from side to side. That was as good an answer as any.

Throwing the door wide open, Amy hurried inside the stall. There was no saddle, no reins, no way she could climb up. She heard footsteps; the paramedics had just entered the barn and were advancing down the central alley, headed right for her. Behind her was a bale of hay. She dragged it over, climbed up, and launched herself onto Little Dipper's back. She then grabbed a clump of Little Dipper's mane in either hand and squeezed the horse's belly with her calves.

"Go!" she yelled. "Go, Little Dipper! Go now!"

Little Dipper obliged with explosive power, rearing onto her hind legs and charging out of her stall at speed. The horse ran straight for the barn's wide double doors, slicing between the two paramedics and knocking them sideways.

Amy had never felt anything like it—the exhilarating rush of reaching full gallop in a matter of seconds. She stuck her head down as they cleared the fence and raced across the field, bracing when she saw the dense wall of trees looming ahead. Little Dipper maintained the same furious pace, plowing headlong into the forest. She galloped hard and let nothing slow her down, weaving between trunks and leaping over every bush and swollen brook as though she had done it a thousand times before. Amy, who was getting lashed by every branch and twig along the way, did her best just to hang on. She prayed that wherever they were headed wasn't far. They may have escaped the ranch, but she was on borrowed time; the specks of light on her skin were glowing brighter and brighter by the second. Any moment this could all be over.

When Little Dipper finally eased off the pace, Amy lifted her head and looked around. The tree cover had disappeared. She could hear the ocean. She realized she was back at the cliffs. *He came out here? Really?* She spun around in every direction, searching for where Ryan might be, when the significance of this location suddenly became obvious.

Of course, this was the spot! This was where he fell.

But Amy was nearly out of time—her skin was shining ever brighter.

"I don't see him, Little Dipper! Where is he!"

They rode up and down the cliffs, desperately searching for him, when suddenly Amy caught a faint cry on the wind and spotted a shadowy blur moving in the darkness.

"There, Lil' Dip! Go!"

When they reached Ryan, he was alone, kneeling on the ground with his head buried in his hands. His own horse was nowhere to be seen. Amy jumped off Little Dipper's back and crouched beside him. She put her hand on his shoulder.

"Ryan, are you okay?" When he didn't stir, she gave his shoulder a squeeze. "It's me, it's Amy."

After a few seconds of silence, he mumbled into his hands, "It's all my fault."

"No, don't say that."

"My father's gone. He's dead. It's all because of me."

"This isn't your fault," Amy yelled, raising her voice above the howl of the wind. "None of this is your fault."

"If only I'd told him. If only I'd done the right thing. I could've stopped this. I could've saved him."

"Look up, Ryan. Look at me, please."

"It's over. There's nothing left. What am I going to do? I've got nothing. I've got no one."

"You've got me! I'm here! And I can help. Here, take my hand."

Ryan looked up. His eyes were bloodshot. He moved to take Amy's hand, but then he saw the luminescence of her skin.

"What the hell?"

"Ryan, don't freak out."

"What is that? . . . What's going on here?"

"It's nothing, it's just—"

"What are you? *Who* are you, *really*?" He jumped to his feet and began blindly stepping back.

"It's me, Ryan, it's Amy."

"No, no . . . you're not Amy. You're not her."

"I am! I'm the girl you spent the day with, remember? I'm the same girl!" She reached out her hand, but he drew back even farther, dangerously close to the cliff.

"No, there's something wrong. You're lying to me. Stay back. Don't come any closer!"

"Ryan, stop moving!" Amy pleaded. "I'm here to help you! Trust me, please! Take my hand!"

"No! I don't . . . I . . . I don't understand. I don't know what's happening to me."

Amy could feel the ground sloping away, could sense they were perilously close to the edge.

"Ryan, *please stop. This is dangerous!*"

"I said *stay back*! You shouldn't be here. You don't *belong here*!"

"And you don't belong here either! Listen to me, Ryan, this isn't where you're meant to be!"

Ryan shook his head. "I don't know *who* or *what* you are, but I want you to get the hell away from me, *right now*!"

Amy refused and reached out her hand again, only this time, while making his retreat, Ryan went back too far and stepped off the edge.

"*Ryan!*"

Amy lunged and caught his outstretched hand, but it wasn't enough to break his momentum and stop him from tumbling backward. She hit the ground but somehow managed to hang on to him, halting his plunge, except now his body was dangling midair. Amy barely had the strength to hold on.

"Don't let me fall! Please don't let me fall . . ."

"I'm not letting you fall, Ryan! *Hang on!*"

Amy grabbed his arm with her other hand and tightened her grip, but the weight of him was dragging her along the ground and pulling her off the edge too. She dug her feet in but couldn't stop sliding. Her arms felt like they were on fire, every muscle burning as she strained to stop him from plummeting to the sea below. She needed to pull him up, needed to get to her feet, but she didn't have the strength to stand. All she could do was hold on tight and try her damnedest not to let go.

34

IT WAS THE STRANGEST THING—one minute Ryan was hanging off the edge of the cliff, clinging for dear life, and the next he was back on solid ground, in the seat of his horse. His left hand was holding the reins and his right was clutching a soggy length of rope with a noose at one end, which he was swinging above his head. He became even more confused when he saw Little Dipper standing in front of him, no more than fifteen yards away. She was stomping the ground and tossing her head, ready to run at any moment. The whole scene gave him an acute sense of déjà vu. It all felt so very familiar. But the weirdest part was that Ryan didn't seem to have any control. He had his senses but no power over his muscles. Everything was happening independently of him. He couldn't turn his head or shift around, couldn't even move his eyes. All he could do was watch, a mere spectator inside his own body.

Certain this must be some kind of dream, he quickly figured out what was going on—he was witnessing a replay of what took place two nights ago. It was the night Little Dipper bolted, the night he'd chased her out to these cliffs. He recognized the scene he'd been dropped into—it was when he'd finally found her, the moment he'd tried to lasso her and bring her in to safety. He had needed three attempts to get the rope around her neck, and that's exactly how the scene unfolded—he watched his first throw fall short, the second bounce off her stomach, and the third hit its mark—precisely as he remembered. Next, he pulled hard on the rope, tightening the noose around Little Dipper's neck, and then he looped the other end of the rope securely around his wrist.

But then his flashback unraveled differently from how he remembered. The moment the knot snapped around Little Dipper's neck, she thrashed her head and threw her weight in the opposite direction.

"Ease up, girl! Stop fighting!"

Every lunge for freedom put more and more tension on the rope, stretching Ryan's arm and burning his skin. "Don't do this, Little Dipper. . . . Work with me."

It was strange hearing his own voice, hearing himself say words he never recalled saying. Stranger still was how fast his heart was racing. All these new sensations, these emotions, these memories . . .

This wasn't how it happened at all. Or was it . . . ?

The rope coiled around his wrist was beginning to twist and tighten against his flesh. His voice sounded more and more desperate. "Come on, Lil' Dip! *Please!*"

The edge of the cliff was nearby. Ryan could hear the roar of the ocean, could sense the vast chasm of air lurking in the darkness. He was doing everything he could to maintain control, but he was no match for Little Dipper's power and size. His strength was fading fast.

Then lightning struck close by, setting fire to a thicket of bushes. Little Dipper bucked wildly in the air and took off so fast that Ryan got ripped clean off his horse. He landed hard on his shoulder and then everything became a blur of mud and dirt as Little Dipper charged off at speed, dragging him behind. There was nothing Ryan could do. He never stood a chance. He screamed Little Dipper's name, tried to untangle himself, tried to wriggle loose, but the rope was wound so tight it was impossible to break free. Then Little Dipper must have seen that she was within a hair's breadth of the cliff because she suddenly swerved and ran the other way, sending Ryan skidding sideways—straight for the edge.

Without any warning, the ground disappeared. Ryan felt himself falling. He didn't have time to scream. He plummeted for a few frightening seconds before the rope went taut, at which point his arm stiffened and he slammed into the cliff face. The collision reverberated throughout his body, spreading pain to every bone and muscle. He dangled like a rag doll for a few seconds, too dazed to move, but was jolted back to his senses when the rope coiled around his wrist began to unwind. His arm was slipping. As dread flooded through him, he lunged for the cliff face, and with his free hand he desperately tried to find something to grab hold of, but this only put more pressure on the rope, causing it to unravel faster. He frantically struggled, clawed at the dirt, tried kicking his feet to gain a foothold, even screamed at Little Dipper to move away in the hope she could drag him back up, but the weight of his hanging body was too great. The knot loosened some more, Ryan slipped even farther, and he knew he couldn't stop what was about to happen next . . . when the knot finally came undone.

The speed of the drop forced his heart up into his throat. Ryan closed his eyes, tried to brace himself, but the impact of hitting the water from two hundred feet sucked the wind right out of him. He plunged into the ocean so deep and so fast that he never had a hope of making it back up to the surface. Seawater poured in a torrent into his mouth and straight down his throat, quickly plugging his windpipe and spilling into his lungs. An enormous pressure built inside his chest, an immense force unlike anything he'd ever known, and in his head he heard himself cry out for help, a desperate plea that no one would hear.

Dad...

And then there was silence, and all was perfectly still.

35

*A*MY STRAINED IN AGONY. Both her arms felt like they were getting pulled out of their sockets. She was perched halfway over the edge of the cliff, her grip on Ryan loosening by the second.

"Hold on to me!" she yelled.

"You can't do this, Amy! You have to let go!"

"*What?*"

Ryan looked down at the ocean, then back at her.

"If you don't let go, you'll fall too . . ."

"Forget it!"

As the rain thundered down and as Ryan slipped even more, Amy noticed the specks of light on her skin were multiplying, rapidly turning into a burning glow that was traveling up her arms and spreading across her body. The emptiness she had felt returned with a vengeance, signaling that her time was fast coming to an end. She was acutely aware what would happen if Ryan fell; she would be banished from this place and Ryan would remain, returned to the beginning of his loop, condemned to this prison without any possibility of escape. If she let him go then his fate would be sealed, but Amy refused to accept that there was nothing she could do. Even if her time was up and all her chances had been spent, she wasn't letting go without a fight.

"Amy, listen to me! There's no way you can pull me back up, and there's no way I'm taking you with me." Ryan then used his other hand to pry away Amy's grip, which caused him to drop farther. "You *have* to let me go!"

"No!" Amy screamed, and she reattached her hand to his arm, but not before he had slipped down even more.

"Don't do this!" he yelled.

Amy shook her head in defiance, tears spilling from her eyes, her skin almost translucent as she fought to hold on, fought to stay in Ryan's world. Her pendant hung low from her neck, and when Amy caught a glimpse of it swirling in the blustery wind, her mind was jolted back to what her mother had said in the lighthouse.

You have more control in here than you think.

A shiver came over her. Those words had made no sense at first, but Amy suddenly understood what they meant. The discovery of her pendant in the attic, the cab mysteriously appearing at the ranch gate—these weren't random coincidences, nor were they the work of Ryan's spirit, either. These events had led Amy to the lighthouse, where she had ultimately uncovered the truth. These events had helped *her*, not him. They were manifestations of *Amy's* spirit, her own attempt to fight back in a world in which she didn't belong— a world in which the rules could be *bent*. This was how her mother could shine a lamp that wasn't there, or how Chloe had been able to lift furniture around the room with such ease, or how she magically had all that money for the cab. Though this world felt tangible and real, it was just an illusion, and inside this illusion Amy had the power to exert her own influence, just like her mother did, just like Chloe did. All she needed to do was *believe* that she could.

"Ryan, hold on tight . . ."

"What are you doing!"

"I'm going to stand, I'm going to lift you up."

"Are you *crazy*? We'll both fall!" Ryan resisted and made a desperate attempt to wriggle free, but Amy had clenched her hands so tight that he couldn't shake her loose.

"This isn't a debate!" Amy shouted. "I'm about to save your ass, so *shut up and hold on!*"

Amy focused her mind, steeled her resolve, then drew a deep breath and began by bringing one leg forward. Her arms felt the downward pressure at once, but Amy was equal to it and dragged her other leg forward, forcing herself to her knees. Then, mustering her will and every scrap of strength she could, she closed her eyes, planted both feet, one after the other, and heaved Ryan out of the darkness, back to the surface.

They clambered away from the edge and fell to the ground, neither able to let go of the other. Ryan stared at Amy in dismay, needing a moment to find his voice.

"How . . . did you do that?"

"Never mind that," Amy said. "Are you all right?" She set about inspecting him, patting his back, his shoulders, squeezing his arms, running her fingers through his hair, every square inch she could reach.

"I'm okay, I'm fine, but—" Ryan turned back around, hesitating as he gazed at the cliff.

"What is it, what's wrong?"

"Amy, while I was hanging there, something happened to me."

"What do you mean?"

"I saw something."

Amy's eyes flicked back and forth between his. "Saw . . . what?"

"I wouldn't even know how to describe it. It was like a vision, or maybe some kind of dream—only, it doesn't feel like a dream at all because I can remember every second of it. It happened right here," he said softly, trepidation creeping into his voice. "It was when I rescued Little Dipper, except it didn't happen the way I remember it, and now . . . well, this is going to sound crazy—"

"It's okay. Say it."

"Now it feels like I've got all these new memories etched into my mind, and somehow they feel more real than the old ones." Ryan took another long, pondering look at the cliff, hesitating before he went on. "Amy, I think something's happened to me."

Amy leaned in closer. "I think I know the meaning behind your new memories. Ryan, I don't know how to say this—"

"It's okay, Amy. I can take it from here."

The new voice gave them both a jolt. They spun around and were confronted with an all-too-familiar face.

"*Chloe?*"

"Hi, Ryan. Hey, Amy," Chloe said, casually greeting them with a smile. "Fancy seeing you guys."

Ryan raised his eyebrows. "What are you doing out here? Where did you come from?"

Chloe's toothy grin grew wider as she exchanged a glance with Amy, who also didn't know what to make of her sudden appearance.

"Chloe? What's going on?"

Chloe gave Amy a wink. "You did amazing."

"You mean . . . it worked?"

"It did."

"What worked?" Ryan gave them both an exasperated look. "Chloe? Amy? Will one of you tell me exactly what is going on here?"

Chloe thrust out her hand to Ryan, who reluctantly took it, then reached for Amy's hand too. After pulling them to their feet, she brought them into a small huddle and told them to close their eyes.

"Um, why?" Ryan asked.

"This will only take a second," she said excitedly.

"What in the blazes is that supposed—"

"On the count of three," she announced loudly. "One. Two—"

36

*T*HE WORLD DISSOLVED around them, everything went dazzlingly bright, and for a brief moment Amy felt a rush of weightlessness.

"Three!"

At the sound of Chloe's last count, everyone's feet found solid ground. Amy opened her eyes and saw that they were no longer standing on grass but sand. Disoriented, she raised her head and spun 360 degrees, and her mouth fell open when she realized they had been whisked away from the cliffs and transported down to the beach. An impossible view of the bay stretched out before her—dunes on one side, waves crashing on the other, and the familiar sight of the lighthouse standing tall in the distance. The time of day had changed too; the sun was high in the sky and no trace of the storm remained, not one single cloud.

"Pretty cool, right!" Chloe said.

"Uh-huh," Amy mumbled, deciding her clifftop rescue kind of

paled in comparison. She was mighty impressed by how Chloe could pull off such a feat.

Ryan, however, didn't seem at all entertained by what was going on and had turned a shade of ghostly pale. He let go of both Amy's and Chloe's hands.

"Enough," he said, stumbling away. "I don't know what kind of game you two are playing at, but this really isn't funny. Someone needs to start talking, right now."

Chloe reached over and took back Ryan's hand, then turned him around and pointed her finger down the beach, at a woman standing in the distance.

"There, look," she said, "can you see her?"

"Who is it?" Ryan asked, glancing at the mysterious woman.

"That's my mother."

"Your mother?"

"She's been waiting to speak with you."

Ryan shifted his bewildered gaze straight to Amy. "You know what's going on, don't you?" He studied her closely. "I know you do. I can see it on your face."

"I do," she admitted.

"Will you please just tell me?"

"I'm sorry, I can't." Amy stood on her tiptoes, squeezed his hand, and whispered in his ear, "You need to listen to Chloe. Go and talk to her mother. This'll all make sense soon. I promise."

Ryan stood still for a moment, then turned and looked back at the woman, who had her hand up in the air, waving for him to join her by the water's edge.

"All right, I'll talk to her. But, for the record, I'm only doing it because I'm finding all of this extremely strange and I'd *really* like to know what's going on."

After he shoved his hands in his pockets and set off, Chloe leaned over to Amy.

"Well done," she whispered. "I knew you could do it."

But Amy wasn't so quick to agree. Declaring this a success was a little premature, she thought, particularly when Ryan had yet to realize the woman he was walking toward was his mother. All Amy could think about were the emotions she had experienced when she had confronted her own mother—the confusion, the disbelief, the heart-pounding shock. She had been so scared she had even tried to run. She hoped Ryan wouldn't react the same way—or worse, reject the news of his fate entirely—because if he did, what would that mean for his snow globe?

"Isn't there still a chance this could all go wrong?" Amy asked. "What if he freaks out? Will all of this have been for nothing?"

"Don't worry, we're out of danger now. Ryan's already been given back his memories—all that's left is for Mom to explain to him what they mean. Time didn't reset. The town's still here, we're still here, and that's the important bit."

"We're still stuck in his snow globe?"

"For now, yes."

"But I thought this town was supposed to disappear? Wasn't that the whole point of him finding out what had happened—to break him out of here?"

"It was, and the town *will* disappear—actually, look, it's already beginning." Chloe scooped up some sand, held out her arm, and let the grains sprinkle out of her fist. While most fell to the beach, some grains flickered and evaporated into thin air, much like what had happened to Amy's mother when she had stuck her arm outside the lighthouse.

"See?" Chloe said. "Bit by bit this place is fading away. There's no one inside any of the buildings. All the people are gone. The town's just an empty shell now, no one left in it but us."

Amy gave a panicked look toward the lighthouse. "Wait, does that mean my mom's not here anymore?"

"Don't worry, she knows how to find you. But first we need to wait till Ryan's spoken with Mom, and that could take a while, so we might as well get comfortable."

Sitting on the sand, their legs crossed and the sun on their backs, Amy and Chloe kept a close eye on Ryan as he made his way down the beach. Neither said a word as his trail of footprints grew; instead, they collectively held their breaths as they waited to see how he would cope with the somber news about to be revealed to him. Part of Amy wished she could be with him, standing beside him, holding his hand, doing anything she could to soften the blow, and yet at the same time she knew this was something he needed to go through on his own.

"Look," Chloe said. "Something's happening."

Ryan had come to a standstill. His mother wasn't moving either. The two of them were standing some twenty or thirty yards apart— too far for Amy to know for sure if Ryan had recognized her or not.

"Do you think he knows who it is yet?" Amy asked.

Chloe dug her fingers into the sand and repeated her trick from before; this time, fewer grains fell to the ground and a larger proportion vanished. "Yep, he knows."

"Wait, why is the sand disappearing so quickly?"

"Because Ryan's starting to let go. And once they start talking and he begins to understand what's happened, it's only going to get faster."

"But I *am* going to be able to see him before that happens, right?"

"You won't have long. By the time Ryan's done talking to Mom, you might only have a few minutes. That's the one problem with helping him get out of here, Amy—there's no longer any reason for this place to exist."

Amy tensed up at the thought. She understood the situation; she knew she and Ryan would be going their separate ways, but that didn't stop her from wishing they had more time. A few lousy minutes were better than nothing, but it would never be enough, not to say everything she wanted to say.

Returning her attention to Ryan and his mother, Amy could see they were no longer stationary. His mother had started walking toward him, albeit very slowly, and Ryan had found his feet too, taking small steps in her direction. It seemed to Amy that Ryan was staying calm, though it was hard to be sure of anything from this far away. They continued edging toward each other, closing the gap with each small, tentative step, until finally they came together and fell into each other's arms. Amy instantly let go of a breath she hadn't even known she'd been holding.

"I think that's a good sign," she said.

Chloe smiled back, her blue eyes shining brighter from the tears welling inside. "I think so too."

Amy and Chloe watched from afar as Ryan and his mother sat down to begin a long chat. To pass the time, they drew pictures in the sand with seashells and spoke about their experience inside Ryan's snow globe, each sharing their relief that they had somehow been able to thwart disaster and save Ryan from eternal imprisonment. They only hoped that, despite the tragedy of his circumstances, he too would be relieved and find some comfort in the knowledge that he'd been set free.

As for how he was taking that news, it was hard to say. What Amy did notice, though, was the speed at which his snow globe was disappearing; by the time Ryan had stood and was ready to return, the sand on the beach had become a sparkling carpet with grains flickering and vanishing everywhere. Time was running out.

"Okay, it's our turn." Chloe leapt up and helped Amy to her feet too, ready to greet Ryan, who was now walking back up the beach.

"Thank you for everything you did," she said, wrapping her arms around Amy's neck. "I couldn't have wished for anyone better to get stuck in here with my brother. You made all the difference. Without you, we never would've gotten him out."

A lump stuck in Amy's throat. "I'm glad I could help. And I'm glad I got to meet you as well, Chloe. I'm going to miss you."

"Me too. I'll go say hi to Ryan quickly, then you can say goodbye, okay?"

Amy smiled. "Okay."

Chloe gave one last squeeze before peeling her arms away, spinning around, and running as fast as she could, straight for her brother.

When she reached him, Ryan was unable to contain his delight. He swept her up into his arms and swung her through the air, grinning and laughing as Chloe's rapturous screams rang out across the beach.

Watching the two of them brought tears to Amy's eyes. She was so happy for them both, but especially for Ryan; amid all this loss, what better news could there be than to discover he'd gained a little sister.

But sand was still vanishing at an alarming rate; the few minutes they had left were dwindling fast.

Chloe was true to her word and kept her time with Ryan short. As soon as Ryan placed her back on the ground, she tugged his arm and pointed in Amy's direction. Amy took her cue and set off toward him, and what started as a brisk walk soon became a run.

They collided in the middle and threw their arms around each other. Emotions took over and Amy instantly lost track of everything she had wanted to say. Words suddenly seemed so inadequate. All she could do was bury her head in the crook of Ryan's neck and try not to cry.

"Probably not how you thought this day was gonna go," he quipped.

Amy was too upset to see a light side to any of this. "I'm so sorry, Ryan."

"Hey, don't say that. You of all people have nothing to be sorry about." He drew her in closer, one hand up by her neck, the other ambling in a long, slow circle around her back. "Actually, it's me you need to forgive."

"For what?"

"Remember how you invited me to come see you in Portland?"

"Yeah."

"Well, in light of recent developments, I think I'm gonna need to take a rain check. Like, a really, really long rain check."

Amy didn't know whether to laugh or cry or punch him in the chest.

"Shut up," she said, sniffing and sobbing into his collar. "That's not funny."

"Not even a bit?"

"Nope."

"Please don't cry. Not for me. We can't change what's happened."

"But it's not fair. It's not fair that you lost your life and have to leave everything you love behind. You're one of the most amazing people I've ever met, Ryan. It isn't fair that this happened to you."

"But it happened, Amy, and there's nothing we can do to change that. And do you want to know something? This will sound a little strange, but once my mom explained everything, I actually felt a sense of calm, and of peace. This whole charade would've continued had you not helped me to uncover the truth. I would've been trapped in here forever, living a lie, never knowing that there was something waiting for me on the other side."

"But your dad, back in the real world . . . Now that you're gone, aren't you afraid of what will happen to him?"

"Of course I am. I'm terrified. Part of me wishes that all this was just a bad dream, that I could wake up and go downstairs and give my father a hug and pretend that everything was normal. Part of me wishes I could go on protecting him forever. But I know that I can't, not anymore. And I can't keep punishing myself for what I did either. The decisions I made, the secrets I kept—they were done out of love, because I believed they were the right thing to do. *You* helped me see that, Amy. Yes, I'm heartbroken that I have to leave him behind, and I'm frightened for what the future might hold for him, but if I've learned anything about my father, it's that he's a survivor. I have to believe that he'll find a way to keep going."

Amy wiped her nose, lifted her head. "So, if your mother told you everything, does that mean you know . . . about me?"

Ryan nodded. "Couldn't believe it at first. I heard all about your dad, how he's connected to all this, and then I heard what happened to you . . . you know, in the bathtub . . . and how you traveled from there to here and didn't know what this place was till Chloe told you to go inside the lighthouse. There's been a lot for me to digest, and I have to confess there's still plenty I don't get."

"Don't worry, I know the feeling."

Ryan gave her a smile. "But then I heard about what happened next, what you did for me, how you chose to help me, the brave decision you made to find your way back to the ranch. The only reason I'm free right now is because of you. Amy, my angel from Portland, how can I ever repay you?"

"Oh, Ryan, you don't owe me anything. I could've easily wrecked everything. I didn't have a clue what I was doing. If it weren't for Little Dipper, I don't even know how I would've found you."

"But you *did* find me. You never gave up. And somehow you managed to pull me back to safety. And now, instead of being stuck inside this prison, I get to leave. I get to be *free*. I owe you everything. I'm not sure how I can ever thank you."

"Please, it's me who should be thanking *you*."

"What for?"

"For the time we spent together. For giving me a day where I felt like a normal, functioning human being again. I haven't felt this way since losing my mom. I can't begin to tell you what it means to me to know there's some hope, to experience what it feels like to actually be happy again. Ryan, if anyone's the angel here, it's you."

"Oh, Amy." He brought his hand to her face, ran his thumb down the side of her nose, across her cheek, down to her lips, collecting stray tears along the way. "We did have a pretty good day, didn't we?"

"The best," she said, smiling.

Then came a drastic change. It was Amy who noticed it first, alerted by a stillness in the air and a strange absence of sound. When she turned her head, she saw the ocean had stopped moving. It was as though someone had hit a magic pause button and turned the sea into a giant frameless painting—every drop of water had been frozen, every wave and whitecap suspended in state. Not only that, but Chloe and Ryan's mother had vanished.

"Wait," Ryan said, suddenly confused. "What's going on?"

"This town you created, it's all about to disappear. You know that, right?"

"I know, yes, but . . . I didn't think it was going to start happening so soon. Can we control this? Is there something I can do to slow it down?"

Amy shook her head.

"How long do we have?" he asked.

"I was told we'd only get a few minutes, but I'm thinking it could be less." She drew his eyes to the ground, where the beach was now shining like a sheet of gold tinsel, with grains of sand fast glittering off into oblivion.

"Dammit," Ryan cried. "Why does it have to be so fast!"

"Because you don't need this place anymore."

"But what if I decide that I do need it? After all, it's my creation, right? Why can't I decide to stay with you a bit longer?"

"I don't think you can. That's not how it works. This was all created for you, not for us. It's served its purpose, Ryan. There's nothing we can do."

Ryan began looking around more frantically. "This isn't fair. A few minutes isn't enough."

"I wish we had more time too," Amy said. "I wish we had met . . . before."

"If only I could go back and change what happened. If only I'd locked Little Dipper away before the storm set in. If only I hadn't wrapped that damn rope around my damn wrist, then I'd still be—" But then a thought swept through Ryan's head, and his voice died in his throat.

"Ryan? What's wrong?"

"I just realized something."

"What?"

"That none of that actually matters, does it?"

"What do you mean?"

"I mean, if things hadn't turned out the way they did, then we wouldn't be standing here. If I hadn't fallen off that cliff, we never would have met. You and I were never going to cross paths. We were never part of fate's grand plan." He held Amy's gaze, a wistful look in his eyes. "Or maybe we were, and maybe one day was all we were ever meant to get."

Amy stepped toward him and fumbled for his hand, threading her fingers between his. "Whatever the universe had in store for us, I'm thankful we got this chance at all. Getting to meet you and seeing your beautiful ranch, riding the trails . . . you holding me in your arms. I'm going to remember the day we spent together forever."

"Me too, Amy."

He shifted even closer and lifted her chin, bringing her face closer to his. As they stared into each other's eyes, a warm breeze blew in from out of nowhere and began to swirl around them. Though gentle at first, it steadily built up speed, becoming so strong that it soon turned into a whirlpool of wind.

Alarm spread across Amy's face as she turned her gaze to the ground and saw a circular wall forming around their feet. Made up of sand, the wall was only an inch high, but it was shifting in a clockwise direction with the wind and gathering mass fast, like a miniature twister rising out of the ground. Using the beach as its fuel, it was sucking in the surrounding sand and growing in height, swirling with ferocious intensity. Within seconds, it had doubled in size and climbed above their ankles, right up to their knees.

"I'm scared, Ryan." Amy stepped in and pressed herself against him, hoping to get as far away as she could from the spinning vortex.

"It's going to be all right," he said as he put both arms around her and pulled her in close. "Just hold on to me. Everything will be all right."

They clung to each other as the wall of sand, which was now so dense they couldn't see out, shot up over their heads and straight into the sky. The inside of the wall was sparkling, and so was their skin, which was taking on the same shimmery translucency that Amy recognized from before. And just like before, she could feel an emptiness spreading through her body, a surreal disconnect between her mind and her limbs, a sign that her spirit was being pulled from this world. Only this time there would be no stopping it.

"Our time's nearly up," Ryan said. "I can feel it. I can feel this place inside me—it's disappearing. I want to kiss you, but I'm afraid of what will happen if I do."

Amy could see it when she lifted her head to face him, the strain in his expression, the struggle in his eyes, the tug-of-war between this world and the next.

"Amy, listen. I need to know if you'll do something for me. A favor."

"Anything."

"It's my father," he said, rushing his words as though every second might be their last. "When you get home, would you check on him?"

"Of course."

"I know he won't know who you are, and obviously he'll think you're crazy if you try to tell him about any of this, but all I want is for you to visit him. I want him to meet you, and I want you to make sure that he's okay."

"Yes, I can do that. I don't know how much help I can be to him, or what on earth I'll say, but I promise I'll go."

"Thank you."

The sandy walls of the tornado compressed around them. The noise was deafening. But it wasn't just the roar of the wind—in her ears, Amy could hear sounds of home: the voices of her dad, her family, all her friends—fragments of a familiar world beckoning her back. There was no time left.

"This is it!" Ryan yelled. "I can't fight it. It's my mother. I can hear her calling."

They pressed their bodies against each other as the spinning vortex swept beneath them and lifted them off their feet. It was just like when Chloe had transported them here—the weightlessness, the disorientation. The world flooded with white. Amy could feel her senses leaving her.

"You're slipping, Amy. I can't hold on to you. I can't hold on to this place any longer."

"Let it happen. Don't fight it."

With time almost up, Amy used their remaining seconds to lean in and kiss him, and she kept her lips pressed against his while everything around her began to fade, until she could no longer see, until she lost all sense of touch, until all she could hear was a whisper of Ryan's voice, his final words before they were pulled apart: "I love you, Amy!"

And in that last flickering moment, she told him that she loved him too.

37

*T*HE EVE of the Lighthouse Festival was the busiest night of the season for The Lookout. Its bar had done more business than a week's worth of happy hours combined. From those seated along the window, to the various groups gathered around tables, or those perched up at the bar, there was a palpable buzz of excitement. Hardly a minute went by without someone raising the festival in conversation or craning a neck to catch a glimpse of the preparations underway in the town square.

But not everyone was so enthused.

Sitting alone in a corner of the crowded bar, Kevin Tucker wondered, not for the first time, if he ought to be checking on his daughter. Amy had been back for a while now, returned from her walk at least a half hour ago. She had seemed upset, though, which was why he thought he'd been doing the right thing by staying at the bar and leaving her alone—but now he was second-guessing himself. The point of this trip was to spend some time together, find some common ground, try to reconnect, but how were they going to do that if they spent the whole weekend apart? He glanced toward the lobby, then back at his watch. He decided he would give it another ten minutes. On the table in front of him was the case file Jack had given him earlier that day; Kevin would first read over his brother's case notes, get prepared for tomorrow, then head upstairs to check on her. Besides, despite Jack's ulterior motives in sending him here, a job was still a job, and Kevin wanted to make sure he was adequately prepared.

Kevin already had a general understanding of the case. A young local man by the name of Ryan Porter had gone missing, and Kevin had been sent to Seabrook to inform the father that the investigation was to be closed. The task was, as Jack had described, entirely routine.

But as Kevin flipped open the folder and read more closely, details of the case began to intrigue him. After Ryan had been reported missing, two horses were discovered in the forest bordering the family property. The local sheriff had suspected something untoward, which is why state police had gotten involved, but a search of the area had turned up nothing. The young man had seemingly vanished off the face of the earth. Ninety percent of missing person cases were runaways, and Jack had concluded that Ryan was one of them. And there were some contributing factors that suggested this might be true.

Ryan had led a challenging life. He'd lost his mother at a young age, then witnessed his father suffer a debilitating stroke, the combination of which had left him with responsibility over the family's affairs. For the last four years, he'd been overseeing his father's recovery while also managing the ranch. But there was a sizeable debt hanging over them, a debt the father apparently had no knowledge of. It seemed that Ryan had drawn a loan against the ranch and gone to great lengths to hide its existence.

Then came the clincher: two days before the disappearance, the bank had issued notice of its intention to foreclose. The debt had spiraled out of control, no payments had been made in months, and the bank was coming to seize the property. Kevin had to admit he could see the logic behind Jack's theory. Perhaps the young man had indeed skipped town. But there was a question niggling in Kevin's head: What exactly were the horses doing in the forest? And why were there *two* of them?

"Well, would ya look at that. Still sittin' here and you *still* haven't touched your liquor."

Kevin looked up from his notes. There she was again, the bartender, the same one who had already called on his table not so long ago trying to refill his glass. Except topping up his drink was probably the last thing on her mind. She had already seen his badge when he'd checked in. She knew that he was a cop. Kevin suspected what she really wanted was to fish for information about his reason for being in Seabrook.

"Guess I'm still not thirsty," he replied.

"Fair enough, but if you leave it sitting there any longer like that I'll be able to water my plants with it." And in no time at all, her eyes drifted off the glass and landed on Kevin's case file. "Doin' some light reading, huh?"

Kevin closed the folder and smiled.

"I'm just spitballin' here, but if you're down here on police business—which you are, right?—then it must be about young Ryan."

"With all due respect," Kevin said, trying not to sound too irate, "even if I was here in an official capacity, it's obviously not something I can discuss. I'm sure you can appreciate that."

"Yeah, I hear ya." The bartender crouched down and tapped the top of his case folder as if to indicate she knew exactly what was hidden inside. "But it's such a shame, what happened, don't you think?"

"Look, I really can't—"

"I knew Ryan, you know. He used to come in here once a month to restock those flyers of his. Spoke to him plenty. Lovely boy. Lots of people been talking, some of them got traps big enough to catch a grizzly, I swear. They all think he took off. Lots think he just snapped and left this place behind, but I don't believe a word of it. He and his father, they'd been through a lot, but that boy was salt of the earth—he'd never do such a thing. Course, playin' devil's advocate, I do suppose this town got a history of people doin' some crazy things. We once had a lighthouse keeper, a looney fellow named Theodore, and you wouldn't believe—"

The bartender cut herself off. She had been distracted by a noise coming from upstairs. She looked up and so did Kevin, for he had heard it as well: the sound of footsteps rushing along the ceiling. Seconds later a young woman in a maid's apron could be seen tearing down the stairs. She was waving her hands in distress, screaming at the top of her voice.

"Help!" she cried out. "There's a girl and she's not breathing! *Someone please help!*"

38

AFTER RYAN'S dramatic departure, Amy found herself adrift, lost in a place that felt empty, dark, and eerily still. It was as though her spirit had been cast out into some soundless, bottomless chasm where there was nothing to see, nothing to touch, nothing but the echo of her own thoughts.

But she wasn't alone, for somewhere in the void there was a voice calling to her:

"Sweetheart. It's me."

The voice lit up Amy's senses, rousing her from the shadows, bringing her back to the light. She could feel the world rushing back to meet her, could feel the flat of the earth beneath her body again as bit by bit the darkness began to fade.

She opened her eyes, tried to blink away the haze. A cloudy white sky loomed above her. The air was quiet. Too quiet. She moved her hands and felt grains of sand between her fingers. Had she been returned to the beach? But that couldn't be right because Ryan had left and taken his snow globe with him. Unless . . . this wasn't the same beach?

Amy pulled herself up, looked hesitantly to her left, then to her right, searching for clues as to where she might be, and then she looked behind . . .

"Mom!"

Waves of joy and relief swept through Amy as she hurried over and fell into her mother's arms. She was so overcome with emotion that her whole body started to shake.

Her mother brought her in close, wrapping her in a warm embrace. "I promised you I'd be here, and I meant it."

"I didn't know what was going to happen next," Amy cried. "I didn't know where I was going. Didn't know how you were going to find me."

"Shhh, everything's going to be all right. I'm here now."

"But where are we? Ryan made it out, didn't he? He's safe?"

"Relax, sweetheart. He's found peace, and that's all because of you. I'm so proud of you. But now we need to move. It'll be dark very soon, and we mustn't linger."

39

$\mathcal{K}$EVIN LEAPT TO HIS FEET, knocking over the table and sending both his drink and case file flying. He pushed his way out of the bar. The maid, visibly shaken and upset, had to lean back as he charged up the stairs.

When he reached the second floor, he could see the door to his room was open. There was a pool of water. People were standing outside the room, hands covering their mouths.

"Get out of the way!" he screamed as he came barreling down the hall. "Move!" He flew through the door and followed the trail of water, which led straight into the bathroom.

The floor was flooded. Water everywhere. And there was his daughter lying in the bathtub. Her skin was pale, lips blue. There was another woman in the room already trying to help; she was standing at one end of the tub with her hands beneath Amy's shoulders, keeping her head above the water. Kevin took over from the woman and ordered her down to the other end to grab Amy's feet.

Together, on the count of three, they lifted Amy out of the bath and set her down on the floor. Kevin covered her body with towels, then sent the woman to go and get more. Tilting back her head, he lifted Amy's slack jaw and put his ear to her mouth and listened for any sign of breathing.

Nothing.

The bartender burst into the room, pink faced and sweating. "Sweet Jesus! *What's happened?*"

"Call 911!" Kevin yelled. "Now!"

Fumbling for her phone, she dialed the number and smacked the phone against her ear. Kevin, doing his best to stay calm and engage what he could remember from his first-aid training, pinched Amy's nose shut, leaned in, sealed his lips around hers, and breathed air into her lungs. Her chest rose and fell. He breathed in again then lifted her arm and checked for a pulse, holding his fingers on the underside of her wrist for a few seconds.

Nothing.

He put his ear to her chest.

Still nothing.

He saw an empty container rolling on the floor nearby—his sleeping pills.

"Dammit, Amy, *what have you done?*" Locking his fingers together, he put the heel of his hand to her chest and started compressions, furiously pushing in and out for nearly twenty seconds before stopping and giving another two breaths. A god-awful panic stirred in his gut.

40

$\mathcal{A}$MY STOPPED SOBBING into her mother's chest long enough to raise her head. Her instincts had been right—this wasn't the same beach. The lighthouse was gone and so was the town. There was nothing around her, nothing but sand and seawater and a small wooden rowboat, beached nearby. There were no dunes, no bush-covered cliffs, no craggy outcrops—what had previously been a curved bay was now a straight beach, a perfectly uniform strip of sand that seemed to stretch to infinity in both directions. The sky was a single shade of blue, and the ocean was so still it could have been mistaken for a sheet of glass; mirrorlike water extended from the shore and kept going and going and going as if there wasn't any horizon.

Everything was so artificial, so neat, so sterile. Even the air tasted strangely stale. Amy didn't have a clue what to make of it. Why were they here? Had her mother created this as somewhere they could meet, or had Amy traveled to *her* and this was what heaven looked like?

"Come, sweetheart. We'll have more time if we leave now."

Amy stared back. "And go where? What is this place?"

"I'll explain once we get going, but right now we have to get off this beach." She nodded to the boat, which had two oars balanced across its gunwales. "Hop in."

Amy followed apprehensively. Barefoot already, her mother waded out to the boat and pulled it in by its bow.

"Slip off your shoes," she said.

Amy did as she was asked and climbed into the shaky little boat. She sat on the front seat and held on to the sides, trying to keep the vessel, and her nerves, steady.

"Mom, I'm not sure I can do this."

"You can, Amy. You're going to be fine." She gave the boat a push and hopped in, positioning herself in the middle and taking the oars in her hands.

Amy began trembling. "I'm scared, Mom."

"Just breathe. You have nothing to be afraid of." She pulled on both oars and the boat began moving. Next, she removed her hands from the ends of the oars, and with a twirl of a finger made them come to life. The blades slid into the ocean and began slicing through the water like magic.

Twilight turned to dusk as Amy watched the shoreline recede, then dusk became night, all in a matter of seconds. A bright moon appeared from nowhere and hung above them like a giant porcelain plate, casting an ivory glow across the surface of the sea. A chill raced up Amy's spine.

"Mom, will you tell me where we are? I don't like it here. This place feels . . . wrong."

"We're in another snow globe. Except this one's different—this one is yours."

"Mine?"

"Your spirit made one so that we'd have a way to see each other." Her mother fell silent for a moment as she threw a wary glance up at the sky. "You weren't ready to go home, but with Ryan gone there was nowhere left for you to stay, so your spirit had to create this place instead."

Amy looked out across the water, stunned. "Wait, so you knew this would happen? Back in the lighthouse, when I said I wanted to see you one last time, you knew the same thing that happened to Ryan would happen to me? You knew I'd get stuck in my own snow globe?"

"Oh, Amy, no, you're not stuck. This isn't the same situation as Ryan's. Your spirit isn't trying to fool you or keep you trapped. Its only purpose is to give us a place where you and I can safely say our goodbyes." She cast yet another ominous look skyward, where something was clearly drawing her attention. "But we don't have a lot of time. Can you see what's happening? The moon's getting bigger and brighter. Soon its glow will cover the entire sky and turn everything white, and then our time will be up. We mustn't delay. We need to get you home."

Standing up, but taking great care not to rock the boat, her mother moved to Amy's end and squeezed onto the seat beside her. "You trust me, don't you?"

Amy swallowed uncomfortably when she saw her mother glance over the edge of the boat. "Of course, I do."

"Good, because the only way out of here is for you to get in the water—and I need you to get in now, sweetheart, before it's too late."

"What?"

"You need to jump in and swim, as deep as you can go."

Amy instinctively grabbed her pendant, clenched it tight. "Mom, you can't be serious."

"Everything will be okay. You'll know what to do. When you reach the bottom, you'll find the way out, I promise."

"Mom, no, I can't." The mere thought of it left Amy teetering on the edge of panic.

"You can do this. I know you can do this. You *must* do this."

Amy looked up and saw the moon was twice as large as it was a moment ago, its glow spreading like an enormous ink stain across the night sky.

"I don't understand. Why isn't there another way out? Do I need to prove myself worthy? Is that it? Is this all just one big test?"

"No, it's no test, but you've been lingering away from your body for far too long. The connection is growing weaker and weaker, and the pull of the light—of me—it's getting too strong. We're out on the ocean because this is where your spirit has decided you needed to be, and now an act of courage is needed to force your spirit back home. But the more time we spend together, the longer we wait, the harder it's going to get."

41

A CROWD HAD GATHERED in the doorway. Kevin looked up and screamed out orders. "Someone see if there's a doctor here. A nurse! Check every room, check downstairs! Go!"

One by one they scattered, leaving behind Kevin and the bartender, who had just gotten through to emergency services and was busy taking instructions.

"Yes, he's already doin' that," the bartender said into her phone, her hands shaking. "Yes, yes, that too."

"How long will they be?" Kevin yelled. "Where are they?"

The bartender relayed the question, waited a second, then grimly shook her head. "Fifteen minutes. They say they're on their way . . ."

"*Fifteen minutes?* Dammit!" Kevin pressed harder, but his daughter remained unresponsive. There was no color, no hint of life. He shook his head as tears spilled from his eyes, his despair mounting and his heart breaking at the sight of his little girl, lifeless in his arms.

42

$\mathcal{T}$HIS IS BECAUSE OF YOU," Amy cried out. "This is all your fault. If you hadn't died, if you hadn't left me, then we wouldn't be here and none of this would be happening!"

"Sweetheart, you have no idea how much I wish I could go back and change what took place that morning. I can feel the pain you've been in—it hurts me more than you can possibly know. But I need you to forgive me, okay? I need you to concentrate all your energy on getting home."

"And what do I tell people when I get back? After everything I've seen, am I supposed to just keep all of this a secret?"

"You won't have to worry about that."

"How can you say that?"

"Trust me, Amy. Everything is going to be okay."

"No, I want to know what you mean."

"There isn't time."

"Mom . . . what are you not telling me?"

Her mother wrapped her fingers around Amy's hands and held them tight. "It makes no difference. What's happened in here will stay here. All that matters right now is getting you home."

"Wait . . . what are you saying? That I'm not going to remember any of this?"

Her mother cast her head down.

"Tell me I'm going to remember you, Mom. Tell me I'm going to remember *something* about what's happened in here."

"I'm sorry, Amy . . ."

"No, no, that's not fair . . ." Amy violently swung her head from side to side, her lips beginning to quiver. "I need to remember this, Mom. I can't go back to the way it was before. I need to know you're out here. I need to know I'm not alone. *Please*, Mom."

Her mother squeezed Amy's hands even tighter, perhaps hoping it might absorb some of the shock. "You're not alone, Amy. There are people back home who love you and miss you, and that's all that matters. All you need to focus on right now is getting into the water."

And, to Amy's horror, it seemed that moment was now upon her. The moon's burgeoning glow had transformed the sky into a dome of solid white, just as her mother had said it would. But there was an even more disturbing development: it was beginning to snow. Thousands upon thousands of pirouetting little flakes were drifting down and settling everywhere—on their clothes, their boat, the surface of the water—slowly turning the world white.

"This is it. Here is where it has to be." With a wave of her finger, Amy's mother froze the oars midspin, tilted them to a forty-five-degree angle, and sent them plunging into the water. The boat came to a stop. "Don't pay any attention to what's happening. Don't think about the snow, don't think about the water. Focus on me, Amy."

But this was hard when the weather was deteriorating so fast. The temperature was dropping, a strong breeze was building, and their boat was beginning to seesaw in the rapidly rising swells. Swirling gusts were whipping the snow into a frenzy. Conditions were turning hostile and blizzard-like, giant waves rising up around them. Hunkered down next to her mother, Amy wondered whether her spirit wanted her to go home at all.

"Hold on! This is going to get rough."

"What's going on?" Amy shrieked, her voice almost lost in the howl of the wind. "Is it *me* who's doing this?"

"Your snow globe is collapsing. It's the end."

"But I can't get out of the boat in this! Can't we make it stop? Just for a minute!" Two waves struck the hull in quick succession and caused the boat to lurch violently to its side, nearly tipping them into the ocean.

"Amy, are you all right?"

Amy shook her head, snow and salt water blasting across her face. "I'm not saying goodbye like this, Mom. Not like *this*!"

"There's nothing we can do."

"It isn't fair!"

"I know it isn't, and I know so much has been asked of you already, but I need you to be strong. Think about your father, your friends, your life back home—think about everyone waiting for you! This is your last chance. The longer you stay, the worse it's going to get. This is it, Amy! It's time to go!"

"And if I don't jump?"

"What?"

"What if I went with you instead?"

"Amy, no—"

"I mean it. You just told me I had a choice about where I go next. What if I'm ready to go with you? What if it's my time, Mom?"

"It isn't!"

"But what if it is?"

"Amy, it isn't, because I'm your mother and I'm telling you that it isn't! You are the most precious thing in the world to me. I love you. I'd do anything for you. You know that. But there's no way I'm letting you come with me." The boat continued to lurch this way and that.

"I know you're hurting, and I know this isn't what you expected your life to be, one without me in it, but you can't let that stop you from going home. You're strong enough to do this. I believe in you, Amy."

Amy raised her head and wiped her tears. Clutching the pendant around her neck, she remembered what Ryan had told her up in his attic; the story of his two rocks, and the memory of his words, gave her a glimmer of hope, enough to make her believe she could do this, that she had the strength she needed to say goodbye to her mother—the courage she needed to return home.

"All right, Mom. I'll do it, I'll try."

"That's my girl."

Amy glanced sideways and saw the ocean heaving beneath her like some ravenous monster.

"This will all be over soon," her mother said. "All you need to do is dive in and swim to the bottom. Before you know it, you'll be home."

"I love you so much, Mom."

"I love you too, sweetheart."

"Promise you'll be watching over me."

"Always." She leaned forward and placed both hands on Amy's shoulders, steadying her against the waves, which were intensifying by the second, rocking the boat more violently than ever. "I'm so proud of you. I probably never told you that enough when you were growing up, but truly, I am. You're not my little girl anymore. You're a strong, confident young woman, and you've got your whole future ahead of you. Never take a single day for granted. Always be true to yourself, experience the world and discover what makes you happy, and never, ever be scared to follow your heart. Life won't always be easy, sweetheart, but just remember that all the strength and courage you could ever need is *right here*." Her mother placed her hand on Amy's chest. "And that's where you'll find me—all you need to do is think of me and I'll be there."

"Oh, Mom, I'm going to miss you!"

Amy leaned in and put her arms around her mother and hugged

her for the very last time. As they embraced, the snow began to fall thicker and faster; the sky and the sea were fading to white. Their skin shimmered, turning translucent. The boat, their bodies—they were all starting to glow.

"We can't wait any longer. We're out of time." Her mother drew back, kissed Amy on the forehead, then nodded to the water. "You have to leave."

"I love you, Mom. I love you."

"I love you too! Take a big breath. Go home, sweetheart!"

Fighting back tears, Amy moved to the side of the rowboat, careful not to tip it. With every single part of her trembling, she sucked in the deepest breath she possibly could and gave her mom one last look. Then, with not a second to spare, as the last of her snow globe was swallowed up by wind and light and shining snow, she closed her eyes, slid off the edge of the boat, and disappeared beneath the waves.

43

*H*ELP WAS NOWHERE in sight. By the time paramedics arrived, by the time they set up with an AED, it would be too late. Kevin needed to be the one to revive Amy, right here, right now, and if he couldn't do it then she would die.

It was all his fault. While he had been downstairs, his daughter had knocked herself out with pills and drowned in the bathtub. He thought of Helen and how distraught she would be if she were here. Amy was his responsibility and he had failed her. He had failed them both.

"Dammit, Amy! Don't do this! I'm not letting you do this!"

Kevin could sense the presence of others in the room: the bartender, the woman who had helped lift Amy out of the tub, each of them no doubt thinking that he was wasting his time, all thinking him a fool for persisting when it had been so long already, when it was obvious that his daughter's body didn't hold the slightest sign of life.

But Kevin didn't stop. It was physically and mentally impossible for him to stop. He kept up the CPR, kept counting off the beats, kept breathing air into his daughter's mouth.

"Come back to me!" he cried. "Come back to me *now*!"

———⟋𝓋𝓋𝓇———

Amy couldn't see a thing. The surface had frozen over. Beneath her loomed an empty abyss. She had swum deeper than she thought was possible and still hadn't found a way out. Every second was precious. Pressure was building in her body, the air in her lungs dwindling fast. How deep did she need to go? Her mother had said this would lead her home! She'd *promised* she'd be able to find the way!

Come back to me.

Amy stopped kicking.

A voice.

She had heard a voice.

She flipped upright and twisted around, trying to pinpoint where it was coming from.

Come back to me now . . .

The voice surrounded Amy, growing louder and louder, and as it did the pressure inside her body became immense. An unbearable pain shot out from her chest, up into her throat, then something else stirred inside, something infinitely cold and rigid, like ice crystalizing around her heart. Then she no longer felt the movement of the water, no longer felt much at all. The chill inside her spread out across her body, curling around every muscle, numbing every limb, until the only thing she had left was a vague, distant sense of consciousness.

———⟋𝓋𝓋𝓇———

There was nothing more Kevin could do. Despite his desperate attempts to revive her, Amy remained unresponsive. He felt his own life draining away at the sight of her body lying flat on the floor, limp and cold and chillingly pale.

But then, just as Kevin's last scrap of hope was fading, as his agonized cries were ricocheting off the tiled walls of that tiny room, something impossible happened, something miraculous—it was ever so faint, barely perceptible, but Amy's skin was beginning to stir with color.

"Amy!"

Kevin bent down, breathed in more air, then put his ear to her mouth and listened—and there, from the depths of her throat, he heard a faint gasp.

"That's it, Amy! Come back, *come back to me . . .*"

Her skin warmed even further, her eyelids twitched, then her lips moved, and she gave a little cough. Then, with sudden, violent force, she arched her back in the air and coughed much harder, causing water to come bubbling out of her mouth and splutter across the floor.

"Amy, Amy . . ." Kevin rolled her onto her side and rubbed her back, desperate to help expunge the water. "Can you hear me? *Are you all right?*"

Amy remained on her side for a minute, coughing uncontrollably, holding her hands on her chest, taking quick, short breaths. Noticeably groggy, she sat up and took a long, confused look around the bathroom, and at those standing by the door. She coughed again, grimaced a little, then turned to Kevin, who couldn't do or say anything except cry with hysterical relief and wrap his little girl up in his arms.

"Dad . . . what happened?"

PART
THREE

44

THE PARAMEDICS ARRIVED not long after Amy regained consciousness. Even they were visibly stunned when they heard what had happened. They performed a few quick checks—listened to her heart, took her blood pressure—then loaded both her and Kevin into an ambulance and drove them to the nearest hospital in a larger town two counties over.

Arriving a little after midnight, Amy was seen by the attending physician, who made the decision to admit her for the night. He ordered a battery of tests to be done, expressing concern on a number of different fronts—the pills still in her system, the water that might still be sitting in her lungs, and the amount of time her brain had been starved of oxygen. Though the tests took less than ninety minutes, to Kevin the wait felt like an eternity.

When the tests were over, a nurse came to get him and together they wheeled Amy into a room. The nurse dimmed the lights, prepared a bed by the window, then put a needle in Amy's arm and hooked her up to a drip. She told Kevin the doctor would be in shortly to go through the results of the tests. As soon as the lights were turned off, Amy fell asleep.

A half hour later, the doctor knocked. Kevin tiptoed across the room and joined him out in the hall.

"How are you doing, Mr. Tucker?"

"Nerves are shot. How is my girl?" By this point it was 3:00 a.m. and Kevin was running on adrenaline.

"Let me set your mind at ease and tell you that your daughter is going to be okay. The results came back fine."

"Thank God. There's no permanent damage?"

"Brain activity is fine, lungs are clear." The doctor looked down at a clipboard. "She's a lucky girl, but I'm not surprised to see that she's asleep—she's been knocked about a bit by the pills. They were yours, yes?"

"Yes . . . they were mine. Is she really going to be all right? Don't you think we ought to be pumping her stomach or something?"

"That won't be necessary. The fluids we've given her will help flush out any remaining DPH still in her system." The doctor flipped to another page and read some handwritten scrawl. "The on-call psychiatrist will be here in the morning—she'll pop in to have a word with Amy when she's awake. She'll do an assessment, then recommend what steps need to be taken next."

He scribbled something in his notes, signed another page, then looked up and glanced into Amy's room.

"Mr. Tucker, Amy has been through an awful lot tonight. Her heart stopped—for how long, we don't really know. That she's come through as strong as she has is nothing short of a miracle. By no means am I a religious man, but if you want my opinion, I'd say someone up there was looking out for you and your daughter tonight. You're both incredibly lucky." He gave Kevin a pat on the arm. "Try to get some rest."

—⟊⟊—

Kevin fell asleep in a chair and didn't wake until long after sunrise. His back was stiff and there was drool running down his chin. A little dazed, he wiped his face, opened his eyes, and felt a sudden rush of panic as the hospital room slowly came into focus.

"Amy! Where *are* you?"

"Dad, it's okay . . . I'm right here."

He spun around and saw his daughter staring back at him. Propped up in bed with a stack of pillows behind her back, she had a tray positioned across her lap filled with food—a bowl of fruit, toast, some water, and orange juice. Kevin jumped up from his chair and threw himself across the bed to hug her.

"I thought I'd imagined it, Amy. For a second, I thought you coming back to me had all been a dream!"

He straightened, looked her in the eyes, then went quiet when he noticed the wedge of buttered toast in her hands. "And you're eating!" he laughed, so happy he could cry. "I can't believe it, Amy . . . you're eating something!"

Amy managed a smile. "I'm trying."

"How are you feeling?"

"Got a headache," she said, speaking slowly. "And I'm a bit woozy, but not too bad."

"Has the doctor been in to see you? Have they checked you over, have they—"

"She's doing just fine, Mr. Tucker. Someone's already been in."

The polite interruption came from a woman who had just entered the room. Professionally dressed in a pin-striped skirt suit with dark-red hair sharply pulled back into a bun, she approached Kevin and offered her hand.

"I'm Dr. Grace Kennedy," she said, introducing herself. "Psychiatrist." She smiled at Amy, then looked back at Kevin, gesturing toward the door. "Amy and I have already spoken. How about you and I step out for a moment?"

Kevin nodded and followed Dr. Kennedy into the hall.

"How is she?" he asked.

"As you know, your daughter went through a traumatic experience last night. She's dealing with it admirably well, but the days ahead may be tough, and she's going to need a support network around her—people who love her, people she can trust."

"And she'll have it, absolutely."

"Good to hear, because that will be important." Dr. Kennedy took off her glasses and slipped them into the top pocket of her suit. "As for what happened, your daughter and I had a good chat, and after hearing her speak on the matter, I'm comfortable that she didn't take those pills with the intention of causing herself any harm."

"But she nearly emptied out the whole container, Doc. What else could she have been trying to do?"

"Quite simply what they were designed to do: help her get to sleep. Don't misunderstand me, it's still concerning—that a young girl should be so desperate she feels it's okay to take her father's medication without him knowing is very serious indeed. That's a girl who needs some help. But there's a difference between someone who is tired, grieving, and desperate for a break, and someone who genuinely wishes to cause themselves harm. Your daughter doesn't present to me as that sort of person. Her memories of last night are very lucid. She remembers exactly how she was feeling before she took those pills, and she regrets it enormously."

Kevin stood there quietly for a moment, processing it all. "What happens now?"

Dr. Kennedy pulled out a piece of paper from her pocket and handed it over. "These are the names of some colleagues of mine up in Portland. When you get home, pick one and set up an appointment for Amy. It's important that you're a part of this process going forward," she added.

"Of course. I'd do anything for her."

"Of that, I have no doubt. But during our talk this morning, I got the sense there's a distance between the two of you. Amy explained to me that she has difficulty communicating with you. She says it's been like that for some time, but that this lack of connection has been exacerbated since your wife passed. Those are my words, of course, not hers, but that's how I interpreted the situation. Would you agree with that?"

"Yes," Kevin said, dropping his head.

"You mustn't blame yourself, Mr. Tucker. You've both been through an awful lot. You're grieving, and you'll be grieving for a while longer yet, but what's important is that you two find a way to move forward together as a family. That's what your daughter wants, and I can see that's what you want too."

"It is, very much."

Kevin thanked the doctor for her help and returned to the room. He wheeled the tray away and sat on the bed beside Amy.

"Last night was the scariest moment of my life," he said. "You're all I've got left. I have no idea what I'd do if I lost you."

Amy wriggled around and slid up next to him, her legs dangling off the edge of the bed. "I feel terrible. It was a stupid, stupid thing for me to do. I'm so sorry I put you through that."

"You've got nothing to be sorry for. It's me who should be apologizing to you. I'm your father. I should be doing a better job."

"Please don't blame yourself for this. It isn't your fault. You're doing the best you can. I know that. The last month has been hard enough as it is."

"I know, but I'm not just talking about the last month. I'm talking about the last eighteen years, years I've missed out on because I was never there for you. It's too late for me to get those years back, but that doesn't mean we can't start fresh." He took her hand in his and squeezed it gently. "Amy, I want to make you a promise, right here and now, that from this point on it's all going to change. Everything's going to change. *I'm* going to change. And it's all going to start the moment we get home because the first thing I'm going to do is quit my job."

Amy looked up at him in shock. "What?"

"You heard me."

"No, you can't do that."

"I can, and I intend to."

"But, Dad—"

"It's the right thing to do. It's time."

"But it's too sudden, far too sudden."

"Not as sudden as you think. I've been giving it plenty of thought. It's a decision I should've made a long time ago, I just never had the guts."

"Dad, you're good at your job."

"And I'll find something else that I'm good at."

"But it's your career you're talking about here. The state police has been your whole life."

"That's the point. I don't want this to be my life anymore. If I keep doing it there'll be nothing left, and I don't want that. It's already taken so much."

Amy stared out the window for a moment, speechless. "This doesn't feel right," she finally said. "I feel like you're making this huge decision and you're doing it all because of what just happened . . . because of me."

"Because of *us*," he whispered. "I'm doing this for us. I promise, from now on, everything's going to be different."

45

*L*ATER THAT AFTERNOON, Amy was given the good news that she could go home. While her dad was signing the discharge paper-work, she visited the restroom to freshen up. She removed her hospital band and gown and shoved them in the bin, changed back into clothes her dad had brought from the hotel, then tied her hair back and splashed her face with water. When she was done, she tore some paper towels from the dispenser, dabbed her face dry, and stood and stared at the mirror.

It was the first time that Amy had faced her own reflection since last night, and she found the experience confronting.

There it is, she thought, her body . . . the same body that had narrowly avoided arriving at this hospital under a sheet and being taken to the morgue.

Even now, twenty-four hours later, she had trouble coming to terms with what had happened. She couldn't comprehend the idea that her heart, her own precious heart, had stopped beating, that clinically speaking, she had *died*.

The doctors believed she had been gone for two to three minutes at least, but no one really knew. Amy remembered taking the pills, getting into the bath—and she remembered the violent force with which she awoke, that awful sensation of water clogging up her throat—but everything in between was a blank. There had been no out-of-body experience. She hadn't walked through any pearly gates or seen a blinding white light. The truth was that it had felt no different from being asleep, and that's what really scared her.

The psychiatrist said she'd need time to process the event, but Amy doubted if that would ever be possible. Even with all the time in the world, how was she ever going to make sense of the fact that, for a short while last night, for a few missing minutes, she had simply ceased to exist?

There was a knock on the door.

"Amy, we're all done out here."

"Okay," she called out. "I'm coming."

They exited the hospital and sat on a wooden bench, waiting for a cab that would take them back to Seabrook. The road was busy; a continuous procession of cars turned in and out of a nearby parking complex while a steady stream of buses, painted in unfamiliar colors, arrived and departed like clockwork.

"This is going to sound a little strange," Amy said, "but what town is this?"

The question made her dad think for a moment and smile. "Do you know something? I'm not even sure I remember myself."

She smiled too, noticing how different he seemed. His demeanor had changed since his big announcement. It was as though the decision to quit had taken a huge weight off his shoulders. Amy was happy for him, if still a little surprised, but mostly she was curious about what the future now held. He had been with the state police for so long that it was impossible to imagine him doing anything else. She was also curious about Uncle Jack. Her dad and her uncle had worked alongside each other their entire careers. What was his reaction going to be?

When she raised that question, Kevin instantly tensed up.

"Yes, well, that's sure going to be an interesting conversation," he replied through gritted teeth. "I think your uncle thought we'd be seeing out the rest of our days in that place, collecting our gold watches, photos put up on the wall, the whole nine yards. I'll wait till we get home before breaking the news."

Amy smiled, not knowing what else to say. This was the most she and her dad had spoken in a month. It was unfamiliar territory. For him as well, she imagined.

"Speaking of which," he added, "when do you want to head back? We can get going as soon as we've grabbed our bags, or we can stay another night and head off in the morning. Depends how you're feeling?"

"I'm all right if you want to leave today," she said.

"Are you sure?"

"Yeah. I can handle sitting in the car for a few hours."

"I do have to make one quick stop on the way, but it shouldn't take long, fifteen minutes or so. We'll be back in Portland before dark." He reached into his pocket and pulled out his phone. "Do you want to call anyone? Your phone is back at the hotel—I forgot to grab it, sorry."

"Not right now, but thanks."

"Not even Sam?"

Amy shook her head. "Sam's gonna freak out when she hears about this. I'll call her soon, but that's a conversation I need some time to prepare for."

He swung his arm over and gave her a hug. "Sounds like we're in the same boat, then."

"Yeah," she said with a smile. "Sounds like we are."

The town square in Seabrook was cordoned off for a festival, which meant they had to be dropped on a side street two blocks away from the hotel. As soon as they were back in the lobby, there was a raucous shout and Amy was set upon by a large, redheaded, apron-clad woman.

"Jesus, Mary, and Joseph! Just look at you, all in one piece, living and breathing. What a beautiful sight!"

Amy was swallowed up in a rapturous hug before she even had a chance to speak. She looked to her dad for help.

"This is the bartender, Amy. This kind lady helped and called 911." His voice trailed off at the mention of last night. "Sorry, I don't think I remember your name?"

"Peggy's the name, but don't you go worryin' about that. I'm just mighty relieved your precious girl is standing on her own two feet and got color back in those beautiful cheeks. I've been so worried, me and the entire staff."

"I appreciate that," Amy said. "I'm okay now."

"Wonderful. Wonderful. And don't concern yourselves over the room," she added, looking at Kevin. "Everything's been tidied up, floor mopped, good as new."

"Thank you," he said. "We just need to collect our belongings, then we must be moving on."

"Of course." Peggy fixed her eyes on Amy once more. "You be takin' care of yourself, now. Gave your old man quite the fright."

"I will," Amy said. "Thank you."

Peggy returned to her post while Amy and Kevin headed upstairs. Amy's phone was on the bedroom dresser, her flats, which she had worn last night, were sitting beside the couch, and her pendant was lying on the bed, its chain snapped in two. Before zipping up her bag, she headed to the bathroom to check if she had left anything in there.

She pushed open the door and flicked on the lights. Just like Peggy had said, the room was spotless. Fresh towels hung from the railing, boxed toiletries sat in a neat row on the vanity sink, and the scent of pine cleaner wafted up from the floor. And there, across the room, looming ominously in the corner: the bathtub. Amy peered inside. The sight of her ghostly image reflected in the porcelain instantly gave her goose bumps.

"Amy, you okay?"

She startled and turned to find her dad standing in the doorway. "Yes, I'm all right." She backed away from the tub. "Feels strange to be in here, that's all."

"There's probably plenty about last night you don't remember." He walked over and put his hand on her shoulder. "I'm not sure how much help I can be, but if you've got any questions, I'll do my best to answer them."

"It's still a blur, to be honest." Amy composed herself and gave the bathtub a second look, imagining what it must have been like for those few minutes, to be lying in there, alone and unconscious while the taps continued to run, spilling water over the edge.

"Wait . . ." She turned to her dad. "You weren't the one who found me, were you?"

"Not the first, no." He looked at her strangely.

"Who was it then?"

"It was one of the maids."

Amy stared at the door. "A maid?"

"Yes. Why?"

"Nothing, it's just . . ."

"Is something wrong?"

"No . . ."

"Thank goodness she was walking by. She had the master keys on her. She saw water in the hall, knocked, and when she didn't get an answer, she decided to come in and check. We were very lucky."

"Right, yes . . . very lucky."

"You look surprised. Had you thought it was me?"

"No . . . maybe. I don't know."

While her dad left to grab the last of his stuff, Amy hung back in the bathroom. A maid had raised the alarm? She had no reason not to believe that, and yet something felt off. Exactly what it was, she couldn't say, but in the back of her mind there was a twinge of doubt: a niggling thought that something wasn't right. Amy couldn't explain it, couldn't put her finger on what was bothering her, couldn't even describe it except to say it was like listening to an orchestra but hearing a single instrument that was slightly out of tune. It may have been quiet and faint, but it was definitely there, lurking somewhere on the fringe of her thoughts, a lone discordant note.

46

THE "STOP ON THE WAY" was police business. Amy had assumed this would be the case since that was the main reason for their trip, but it did strike her as a little strange to be accompanying her dad while he attended to the actual job.

"Are you sure this is okay?" she asked as she got into the car and slipped on her seat belt. "Doesn't me tagging along break a hundred different rules?"

"Not at all," Kevin said, checking for an address in his folder before keying it into his phone. "It's just a routine stop I have to make—a formality, nothing more. Someone went missing a couple of months back and the investigation is about to be closed. I was just sent here to notify the father."

"Oh, I see."

The GPS directed them to leave Seabrook and head north. They traveled for ten minutes along the highway, past fields and farms and expansive orchards, then made a left turn toward some tree-covered hills and a valley. Another left turn took them down a gravel road, which soon narrowed and turned to dirt as it wove through a dense forest. As Amy was watching the sunlight try to crack through the tops of the trees, the car made a turn and came to a stop.

She looked over and saw a driveway out her dad's window. There was a rickety mailbox poking out from behind some shrubbery with the words *Porter Ranch* stenciled in white, as well as a handmade sign strung to a tree that said *Horseback Riding*.

"This is it?" she asked.

Her dad stared at his phone, but coverage was fading in and out and the friendly GPS lady was nowhere to be found. He reached for his folder, checked the first page of the case file, then nodded his head. "Porter. Yes, this is it."

Though by no means large or sprawling, the Porter Ranch was certainly majestic. The property was hidden at the end of a long driveway, nestled on a modest, sunlit piece of land bordered by forest and rolling hills. There was a patchwork of fields and a smattering of buildings, including two sheds, a carport, a magnificent pitched-roof barn—which could have been mistaken for a church were it not for its hayloft and lack of a cross—and a charming single-level house complete with a wraparound porch and creamy-blue door and shutters. Towering trees, a garden, and two timber-walled vegetable patches marked the area between the barn and fields, and between the house and the barn sat a dusty fenced-in arena that Amy assumed was used for horseback riding.

Not everything was perfect. She could see the property was a little unkempt. The fields were overgrown, vines were attacking the house and creeping up the banisters and along paint-chipped walls, weeds had overrun flower beds, and the barn roof seemed to be missing a few planks of wood. But to Amy this only added to the appeal. There was a fairytale sense of grandeur about the place, a raw, wild, undeniable beauty.

"Wow, this is certainly somewhat impressive, isn't it?" Kevin said as he circled the car around the forecourt and stopped outside the house.

"Uh-huh," Amy mumbled, thinking "somewhat impressive" was selling it short when this was perhaps the most gorgeous property she'd ever laid eyes on. Everywhere she looked was like staring into a postcard.

"You know something? This reminds me of the farm your mother grew up on. It looked nothing like this, but it was beautiful all the same. You had a sense when you were there that the rest of the world was a million miles away." He went quiet, gazing out past the fields to the hills and blue sky beyond. "She never talked about it much, but it was always her dream to move back to the country one day."

"I always wish I'd seen where she grew up. Mom loved telling me stories about her childhood."

"That farm was her favorite place in the world. Broke her heart when her folks had to sell."

"That's where you two got engaged, wasn't it? The place where she had buried that letter?"

"Yep, right next to her favorite tree—that big ol' cottonwood," Kevin said wistfully. "I've still got lots of photos from when we used to visit, still got all her albums from when she was young. When we're home, maybe we can get them out and have a look."

"I'd like that," Amy said.

He then gave her a smile, the kind of smile that made Amy believe what he said was true—that from now on everything really was going to be different.

47

$\mathcal{A}$MY AND KEVIN were still admiring the scenery when the front door to the house swung open. A man hobbled onto the porch. He was smartly dressed, slight in build, and had a noticeable limp in his step.

Kevin acknowledged him with a polite wave before unclicking his seat belt and reaching for the case file. He tucked it under his arm, told Amy to sit tight for a bit, then stepped out of the car and made his way up the steps, stretching out a hand to the waiting man. "Mr. Porter? I'm Detective Tucker."

"Good afternoon, Detective. Thank you for making the drive out." Mr. Porter leaned on his cane as he came down a step to shake Kevin's hand. "Come inside, and please, call me Roger."

Kevin was led into the kitchen and offered a seat at a lime-green Formica table. The interior was sparse. There were no pictures hanging and what little furniture there was had been wrapped in plastic and slid against the walls. Scattered around were cardboard boxes, newspapers, and reams of bubble wrap.

Roger put a glass of water down in front of Kevin and awkwardly collapsed into his seat. "Excuse the mess, will you?"

"Moving someplace, Roger?"

"Have to, I'm afraid. Bank is foreclosing on me next week."

"I heard about that. I'm very sorry."

"Not your fault, Detective. They've given me time to sort out my affairs, and it's for the best. I can't run this place on my own— nor would I want to, not with my son gone. Doesn't feel like home anymore."

Roger looked around the room and mustered a brave smile, which wasn't so much a smile but a faint turning up of the lips. Kevin could tell just by looking at the poor man that he had been through hell these past two months; he looked weak and tired, and his battle-hardened face expressed nothing but grim emotion.

"If you don't mind me asking, where will you go?"

"Up north, to Montana. My brother has a farm there. We both agreed it might be good for me to stay with him and his family for a while."

He went on to explain that he and his brother hadn't spoken in over twenty years, the unfortunate result of an old, long-forgotten feud, but that his son's death had prompted them to get back in touch. "And I'm glad we did," he added.

Kevin shifted forward in his chair. "Roger, just so I'm clear, I'm not here because we're pronouncing your son deceased."

"I know, Detective. But his case is being closed, right? Isn't that why you've come to see me?"

"I'm afraid so. With the way things stand, there's nothing more we can do."

—⁓—

Amy buzzed her window down and leaned back in her seat. The sun was warm, the air smelled sweet, and she couldn't hear a thing except for birds, insects, and the distant rustling of leaves. But the pleasant surroundings did little to help her relax. Not only was she still trying to come to terms with the events of last night, but she was also beginning to worry about what the reaction was going to be back home, particularly that of her best friend. Having already been worried about Amy's wellbeing, there was every chance Sam would flip out when she heard what had happened, especially if Amy took too long before telling her. And Amy had to admit, if the situation were reversed, she would want to know as soon as possible too. Revealing the news wasn't going to be easy, but it had to happen—and sooner rather than later.

Amy took a deep breath, pulled out her phone, and began typing her message. Three screens were used in the telling, and she didn't leave anything out. And while putting it down in words did make her feel a little ashamed—after all, she had never thought of herself as the kind of person who would overdose on pills—she admitted to feeling a sense of catharsis when she reached the end. Now all that was left to do was hold her phone in the air, find a signal, and wait for the message to swoosh its way north to Portland.

—◦◦◦—

"So, where does this leave my son?" Roger asked.

Kevin put one hand on top of the case file, which was sitting out in front of him. "Officially, Ryan is a missing person. His details will be transferred to the FBI and entered into their database."

Roger sat motionless for a moment, his eyes wet with tears. It took him a long time to gather the strength to speak. "I know what you think, Detective. I know what everyone thinks: that he ran off because of the money and the problems here at home, but that isn't what happened. My son was a good man—the best—he'd never do such a thing."

"You have my sympathy, Roger. I can only imagine what an awful ordeal this must be."

"Can you? Really? Because sometimes it feels like I'm the only person who sees reason in all this madness. Everyone wants to give up and accept some ridiculous answer that simply isn't true. My son isn't missing. He didn't run off. Something happened—an accident of some kind. For Pete's sake, they found two horses in the forest. One of them was *his*. Why does everyone seem to forget that?"

"We haven't, but that particular lead went nowhere. For the record, I agree with you—the circumstances are strange—but the forest has already been searched and nothing was found."

"Then search someplace else. This is what I've been saying from the beginning. The area needs to be wider. People need to search beyond the forest—out by the cliffs, along the coast."

"You have reason to believe that's where your son went?"

"I do. That second horse they found is very temperamental—she spooks easily—and my gut tells me she escaped the ranch and my son gave chase."

"I don't recall reading anything about this in the report."

"Probably because everyone has chosen to believe that *both* horses spooked and somehow got lost in the forest, because that better suits the preposterous fiction that my son ran away." Roger pointed out the window, indicating a small clearing in the woods where the boundary of the ranch met the forest. "She would've bolted through that gap, and from there it's a straight shot to the coast. It's entirely possible."

Kevin glanced down at the file. "Did you run your theory by the other investigators?"

"Yes."

"And?"

"They didn't buy it. They said there was nothing to indicate any movement in that direction—no tracks. But what they don't understand is that it rained solid for twelve hours that night, so any footprints— or hoofprints, for that matter—would've been washed away."

"And I presume you passed that information on as well?"

"Of course, but no one seemed convinced. They put a chopper up in the air, did an aerial sweep, said it was the most they could do."

"I see." Kevin stared at the table, scratching his chin.

Are you shitting me Ames?! Is this a joke?? Are you okay?

As Amy typed her response, assuring Sam that she was indeed okay, she caught the sound of a croaky engine making its way up the driveway. She finished the message just as a beat-up black truck rounded the corner. Towing a large trailer, the truck rumbled past in a plume of dirty brown smoke and parked outside the entrance to the barn. The words *McGuire Bros. Horse Transport* were cheaply stamped on the door. Amy's phone beeped again.

I'm trying to call. It says you're out of range. Where are you?

Amy tapped back a quick reply, telling Sam all about Seabrook and how Uncle Jack had sent her dad down here to deliver some news about a local case. Then she held up her phone and snapped a picture of the view.

Her attention went back to the truck. Two men, presumably the McGuire brothers themselves, had gotten out and were readying their trailer for transport. Identically dressed in dirt-splattered jeans and tank tops, one tall and lanky, the other heavier set, they were both laughing and joking as they rolled out a gangway and opened the trailer door. Once done, the tall one swaggered off toward the barn.

Another beep.

OMG that's beautiful. When are you coming home??

Tonight.

Is it all right if I come over later? I need to talk to you.

Amy smiled and sent back: *Yes.*

Ok. Call me the MINUTE you're back.

After switching off her phone, Amy saw the brother re-emerge from the barn. He had retrieved a horse and was yanking it by its chin straps, aggressively pulling it toward his truck. Amy watched in disbelief as he dragged the poor thing up the gangway, shoved it into the back of the transport, then strutted back to the barn, presumably to fetch his next victim. The next horse was far less cooperative. Far bigger, far stronger, it came out thrashing its head so hard that he stood no chance of getting near it, never mind getting his hands anywhere near its straps. Swearing audibly, he backed off and spun a finger in the air, a signal for his cohort to go fetch something from their truck—a whip—which he then proceeded to crack right in front of the horse's face.

Having seen as much as she could stomach, Amy swung open her door, leapt from the car, and stormed toward the barn, her hands balled into white-knuckled fists.

"Hey! What the hell do you think you're doing?"

"Were you expecting company?" Kevin asked, twisting in his seat at the sound of a truck rumbling onto the property.

"Yes, some people are coming to take my horses to their new home. I must see to them. But before I do, I want to show you something." Roger got up, hobbled into the kitchen, pulled a tube of paper from a drawer, then returned and unrolled it in front of Kevin. It was a map of southwest Oregon. There were circles around Seabrook, the ranch, the forest, the cliffs, as well as two dozen red circles stretching down the coast.

"I've been doing calculations based on the tides and the currents since the night my son disappeared. There's a number of beaches down the coast, but these bays and inlets are remote and inaccessible by foot, which means a body could wash up without anyone knowing."

Kevin studied the swirling arrows and plotted lines.

"You think your son fell into the water?"

"I don't know, but it's the only explanation that makes any sense. I assure you, I'd much rather believe the other version of events. It would be easier to pretend that my son ran away, because then at least he'd still be alive. But I'm his father, and sometimes a father has a gut feeling about these things. Ryan would never abandon me. He'd never abandon this ranch."

Roger sat back down in his chair and took a sip of water, taking off his glasses to wipe away a tear. When he looked back at Kevin, he had a pleading look in his eyes. "Detective, are you a father?"

"I am."

"And if you were in my place and your own child needed you, wouldn't you be doing the same? Wouldn't you be doing everything in your power to help them?"

After the events of last night, Kevin didn't hesitate to say yes.

"Then please, help me. Help me find my son."

Kevin sat very still, working through the situation in his head. He had to consider his next words carefully. He'd been sent here by Jack to relay news, not to indulge a father's theories about what might've happened to his missing son. But even though this wasn't his case, he couldn't deny the merits of the argument, nor could he deny that this was a line of inquiry that needed to be pursued.

"Roger, you should know that I cannot make any promises . . . and I would suggest there's a very low probability of us being able to find anything this many weeks on. But I'll speak to the detective in charge, and my captain, and see what I can do. Maybe we can get a small team to take a look at the cliff, and maybe we can get the coast guard to take a look at your map, send a few boats to investigate."

Roger fell back into his chair, overcome with emotion. "Thank you, Detective. You don't know what this means."

"Don't thank me yet. I'm not the one who has the final say, and I can't be sure what the answer will be."

"Just so long as you'll try."

"I will."

As they were shaking hands, a commotion erupted outside.

⸙

"Who are you?" the taller of the two brothers sneered at the sight of Amy approaching.

"Doesn't matter who I am," she snapped back.

"This your wild beast, is it?"

"No, but I'd like to know what makes you two think you've got the right to treat an animal like this? It's disgusting."

"Disgusting?" They screwed up their faces and sniggered. "How 'bout you run along. We don't want you gettin' hurt." The horse gave a loud snort and bucked high into the air, slamming its hooves into the wall of the barn.

"The poor thing is terrified!" Amy yelled. "Can't you see that?"

"Beat it, princess. Leave us to do our work."

Amy shook her head and boldly took another step forward, wedging herself between the brothers and the horse.

"Are you damn *crazy*? Do you want to get yourself *killed*?"

Amy stood her ground. If they expected her to back down, they had another thing coming. Taking a deep breath, she turned around and faced the erratic animal head on. Then, with just a few feet of dirt between them, without having a clue what she was doing, fully aware that at any moment she could be trampled to the ground, she stepped even closer, close enough to see the whites of the horse's eyes, close enough to feel the air snorting from her nostrils . . . and reached out to touch its neck.

"Amy!" Kevin cried out in the distance. "What are you *doing*? *Get back!*"

Amy ignored her dad's pleas. She switched off from the commotion unfolding around her. The horse was panting heavy and fast, its sweaty skin pulsing beneath her palm, but she let nothing distract her. Determined not to show any fear, she rested one hand on the horse's nose while running her other hand along the side of its neck, making long, gentle strokes, back and forth, back and forth.

"It's okay," she whispered. "Everything's okay . . ."

Amy repeated the same motion, the same words, never letting her voice waver, never letting her hand deviate. The horse resisted at first and continued to buck its legs and grunt and swing its head, but then something extraordinary happened—it began to calm. As though cast under a spell, the horse pricked its ears forward, gently padded the dirt, then bent down and nuzzled its nose into Amy's shoulder. Amy couldn't believe what she was witnessing. She raised her other hand and stroked the other side of the horse's head, and an affectionate nicker rose from the horse's throat. For a moment, Amy wondered if she might cry.

After kissing the horse on the nose, she gripped its straps and turned around. Four wide-eyed faces were staring back at her. No one knew what to say. Not her dad, not the owner of the ranch, not even those two louts from McGuire Bros. Horse Transport.

48

$\mathcal{R}$OGER, who couldn't stop staring at Amy, his gaze a mix of both curiosity and wonder, mumbled, "Who are you?"

"This is my daughter," Kevin said, stepping in, "who was *supposed* to be waiting in the car."

"Sorry, Dad, but these two were being cruel to this horse and I had to do something."

"Whoa, now hang on just a minute," one of the McGuire brothers huffed. "Cruel? Hardly."

Roger jerked his head and gave the two men a scowling glare. "Is that a whip?" he cried out in disgust. He was so angry that he had to lean down hard on his cane to keep his balance. "I don't appreciate you coming here and threatening my horses, so I'd like you to get off my property—*right now.*"

"We ain't movin'. And that horse that's already in our trailer? He isn't going anywhere, not till we get what's owed to us."

Kevin took that as his cue to intervene. "I don't think it's wise for you to be making threats," he said as he pulled out his wallet and flashed his badge right in the faces of the brothers.

The two men looked back at Kevin, each with the same dim-witted expression. "You're . . . a cop?"

"That's right, and I believe I just heard the man order you off his property, so how about you clear off before he accuses you of trespassing."

"But—"

"*Now*, fellas, before you say something you'll regret."

The brothers promptly gave up the fight, sulkily retreated to their truck, and unloaded the horse. As they were driving off, Kevin was sure he heard Roger mutter "good riddance" under his breath.

"Thank you, Detective. And you," Roger added, staring at Amy, "what you did just now was remarkable. I didn't catch your name."

"It's Amy."

"Thank you, Amy. You obviously know your way around horses."

"Not really. But what I saw wasn't right and I had to do something. I'm sorry if I caused you any trouble."

"Hardly. You did me a favor, and you saved that poor horse from an awful lot of distress."

Amy smiled. "I'm just glad I could help."

Kevin gave Amy a nudge. "Why don't you go wait in the car. I'll only be a minute."

Before leaving, Kevin helped Roger secure the horses back in their stalls and close the barn. "There are others who can come take them?" he asked as they walked back to the car.

"Yes, I'll find someone far better. How those two are allowed to operate, I have no idea, but you can be sure I'll be laying a complaint."

"If you don't mind me asking, since your son's been gone, how have you been able to keep this place running? The horses must be a handful?"

"They are, but I've had plenty of help. A group of folks have been volunteering their time. Each morning and night someone comes to tend to the horses and check in on me. Everyone in town has been so kind, so generous."

As they arrived at the car, Kevin stole one last look at the view before turning to shake Roger's hand.

"Like I said, Mr. Porter, I will speak to my superiors. No promises, but I will do my best."

"Thank you, Detective. Please get in touch once you learn the decision. Oh, and one more thing . . ." Roger came in close, turning his back to the car. "Is that really true, about your daughter? That she hasn't been around horses?"

"I'm afraid so. No horses about when she was growing up. Her mother grew up on a farm though—maybe she got the special touch from her."

"Detective, it took my son months to form a bond with that horse and your daughter managed it in only sixty seconds. Whatever she's got, she sure got it from somewhere."

49

THE MOOD WAS QUIET as they left the ranch. Kevin steered the car out the gate and drove well below the limit, both hands on the wheel, eyes ahead, not because the road demanded it but because he was finding it hard to concentrate. A wild thought had tumbled into his head. Precisely where it had come from, he couldn't say, but it had him so excited that he had to tell Amy all about it. After coming down the hill, he swerved onto the shoulder, brought the car to a stop, and switched off the engine.

"Dad, what's wrong?"

"Amy, I need to talk to you."

"I know what you're going to say, that it was dangerous and dumb of me to get so close to the horse and that I could've been hurt, but I was only—"

"No, that's not it. You saw something wrong and you took action. I'm proud of you. You did the right thing."

His praise caught her off guard. "Oh, thanks. What is it, then?"

Kevin stared at her for a moment, tapping the steering wheel with a hesitant smile, which only heightened Amy's curiosity.

"This might sound crazy," he said after a long pause, "but what would you say to a change of scenery?"

Amy squinted back at him. "What *kind* of change?"

"The permanent kind."

Her confusion intensified. "What are you talking about?"

"I'm talking about doing what your mother always wanted to do—selling the house, getting out of the city."

"Um, and where would we go?"

"Well, you know that ranch we were just at?"

"Yes . . ."

"The bank is foreclosing on it. The owner, Mr. Porter, is moving out in a few weeks."

"And . . . ?"

"And I think we should buy it."

Amy reacted with a slow, facetious laugh. "Very funny. What's the punchline?"

"There isn't one. I'm being serious."

She studied his face, but his expression wasn't budging.

"Wait, you *are* being serious . . ."

"Imagine it, Amy. Imagine living in a place like that. It was stunning, don't you think?"

"Of course it was stunning—it was amazing—but we're two hundred miles from Portland. Our lives are back in the city."

"That's the whole idea."

"To what, run away?"

"No, to start afresh, something new, to embark on a project that you and I can work on together." Kevin could tell by the look on Amy's face that she was probably trying to gauge if he was joking or downright nuts. "It's crazy. You think it's crazy."

"Slow down, Dad. This morning you said you wanted to quit your job, now you want to move to the country? Are you sure you're feeling all right? And what do we know about running a ranch? Or looking after horses?"

"Right now, not a lot, but I'm sure it's nothing we can't learn. It would be a leap of faith, but we'd do our best and make a go of it, together, you and me."

Amy stared out the windshield, her eyes flickering with confusion, but also a glimmer of excitement. "I'll admit, on the one hand, it does sound kinda tempting . . ."

"And on the other?"

"And on the other, it all sounds sudden and drastic."

"Too drastic?"

"I don't know. I honestly don't know."

Kevin fell silent, stared out the window, then laughed and shook his head. "Actually, forget it," he said, turning the engine back on. "Let's just go home. It's probably a terrible idea. I'm sorry, I'm not sure what got into me."

"No, wait . . ."

"No, honestly, it's ridiculous. It wouldn't be sensible, not after everything's that happened."

Amy reached over, twisted the key, and switched off the engine. She then reached into her pocket and pulled out her mother's pendant, which she turned over in her hands for a moment, brushing her fingers over its luminous moonstone. For reasons that weren't entirely clear, she found herself warming to the idea.

"Dad, maybe this wouldn't be the craziest thing in the world."

"Really?" He spun around in his seat, startled. "You don't think I've lost my mind?"

"I did at first, but now that I think about it, it actually seems to make sense."

"You think so?"

"Strangely enough, yeah, I do."

"But you do realize what it would mean? With a move like this—everything would change."

Amy looked down at her pendant again and caught the sunlight reflecting off the silver, almost as though it was winking back at her. "I know, but maybe we have no choice."

"What do you mean?"

"I can't explain it, but something about this feels right. I mean, what if we were meant to come here today? What if this is something we were meant to do?

Kevin leaned back in his seat, quietly smiling at his daughter. "Do you know something? You sound just like your mother. That's exactly what she would've said. Everything happened for a reason, according to her."

"And what do you think she would say if she were here? What would she tell us to do?"

"That's easy," Kevin said, who didn't need to consider that question for long. "I know *exactly* what she'd tell us to do."

Amy smiled back at him. "Me too."

Kevin took a deep breath, turned the engine on once more, released the parking brake, then flicked his indicator in the direction of Seabrook.

"What do you say we head back into town and stop by the bank, see if this crazy idea is even going to be possible."

Amy nodded her head, letting slip a quiet squeal of excitement. "I can't believe we're actually doing this . . ."

"Neither can I," Kevin laughed. "Believe me, neither can I."

50

AFTER SPEAKING with the manager of the local bank, and after a few calls to realtors back home, the logistics of purchasing the ranch proved to be more straightforward than Kevin had expected. Through sheer good luck and timing, he and Helen had bought in what had become one of Portland's most sought-after neighborhoods; that, combined with the payout from Helen's life insurance policy (it was pressed upon every officer in the force to take out comprehensive policies for both them and their spouse), and the fact that the bank had given Mr. Porter a period of clemency and was yet to formally serve the foreclosure notice—meant that Kevin didn't need to wait around. He was able to approach Roger without delay and make an offer direct.

But rather than jump to any sudden decisions, Kevin and Amy decided to stay in Seabrook one more night. They checked back into the hotel and spent the night in vigorous discussion. During a light dinner, they even made a pros-and-cons list in which every potential issue was noted down, every pitfall objectively weighed and considered. But by the end of their deliberations, they were in unanimous agreement: this wild idea of theirs was a leap worth taking.

—⟨⟨⟩⟩—

After a short interlude back in Portland in which Amy caught up with friends and Kevin managed to convince Jack to keep the case open a short while longer, they returned to Seabrook and visited Roger at the ranch. Sitting out on the porch in two low-slung wicker chairs, Kevin delivered the news that state police would indeed be taking a second look at his son's disappearance, and that the green light had been given for another search, this time over land *and* sea. The news was met with heartfelt relief.

"Thank you so much, Detective. But you didn't have to come down here to tell me this."

"Roger, I'll level with you—there's another reason why we're here." Kevin eased forward in his chair, broached the subject of the ranch's impending sale, and asked whether Roger would consider bypassing the foreclosure and accepting an offer direct.

"An offer? From who?"

"From us." Kevin pulled a piece of paper from his pocket on which he had written down a number, a large number, a generous sum of money that would cover Roger's loan and even put some cash into his back pocket. It was a number so generous that Roger couldn't help but put the paper down as his eyes welled up with tears.

"Are you serious? You would do this for me?"

"If you'd let us, yes."

"But, Detective, this is more than—"

"Think of it as payment for future services. If you agree, and I hope that you do, we intend to make good use of you. You know this property better than anyone, and it's in our own interests if we can pick up the phone and talk to you whenever we need help. We're newcomers to all this, my daughter and I, but we're eager to learn, and we'd love for you to be involved, as little or as much as you would like."

"And the horses?"

Amy leaned forward. "Them too," she said. "This is their home, and we'd love to keep them here, but only if that's okay with you."

"You don't know what this means to me. I don't know what to say."

"We're hoping you'll say yes," Kevin said.

"Yes," Roger said, his voice choking up with tears. "Of course, my answer is yes."

———

"Are you *mad*?" Jack spluttered, nearly ejecting a mouthful of beer. "Kevin, I sent you down there for the night, not to quit your job and buy the place. *Jesus*."

"It's a little out of the blue, I know," Kevin said.

"*Out of the blue?* It's *extreme* is what this is. Isn't there some rule about making life-changing decisions when you're in grief? You only lost Helen a month ago. You're still hurting. Are you sure everything's all right? Are you sure you're thinking straight?"

"My leaving CID has been a long time coming, you know that."

"Maybe," Jack conceded. "But to uproot your life and move to the country? Is *that* really necessary?"

"I've got you to thank, Jack. You thought we needed to get out of the city, and you were right."

"Gee, that makes me feel a lot better." Jack set his bottle down and slumped against a banister on Kevin's back porch, shaking his head. It was a good few minutes before he managed to speak again. "You do know what you're doing, don't you?"

"Do any of us really know what we're doing? I lost my wife a month ago and came this close to losing my daughter. Is moving away the answer? I don't know. But I have a good feeling about what we're about to do, and I'd love to have the support of my brother, because heaven knows I'll need it in the coming months."

"Hey, I'll always support you, and I'll always be there for you and Amy, no matter what. But that doesn't mean I don't reserve the right to think you're out of your mind."

"Thanks, Jack. You know, you're welcome down there whenever you like. You might even get a taste for country life. Trust me, wait till you see it."

"I'll be coming down, all right," Jack retorted as he bent down to pick up his beer. "But only to make sure you haven't completely gone around the bend. Oh, and if you think you're gonna see me gallivanting around the countryside on the back of a horse anytime soon, you've got another thing coming."

Kevin grinned. "We'll see, Jack. We'll see."

51

*W*ITH A DATE LOCKED IN and excitement surrounding the move beginning to build, there was packing to do, and plenty of it. Amy and her dad went about the house making a list of what they needed to take and what could be sent to storage, and then, together, they moved from room to room and boxed everything up.

One night, when they were in the master bedroom sorting through her mother's things, Amy came across the stack of photo albums. Remembering what she and her dad had promised each other back at the ranch, they boiled the kettle, sat down on the couch, and went through the albums together, page by page, photo by photo, laughing, crying, remembering a mother and a wife who they knew would have given everything she could to be with them right now, joining them on this great adventure.

"Are you okay?" Kevin asked.

Amy pulled a clump of tissues from her pocket and dabbed her eyes. "I'm okay. I just miss her so much."

"I know. So do I."

As she flipped to the last page of the final album, Amy arrived at a photo of her parents taken over twenty years ago on her mother's childhood farm.

"This is the famous photo, isn't it?"

Kevin nodded, smiling. "We took it with her old Polaroid camera, right after I had dug up that box and read your mother's letter."

"Didn't you used to carry that letter around with you?"

"I still do," he said, as he reached into his pocket and pulled out his wallet, where the letter had remained safely kept.

Teary-eyed, Amy opened the letter and spent the next few minutes lost in her mother's words:

Dear Stranger,

Today is a special day. I have brought you here, to my favorite tree, because there's something important I want to tell you. I want you to know that I have found someone . . . someone special . . . someone I want to spend the rest of my life with.

Yes, dear stranger, I found <u>you</u>.

Right now, I don't know a thing about you. I have no idea who you are, or where you're from. I don't even know your name. But somewhere in the ocean of time, somewhere in the days, months, or years that lie between now and the moment these words next see the light of day, you and I will have met, and I will have fallen in love.

Thank you for making my dreams come true. I don't know what the future holds, but wherever our lives should lead, wherever the road should go, my heart and my mind are made up: it's you who I want by my side . . . it's your hand I want to hold along the way.

Forever yours, no matter what,

Helen

P.S. Will you marry me?

"I can't believe Mom was such a romantic," Amy said, dabbing at her eyes.

"We used to joke about how she was probably the only person in history who had proposed via postscript."

Amy laughed through her tears. "I think it's more amazing that she popped the question on a piece of paper that had been buried for . . . how long was it again?"

"Nine years!"

"Wow, go Mom."

"It's incredible to think she wrote those words when she wasn't that much younger than you, never knowing who would one day read them."

Amy delicately folded the letter and handed it back. "Do you think she's looking down on us?"

"I don't know, sweetheart, but something tells me that she is."

Amy rested her head on his shoulder. "I don't want to forget her, Dad."

"That's not going to happen."

"But we're moving, we're leaving our home. What if this means we——"

He put his arm around her. "Your mother's memory lives on inside of us, not between the walls of this house. No matter where we are, whether it's Portland or Seabrook or anywhere else, we're the ones who will keep her memory alive. And we're going to do that by thinking about her, and talking about her, and remembering the amazing woman and mother that she was. You have my word; we won't ever forget her."

52

*T*HOUGH THE MOVE went off without a hitch, it took a week before Kevin and Amy were properly settled in. When they weren't inside mulling over what to unpack, or deciding which couch should go where, they were outside roaming the ranch, investigating unseen corners, prying into the outbuildings, fiddling with equipment, trying to familiarize themselves with how everything worked. Roger had left them a list: a city dweller's survival guide—tips on keeping the rainwater tanks clean, what to do if the power was cut—but Kevin refrained from looking at it too much. He figured it did them no good to pick up a phone or refer to a cheat sheet every time they had a question. Besides, Amy seemed to be enjoying the pioneering thrill of inspecting everything for herself, particularly if it had anything to do with the horses. She'd made the barn her second home, camping out there for hours on end with books borrowed from the local library: basic care, grooming, feeding, behavior, handling, and safety. Anything to do with horse keeping, she read from cover to cover.

Even the ranch hand they hired, a friendly local man by the name of Zack, with twenty-five years' horse-keeping experience, was impressed by how much Amy had learned in such a short space of time. None of this was news to Kevin, of course, for he'd already witnessed her ability firsthand. Seeing her work her magic with Little Dipper was a sight he'd never forget.

—⁓—

A month after the move, on one sunny, cloudless morning, Kevin grabbed Helen's old Polaroid camera, a pen, a sheet of paper, a tin box, and a shovel from the shed, and went to find Amy. She was in the barn with Zack, getting a lesson on first aid and monitoring the horses' health.

"Mind if I interrupt?"

"Sure, Dad. What's up?"

"I need a favor." He held up the camera. "Zack, would you mind taking a photo of us?"

"Certainly, Mr. Tucker."

Kevin headed outside and found a spot beneath the spindly branches of an old sycamore tree. Amy followed a few minutes later, emerging from the barn carrying an old-fashioned cowboy hat.

"Look what I found gathering dust in the tack room," she said, sticking the hat on her head. "What do you think? How do I look?"

Kevin grabbed the brim of the hat and tipped it forward, laughing as he brought her in for a hug.

"You look perfect," he said.

Standing in sun-dappled shade, with a view of the valley as their backdrop, Kevin and Amy put their arms around each other and faced the camera. Zack told them to smile, counted to three, then snapped the picture. There was a click and hum as the film fed through the camera and slid out the front. Zack handed the camera back to Kevin.

"Great stuff, Zack."

"Happy to oblige, Mr. Tucker."

Kevin and Amy stayed by the tree, waiting as the white sheet of Polaroid film slowly bloomed with color.

"Thanks, Amy," Kevin said, watching their faces emerge. "This is exactly what I need."

Before returning to the barn, Amy gestured at the pen and paper in her dad's hands and gave him a smile. "Say hi to her, okay?"

He smiled back. "I will."

Sitting down with his back to the sycamore's trunk, a blank page laid over his lap, Kevin closed his eyes and let his thoughts drift backward through the years, and to those still ahead. Then, after a minute of reflection, he took the pen in his hand and began to write:

To my dear wife,

Hopefully these words will somehow find their way to you, wherever you are.

The last few months have been more difficult than you can possibly know. Every day is a battle, every moment tinged with an unbearable ache. There's nothing I wouldn't do to have you back, Helen, nothing I wouldn't do to hold your hand again, to see your face and kiss your lips, to breathe in your scent, to just be around the woman that I cherished and adored. The world isn't the same without you in it, my love, and it never will be.

As for Amy, she has struggled too. Soon after we lost you, she had an awful accident. It wasn't her fault. You were her whole world, and she took your death extremely hard. All she wanted was an escape from her grief, but in doing so she made a terrible mistake, one that nearly cost her her life. Even now, just writing those words makes me feel sick to my stomach. Helen . . . for a while there, our precious baby girl actually left us. The doctor who saw her afterward, he said it was incredible she had no lasting damage, even said it was a miracle she woke up at all.

Now, I haven't a clue what happened to Amy while she was gone, but I believe her returning was more than a random miracle. Somehow,

I don't know how, but I think you played a part in what happened that night. I think you helped our daughter find her way home.

Or maybe I'm crazy. Maybe we got lucky. Maybe the gods just decided to be kind. I don't know. I guess I'll never know. But what matters most is that Amy was given a second chance, which means I've been given a second chance too—a second chance to make you proud.

Helen, this is my second chance to be the man I always should have been. I promise I'll take good care of our daughter. I promise that, for as long as I can draw breath, she will have my unconditional love and attention. I'll make sure she comes through this and goes on to live the fullest life she can, which is just what you would have wanted. And as for me, I shall try to do the same.

Till we meet again, whenever and wherever that might be, you will always be in my thoughts. You've left me with the memory of a love I won't ever find again. You were the woman who turned me into a man, the luckiest man on earth, and I will remain forever grateful that I was the one you chose to share your life with, that it was my hand you chose to hold along the way.

Wherever you are, I hope you're at peace.

I love you, and I miss you.

Your husband,
Kevin

P.S. Amy says hi.

Kevin folded the pages in half and placed them inside the box. He also took the photo of him and Amy, father and daughter, cheeks pressed together, smiling for the lens, and tucked that inside too. Then, after digging a small hole, he laid the box in the dirt, knelt on the ground, kissed his fingers, and placed his hand down on the tin lid.

"Rest easy, my sweetheart."

53

*L*IFE HAD BECOME a nonstop crash course in horse keeping, and Amy loved every minute of it. Their ranch hand, Zack, had a natural rapport with the horses and made for an excellent teacher. A little younger than her dad, he was quiet and reserved but could explain everything in a way that made perfect sense. The funny thing was, Amy had never once considered herself a "horse person," yet in just a few short weeks these wonderful animals were already the center of her world. She loved them dearly and couldn't imagine life without them.

Her best friend, Sam, was also smitten. She had become a regular visitor, driving down every weekend to see Amy and the horses, often staying the night. No matter the activity, whether it was riding or grooming or feeding, she loved being part of the action. She always made herself useful, helping muck out the stalls, doing whatever she could to put off going back home. She even suggested in a vaguely serious manner that she adopt one of the horses as her very own.

"Actually," Sam said, her eyes glowing as she ran a brush down the length of Snowflake's mane, "maybe your dad could just adopt *me*, and I could live here full-time."

Amy burst out laughing. She was up in the hayloft grabbing a few small bales for the horses' dinner.

"You're nineteen, Sam," she yelled back. "I don't even think you can be adopted anymore."

"Oh yeah." She laughed. "Awesome, so I can just move in right away. Why don't I start packing?"

"Why not?" Amy grinned.

Elsewhere around the ranch, her dad had been keeping himself busy tidying up the property and restoring it to its former glory. So far he had cleared the gutters, fixed a few tiles on the roof of the house, replaced the rotting timber around the vegetable garden, dug new soil, sown new seeds, replaced a dozen or so fence posts, hacked away what seemed like a mountain of weeds, mown the fields (after spending a whole day troubleshooting why the riding lawn mower's engine cranked but wouldn't start, which turned out to be because of a clogged fuel filter), and was halfway through sanding and repainting the barn. He was, by his own admission, not a natural handyman, and although there had been a couple of minor incidents—one with a rusty nail, the other involving some hay and a buried rake—on the whole, he thought he was acquitting himself quite well, or at least that's what he liked to tell Amy.

Such industrious productivity outside the barn meant he was always a step behind with the horses, though, especially compared to his daughter. He was capable, but his skills weren't comparable to hers, which, from Amy's perspective, worked out fine because it gave her a chance to sharpen her own.

"No, no, you need to sit straighter, and loosen your hands," Amy told him one afternoon as they were taking Snowflake and Bella on a walk somewhere in Seabrook State Park. "And you need to shift your feet forward," she added, pointing down at his stirrups. "The back of your heel should be resting on the bar, not hanging off the edge."

He did as he was told and adjusted accordingly. "How you've learned all this so quickly, I have no idea. Are you sure we're not lost? Everywhere looks the same to me. Haven't we come this way already?"

Amy reached into her pocket and pulled out a map, left for them by Roger. "I know exactly where we are. Sam and I have been riding the trails, scoping them out. This is one of the trails that Mr. Porter's son used to ride. Ryan, right? This is where he took people."

"Ah, I see," he said, bobbing in the saddle. "You know, I thought it would be another six months before we could begin thinking about opening up the trails, but do you know what? You look like you're almost ready."

Amy smiled. "Yep, I think I am."

As for the case of the boy who had previously lived on the ranch, Amy only knew what her dad had been willing to share—that Ryan Porter was a missing person, and that his disappearance was either purposeful or he'd suffered some kind of tragic accident. But Amy could draw her own conclusions. She was aware that a new search was being organized, this time with the coast guard involved, which suggested to her that they were looking for a body and not a runaway—and, sadly, it turned out she was right.

Ryan's body was found twenty-three miles south, on the shores of a remote bay at the very edge of the marine search zone. Carried down the coast by strong seasonal currents, the body had lain undiscovered for months before being spotted by a local fisherman, one of many who had volunteered to help. He had reported seeing something unusual on the sand, something out of place among all the washed-up seaweed and kelp. Prompted to take a closer look, he dropped anchor and rode his dinghy ashore, and that's when he made the discovery and radioed in the news that no one in Seabrook wanted to hear.

For the next week, confirmation of Ryan's death consumed the town. The *Seabrook Beacon* ran front-page headlines every day, reporting on the recovery of the body, identification, and burial plans, and, on the eve of the funeral, they ran their biggest piece yet, a four-page obituary entitled *Remembering Ryan—Our Beloved Son.*

Half was a biographical account of Ryan's life, the rest a collection of eulogies contributed by those who had known him. There was one from his father; one from Joe and Linda, owners of the local diner, where Ryan had worked part-time; one from Peggy, proprietor at The Lookout; there was even one from the local bank manager, Tom Tippenworth. It seemed the town was full of people whose lives had been touched by Ryan, many wanting to share their memories. Even those who had never met him were prompted to write in and express their sympathies:

> *Ryan and I weren't acquainted on a personal level, but it is clear, after learning all about him, that we have lost someone special. He sounds like he was a young man of unimpeachable character, and he has been taken far too soon. To Roger, we send our deepest condolences. We have shed tears this week. Words cannot express how sorry we all are for your loss. I have two young boys, and if they grow up to possess even half the heart and valor of your son, then I should be a very proud father indeed.*

That night, while reading through the pages of poignant tributes, Amy shed a tear too.

—◦∿◦—

The funeral brought the town to a halt. It was standing room only in the church. Amy and her dad were given seats near the front, not because they were the new owners of the ranch but because Roger had asked her dad to be a pallbearer. It was surreal for Amy to see another casket resting on his shoulders, so soon after her mother's burial.

After the service, the casket was carried outside and loaded into a hearse, which made a slow procession around the town square. People lined the sidewalks, clapping and throwing flowers at the sleek black car as it crawled by in the midday sun. A large contingent followed on foot to the cemetery.

Gathered around the grave site, Amy and Kevin stood and listened to the final prayers, then watched as the casket was lowered into the ground. When the formalities were over, the crowd of mourners formed a line and approached Roger one by one to pay their respects. Most grabbed some dirt to throw on top of the casket; others picked up a spade. Some had brought flowers and cards. One person even threw in a horseshoe. But Amy had brought along something else . . .

Earlier that morning, while up in the attic, in the room that had once been Ryan's, while she was staring at lines of dust on the floor and pinholes in the roof and feeling sad for a boy she hadn't even known, two small rocks had caught her eye. They were sitting on the windowsill. One was smooth and rounded, the other misshapen, jagged, and rough. Whether they'd been forgotten by the movers or purposely left behind, Amy didn't know, but she felt a duty to return them, especially if there was a chance they had once belonged to Ryan.

When it was her turn to speak with Roger, she reached into her pocket, ready to pull them out.

"I'm so sorry for your loss, Mr. Porter," she said, leaning in to give him a hug.

"Thank you, Amy. Thank you for coming today." With a cane in his hand, he could hug her back with only one arm. "How are the horses?"

"They're doing well."

"And Little Dipper?"

"Absolutely fine. She and I are getting on very well."

"Thank goodness. It's been a great weight off my mind. My son would be so pleased knowing that someone like you is there to look after her."

"I've been reading everything that's been written about him. He sounded like a very special person."

"He was, Amy, he really was. And he would have liked you very much. The two of you would have gotten on well, I suspect."

Amy smiled, then showed Roger what she had been holding in her hands. "I don't suppose you recognize these? I found them upstairs."

"Mm?" Roger glanced down and then went very still. His mouth dropped open. "Oh my God." He gasped as he grabbed both rocks, inspecting them closely. "Where did you find these?"

"In the attic."

"I had no idea that he'd kept them all these years. I . . . I can't believe it."

"They mean something to you?"

"Oh yes, they mean a great deal—more than you could possibly know."

His cane fell to the ground and he gave her a second hug, this time with both arms. He couldn't bring himself to let go. "Thank you so much, my dear girl."

"That's all right," she said. "And remember, the ranch is always open to you. Please come visit us whenever you like. Promise that you will?"

"I will, I promise," he said, nodding his head, still clutching the rocks tightly in his hands. His eyes were red and watery and his bottom lip was quivering. "Thank you, Amy. Thank you for bringing these to me. And thank you for all that you and your father have done for me. It means so much." He went to pick up his cane, but Amy bent down and got it for him.

"It's okay, Mr. Porter. And again, I'm so sorry."

"Thank you. Thank you for everything." Glancing at the line of mourners waiting to pay their respects, Roger wiped his nose with his handkerchief and mustered a tired smile. "You head along now. Go be with your dad."

"Goodbye, Mr. Porter."

"So long, Amy."

Amy turned and headed over to Ryan's grave. There were at least a dozen others there as well, many weeping, many of them with their arms around each other. She stood beside her dad and peered down at the casket, which was nearly completely covered in flowers and cards and dirt. She grabbed a handful of dirt for herself and sprinkled it down, concealing the very last patch of the polished oak.

Bowing her head, Amy closed her eyes and whispered her final goodbye. Then, as a cool breeze drifted through her hair, as birds sang in nearby trees, and as the world turned beneath her feet, she smiled and took hold of her father's hand.

"Come on, Dad," she said. "Let's go home."

EPILOGUE

*S*PRING HAS ALWAYS BEEN my favorite time of year on the ranch. The branches of trees stripped bare during the winter months begin camouflaging themselves in new growth, migrating birds return to nest in the woodland and fill the forest with song, and the hillsides experience their own rebirth, their frosty, sun-starved slopes slowly turning from tawny to emerald green. Tiny bulbs sprout everywhere, in the gardens and along the pea-gravel paths—future lilies, suncups, and bright yellow arnicas to name but a few—and sometimes, if I'm lucky, I'll see deer and their fawns grazing nearby, feeding on the red huckleberries that fall by the forest's edge.

Our business comes alive too. The season kicks off in early March and runs strong through to Christmas. From young schoolchildren learning to ride in the arena, to the large groups who come to experience the forest trails, a day here rarely sees a quiet moment. And that's just the way I like it. In the afternoons, once it's warm enough, I'll throw open a window and sit in my favorite chair, just so I can be a part of what's going on outside. Whether it's the rapturous laughter of a budding rider who's just climbed into the saddle for the first time, or the adorable giggles of a honeymooning couple heading off on a sunset trek, these small delights warm the soul and make this old woman incredibly happy. I only wish I was able to share in that same joy again, the kind one can get only from being on the back of a horse.

Regrettably, my riding days are far behind me. These eyes of mine have seen many a springtime—ninety-two and counting—and I confess there are moments when I wonder how many I have left. But if you think I am frightened of what's to come, you would be mistaken. I have lived a great life, one blessed with good health, a beautiful home, and a loving family that continues to grow. That's not to say I haven't experienced my fair share of heartache, because I have, and I'll be the first to admit that sometimes my life has ventured down paths I rather wish it hadn't, but more often than not I feel like good fortune has shone down on my little corner of the world, and for that I'll always be grateful. My family, my dear friends, and the wonderful animals with whom I share my home—these are what keep this old lady content. Even in my lonelier moments, when I have only my thoughts and I begin to contemplate what may come next, I am comforted by the memories of a life well lived.

And in the end, what more could anyone want?

⟞⟋⟍⟞

For some, their twilight years are a chance to put their feet up and relax, but that was never the case for me. Whether it's fundraising for the elementary school or volunteering each Christmas at the local shelter, I have always stayed active in the community, always tried to give something back. Which is what makes today a very special day indeed. You see, a humble little project of mine—or a "preposterous longshot" as the *Beacon* once called it—has finally reached completion. After eight long years, the hard work of myself, and countless others, is at last ready to be unveiled to the town.

Few thought it could even be done. Indeed, when I first formed the Seabrook Lighthouse Preservation Committee and announced my lofty goal of restoring the decrepit tower to her original, nineteenth-century condition, the plans were met with a chorus of skepticism. I wasn't surprised. After all, the council had been at a stalemate for decades over the issue. Some considered it an exorbitant waste of money; spending millions on such a folly couldn't be justified, they said, not when there were more pressing matters to be addressed. And there were of course the superstitious few who brought up old ghost stories from the past, claiming that hell and damnation would rain down upon the town if anyone dared step through the door. Mustn't disturb Theodore's spirit, they cried out—for anyone who did would surely feel the lighthouse keeper's wrath!

But despite the opposition, despite the endless debates and bureaucratic red tape, I pushed on undeterred, and not only did I generate a groundswell of support, but I also managed to convince the powers-that-be—through a very impassioned speech, I might add—that the heart of Seabrook was at stake, that our crumbling tower wasn't just a relic from the past but a beacon for the future, a towering monument that urgently needed to be saved. Countless meetings and fundraising drives were to follow before the restoration work could begin, but the fact that we've finally reached this moment, that our precious lighthouse is now on the cusp of her rebirth, at last ready to reveal herself to the world, fills me with enormous pride.

—⚬⚬⚬—

A grand celebration was put on for the unveiling. Seabrook's beach was transformed into a parade of festivity with thousands gathered along the shoreline to enjoy the food and live entertainment. For the ceremony itself, as official guest of honor, I was escorted by the mayor onto a podium in front of the tower, where I made a few remarks and cut a giant blue ribbon with a pair of equally oversized scissors. A giant holographic curtain had been keeping the building hidden— technology that I admit I'm far too old to understand—but the effect, when the curtain magically came down, made for a dramatic unveiling. The tower, in all her grandeur, was suddenly revealed for all to see, and even I was taken aback at how marvelous she looked. Her walls, now solid and lustrously white, rose boldly to the sky, her lamp room glistened behind newly minted glass, and her dome sat proudly at the top, painstakingly restored, freshly painted in its original navy blue.

"Heaven's above," I said, stunned by her beauty.

The mayor gazed up in wonder, equally impressed. "For 232 years old, she scrubs up pretty well, wouldn't you say?"

"She most certainly does."

Then, as the sun began to dip below the horizon, I was led toward the building's imposing arched door, where the mayor confessed that my official duties weren't over yet, that there was one last job he wanted me to complete.

"Our lighthouse needs to do what she was designed to do, Amy. This little project of yours won't truly be finished until we fire up the lamp and her light shines across the bay. It's all set up and ready for you."

"Oh my . . . but I don't think I can possibly make it up those stairs."

"We'll take as long as you need, and I wouldn't worry about the crowd—they're not going anywhere."

Ascending the twisting staircase was painfully slow, but with the help of the mayor's steady hand, and a few breaks along the way, we made it to the top.

Like the rest of the building, the lamp room was a sight to behold. An authentic Fresnel lens sat in the center, exquisitely refurbished, glass prisms sparkling, brass polished to a golden finish, while to the west, framed against the tall windows, was the most staggeringly beautiful view of the Pacific Ocean, laid bare in all her shimmering splendor.

To be standing in a room I had gazed upon nearly all my life, a place that for so long had been impossible to reach, left me humbled and awestruck. But that wasn't all I felt, for as I made my way around the lens, running my fingers across the bumpy ridges of glass, something else crept over me, a most peculiar sensation, a tingling that spread from inside my chest all the way to the ends of my fingertips.

"Amy, is something the matter?"

The mayor, who had just returned inside from delivering a speech via megaphone to the expectant crowd below, picked up on the fact that my mind was elsewhere.

"This might sound strange," I began to say, "but I swear I've been in this room before."

"I know what you mean," he joked. "We've all been staring at sketches and studying old photographs for so long that everything about this building now feels very familiar, doesn't it?"

"No," I said, feeling awfully lightheaded, "it's more than that . . ."

The mayor put his hand on my shoulder and asked if I was okay, but his voice was starting to fade. So too were the sounds of the crowd, their cheers becoming more and more distant. Soon I couldn't hear them at all. Even the sound of the wind, quietly whistling through the windows just a moment ago, vanished.

Suddenly I could no longer feel the mayor's hand on my shoulder. I turned to find him, but he wasn't there. I moved around the lens, uncertain, but not afraid, and that's when I noticed something stranger—my body no longer felt like my own. I had a lightness in my joints, strength in my muscles. I could move more easily, more freely, and when I looked down at my hands, they were different too. My skin was smooth and wrinkleless, the skin of someone much, much younger.

I lifted my head and gazed into the lens, and as I peered into the glass, a reflection appeared, not of an old woman, but a vision from a different time . . . a girl from long ago. She put her hand to the glass, and I did the same, and as we touched the years were instantly wound back. Emotions from the past returned. Faded memories became clear again, and alongside those old memories new ones emerged, memories I didn't recognize, memories that flickered and flashed inside my head like embers from an unseen fire, illuminating an experience I had long since buried and forgotten. But before I could make sense of everything, the girl in the reflection gently nodded her head and shifted her gaze. Her eyes drifted past me, behind me, down toward the beach.

Following her lead, I turned and approached the window, and there in the distance, beneath a dusty pink sky, I could see two figures—a boy and his horse. They were riding in the shallows, headed in the opposite direction. Moments after my eyes landed on him, the boy brought his horse to a stop and turned around. He lifted the brim of his hat and looked up at the lighthouse, and I looked back at him. We stared at each other for a while, neither of us moving, until his horse suddenly reared up on its hind legs and began stomping and splashing in the water, as though impatient to get riding again. The boy took off his hat and waved it high in the air, his smile visible even from the distant shoreline. I too raised my hand, waved, and smiled back.

—ɷ—

"Amy, can you hear me?"

"Pardon?"

"I said, are you ready?"

The mayor was once again standing beside me, his hand returned to my shoulder.

"Sorry, yes . . ." I lifted my head and squinted at my reflection in the lamp, trying to regather my thoughts.

"Are you feeling okay?"

I gave him a reassuring nod. "Yes, I am," I said. "Now, please explain what I have to do."

The mayor showed me around the lens and pointed out that everything had already been prepared—the lamp, wick, oil, and gas—all I needed to do was turn on a small green switch near the base, wired to light the fuse.

"You're certain everything's all right?" he asked again. "You seemed to disappear on me just now."

"Oh, that was nothing. Just a bit of déjà vu."

"Déjà vu?"

"Happens from time to time."

"You're sure?"

"Quite sure," I said, smiling softly, and I bent down, reached out my hand, and flicked the switch.

Christopher was born in Takapuna, a seaside suburb in
Auckland, New Zealand, where he currently lives with
his daughter. Having loved writing stories growing up, it
was a walk along Takapuna beach and a chance glimpse
at a distant lighthouse that made him want to revisit his
childhood passion and try his hand at producing a novel.
Nearly ten years on from that fateful stroll, he is proud to
finally share his story.

    The Lighthouse is Christopher's first novel.

christopherparker.com

Made in United States
North Haven, CT
31 October 2023

43091132R00221